S.WRIGHT

TEMPEST

Bermuda, 1609

Dedicated To the many beautiful Cahows slaughtered almost to extinction through the wanton greed of man.

(http://www.audubon.bm/ for information on Cahow preservation)

Be not afeard; the isle is full of noises,
Sounds, and sweet airs, that give delight
and hurt not.

William Shakespeare, The Tempest

Pink, blue, green, yellow. Warm, soft, sinking
Joy, Life, Nature, no chains here
He is large gentle, no guile
Out of the blue sky, framed by the sun,
landing, trusting, large brown eyes seeing
a new world; man.
His tears of blood are all there is now...

Contents

Foreword

Since my history lessons at Bermuda High School, historical stories have always fascinated me.

However, none of my lessons taught me anything about the history of Bermuda. Thirty years later, when I finally decided to seek out details of how Bermuda was founded, I was blown away by one of the most fascinating and exciting stories I have ever read.

Reading "A tale of Two Colonies"(V. Bernhard), and The Shipwreck that Saved Jamestown (L. Glover and D. B. Smith) whose factual accounts were riveting, I started to imagine what it must have been like in 1609, journeying across the Atlantic in a ship powered only by sails, encountering a hurricane of monumental ferocity.

As a psychologist, I find the concept of people of differing backgrounds fighting for survival as equals and then marooned on a paradise island, also made for a study in human nature. How people survive, the hierarchy of people's needs and how power struggles turn potential harmony into murder and mutiny seemed a blueprint for many of the human behaviours that we see to this day, illustrating the unchanging nature of humanity.

The core facts in 'The Tempest 1609' are true, however I have had to imagine what the real people were like, - the personalities and the conversations that they might have had are from my imagination. I have also had to imagine the flora and fauna of the Island, as this was very different to that of the colourfull vegetation of Bermuda where I grew up. This is a story not a text book. Whilst I have done the best I can to research the facts, I extend my apologies for any errors . The beautiful Island of Bermuda is portrayed from my own childhood memories. I had to elaborate the relationships and struggles of the individual characters as a way to bring the story to life, creating heroes and villains from my imagination, as very few of these facts are recorded in the history books. The characters are all named in the records of the passenger list for the 'Sea Venture'. Marriages, mutinies, murders, births, executions and the killing of innocent wild life, all took place, but specific details of conflicts have been written from my imagination - villains have been created purely to advance the story.

The novel is called 'Tempest 1609' because Shakespeare knew many of the people that boarded the "Sea Venture" and it is generally thought that he based his famous play on the stories that they brought back. These included William Strachey and Sylvester Jourdain who both wrote factual accounts in 1610. Most of what we know about this historical adventure is from these two documents.

A special thanks must go to my husband, Nige who has put up with my spending hours researching, writing, and re-writing. He also spent many hours reading, editing and supporting me throughout.

S. Wright

Acknowledgement

A special thanks to Christopher Grimes who supplied the artwork for the front cover. Christopher M. Grimes is a Bermudian artist working from a studio in the old Royal Navy Dockyard in Bermuda. He specializes in historical paintings in oils primarily of Historical Bermudian scenes and events.

Heacham Manor, Norfolk 1593

Something had changed. John sensed a stillness in the school room and forced his attention from the birds nesting outside the window.

Out of nowhere, a ruler came crashing down on his hand. The pain was instant. Tears stung his eyes as red weals started to form. Eustace, his twin brother put his hand over his mouth, his face drained of colour.

The Professor stood staring at John, the ruler poised. "Boy, you have done this to me too many times. My job is being made impossible by your insolence and stupidity. I shall have to inform your father and mother." Professor De Courtney was shaking with rage, as he crouched down looking into John's eyes. "Do you hear me boy? You will *not* get the better of Professor de Courtney. I will always win, do not be mistaken." His voice was soft and menacing.

"Please sir, don't tell my parents. I will try harder, I promise. I was just interested in the birds nesting . I will not do it again." John whimpered through his tears. The Professor rolled his eyes.

"Blubbing like a baby does not help" the older man said as he grasped his mortarboard from the coat hook and marched towards the door. "I have had enough" he grunted as he left the room slamming the door, forcing lumps of plaster out of the surrounding wall and leaving the twins staring after him in silence.

Left alone, they looked at one another. "Why does this keep happening? I do try and concentrate, but it is so boring. I don't understand how you can sit for hours listening to him droning on in Latin. It is much more interesting outside. *You* should be Lord of the Manor, you are so much better at lessons than me." John's face was pale and his shoulders hunched.

He looked at his brother and saw tenderness in his eyes. He felt the strength of their bond, something he instinctively knew he would always have, no matter what. He gave a weak smile and raised his fist, Eustace gently returned the gesture, forcing a smile.

"It won't always be like this John. When we are grown-ups you will be in charge and everyone will have to do as you say."

"But I don't *want* to be Lord of the manor. I would much rather come with you to The New World. I wish I had been born second."

John looked at the floor as a picture crept into his mind... A brightly painted schooner was waiting on the quayside. Side by side the two brothers were being piped aboard to the roars of the crowd. Then his imagination switched to running through the forest, splashing in crystal clear streams on painted ponies chasing savage Indians. How he would have loved to become an adventurer and sail the seas with someone like Sir Francis Drake, Eustace at his side.

But Eustace was born to do it alone. John would be Lord of Heacham Manor. It was his destiny. His face fell as he was jolted back to reality with the noise of his brother's shouting.

"Come with me! Come with me to Virginia John! You can do whatever you want when you are Lord of the Manor!" Eustace's eyes were wide with innocent anticipation.

Even at John's tender age, he knew it would not be possible, but he did not want to dampen his brother's dream. "Yes, you are right. We could both go." He sighed as he tried unsuccessfully to sound enthusiastic. Another vision came into his mind. This time, it was of Eustace boarding the ship alone. Eustace was oblivious to his brother's skepticism as he jumped up and down with glee, brandishing a pretend bow and arrow and aiming at an Indian hiding behind the desk.

John's eyes welled up as he thought of the reality of the different worlds that they would inhabit as adults.

* * *

Their Mother and Father had gone up to London and there were no tutors as it was a Sunday. The children had been left in the care of the housekeeper, Mrs. Jenkins. She was too busy looking after Henry who was six and Edward who was only two, to care about what the twins were up to, so they were free to do as they pleased, and it felt like a rare liberation.

Eustace bounced up and down on the red taffeta couch in the morning room, throwing the embroidered cushions flying, laughing as the escaped white feathers floated down to the exquisite Turkish carpet below.

"No more 'Chalky', no more 'Chalky', no more Latin, no more canes!" The springs on the couch squeaked and groaned as he bounced higher and higher. "Why don't we go outside and play? Savages beware" he bellowed as he landed on the floor with a thump, falling over laughing and throwing a cushion at John, crouching behind the sofa and peering at him gingerly with his finger in the shape of a gun. "Pow, pow! You are dead, you savage Indian. What do you say? You can be an Indian and I can be a Settler. I can track you down and take you prisoner."

Any opportunity to act out the stories of settlers and Indians opened up their imaginations and took them a world away from the boring confines of the Heacham Estate. "We can use the whole estate and pretend that it is the New World. Old stodgy Jenkins won't care, and even if she does, she won't be able to find us. We could explore the parts of the estate that old Mr. Jenkins the gamekeeper has fenced off? How dare he fence off our estate - we should be able to go wherever we want to! After all you are the Lord of the Manor!"

"Maybe not Eustace. He must have fenced it off for a reason." His hand was still throbbing and he wanted to avoid further punishments for a while.

"Don't be an old fuddy duddy, twinny" Eustace stuck his tongue out at John and roughly pushed him towards the door, his cheeks glowing with mischief. John pursed his lips and shook his head but as he saw Eustace laughing, a twinkle came into his eye and a smile spread from one of his ears to the other. "I don't call you 'Mister Mischief' for nothing." He whooped like an Indian as he came up behind his brother, putting his arm around his neck pretending to strangle him. Eustace had won him over again with his antics.

"Race you!" John shouted, releasing him and making a dash for it. As they raced each other through the warm glowing kitchen with its lingering aroma of eggs and bacon and into the musty boot room, both twins grabbed warm apparel and stumbled outside.

It was a lovely crisp winter morning with the frost coating the slippery blades of grass, crunchy diamonds twinkling in the watery sunlight. "Come on" screeched Eustace, his boots slipping alarmingly on the icy surface. "I will give you a head start and count to ten before I start looking for you" he shouted.

"OK Mr. Mischief, we'll see who is the better twin." John ran down the front of the lawn heading to the copse at the bottom, putting as much distance as he could between himself and his brother who was counting slowly "four, five, six ...."

"I am free, I am free ...no rules, no Latin, no French...I am going to win, win, win!" the glee of the moment turned John's cheeks pink and his eyes sparkled.

As he approached the bottom of slope, John saw that there was a tall hedge marking the end of the garden. There was also an old rotten wooden gate lying on the grass as if, at one time, the area beyond the hedge might have been out of bounds, but seemingly no more.

He was able to navigate through the opening to the clearing behind the hedge. He made sure that his footprints were obviously planted in the frosty grass in the direction of the gate so Eustace would follow them. Having bypassed the gate, giving it a little kick as he passed, he walked forwards for several steps creating a misleading clue, and then walked at right angles erasing any footprints that might give away his true location. The plan was to come up behind Eustace when he was least expecting it and push him onto the cold ground. He imagined sitting on him, raising his hands in the air in victory.

He heard Eustace shout "Ready or not here I come", his voice quivering with anticipation, he put his hands over his mouth to stifle a giggle and held his breath, silencing the freezing rush of air that went in and out of his nose like a racehorse. Eustace's eyes were wide with concentration, and he was tiptoeing through the long slippery grass, stumbling from time to time on the frozen vegetation.

John watched from afar and then stealthily and quietly, followed *him,* revelling in having deceived him so cleverly, just like a real Indian would have done.

He followed for several minutes seeing Eustace's dark head duck and weave through the undergrowth, delighted with his clever plan. Then he lost sight of him for a minute. Suddenly John was jolted out of his preoccupation with the game when he heard a blood curdling scream that made him stop in his tracks.

"Help, help...!" Eustace was screaming with terror.

John ran slipping and stumbling towards the sound of Eustace's voice, and had to stop suddenly when he was faced with a sheer drop. He ventured as close as he could get to the cliff edge, clutching the undergrowth to stop himself falling. He peered over and saw a scene that he would never forget.

Eustace, was clinging for dear life to a large protruding root at the edge of the cliff. For a moment John was glued to the spot unable to move, as if his legs had turned to lead weights.

"Hold on to my hand" he shouted as he plunged on to his stomach, feeling the icy dampness on the front of his body. He reached for Eustace's free hand, and strained to hold it as tightly as he could as he used every last ounce of energy to haul his body towards safer ground. Eustace was screaming, his brown eyes full of fear and helplessness. His screams turning to sobs. The strength was draining from him and the sides of the cliff were crumbling, with rocks disappearing into the vast emptiness below.

"I can't hold on...!" Eustace sobbed. His face was red and contorted with pain.

"You can, and you must" screamed John.

"I am slipping... John, help me; I am slipping... it hurts..."

"No, I have got you, please Eustace, just HOLD ON."

He had a renewed bout of energy and jerked at Eustace's hand, inching his body up slowly bit by bit, despite the burning sensations that overtook his whole body. He said to himself over and over "just hold him, hold him, hold him,... You can't let go no matter how hard it is"

Just as John felt he was making headway, Eustace's strength seemed to diminish and his body became heavier as his muscles began to fail. John was finding it harder and harder, and the burning sensations were getting stronger and stronger as Eustace's weight seemed to increase. John was starting to slip on the icy grass, but fought to dig the toes of his shoes into the ground.

No, don't let go Eustace... don't give up... I will save you......" John screamed.

"John... I can't... "

Slowly and with an overwhelming feeling of powerlessness and panic John started to feel Eustace's hand slipping from his. Slipping... slipping... the sweat, mixed with dirt and tears facilitated their hands moving apart. Gouging, dragging, clawing... Then the unstoppable sliding began. His palm, his fingers, the look of terror in his eyes as his strength seeped away. Eustace's hand released from the root of the tree, and he tried to grasp hold of the edge of the cliff, but the stones crumbled with his touch... It was the fastest and slowest moment of John's life. It went on and on until the final lingering trace of contact was lost between the beloved twins.

"Nooooo... " John cried, watching, powerless, as Eustace's small body tumbled down the cliff like a rag doll. All he could see was the panic in the large brown eyes that, even in free fall, were pleading with John to save him as he fell further and further down, until he could look no more.

John continued to look down to where he had let Eustace fall. He stared in disbelief, at the limp figure at the bottom of the cliff, willing him to move and jump up and laugh. That did not happen and he screamed a scream of pure agony. He slumped away from the edge, unable to think or to move. Suddenly he thought – I must be dreaming. Surely Eustace is just playing another trick on me. He didn't want to look again, because that way, he could turn the clock back two minutes.

He had to look again though, and he summoned enough energy to drag himself towards the edge. As he looked over, he saw more clearly the small figure, his head battered and bleeding, his dark hair matted with blood and his limbs spread out at awkward angles, with no sign of movement. John turned away as nausea overtook him and he vomited violently.

As John lay, stunned at what he had seen, he heard movement, and when he looked over the cliff again, he saw the old game keeper emerging from the trees. Mr. Jenkins ran towards the figure lying on the ground faltering and whimpering as he got near to the place where Eustace lay.

"Oh no, my little Master" he said, as his lined face became distorted with the pain and horror of what he was seeing.

For one moment John thought, as the old man picked the limp bundle up, that it was going to be ok. Perhaps Eustace was hurt but alive and Mr. Jenkins could take him back home and they would be able to play some more tomorrow.

"What have you done boy?" the old man shouted as tears started to stream down his face as he looked up at John. He crumpled to his knees, not through the weight of the tiny body, but through the weight of the sheer emotion that was etched on his gnarled brown face. "Your brother is dead." He was sobbing as Eustace's blood ran down his arms. John scrambled down to where Mr. Jenkins was holding Eustace. He looked at the little broken body. He bent over his small form, pausing as he tried to absorb the horror of the reality in front of him. Taking a deep breath he made a fist and lightly touched his brother's hand as a final loving goodbye. As he did so, he noticed that Eustace was holding something – his last act of life. John opened Eustace's hand and saw a stone. He picked it up, knowing that the stone had come away in Eustace's hand when he was struggling for survival trying to grasp the edge of the cliff. The stone had let Eustace down, and so had he. As he touched Eustace's hand, he looked at his face and saw a flicker of his eyelids. "Eustace, Eustace, you are alive!" John shouted. He saw Eustace struggling to say something, and bent down to hear his small voice.

"Virginia" he whispered, a tear rolling down his cheek.

John nodded. Eustace smiled as his hand went limp, releasing the stone, and his hold on life.

As John collapsed with screams of agony, he took the stone holding it to his heart. He would keep the stone forever. He knew it would always be a concrete reminder of his "Mr. Mischief". As he sobbed with grief, looking at the innocent battered face of the only true friend he had ever had, it came to him. He would not let his brother down again. "I don't care what they say, I will go to Virginia." John said to himself. He was not to know what lay ahead.

Aftermath

J ohn lay on his bed in the foetal position, holding on tightly to the small stone which was a reminder of Eustace's final desperate attempt to save himself. The curtains were drawn and so many tears had been shed, that his eyes were now dry and staring, looking up at the blank ceiling. The sounds of the household filtered through his consciousness, and he flinched and cried out as Eustace's terrified face appeared in his mind. Once again John shouted out in anguish, this time he would save him.... But no... again he saw the small form tumbling downwards, brown eyes pleading for John to do something. Yet again, the feelings of loss and failure overwhelmed him and he banged his head against the wall to try and rid himself of the repeating images. Despite this, the same pictures kept intruding, hour after hour, week after week month after month. Banging his head repeatedly transferred the pain from his heart to his body, but relief never lasted. Again and again, the scene was repeated, torturing John almost to the point of madness. He clutched the stone, a small reminder that started the cycle of pain yet again.

In his distress he heard a knock on his bedroom door. "John... John..." It was an urgent whisper. He knew what was coming. "John, your Father wants to see you." It was Mrs. Jenkins, sent again to pull him out of his hell hole. John struggled to sit up.

"I am so sorry Master, but your father is in a state again, and I am afraid you must come, or he will come and get you – which will make him even angrier. Your mother is crying and Henry and Edward have been banished to the nursery. All hell is breaking loose John. You must come quickly."

John stumbled to the door, his head spinning.

As he opened the door, he looked at Mrs. Jenkins' troubled face.

He wandered through the long badly lit corridors of the cold inhospitable house, and arrived at his father's study to see him kicking over a chair in anger. His mother cowered in the corner sobbing, and turned her face away when she saw John approaching. "Come here boy" his father bellowed. His father's red and bleary eyes glimmered with hatred, and his breath reeked of alcohol. Several empty bottles of brandy lay scattered on the floor. Grief had transformed him, and alcohol had taken him over, blurring his pain and deadening his heart. John's father was never to be the same - nothing was to be the same after Eustace's death, of that, John was certain.

"Ah Eustace" his father staggered towards John.

John inched backwards. "Sir, I am John".

"John - no I do not want John, I want Eustace" he slurred.

"Sir, you know he had an accident" John mumbled.

"No, Eustace is my boy. Bring me my boy"

John looked towards his mother, but she stared at the floor.

"Eustace is dead father" John murmured.

"You are a liar" he said as he collapsed on the sofa grunting to himself with tears rolling down his cheek.

To John, it was like a knife to his heart. Not only had he lost his brother, but it seemed as though he had also lost his father. He looked at the pathetic creature now snoring on the sofa and his stomach

11

churned. The only way his father could understand Eustace's death was to blame John. He felt sadness and pity. If only he could turn the clock back - for himself and for his father.

John's mother walked forwards and put her arm around John's shoulders. "He knows Eustace is not with us John, he just struggles to remember sometimes when he is 'tired'. He is not a bad man; he is just very upset about the loss of Eustace. He has to find a reason for his death, and in his head he blames you. They were so very close you know... I think it best that you keep away from him as much as possible. With time, maybe he will forgive." She looked away having done her motherly duty to protect her son.

"The reason that he wanted to talk to you this afternoon was to tell you about your future. We thought that perhaps instead of lessons with the Professor you could learn about the farm and agriculture. It would be more suited to your temperament. You would like that, wouldn't you dear?" She sighed, looking over at a painting of Eustace that was hanging on the wall. I am so sorry John, but your father has removed you from his will. You are no longer the Heir to Heacham Manor."

Part of him was relieved. He never had wanted his father's money or title, but he did want his love. He looked at his mother with disbelief. "But Eustace's death was an accident Mother. I tried to save him but I was not strong enough." John had told himself this many times, but still failed to truly believe it. Maybe he was just not good enough. He was not to be the Lord of the Manor - but that was the least of his concerns. He had lost his brother and his father, just because he was not strong enough. His mother shrugged her shoulders and sighed.

John looked at his father asleep on the sofa. If only he could explain the truth. But his father was insane with grief and he would never listen. His twin brother, Eustace's face was mirrored on John's face, and it was a living reminder of the loss. John had to go. He would be completely alone in the world. His fate had been decided. He and his tortuous memories had been disowned by his family and he knew it could never change. What was he to do?

The Farmer's Daughter

rom that day onwards John's life changed. He no longer ate with the family, taking meals by himself in the kitchen, and whilst he still slept in the house he left in the early mornings like an unwanted guest, wandering the estate and surrounds. He was, in effect, disowned.

At least the dubious pressure of inheriting The Manor had been removed from his shoulders, but it left an uncertain future.

His dream was to carry through his promise to Eustace and head to London in a few years to join a ship travelling to Virginia, but he did not know where to begin with such ambitious plans. He wandered across the fields, taking in the beautiful colours of the spring morning. Winter was starting to disappear and spring was showing herself in the form of new bright green leaves decorating the old brown sticks of winter.

John sighed. His mind wandered back to that fateful morning. He relived the joy of being with Eustace as his thoughts meandered through the events – the smell of the bacon as they rushed through the kitchen, Eustace shouting as he counted to ten. Then reality hit him like a sledgehammer once more. His stomach turned over. He was totally transported, reaching, reaching, and trying once again to get Eustace up from the cliff edge. He felt the icy frost on his stomach and heard the pitiful cries, both from himself and from his brother. He lay on the grass in a world of his own, immersed in tragedy.

"Hello, are you alright?" A distant voice permeated his mind. "Are you alright Sir?" The voice came once again but this time it was clearer and louder, more insistent.

He came back to reality slowly shaking his head and trying to focus, and as he looked up he saw a girl, a little younger than himself standing a few feet away watching him, eyes wide with concern. She was dressed like a peasant. Her hair was auburn with flashes of red, and it cascaded down her back like a waterfall. Her blue eyes twinkled with kindness.

"Hello" he said shyly, smiling and trying hard to look friendly. "You caught me talking to myself. How embarrassing." He laughed in his confusion.

"Don't fret" she smiled. "I talk to myself all the time." She giggled and lowered her eyes.

He had not met many girls before, and he was both excited and unsure of himself. "What is your name?" It was the only thing he could think of to say.

He found himself staring at her.

"I am Sarah Hacker" she said. "I live at Heacham Manor Farm, where my father farms the Estate." Sarah looked proud of her position as farmer's daughter as she stood erect, trying to make herself look taller and older than she really was to impress this strange boy. She thought he looked a bit like a ragamuffin, but his clothes seemed as though they might have been cast offs from toffs. She wondered where he was from and why he was wandering the woods alone.

"I haven't seen you here before. Who are you?" Sarah had always been outspoken and the most confident and inquisitive of her nine siblings. She was the only girl, which made her not only her father's favourite, but a rough and tumble tomboy who could give as good as she got with her older brothers. This lad looked more delicate than the hooligans at home, she thought.

"Well... " He wanted to move the focus from himself to something interesting and engaging. What did girls like? How could he impress her and make her feel at ease? He skirted around her question.

"Have you seen the baby foxes?" he asked.

Sarah's eyes widened. "No, I haven't. Do you know where some are? Can we go and see them?"

"We must be very quiet. I have been watching them for a few weeks now. They are quite shy, but they are getting used to seeing me... but you must tiptoe." He was pleased that she seemed interested.

"Don't be silly. I am a farmer's daughter. Do you not think I *know* how to behave around baby animals" she said, feigning offence. "Anyway, I can't possibly go anywhere with you if I don't know your name, can I?" Her blue eyes were smiling as she teased him, tossing her auburn hair back to catch the sunlight.

He paused for a moment unsure what to do next, staring at the ground, waiting for inspiration to come. There was nothing left for it, he had to come clean and tell her his name. He took a deep breath. "I am John Rolfe" He blurted.

"No. You are teasing me. John Rolfe lives at the Manor. My father works for his father. I don't mean to be rude, but you are too scruffy to be the son of the Lord. Anyway, I couldn't talk to you if you were John Rolfe, you would be too grand for the likes of me."

"I promise you I am John Rolfe."

He could see she was confused, and seemed ready to turn around and run away, just as he thought she would.

"I *am* John Rolfe and I *want* to speak to you, I *want* to show you the foxes. Please don't go."

Sarah pursed her lips, and frowned. She believed every word now, but the atmosphere between them had become strained. She was struggling as much as he was.

He took a deep breath. He knew he had to take action or she would run away. "Let's just be plain John and Sarah" he said brandishing a huge smile. "A farmer's daughter and her friend just getting to know one another. I can manage that, if you can?"

She looked at him from under her long dark eye lashes, the rebel in her returning. "Why not? Maybe I can order *you* around… " she said testing his sense of humour.

"Your wish is my command m'lady" he said laughing. Eustace would like her, he thought. She had real spirit. She was like the Indian squaws they had read about – pretty, but feisty.

"Show me those foxes then, and be quick about it." She commanded.

* * *

For many months thereafter, John and Sarah met in the woods. John looked forward to catching sight of her every morning as she navigated her way through the trees in the changing seasons to the place that they called their own.

They had built a den out of sticks in the shape of an Indian Wigwam, and Sarah had brought blankets for them to huddle up in. She also brought food every day to share with him, usually large chunks of homemade bread and great wedges of the cheese made on the farm. He had never tasted such flavours. The soft bread covered in yellow salty butter, mingled with the sharpness of the crumbling cheese, washed down with fresh warm milk.

They spent hours playing at being Indians. She was his Indian Squaw, and he the warrior. She usually won the games, but if she didn't, John let her. It was not the same as the games he had played with Eustace, but almost as much fun.

He began to feel a similar closeness with Sarah, but it felt more than brotherly camaraderie - she was like a magnet that pulled him in. He could tell from her eyes and the way she reached out to him that she felt the same way. They had watched the fox cubs grow and thrive, leaving their burrow, and seen how as the winter approached, everything died down leaving the woods with a different kind of sparse magic.

John began to realize as the weather turned colder, that his months playing with Sarah, whilst idyllic, probably had to come to an end when the snow started to fall. She would no longer be allowed to spend the colder days in the woods, and she would be drawn to the warm fire of the farmhouse rather than the draughty wigwam.

It was about a year since the fateful day that Eustace had fallen, and John's mother had not made any arrangements for him to learn farming as she had promised. He only saw his mother every now and again, and each time he did, she was kind and reassuring, but she never mentioned his future or his father. She did not seem to understand that he was like a rudderless ship in a stormy sea. She never saw the fear in his eyes or gave him the comfort he needed. The death of Eustace had left her vacant of any emotion except grief. He could only feel pity for her. He never made demands on her, or told her how he felt. His heart ached in silence.

John sat alone in the cold forest waiting for Sarah to come. He covered his face and considered his fate. There was no one to help him. He had not faced this fact head on until that moment. He was a small boy living like a fox in the woods, spending his days playing games. Was it delusional to believe that he could ever get to Virginia? Sarah was kind, but she was a child too. She could not save him. How was he going to manage through the harsh winter, having to spend his days furtively in the manor, keeping himself out of the way?

He felt the cold ground beneath his legs. He was nine years old and had nowhere to go and no future. He had been forgotten. With the absence of adult protection he had made a valiant effort to be a man, but his fear was coming to the surface. A slow tear slid down his cheek as he gave in to the childish feelings that had been withheld for so many months. He did not hear Sarah approaching.

Sarah came towards him smiling with the anticipation of what fun she was going to have with John today. She saw her friend bent over, his hands over his face as his tears fell.

"John, whatever is the matter?" To her it was just another 'play day' and she was stunned to see him so distressed.

"It is alright Sarah" he said, knowing his appearance belied his words. He had always deflected her questions about his family and his past, not wanting to spoil their carefree days together.

She stooped down in the makeshift wigwam and scooted herself next to him, looking into his eyes. "It is not alright, is it John?" She put her arm around him. "Is it your family? Are you ill? Tell me John."

John knew he had to tell her. He had avoided it for too long.

When he started to tell Sarah his story, at first he was hesitant, fearful that she might not be interested in such a sad tale. As the story started to unravel and he saw that her eyes were focussed on his every word, and her face was soft with compassion, not pity, he spoke faster and faster. It all came out; his love for Eustace, his parents' rejection of him, and the horrible accident, the blame for which had fallen on his shoulders. At times he cried, at others he looked stony-faced and emotionless, but Sarah never took her eyes away from him.

Every now and then, when she could tell that the emotions were almost too unbearable for him, she reached her hand towards him and reassured him with a gentle hug. He knew she was there, but he continued with his rush of words as if, in throwing the words out of his mouth, he was cleansing himself.

When he had finished the story, the two children sat, side by side looking at one another, stunned. Sarah's face was stained with tears. John's body was slumped with the emotion of telling the story. The only sound was the sound of the birds singing and the wind blowing through the trees. They sat in tearful silence holding hands, no words were necessary. Two children with many questions, but no answers. How was he going to get to Virginia? He felt Eustace's stone in his pocket.

Refuge - (14 years later)

❧

John had been welcomed with open arms by Sarah's mother and father when he walked in the door looking bedraggled, pale and breathless. When Sarah had explained John's situation, her mother had taken pity on the young lad. Everyone could see he was only a child and they were shocked the former heir to the Manor had been rejected in such a way.

For fourteen years Sarah's mother and father had nurtured him as if he were their own. The arrangement had been keenly accepted by John's mother, her guilt assuaged as she thankfully handed her son over to Mrs. Hacker, fooling herself that at last his "apprenticeship" aspirations had been catered for. It was for the best.

Over the years of being with Sarah's family, John and Sarah's relationship continued to grow in strength as they turned from boy and girl to young man and young woman. Opportunities were never lost for them to be together. A secret glance, an innocent touch. Never overt, but very real to both of them.

John's longing for Sarah grew. He would lie awake at night imagining holding her in his arms, running his hands down her body. He imagined her close to him, her auburn hair falling over his body, triggering a passion that was unfulfilled in reality. However, he knew it was never to be. God would never allow it.

Through the many years spent with Sarah's family he had come to understand how important the Catholic faith was to them. There was a strong bond between Sarah and her family that was cemented by their faith. Sarah's rosary was everything to her, something that she carried with her everywhere, just like he carried Eustace's stone. He understood that Sarah would never be happy leaving Heacham and her family, and he knew she would only be content if she married a Catholic. He did not have a chance. He had to be content with a glance, and a tender touch. He had lost everything, and could offer her nothing. He loved her too much to try to do anything about it, but his attraction to her was so strong that he could not break away and leave her. She was like opium to him. Any small gesture kept him wanting more, but pulled him into the abyss, knowing he couldn't have it. His dreams of a future in Virginia were overshadowed by her presence, even although he would never have a future with her.

✳ ✳ ✳

"Piss off John! You are not even a part of this family. I wish you would just potter off back to your Manor and leave us alone!" Jake was one of Sarah's elder brothers and he had never taken kindly to John having moved into the farmhouse and becoming one of the family. John made him feel inferior, and his hatred had grown over the years as John had become more and more competent as a farmer, leaving Jake in his shadow.

Jake knew there was a special bond between Sarah and John, something he could never be a part of. Ever since she had brought him home and pleaded with her parents to let him stay with them, Jake's life had changed. He used to be close to Sarah. Not any more. John and Sarah would huddle together laughing and playing and Jake felt an outsider in his own home. John had blossomed into a handsome young man, who had time for everyone and was well liked. Jake's resentment had intensified over the years. He knew he was often unkind to John, but he didn't care.

"Jake, I don't know what your problem is; I was just trying to help you." John stood looking, hands outstretched in frustration his eyes pleading. He had tried so hard to be helpful and to be a friend to Jake, but he only received bullying in return.

"I don't need your bloody help. I just need you to leave me and my family alone. I especially want you to leave Sarah alone. I have seen you smooching up to her being all sickly sweet and touching her you dirty bastard. You just want to sink your pizzle, that is why you stay. No other reason."

John's face went red, and he was lost for words. Jake had struck a chord of truth.

Jake laughed. "Ahhhhhhh yes. I see from the look on your face that I have hit a nerve now haven't I, Lord of the Manor? You do harbour unsavoury thoughts about Sarah. Well you can forget it, apart from the fact that you are undoubtedly a milksop; you aren't even a Catholic. Sarah would never look at a man who wasn't Catholic, and Papa certainly wouldn't agree to it, so do yourself a favour and forget it, put it out of your mind you churl. If I see or hear of you being inappropriate with my sister, I will beat you black and blue and make sure that you never cross this threshold again – do I make myself absolutely clear?" Jake's eyes were staring. He was several inches taller than John, and he was strong and wiry with ugly scars on his face as a result of having suffered with the pox as a child. He picked up the pitchfork and thrust it towards John in a threatening gesture.

John jumped back cursing as the pitch fork just missed his foot. He was used to bullying and abuse from Jake, this was the one difficulty that he had had to contend with since coming to live with Sarah's family. He just had to accept it and not rise to the bait. Jake had obviously been drinking and was more abusive than usual.

Jake couldn't leave it at that, the drink accentuating his aggression. A nasty thought came into his head. "Come to think of it, Johnny boy, I have noticed you flirting a bit with the baker's daughter Polly when she delivers the bread. Now she's a pretty little wench." John looked surprised as he had never noticed this girl.

"What the hell are you talking about Jake? You know that is a lie." John's voice was getting louder trying to defend himself against slanderous insinuations, but he knew it would be futile.

Jake continued, enjoying the fact that John was squirming. "In fact, I have had several samples of Polly's wares myself up against the barn door and she is quite willing to pass around more than bread... if you know what I mean?" Jake gave John a wink. "I think I must mention her to Sarah. I am sure she would like to know that you are interested in that little pox ridden slut. Yes... come to think of it, I am sure Sarah would be grateful to know that you are all set up in a relationship. She will be happy for you and I know you will enjoy Polly, as she is far more willing than the sainted Sarah." Jake gave a self-satisfied smile when he saw John's look of horror.

John didn't know what to say. He decided that it was pointless to say anything to this mean bully. Whatever response he gave was going to be fodder for further bullying so he turned and walked away.

He could hear Jake laughing and shouting after him in a singsong childlike manner "John and Polly, John and Polly...Dah Dah Dah Dah Dahhh Dee..."

John walked into the warm farmhouse kitchen, hoping that no one else had heard Jake's lies. Sarah's plump mother was at the stove stirring the stew for the evening's dinner humming to herself as the delicious aroma wafted through the steaming kitchen. A huge fire roared in the grate and the black cat nestled on the rocking chair nearby. Sarah was at the sink peeling potatoes. She had grown into a beautiful young woman. Her hair was still auburn, but with maturity her body had taken on a soft roundness and her complexion was clear and unblemished. Looking at her, John felt that his heart would break. These last few years had been a refuge from the past and from his family, and John was grateful for every moment, especially those spent with this beautiful girl, but he struggled with feelings of failure, knowing that Sarah would never be his.

"Oh John, it is you. You look a little upset, whatever is the matter. It's not your memories again is it?" Sarah's eyebrows were pushed together in concern, as she turned to look at her friend.

"No, it is nothing really; it is just a little cold out there. Shall I come and help you with the potatoes?"

"Yes, that would be good. Here, take a knife"

As John started to peel the potatoes, Jake pushed open the large oak kitchen door which crashed against the wall behind it. He was laughing and blaspheming as he staggered across the threshold. An icy draft accompanied his dramatic entrance making everyone turn to see who it was.

John's heart sank. Jake was staggering and smelling of alcohol. Goodness knows what he was going to say, but whatever it was, John knew it would cause trouble.

"Well, isn't that sweet... the lovebirds peeling potatoes together – a scene of domestic bliss." Jake grinned as he turfed the cat out of its comfortable chair, dodging its spitting clawing response, and plonked himself down next to the fire.

"Although – it is not *quite* domestic bliss, is it Lord John? I was shocked to the bone to see you with the baker's daughter earlier. I had to avert my eyes in case you corrupted my innocence. Looked like *more* than domestic bliss you tasted with *her*." He shook his head, tutting at John, a look of superiority on his face. "Didn't know you had it in you Lordy boy."

John did not know what to say, he stood like a statue, trying to control the feelings that were whirring around his body. He knew if he gave in to them, he would disgrace himself. He wanted to march over and give Jake the hiding he deserved. He clenched his fists and looked down, trying to control the volcano inside of him.

John watched as Sarah's face fell, her eyes welled up and her complexion took on a crimson hue, and his heart skipped a beat.

"Oh, I see Sarah is a little surprised with the news of your liaison." Jake said in a mockingly sympathetic voice, nodding in Sarah's direction as he noticed her stricken face.

Sarah tried to concentrate on peeling the potatoes, avoiding looking at anyone, especially John.

Sarah's mother broke away from attending to the dinner and rounded on Jake. "Jake, for goodness sake, Sarah and John have grown up together; don't start trying to stir things up. There is nothing romantic between them, there could never be as John is not a Catholic. If John wants to start up a relationship with someone from the village, he is entitled to do so without your commenting on it! Why don't you get off your arse and come and help with the dinner. I want to hear no more about it."

Jake slouched back in the chair and put his feet on a nearby stool smirking and laughing as he watched John and Sarah trying so hard not to react. He could see that he had touched a raw nerve in both of them, which had confirmed his suspicions. It was only a matter of time until he was able to catch them together, and he would make sure that John was sent away in disgrace for even thinking about Sarah in that way. He had been waiting for years to put the 'goody two shoes' 'Lord of the Manor' in his place, and he rubbed his hands with glee to think that he was finally going to get the better of him.

Sarah could hold it in no longer. Hearing that John had someone else was one thing, but hearing her mother pronounce that she and John could never be together was the final straw. She had always known it to be the case, but she had not allowed herself to confront the reality of it. She threw down the knife and ran from the kitchen.

John wanted desperately to follow her and comfort her, but he knew this would be playing into Jake's hands, so he continued to peel the potatoes, his body rigid and his face set in pain.

Jake laughed once again. "Oh John baby – what *have* you done?

"Jake, that is enough" shouted Mrs. Hacker, marching over to Jake, her finger pointing at him, her large bosom shaking. "I said to drop the subject and I mean it. I will not have you upsetting Sarah anymore." John knew that Mrs. Hacker had always been fond of him. He had never caused her any trouble, unlike her own son Jake, who even *she* found difficult to like.

It had never occurred to Mrs Hacker that there could be romantic feelings between Sarah and John. Apart from the fact that he was not catholic, she would have been happy for them, but because of the religious issue it was out of the question. Her husband was fond of John too; he was a real grafter and had turned out to be a talented asset to the farm. What Jake said had made sense though – John was a very good looking lad, and would be attractive to the young ladies. The way Sarah had left the kitchen surely confirmed that there *was* something between them. Maybe Jake was right; maybe it was time for John to go, to avoid any heartbreak for Sarah, Mrs Hacker sighed, imagining the trouble to come.

It was like torture for John standing in the kitchen, trying to kill the urge to dash after Sarah and defend himself against Jake's cruel accusations. Eventually, he could bear it no longer.

"I think I will go out and help with the hay baling" he said, his voice quivering, his eyes shifty with the lie. Eustace's stone was still in his pocket, and he clutched it for strength.

"I bet you are going to chase after Sarah, aren't you?" Jake mocked.

John ignored the jibe and walked out of the kitchen door towards the barn, banging his right fist into his left hand. He sat on a large hay bale in the warm barn and put his head in his hands. He didn't know where Sarah had gone. Maybe it was better not to see her. Maybe he should just let her think that what Jake had said was true. It might be easier that way.

It was going to be impossible to live under the same roof as Sarah under these circumstances. He had to tell her the truth, but what was the point? Maybe it would be better if she thought he *did* have feelings for Polly. After all, even if Sarah loved him the way he loved her, religion would be a barrier. She would never forsake her God for him. To make it easier for her, he must leave Heacham and let her find someone more suitable. It was only fair. He loved her so much he would do anything for her – even give her up.

He decided there and then that he must leave as soon as possible. He had heard there were ships leaving for Virginia looking for strong young men to start a new colony. If he had to go, this would be an ideal opportunity for him to cut himself off completely from England, and his memories, and leave Sarah to find a better man to spend her life with. By doing this he would also fulfill his promise to Eustace. He felt the stone in his pocket that was now round and smooth with handling. Leaving was the only way.

Having decided what he had to do; John lay down in the hay, feeling the soft and prickly strands, smelling the rich and earthy smell, and listened to the restless horses snorting gently in the nearby paddocks. He started to drift off. He thought back to when Sarah first brought him to the farm. He had been nervous, fighting his flashbacks, but Sarah had held on to his arm, pulling him along and reassuring him that he was going to be alright. He *had* been alright. His memories had haunted him for a long time, but gradually over the years, with Sarah's help and reassurance, they had faded into the background.

For the first time, he had been part of a real family. He loved farming, the smells, the sounds, everything about it. If only he could stay here forever. He never saw his own family, but they did not miss him, and the feelings were mutual. He would be pleased if he never had sight of that house again, it had caused him nothing but anguish. He still held on to Eustace's stone, but the memories of Eustace were now mostly pleasant memories of twin boys playing together.

Lost in his thoughts, he heard a small voice calling him. His stomach lurched. It was Sarah.

She was nineteen now – a woman. She was hesitant as she walked towards him, her face downcast and serious. Her eyes were red from crying and her beautiful clear complexion was blotchy and marked with tears.

John found himself propelled forwards. At first she stood, blinking and looking away with uncertainty, and then as she became more confident, she allowed herself to look at him. Their eyes locked.

They did not speak. He put out his hand and held his breath as she slowly walked closer and reached her hand out to meet his. He could feel her warmth, and see the pulsing of her heart in her chest as her breath quickened. Without thought, he was pulled towards her like a magnet. He shook as he bent forwards and kissed her lips. He tasted her sweetness and felt her soft body relaxing into him, welcoming him, and pulling him even closer to her. She started to sink downwards, pulling him towards her and into the soft pile of hay. The culmination of so many years of repressed emotions erupted.

Like slow motion, he felt the silhouette of her body beneath him as he enveloped her in his arms, feeling the strength of his desire. Neither of them consciously thought about what they were doing, but pure instinct took over. His mind started shouting at him to stop, but his body was beyond the point of no return.

John heard a loud crash and felt cold air around him.

"Well, it didn't take you long did it Lordy boy?" Jake was standing at the open barn door, brandishing a shot gun which was aimed at John's head. Sarah and John pulled apart, rearranging their dishevelled clothes around themselves and stared open mouthed.

Realising what was happening, Sarah sat herself up and placed herself between John and the pointed gun. "Leave us alone! Leave us alone! You pervert – how long have you been listening to us?"

"Oh a fair time, my little love. Never thought my little sister would stoop so low." Sarah covered her mouth with her hand. *"He…"* Jake moved the gun up and down gesticulating towards John, "…will have to leave or I will let everyone know what has been going on. You will have to do what I say, or Daddy will hear what a whore you are and throw you out. You will have nothing." Jake's face was a picture of glee, he had been so clever, and now everything was going to go his way.

John stood up facing Jake, he could think of nothing but how he was going to protect Sarah from shame and destitution. This was his fault. He had taken advantage of her when he knew it could destroy them both. His body had acted, and when she responded, there had been no way to fight what they both wanted. Now the only way was for him to leave, and leave immediately, and hope that her despicable brother would not expose her and destroy her future. It was a gamble, but he knew deep down that Jake loved Sarah, and had always been jealous.

"Alright, alright Jake, I hear what you are saying." John put his arm around Sarah, who was gently weeping, and lifted her chin to look in her eyes. "I love you Sarah, but for your sake I must leave. You know I have no choice now." John turned to look at Jake. "You are a bastard, we all know that, but to do this is the lowest of the low."

"Lowest of the low? How can you say that, when you have deflowered this beautiful girl? You will leave, and Sarah will never see you again, or I will reveal all and Sarah will lose any chance of marrying a good Catholic lad – worse than that, she will have no home and no family. The choice is yours Lordy boy!"

Plans take shape

1607, Offices of the Virginia Co., London

Sir George Somers had been watching the progress of colonisation of Virginia with great interest. He felt it had potential, but he knew there had been some dire decisions made by the Virginia Company that had resulted in the loss of lives as well as money, and as yet, he was not convinced that he wanted to be involved. He did not want to miss an opportunity though, and if the project followed the success of The East India Company, who traded very successfully, there could be a chance to not only make a lot of money, but to make a name for himself in the process. He had cautious optimism, curious as to the outcome of this latest report on the colony.

Sir George knew several of the investors personally, many of whom were at this meeting today, and he nodded genially as he walked into the cramped room that was heaving with sweaty and greedy men. He had dressed in full naval uniform, and looked handsome for his age, his grey hair framing a tanned and regal face. He cut a swathe through the crowd, puffing himself up to ensure he did not go unnoticed, something he needn't have worried about. As they met his gaze, most stood aside in recognition of his seniority. His blue eyes scanned the room. He was surprised and pleased to see so many respected names, and he noted who was there for future reference. They were all very intelligent and well-to-do people, who didn't often get things wrong.

Sir George spied the speaker for the evening, Christopher Newport, a seasoned Seaman who, after the Royal Charter of 1606, had taken it upon himself to see this project through, and was back now after eight months, having captained the latest expedition to Virginia. He had already been to Virginia three times, and was well versed in the trials and tribulations of the new colony there. He was to address the Virginia Company Investors on the state of their investment. Christopher Newport was 49, attractive, dark and serious as he stood tall and proud looking down at the expectant crowd from a hastily erected stage. Despite the fact that he had lost one of his arms in a battle with the Spanish sixteen years previously, Sir George could see that he had lost none of his confidence in himself or his belief in the colonisation of Virginia. Excitement seeped from his pores, and his serious brown eyes were wide and unblinking.

It was hot, smoky and loud. As Christopher Newport took to the stage, the noise ceased as they waited with bated breath to hear his latest report on the state of the colony. Apart from the occasional cough, one could have heard a pin drop.

"Sirs, it gives me great pleasure to address you, following one of the most exciting and promising adventures I have ever had the pleasure to Captain. I bring back news of the Americas that will fill your hearts with gladness. As you know, we set sail with three ships, "The Susan Constant", "Godspeed" and "Discovery" with 100 men and 4 boys. Our main aim was to find gold, convert the heathen Indian population to Christianity and to create a functioning and profitable community, and your money has been put to good use I can assure you." He gave a knowing smile. Their appetite was whetted.

"Can you tell us about the gold Christopher?" asked Thomas Smythe, a rotund and loud man, one of the leading members of the Virginia Company, whose house was being used to host the meeting in Philpot Lane, London and who had been instrumental in the organisation of the project.

Christopher paused for theatrical effect. "Yes, I brought back sample ore with me for testing and there is far more where that came from. I foresee a great profit from the further mining of gold, and I am determined to ensure that this is one of the main focuses for the colonisation." Sir George Somers listened intently, this was the best bit. He knew Smythe of old. He was always one for making a quick farthing, and it did well to watch his reaction as it was a good indicator of how things were really going. So far it sounded almost too positive. Other questions needed answering. Before Sir George could broach these questions, as he expected, Smythe almost took the words out of his mouth.

"That sounds promising, but we know there have been problems with the aggression of the local Indians, what is your experience with them? Have the colonists started to convert them to Christianity, and are there good trading relations with them? We have heard a lot of poppycock about how when you left, Captain Smith was saved by the Indian Princess Pocahontas, but personally I think all that sounds a bit far-fetched." Smythe was looking intently at Christopher Newport, his face had a slightly sceptical look. After all, it would be easy to pull the wool over investors eyes as no one else had actually seen what was happening in America.

Christopher Newport took Smythe's interrogation happily, and gave a slight smile of superiority putting Smythe in his place, as he explained slowly and carefully the success that he had witnessed.

"Yes, there were a lot of rumours about the Indians and Captain John Smith's capture. In my opinion it is unlikely that he would have been captured and even more unlikely that he was saved by a child – he is a fantasist, I assure you.

I know it is difficult for you all to understand as you have not been there, but the colonists have fortified *well* against the Indians, and in fact, trading with them has become extremely easy. They are very efficient farmers, and I personally, forged a good relationship with them. I can see that with time things will just get better and better. Maybe it is just the personalities involved that make this expedition so much more successful than any of the others. It is all about relationships. Now we are on friendly terms, the next step will be to start converting them to Christianity and involving them more in the settlement. Whilst I would say that this is 'work in progress' I see no reason why, with time, the objectives of good trading relations with the Indians *as well as* converting them to Christianity should not be achieved."

Sir George Somers was starting to like what he was hearing, but there were still unanswered questions. There was murmuring in the crowd, as people began to sense the possibility of riches. Another voice from the crowd shouted "Is food plentiful in Virginia? Are the colonists able to sustain themselves sufficiently to expand the colony?"

Christopher looked at the assembled crowd for a minute forming his words thoughtfully.

"Yes, food is very plentiful in Virginia." Christopher reached into a file that was on the desk, bringing out some crumpled and well-worn papers. "I have something here that I think you will be interested in." He placed his spectacles on his nose and drew himself up to full height, pausing to ensure he had the attention of everyone.

"Let me read from letters sent by the Jamestown councillors and colonists, that way you can see the colony from the perspective of other people, which will prove to you that what I am saying is the absolute truth and not my own wishful thinking...

One colonist writes:

'The land is very fruitful; there are oaks, ash, walnut, pine and cedar trees. The water is so stocked with sturgeon and other fish, that we have never seen anything like it.'

Another colonist reports:

'At the mouth of every brook and in every creek there are many kinds of fish, and in the sea, oysters and lots of crabs. The soil is better than in England and so we can produce better wheat, peas and beans. Strawberries, gooseberries, nuts, carrots, potatoes, pumpkins and melons all grow plentifully in Virginia."

Christopher Newport was glowing with pride as he read out the letters from the colonists.

The excitement in the room was rising to a frenzy as people shouted out question after question. Newport was ecstatic. He had given them what they wanted and things could only get better.

"I have returned to London to encourage you, the investors, to keep supporting this lucrative venture. Britain has lagged behind the Spanish in acquiring colonies, but things are changing. With time, the resources from this venture will make us rich, and bring respect to our nation - God Save the King! "

As the speech started to come to an end, there were cheers, whistling and clapping for Christopher Newport. The ale was flowing and the voices grew louder and louder as they chanted "God Save The King! God Save The King!" The mood in the room was jubilant. Christopher Newport was a hero. He had brought them the news that they wanted to hear and they were keen to see another expedition and another ship full of gold. Their greed was palpable.

Sir George Somers smiled. Maybe there *were* possibilities here, he thought as he slipped quietly away.

* * *

April 1608 Philpot Lane, London. (A year later)
"I can't believe what I am hearing Christopher" Thomas Smyth's normally placid voice was rising with panic. "People starving? Leaders locked in conflict? How could things have changed so drastically?" The room was stiflingly hot with a roaring fire, the reflection of which glistened in the four large tankards of ale placed on the table. Large comfortable chairs were arranged in a circle, with Christopher Newport, Sir George Somers and Sir Thomas Gates listening to Smythe ranting with anger.

Christopher Newport looked at the assembled group, crumpled with disappointment, his body shrinking as if trying to disappear. "I know, I know... it is not what I promised. I am as surprised as you are. The whole colony collapsed after I left the last time. That bastard John Smith managed to upset everyone. He was to be one of the leaders of the colony, but his behaviour was so despicable his colleagues imprisoned him – it doesn't get much worse than that. I tell you, I can understand why they don't want him there, he is poison. He upsets everyone with his arrogance. I freed him when he was sentenced to death, but I actually regret it."

"That is as may be, but from what you are saying, there are *many* problems, not just leadership, and I am not sure investors will be too keen to provide yet more money to prop up a disaster... It would be good money after bad." Smythe's reputation was seriously in jeopardy if this turned sour. He picked up his ale taking a large gulp to try and calm himself, then grabbed some snuff and sneezed.

Christopher was sitting on the edge of his chair. "We have to raise more money John. They are starving out there, and the fort burned down, so they have to try and build shelter. I struggle to give them sympathy as they are lazy bastards just concerned with finding gold, but I think we have a duty to save them." He sighed and looked with pleading eyes at the assembled group.

"If *you* struggle to give them sympathy Christopher, how do you think others will feel? How the hell am I supposed to raise more money when it seems these lazy bastards just sit on their arses and do nothing? There are a lot of *reputations* at stake here, as well as money. How can we salvage this without loss of face?"

Sir George Somers was looking grim. He had been excited about the prospect of fame if he became Admiral Of The Fleet for this project but now, it looked as if he would be wise to withdraw his name from any association with this white elephant. It was clearly *his* name that would be tarnished most if this gamble turned sour. In his retirement he wanted to make a good name for himself, not be dragged down with failure. He was not there for a humanitarian mission; he was there to make his name as the founder of a successful colony and to make a pile of money.

His eyebrows knitted together as he grimaced, sighing at the thought of the lost possibilities.

"No, I can't be involved in something like this" he said shaking his head. "A man of my reputation cannot be soiled by this incompetence... and it *must* be incompetence, as they had everything they needed, but just failed to make it work."

Sir Thomas Gates, silent until now, sat forward in his chair. "For God's sake!" He was a fifty year old soldier, well known for his inability to tolerate fools. He stood up abruptly, looking down on the others, banging his glass of ale on the table. "This is a waste of my time. For once I can agree with Sir George." Sir George raised his eyebrows - the two of them had a strong mutual dislike. "How you can sit here listening to Christopher's drivel and still think there is a chance to make things work, is beyond my comprehension. I am a man that succeeds. I will not be dragged down by this" he growled. "This was to be MY mission. I was to be Governor, the one in charge of everything and therefore it is my reputation more than anyone's that is at stake here. I will not be associated with this shambles." He picked up his glass of ale, downed the half a glass that was left, then stomped out of the room banging the door loudly.

Sir George Somers looked after him, his eyes rolling. "That man is a rude pig. Apart from everything else, *I* am to be Admiral of the Fleet. There cannot be two leaders!" He stared straight into the eyes of Thomas Smythe.

"The issue of who is leader is immaterial and the least of our problems at the moment." Thomas Smythe sighed. "I am sorry to say that for once I agree with Gates, this is all a waste of time. Unless we can do something radically different with this colony, I think it is a dead duck". Smythe relaxed back in his chair, taking his ale and finishing off the last dregs. He paused. "Yet more lives will be lost if we do not send them supplies, but we can't pull the wool over the eyes of the investors. There have been so many half-hearted attempts at this over many years. Some of the settlements have even just disappeared under our noses, for God's sake! How can this happen in the so called "land of plenty"? We need to find a way to raise considerably more money. We will need at least ten times what we have raised before, and with these latest reports I can't see that happening."
Sir George Somers and Christopher Newport were both looking at the glow of the fire sparkling in their glasses of ale, transfixed by Thomas Smythe's words. Neither wanted to believe what he was saying, but both were nodding their heads. "My view is that England will never succeed in America – perhaps we should leave it to the

Spanish."

* * *

May 1609 Lyme Regis

Lady Joanna Somers sat in the sitting room of their grand house, looking at her husband with questioning eyes. "What do you mean you are leaving to be the Admiral of the new fleet going to Virginia? We talked about this before. You said it was doomed to failure, and you were not going to be involved with it. You promised that you would stay with me here in Lyme Regis now that you are retired. You are too old anyway. I was so looking forward to finally being able to spend some time with you after all your years of gallivanting all over the world being the hero. Am I not enough for you?"

She was a delicate woman of immense elegance and style. Kindness always shone from behind her dark eyes and she had a softness that endeared her to those that met her. Her now grey hair was tied back in a chignon, and the pearls around her neck matched the luminosity of her crinkled skin.

He nodded. It was true, he had promised her that he would stay and continue his job as Mayor of the town... but this was such an opportunity. Beyond all expectation, they had raised enough money for an expedition. The King had granted another Charter, and they had turned the whole thing into a religious mission, galvanising the great and the good to invest in something that was now conveniently labelled as "God's Will". Investing had become fashionable and if one did not invest, one was seen as sacrilegious, a label to be avoided if you wanted to move in the upper echelons of society. A fantastic ploy that raised thousands of Guineas from inflated egos.

One more big bash. One more chance to feel the wind in his hair and the sea spray on his face. One more chance of excitement. He was born to be on the sea, and to stay here with his wife would be sacrificing whatever time he had left. If he stayed, it would be a time of drudgery, and he could not do it, even for this lovely woman who was his wife. He looked at her pleading eyes, and turned his own eyes to the floor. All he could see was himself at the helm in full dress uniform, commanding the fleet of nine ships. Men all lined up saluting him. "Yes sir!" they would cry.

He was carried away with his thoughts. The room was quiet as she waited for a response. He struggled to find the words. Brought back to reality, he looked over at the shelves and shelves of books lining the parlour, and imagined sitting day after day and reading them one by one. It was something he always swore that he would do, and had never had the time. If he chose to, he could devote whatever time he had left to it. But the thought was abhorrent to him. The large grandfather clock was ticking, the pendulum swinging backwards and forwards marking time that seemed to slow down, as she waited for him to respond. He coughed, placing his handkerchief at his mouth and looked at her, his eyes full of sorrow. She did not know the full truth, and he was not about to tell her.

He did not need to say anything. As she caught his gaze, she knew. Her face hardened. No words were spoken. She rose. Her taffeta gown crackled as she moved, the light catching the dark blue and green of her latest gown. Her cheeks were flushed, and a silent tear rolled down her face, as she dabbed her eye with her lace handkerchief.

41

He could see that she was trying to hold her emotions in, but wasn't fully succeeding. She walked across the room and turned to look at him as she reached the door. "Lunch will be served at noon. I assume you will be there." Then she was gone.

The room was silent. All he could hear was the beating of his heart as it pounded in his chest. He looked down at his handkerchief, quickly putting the blood stained piece of cloth back in his pocket. He did not want to look too closely. He might not have long – who knew. He was certain of two facts. The first was that he had to live, - *really* live, one more time before he died. The second fact was that he was already dying.

The Streets of London

John Rolfe felt himself to be in a foreign land. Walking down a London street, he felt alone and empty. He had left the peace and tranquillity of his home town of Heacham, and remembered with regret the warm bread scented kitchen of the Heacham farmhouse, and the first time he had experienced the joys of being part of a family. Of course, he had felt alone many times before he had met Sarah's family but this was very different. There was no countryside, no wildlife, and most of all, no Sarah to comfort him. When Jake had eventually left him and Sarah in the barn, his heart had ached with the thought of leaving her. He had considered asking her to come with him and marry him, but he knew this was out of the question, for *her* sake rather than his. Class and Religion were barriers that would make her an outcast as his wife. He put his hand in his pocket to feel the worn edges of Eustace's stone, which was now tarnished with his own blood. It brought comfort as well as painful memories both of Eustace and of Sarah. The stone's usefulness had diminished with each year that he had worked at the farm, but now it was his only comfort.

The noise of London was deafening. The rumble of carts on the cobbled streets, partnered with the din of street traders shouting out the benefits of their wares, was in stark contrast to the cool calmness of Heacham woods. The river, unlike the beautiful water off the coastline of Norfolk, was filled with grime as people washed in it, did their laundry in it, and threw remnants of old meat in it. There was scum floating on the surface of the water, and the smell of decay permeated the air.

The streets were teeming with rats; frantic, wild eyed and aggressive. John had heard tales of the Bubonic plague, and now he could see why the disease had been so serious. The rats, in their thousands, openly fed on putrefying fly-ridden rubbish that was left in the streets to rot. The thin and grubby residents of London were unmoved by the intrusion of these large rodents, occasionally giving one a swift kick if it was in the way.

The alehouses were small wooden houses that were dotted along the road. Drunkards and prostitutes were spilling out onto the cobbled streets, at any time of day, staggering erratically and violently. The number of people milling about jostling him and cursing was a new and terrifying experience for him. It took only a disrespectful glance for a fight to break out, so he looked at the ground, making no eye contact to avoid confrontation. Beggars sat at the side of the street in rags, their children running wild around them picking pockets. It was an unkind city.

An older woman of about thirty years with painted lips and a low neckline lined with dirt encrusted lace, started to walk toward John.

"What can I do for you my lovely?" she said beckoning him with her finger, the nail of which was black with grime. As she approached, John could smell the stink of ale and body odour masked with the scent of cheap stale perfume.

"I bet you have a fat purse that could help old Betty out." John looked at the ground, hoping that she would go away without incident, but she came towards him, staggering and grabbing the lapel of his jacket.

He pulled away, feeling light headed and unsure what to do. He held his belongings tightly as he knew he could lose everything if this woman wanted to rob him. He turned to flee and came face to face with another leering prostitute ready to take him on.

"Oh what a pretty one, look at your fine clothes and your flowing locks. I will give you one on the house, if you like my dear. I could teach you a thing or two." She grimaced, showing a mouth full of yellowing rotting teeth, with large gaps. Her obese and flabby frame drew closer and closer. John was being trapped. "Come to mummy, come to mummy" she taunted as she pushed her large bosoms very close to his face, her saliva landing in globules on his jacket.

He dodged adeptly and started running. As he ducked into an indent in one of the buildings, he could feel his heart racing and his breath short and uneven and he knew what was coming.

He started to tremble, and suddenly he was mentally transported back to Heacham watching Eustace fall. Terror took over and he froze. He was transported from one hell to another in a matter of seconds.

Luckily no one had followed him, and a rat, jumping off a nearby wall and landing on his back, startled him back to reality. He was still shaking but started to calm himself down, breathing slowly, and feeling the round shape of Eustace's stone in his pocket. After a while, he was able to gather his thoughts and remember where he was and what he had to do.

He had The Virginia Company's address written on a piece of paper and he had to get there tonight before nightfall. He could not sleep on these streets as he was sure by the morning he would have been mugged or murdered. He was aware that his attire indicated wealth, albeit shabby, and the cruelty and aggression that lived on these streets had no pity for one such as him. He drew his cloak around himself and bowed his head walking quickly in the direction of London Bridge hoping that further approaches from amorous Londoners would be thwarted by his purposeful stride.

He knew that Philpot Lane was near London Bridge, and he was able to duck into, what looked like a reputable Inn to ask directions. Looking around, he saw that the people in the inn were gentlemen like himself. He noted that most of the gentlemen were puffing on pipes as they drank their ale, and the room had a pleasant comforting smell of tobacco and an atmosphere of calm with the low murmur of conversation. This contrasted vastly with the hubbub of the street outside and made him feel more relaxed.

As he ordered his ale, he said to the inn keeper "I am trying to find the House of Sir Thomas Smythe in Philpot Lane, I wonder if you could direct me?"

"Oh you mean the Virginia Company man? Yes – that is not far at all. If you continue towards London Bridge, down Gracechurch Street, past Leadenhall, into Fenchurch Street and take the first right. It should only take ten minutes. I understand there is a big meeting at the house tonight concerning the next voyage to Virginia."

"Oh is there, so I am in time? I wanted to enrol as a passenger."

"I think you had better be quick getting down there, because a man that was in earlier said he was turned away as they already had enough people for the journey. They are interviewing everyone to get the right people, and I hear there are very strict rules".

He thanked the inn landlord, and when he finished his ale, headed in the direction of Philpot House. As he turned the corner into Philpot Lane, he saw a queue of people standing outside a large house.

There was excitement in the air, and as he looked closer he could see two plaques on the side of the house which said "Headquarters of The Virginia Company" and "Headquarters of The East India Company". He knew that he was in the right place. He turned to a middle-aged man, who was well-dressed and appeared educated.

"Sir, can you tell me where I go to enrol for Virginia?"

"We are all hoping to sign up, so you will just have to wait your turn." he said gruffly.

John could feel his panic rising, but dutifully joined the queue, waiting his turn to find out his fate.

A few hours passed and he started to panic, imagining available spaces diminishing but eventually he came face to face with Thomas Smythe. The room was dark and smoky with a roaring fire which made it stiflingly hot. The figure of Thomas Smythe was round and his complexion ruddy with the evidence of good living. He had an air of authority, but at the same time John could detect a humanity and kindness. He looked John up and down evaluating what must have been one out of the many people that he had seen that day.

"Sooooo... what is your name son and why do you want to join the expedition to Virginia?"

John stood awkwardly. He couldn't tell the whole reason, but he was prepared. "I have always had an interest in The New World, even as a child. I have read everything that there is to know about it, and Thomas Gates, in my opinion, is the greatest adventurer of all time. I have also followed the progress of the Virginia Company and have read all about the exploits of Sir Christopher Newport. My greatest ambition is to help found a colony in Virginia and make my fortune and my name."

Thomas Smythe smiled. He liked the look of this young man. There was a spark about him that suggested he would turn out to be a leader. He had intelligence and his eyes sparkled with enthusiasm as he spoke about Virginia. He wasn't going to take him on easily though. He had had to turn down many applicants, and he needed to be sure that this one had something to offer the new colony. "That's as may be." He sighed and looked at John searching his face for clues to his motives. "What skills have you got to offer the colony when we get there? I cannot take freeloaders that are only in it to find gold – that has happened too many times with dire consequences."

John jumped to the challenge. "I am the second son of the Lord of Heacham Manor, and as such I have spent my whole life learning about the farming of the land. I understand all aspects of farming from livestock to crops and I am able to direct workers and manage the farm books. I feel my skills will be put to better use in Virginia." He blurted out his pre-prepared speech. A little white lie about being the second son would not hurt, he thought. It would remove any need for explanations as to why he was leaving Heacham.

Thomas Smythe smiled. This is what he wanted. He had to make sure of the religion of this boy. The whole venture was based on the premise that the expedition was "God's Will". However, it was the Protestant God, not the Catholic. No Catholics were allowed. If it ever got out that a Catholic went on the expedition, there was no doubt that funding would be withdrawn. "What God do you worship son?" he asked smiling at John.

My family are very strict Protestants. My Stepfather (his mother having re-married on the death of his father, an event that had passed by with no involvement from him) is Chancellor of Norfolk." John replied quickly. As he spoke, he thought of Sarah and how he could never have brought her with him as a Catholic. Her religion would have prevented both of them from going. Whilst his heart had broken to leave her, now he was free to go to Virginia and fulfil Eustace's dreams.

At least his family connections were useful for getting to the New World. No need to reveal that his adoptive family were Catholic.

"Ah, I thought so but I just had to make absolutely sure."

Smythe continued with a lecture about the rules and regulations of the new colony. John wasn't really listening, he was thinking of the choice he had made. Maybe he could have stayed with Sarah and brazened it out with Jake. Maybe he could have converted and married her, staying at the farm and having a quiet life. Having made the awful decision, now that he was here and had accepted his fate, he was excited by the thought of riding on the high seas as he and Eustace had always talked about. Sarah had always told him to live for Eustace, she would understand. He felt the stone in his pocket, and smiled.

"Very well, young man. Sign your papers, and you can start helping with the preparations for the journey. We will be leaving in six weeks' time, and there is a lot of work to be done before that. There is a room upstairs where you can bunk down until then, and the dining room is next to the kitchen at the back of the house, help yourself to food."

"Thank you, Sir." He had signed his life away to The Virginia Company, and now he knew, without any doubt, that he would never see Sarah again. He had to finally close and lock that door in his heart forever. The only meaningful thing he had left was Eustace's stone and the knowledge that he had done the right thing, or had he? His heart still ached.

* * *

WOOLWICH DOCKS 1609

John made his way down to the docks at Woolwich the next day. It was a beautiful May morning and the sun was shining. He was surprised by the excitement he felt in his bones. He had imagined how it would feel to embark on an adventure like this for so many years, all the time denying himself the belief that it was possible. Eustace's dream had become his dream and he convinced himself that he could not mar the moment with regrets of what he had left behind. Sarah was in the past, Sarah was gone. Instead, he had a life of adventure before him. He must keep reminding himself.

As he rounded the corner, the scene took his breathe away. In front of him was the most magnificent vessel he had ever seen. The five year old, 100 foot long vessel "Sea Venture", the lead ship of the fleet of nine, towered above him, her newly painted hull gleaming in the sunshine giving the perception of solidness and invincibility. No one looking at her today would doubt her capacity to stand up to whatever stood in her way. The figurehead of The Hound of the Vikings towered over the ant-like creatures that were loading her and preparing her for the journey ahead. Her two flags – the Union flag on the main mast and the Flag of St. George at the fore, fluttered in the warm breeze like kings waving to their lowly subjects.

John was staggered by the spectacle as he looked further down the key to see the other six ships, "Diamond", "Falcon","Blessing", "Unity", "Lion" and "Virginia", plus two small pinnaces. The entire fleet, led by the magnificent "Sea Venture" would be carrying the total of 600 passengers.

Hundreds of people were carrying, bending, throwing, polishing, climbing rigging, and shouting. There was a frenzy of activity that John was keen to be a part of. Apart from those loading the ships and the sailors checking the rigging and sails, there were hundreds of people milling around the dock, all keen to take advantage of a ready market for their wares. Bakers carried boxes of bread hanging from tapes around their necks, smoke billowed from makeshift fires that were lit in old tin boxes cooking every type of food one could imagine. Sausages were sizzling and potatoes baking. The noise and the smells were overwhelming. He suddenly felt in his gut that this was his destiny. Everything in his life so far, had brought him to this moment. At last he was somewhere he felt he belonged and he smiled, his pain momentarily forgotten.

"Hey you, boy! Don't stand around gawping! Get those bags of grain loaded, time is money you know." He looked up to see a weather-beaten man of about fifty, pointing at him angrily.

"Sorry Sir. I am at your service." John started to lift the bags of grain that were at his feet. He was surprised by the weight, but did not falter. He moved up the gangplank carrying two bags and followed the other men, finding a home for them in the hold. Having delivered his load, he stood on deck, feeling the slight movement of the swell, and the warmth on his skin. Yes, this is for me he thought, as he started to make his way back to get more bags of grain. He thought of Eustace, and felt the stone in his pocket. I am really here, he thought. I have made it happen.

At the end of his first day, John's back ached and his thighs were burning from the weight of the bags of grain that he had carried non-stop throughout the whole day. It seemed that everyone felt the same. The weather-beaten boss approached John smiling.

"Well done lad. You did a fine days' work there. Are you joining us on the expedition, or just here for the loading?"

"I am John Rolfe of Heacham Sir, and I am sailing on the "Sea Venture"." John's face was gleaming with the sweat of the day's work, but his voice was strong and proud.

The other man looked him up and down, taking in his youth and enthusiasm and remembering himself as a lad in similar circumstances. "Welcome. I am Sir Thomas Gates, and I will be sailing with you and taking up the post of Governor when we reach Virginia."

John was taken aback. He had never expected his boyhood hero,

Sir Thomas Gates to acknowledge him, let alone speak to him. "I am honoured Sir" he stammered, as he took a slight bow in acknowledgement.

Sir Thomas looked over his shoulder. "Yeardley…, Pierce…, take this lad for a drink. He has done his first hard day's work of, what I am sure will be, a long and distinguished career. Show him the ropes and tell him who his friends are. I can see that he is 'one of us'.

John saw two men approaching, who he assumed were Yeardley and Pierce. They both looked like experienced soldiers, older than him, and with the weathered complexions of the sea. The taller of the two, had strawberry blond hair that had been bleached in the sun and freckles peppering his bronzed face. Some would say he was handsome, but for his rather sharp facial features.

"Come with us lad" he bellowed as he banged John on the back, a little too hard.

"Ale it is for you, on your first day."

As they entered the tavern, John coughed and blinked through the strong haze of tobacco smoke as he fought through the crowds of merry men to find a seat in the corner.

"Yes, it is a bit fuggy in here, isn't it?" said the shorter darker man. "By the way, I am William Pierce and this reprobate is George Yeardley" he said pushing his companion roughly in a playful way. "We go back a long way with old Thomas Gates - he has been our commander in many raids in the Netherlands. As we are both married now, we thought we would have a bit of a change from fighting Spanish, and join him on this little venture. Our wives are with us, but will be traveling on different ships as there isn't room for them on the "Sea Venture". So, we can do what we like while the old girls can't see." He laughed in a mischievous way, but his eyes were sad thinking about his wife and four year old daughter. He pulled himself together, taking his mind away from his family. "Anyway, Yeardley

- why haven't you got the ale yet, you slacking bastard?" Yeardley laughed sticking his two fingers up at Pierce.

"I don't know why I stick with you, you bully" Yeardley shouted as he disappeared into the throng of drunken sailors to find some ale for them all.

John sat deep in thought as he waited for Yeardley to come back. These two men were bringing their wives, maybe he could have done. But no, their wives weren't Catholic, so it wasn't the same. He must stop thinking about Sarah. This was such a wonderful adventure. These two had actually been a part of the battles that he and Eustace had read about. They had fought alongside Sir Thomas Gates, and now he was one of them.

George Yeardley staggered back with three pints of ale. "There are three steaming beef pies on the counter - I have paid for them, so you had better go and get them before some other bastard nobbles them John" he shouted over the noise of the tavern that was creaking at the seams with drunken men.

John jumped up and tried to forge a path through the crowd squeezing himself through narrow gaps, avoiding pints of ale spilling down as he pushed and levered himself between the laughing punters. At last he was in sight of the steaming pies on the bar top. As he went to reach up for them, he saw a large arm sweep across his path, grabbing the pies.

"No, stop, those are my pies" John shouted. He was desperate not to let his two new friends down, and he was very hungry. The thief obviously couldn't hear John as he paid no attention to John's pleas. John tried harder "Sir, please, I think you are mistaken." John shouted.

The thief stood like a brick barrier in front of him, glaring down at him, daring him to take the pies. "Push off, I was here first. What you gonna do about it posho matey? Possession is the law, I think you will find." John could tell that this monster of a man meant business. He was huge, his chest heaved with anger, and his shiny bald head was sweating in the heat of the tavern. His small piercing eyes glared at John, as if one wrong move and he would swat him like a mosquito.

The tavern owner saw what was happening. "Want - I will not have your antics any more in this tavern. I have had enough. Get away from those pies; they don't belong to you, as you well know. Any more from you and you will be banned from this tavern!" He marched towards Want, and grabbed the pies, handing them to John with a wink.

"You little posh bastard!" Want shouted at John as he made his way back to the table in the corner and his two waiting friends who were getting up to leave. "I will remember this... I never forget a face, and I will get you back one day. Come on Robbie, I don't need this." He growled like a wounded dog, kicking over a chair as he turned and put his fist up at John before he followed his friend through the door.

"Whoops" said Yeardley raising his eyebrows. "He is not one to have as an enemy. Be careful John - he is sailing with us on the "Sea Venture" so watch your back. He has very few scruples. I saw him giving the poor little stable boy, Davey Jones a hiding yesterday just for sport. I don't understand why Smythe put him on the list. He is bad news."

"So that is what Sir Thomas meant about friends and enemies then?" said John, as he took a swig of his ale to hide his rising panic. That guy was big, very big he thought, feeling his stomach turn over. The boat was a confined area, he was sure to bump into him again.

"Yes, keep your wits about you John. Not everyone is as friendly as us." said George Yeardley smiling and handing John a clay pipe, the like of which most of the men in the tavern were drawing on.

"Thanks" said John, taking the clay pipe and looking around him to see what others were doing with it. He took their lead and sucked in the aromatic smoke, closing his eyes for a moment to savour the taste.

It was warm and fragrant, and he could understand why everyone wanted to partake. Suddenly he felt it tickling the back of his throat, and he coughed and spluttered, trying to catch his breath, fighting for his dignity.

His two companions looked at one another and laughed. "No worries John. You will get the hang of tobacco if we have anything to do with it."

"It seems as if there are a lot of things I will have to get the hang of" said John shrugging his shoulders. If only Eustace had been here - they would have made a formidable team he thought wistfully.

Dilemma at Philpot Lane

T he day had ended well. He was feeling mellow after the tobacco and ale that he had shared with George Yeardley and William Pierce. He was happy. At last he felt that he was part of something that was worthwhile. Something that he and Eustace had been dreaming about for years. Everything was going to be fine, he had to just keep himself busy to stop any thoughts of Sarah. He sauntered along the road, whistling, and kicking the odd stone, the dull ache of his lost love starting to give way to the excitement of his new adventure .

As he approached Thomas Smythe's house, he saw a figure standing outside the Philpot Lane house, shrouded in a cloak obscuring his face. John grew wary, thinking back to the violence he had witnessed on the streets and remembering the staring eyes of Want, the ruffian who had tried to steal his pies. A figure lurking in the dark would only be doing so for one reason. Robbery. He continued walking as quickly as he could with his head down. Thomas Smythe's house was only a few yards away, and with any luck he could dodge the dark stranger and get to safety. He hoped it was not Want come back for revenge. As he drew closer, the figure threw back the cloak.

His heart was in his mouth, he did not know what to do, say or feel.

"Sarah... what are you doing here?" He took in her lovely auburn hair, the sprinkling of freckles on her face, and the intense pleading look in her eyes.

"I couldn't bear it any longer without you John. I had to come and find you."

He could not stop himself as, impulsively he ran to her and grabbed her hands, he wanted to encase her in his arms, but in the middle of a London street, this would cause a spectacle that could have consequences. What could he do? This was so unexpected. He had come to accept that she was no longer in his life - but here she was. He would have to secrete her into his room in Philpot house, until he could think of a solution. He looked around the street, and fortunately there seemed to be no one around.

"Come with me quickly, and pull your cloak around you so people can't see you". He was confused and frightened, ecstatic she was there, but scared because he didn't know what to do. He looked from side to side, checking that there was no one coming, and pulled her into the house and up the stairs. He opened the door to his room and gently pushed her through, praying that they would not be seen or heard.

"Oh my sweet Sarah" he said pulling her to him. He did not care about the consequences now, his goal of getting to Virginia was forgotten, his body was craving the feel of her touch, just the way it had the first time, only this time the feelings were stronger. She melted into his arms, it was like he had been dying of thirst, and she was all he needed to quench it. He realised that his feelings for her were not something that he could dismiss. The weeks of being deprived of her, seemed to instantly dissolve into overwhelming feelings of joy. He was alive.

He ran his finger over her face feeling the soft velvet skin, looking at each freckle as if it was a piece of gold. He removed the hood from her head, and her long auburn hair tumbled out down her back. He was breathless, lost in a dreamlike state from which he did not want to waken.

She ran her fingers through his hair and he felt a tingling at her touch. Their eyes locked as each looked into the soul of the other, hardly daring to move in case they broke the spell. Her fingers traced the line of his face, and gradually moved downwards undoing his garments button by button.

* * *

John's dilemma was overwhelming. He could not leave Sarah now, and respectability demanded that if they were to be together, marriage was the only solution. His happiness at boarding the "Sea Venture" had turned into confusion. He still had to do the honourable thing for Sarah, and that must take precedence over everything else.

If they married, he could not take her to Virginia like Pierce and Yeardley had done with their wives – Catholics were forbidden. He would have to abandon that idea, and maybe get a job as a farm labourer or some other lowly means of livelihood. They would be very poor, and alone. He looked over at her sleeping form. She began to stir, and he reached over and gave her a kiss on the cheek. She opened her eyes startled, as if she didn't know where she was, and when consciousness took over, she gave him a mischievous smile.

"Good morning" she sighed. Her cheeky grin spreading from ear to ear.

"Good morning" he said as he snuggled back down next to her. He looked into her eyes and sighed. "Sarah, I can't let you go, we must be together, but we have a lot of thinking to do. There are so many obstacles in our way."

"I know, I know…" she said reaching for him." I don't know what to do either." As she said this, the sparkle previously in her eyes diminished, and her body became slumped as if defeated. I am Catholic. My family have faced many dangers for the cause. It would feel a betrayal for me to convert. But I know I can't live without you. We can't live in sin, we would be outcasts". As Sarah spoke, her fingers gently fondled the rosary that hung around her neck, a symbol of her love not only for her God, but for her family. Her mind drifted back to when John had left her and a shadow crossed over her face.

She had moped around the farm, unable to think or function. Her family became worried about her, as they could see she was ill – she was not eating or sleeping and she never smiled. Even her Father could not put a smile on her face, and he became very concerned as the robust young woman he knew, became a shadow of her former self. Sarah constantly prayed, her rosary was never out of her hands as she murmured prayers over and over seeking comfort that was never forthcoming.

She had thought John loved her and felt the same as she did, but his choosing to leave without her told a different story.

Surely he could have convinced Jake to leave them alone? Surely their love was stronger than her brother's hate? Eventually, she could stand it no longer. She had no life without John, but she had to be sure that he felt the same. The only way was to go to London and confront him again- it was either that or live the rest of her life as an old maid constantly questioning her existence and wondering what might have been.

She left in the middle of the night leaving a note for her Father, explaining that she had to go to London, but giving no details. She wanted the family to know that despite her having left them, she would always love them.

Now she was here with John – it was as she had thought – he did love her as much as she loved him. She felt the rosary in her hand as she looked up at him. He had turned into the most handsome man she had ever seen. He had hair that was touched with gold from the outdoor work on the ships, his skin had a chestnut glow, but his lovely hazel eyes that usually sparkled when he laughed, were now clouded with the fear of what they were facing.

He looked at her, his brows pulled together. "What are we to do?" He threw himself back on the bed and stared at the ceiling puffing on the tobacco that had become his new found habit. "I want to marry you, I want to go to Virginia with you, but neither is possible.

She paused for a moment, looking at the floor. "Would you marry me if it were possible?" she whispered. Her words were so quiet that John could hardly hear what she said, but when she said it again with slightly more conviction he understood.

"Of course I would" his eyes turned from the ceiling flashing with desperation as he searched her face for some indication of the thoughts behind her words.

"I want to marry you" she said, her face crumpling, and her mouth quivering as she fought back the tears.

John knew by the look on her face, the dreadful struggle that she was going through.

He knew how important her religion was to her – it was part of her.

He remembered how her family had assembled in the warm steamy kitchen at Heacham, their love for each other cemented by the shared belief in Catholicism. How could such an innocent ritual performed by good upstanding people command a death sentence for a priest and prevent her from being with the man she loved?

"I will convert" she blurted out. "... and we will go to Virginia." There – she had said it – and there was no going back. Her heart was racing.

"If anyone ever finds out that you worshipped the Church of Rome, life will be very difficult for you, even if you converted. You could face a death sentence... I want you to be safe." He was struggling to convey what he wanted – as he wasn't sure what that was. Thoughts were rambling in his head - going one way, and then going another.

Sarah looked deeply into his eyes. He fought to hide his hope that she would choose him over her religion. She had said she would convert, but he wasn't sure if she meant it. Holding his breath. Waiting.

"No, I have decided that we must go to Virginia." Her voice was overly strong and unflinching as she tried to hide the pain of her decision. A life with John as a farmer would only be a life of resentment and guilt for his sacrificed dream, and she could not bear that. If she wanted to be with him, she had no choice.

"There is one thing though..."

"Anything" he replied, looking at her, his eyes filling with fear, wondering what she was going to say.

"I must keep my rosary. My rosary is my connection with my family, a little like Eustace's stone is your connection to Eustace. I will keep it well hidden, but I must keep it."

"It is dangerous to have such things on your person Sarah. You must be very careful, because if it is ever discovered there could be dire consequences.

She picked up her rosary, moving the beads between her fingers. "I know John, but please don't make me throw away my rosary."

He knew this was the only way, despite the dangers, and he nodded in agreement with her.

She pulled him to her, and wrapped her arms around his neck.

"One more thing…" she said.

She gently placed his hand on her stomach and held her breath, pausing while she waited for him to look into her eyes. " I am having your baby… "

Beth

She was only fifteen years old, and had lived solely with her father, Eddy Samuel, since she was five, when her mother had died of the plague. She and her father had struggled to survive. He had work periodically and she, as a very young child, stayed in the one room that they shared, alone and terrified most of the time.

Her name was Elizabeth, but her father called her Beth. She missed her mother and the very different life that she had known in the first five years of her life. She couldn't understand it when strangers came to take her mother's body away and said that it had to be burned. No amount of tears brought her mother back, and she was left numb. Her father didn't talk to her or explain what had happened. She had never been close to her father, but as he had grudgingly been forced to care for her, a bond of sorts grew between them. They were not close, but they needed each other. They were both trying to survive in a world where everything was against them.

When she was eight, Beth's father taught her how to steal and pickpocket on the streets of London - and she had been extremely good at it. Her appearance helped their cause. She was of delicate build, with flaxen hair and bright blue eyes. When she smiled, people could not help but smile back, as she was so engaging. With some of the money that she managed to steal, her father bought her fine clothes of silk and velvet, making her appear to be a little lady. Her expensive clothing was very successful at disarming unsuspecting gentry as she mingled in the crowds, slipping her little white hand in and out of handbags and pockets smiling with the confidence of someone who had been brought up in a stately manor.

Beth's career as a pickpocket had ended quite suddenly. It wasn't that long ago, and she knew that as she was getting older, she was not quite as cute and inconspicuous as she had been a few years ago. She had seen a tall dark man standing talking to a very pretty lady, and it looked like they were engrossed in conversation. She sidled up to the man, as was her usual tactic, and deftly cut his purse from his belt with a sharp knife in one swift movement. Unfortunately, the lady talking to him saw Beth in the corner of her eye.

"Stop thief" she shouted, as the man turned quickly enough to grab Beth by the wrist.

"Sorry sir" she said weakly, looking at him and trying to be as sweet and vulnerable as she could. "My mam is dying, and I need money for my little sister that is only three days old." She quickly thought up a sob story that might soften his heart, and she could see that his eyes were softening as he was starting to let go of the grip he had on her wrists.

At that moment, the Constable came over to see what was happening. "Good day, fine sir, is this girl bothering you" he nodded in Beth's direction. "Beth, you are not up to your old tricks are you?" He looked at her sternly. He had let her off several times, but this was one time too many. He walked over to her and roughly put handcuffs on her. She looked at the Gentleman with pleading eyes, but he turned and walked away.

This had led to a night in gaol for her. A night she would never forget.

She was flung in a stone cell with three prostitutes and two drunken sailors. It was only to be over night, so the jailer had not bothered to segregate his prisoners, he didn't care for the well-being of the inmates. They had misbehaved and deserved no respect. The girl looked a little young, but she had survived on the streets, she could survive in jail. What the hell?

Beth was roughly shoved into the cell.

"Hello little love" the prostitute crooned when she saw the fifteen year old land on her knees which were now bleeding and sore.

"What you doin in ere then? Been a naughty little girl, ave we?" The prostitute was in her forties, with grimy clothes and bright red lipstick. "Best do as yer told in ere" she said winking knowingly.

"A nice little morsel you are" one of the other prostitutes said. "Could make a packet in our game. What about it. Want us to introduce you to our minder then?"

Beth recoiled with horror. She and her father may have been poor, but she would never stoop to such depths as these women.

"Just leave me alone" She shouted. Her face was wet with tears and crumpled with fear and loathing. "My father will get me out of here" she shouted

The prostitutes laughed.

At that the two drunken sailors shook themselves from their stupor. "Oh, I see we have top class company with us now. What a little treat" said the larger of the two, smiling and rubbing his dirt encrusted hands together. "What do you say Jim?"

"Mmm..." his companion was walking towards Beth with a purposeful look on his face.

"Daddy, daddy" he said, his voice mocking her. "Come to Daddy. Daddy will make it all better."

The three prostitutes laughed louder. They could see what was on the minds of their drunken companions. "Oh come on, you two. She is only a baby" said the first one.

"Nice and tender" retorted the sailor who was now towering over the terrified Beth. "Perhaps you will need to hold her down for us though; she doesn't look very loving at the moment." He laughed at his understatement.

Beth curled herself up into a tight ball, trying to fend off her attackers, but it was no use. She screamed and screamed, but no one came.

She smelt the sweat and closed her eyes. She was no match for them.

Sarah

arah had finally summoned a degree of excitement at her impending nuptials.

John had given her some money from his wages on the "Sea Venture", to buy a new dress for the ceremony. She chose a green dress which she embellished with fresh daisies, making herself a crown of white roses that contrasted beautifully with her long auburn hair.

She stood, on her wedding day, looking up at her handsome young husband, imagining the small life growing inside of her. He looked down at her as they took their vows, smiling, holding her hand as they finally became man and wife. They had sipped spiced wine to celebrate, and John had hired a carriage to transport them back to Philpot lane for their first night as man and wife. He had showered her with kisses in the carriage until she felt he was going to consume her with love.

She thought about her family on her wedding day, knowing that she had to accept that she would probably never see them again as tears pricked her eyes. She had her rosary safely in her pocket, and felt it's shape as she took her vows. On the face of it, she had renounced Catholicism for John, but a part of her would always remain close to the religion of her family. She knew the rosary would keep her safe and she would never let it go. It was her strongest security and her strongest danger all rolled into one.

They had spent a blissful few weeks as man and wife before they boarded the "Sea Venture". John would leave every morning to continue his work preparing for the journey at the docks. She always brought him lunch, continuing the childhood ritual of providing fresh bread and cheese, but now washed down with ale instead of milk. John talked to her for hours about his dreams of going to Virginia to fulfil his brother's dreams.

"Sarah, Sarah, listen to this... I have just found an excerpt from John Smith's book. You know he is one of the settlers in Virginia? It is just like Eustace and I used to imagine... The Indians captured him and took him before Powhatan, the Indian Chief. This is what he writes:

"before a fire upon a seat like a bedsted... On either hand did sit a young wench of 15 or 18 years, and along on each side the house, two rowes of men, and behind them as many women, with all their heads and shoulders painted red; many of their heads bedecked with the white down of Birds; but every one with something: and a great chayne of white beads about their necks..... two great stones were brought before Powhatan: then as many as could layd hands on him, dragged him to them and thereon laid his head, and being ready with their clubs, to beate out his braines, Pocahontas, the Kings dearest daughter, when no intreaty could prevaile, got his head in her armes, and laid her owne upon his to save him from death; whereat the Emperor was contented he should live." John's eyes were sparkling with excitement imagining the picture" of what had happened.

"Wow, a real life Indian Squaw... imagine that." he said.

Sarah smiled. "Let's just hope you don't need saving by an Indian Squaw" she laughed. She was a little disconcerted by the story. What kind of place were they going to?

On the morning of 7th May 1609, John and Sarah walked to the Woolwich docks together, ready to board the ship and leave England forever. He held her hand, squeezing it with excitement as they approached the bustling pier. Suddenly, she broke free.

"Catch me" she said as she started to run.

"Sarah, wait" he ran after her, catching her just as they reached the gangplank. He picked her up and buried his face in her neck. She laughed, throwing her head back with mirth as he carried her up the gangplank. All those on board, seeing the happy couple, clapped and whooped as they arrived on deck.

Sarah had thought the "Sea Venture" was beautiful, when she had first climbed the gangplank at Woolwich. She had been excited, thinking about the journey ahead with her new husband who had regaled her with tales of the beautiful ship and the excitement that he felt in fulfilling Eustace's dream.

All of that was three weeks ago. Now she had lived on the ship she had experienced the reality of the conditions; conditions that were bound to deteriorate more once they reached the open seas. She remembered her first twinges of doubt as she made her way skipping hand in hand with John down to the gun deck that first day, excited to see the cabin that was to be theirs over the next nine weeks.

Instead, of a cabin, what she found was a small dark area full of makeshift beds made of rammed straw. There was very little space between the beds, and she could see that privacy was a thing of the past. John had managed to get some sacking to hang around their beds in an attempt at hiding her modesty, but the reality of the lack of space and the forced intimacy with strangers began to become a horrible reality.

She had held John's hand as they stood on the deck with the other passengers, watching England become a small dot on the horizon. He was handsome and strong and she loved him. But as she watched

England fade into the distance, she would have given anything to be those two children again... Just John and Sarah. Now they were husband and wife, with a child on the way setting out on an adventure that most people never even dreamed possible. Perhaps she would have rather been with John in a country kitchen as a farmer's wife instead of sailing into the unknown. She had to put those thoughts out of her mind. She rose up on tiptoes and kissed his rough bearded face.

"I am so tired John. I have to go down to the gun deck to lie down." She smiled at him.

He looked concerned. "Are you sure you are alright Sarah? Is there anything that you need?"

"No, my love" she shook her head. "It is just that with the baby, I am not sleeping well, and I am more tired than normal." She gave him a hug and turned away.

He watched her go. He was concerned about the conditions that she had to put up with. He had no idea that things would be so bad, but there was little he could do now to change anything. It would not be long, and they would reach Virginia where the settlement would give her all the comforts she deserved.

As she reached the gun deck she looked around her, wrinkling her nose and retching with the stench of the place that she had called home for the past three weeks. She thought with horror that it would only get worse. They were only just leaving Plymouth for the open seas and already the deck was the most disgusting swirl of human fluids imaginable. The journey from Woolwich to Plymouth had been a little stormy, but she knew it had been *nothing* like they were likely to experience on the open seas. But even so, almost everyone had been sick, with nowhere for the vomit to go, but the floor.

The light in the gun deck was dim, as daylight could only be seen through spaces that had been left when the guns were moved up to the main deck. There was just enough light to see the rats scurrying about looking for detritus as sustenance. She shuddered remembering how at night when darkness fell, and visibility was low, the rats made their presence known by their high pitched screams and the feel of their little paws with sharp nails as they ran over her body. She lay tense with fear, clutching her rosary and praying they did not bite her. Small wonder that she was not sleeping well.

Going to the toilet, which her pregnancy made her do with increased frequency, was a feat of complete indignity. She felt like a farm animal as she squatted over a china bowl that had to be emptied in the bilge on the deck below - a task she had to leave to her new husband as women were not allowed on the lower decks. With the shame of it, her face went red, just thinking about it. Just married, She had had to reveal to John, a side of her that most women keep hidden from their husbands for their whole lives.

Most people didn't bother with the niceties of the disposing of their bodily fluids in the bilge as she did, and even in the short time they had been on board, the floor was awash with not only vomit, but urine and faeces as well. The stench was unbearable. Sarah tried to block it out by breathing through her mouth, or holding a handkerchief to her nose, but gave up in the end. Nausea was something she would not be able to escape from - pregnancy, the vile smell, and the rhythmical rising and falling of the ship were all contributors to her sickness, and none of them were going to diminish over the next six weeks. Her increasing nausea meant that her own vomit mingled with that of many others on the gun deck. At least one godsend was that with her pregnancy, her bleeding had stopped. That would have been the ultimate humiliation.

She caressed the rosary that she kept in the deep pocket of her now dirt stained dress, and looked around her again knowing that the first three weeks had been hell, and realizing that it had only been a mild taster for the next six weeks, when the seas would be rougher, and the rations scarcer. Her eyes welled up and a silent tear slid gently down her young face. Of course she loved John, but why did things have to be so hard? She felt the first bead of her rosary through the cloth of her dress to be sure that no one saw, and mouthed "The Apostles Creed". "I believe in God, the… " she said in her mind soundlessly.

"Are you alright love?" Sarah jumped, she had thought she was alone and didn't see Alice Eaton sitting in the corner in the dim light. She rubbed the tears from her face, let go of the rosary in her pocket and sat up straight, trying to pretend that there was no problem, and then slumping when it occurred to her that Alice must have been watching her for some time.

"Oh Alice, I didn't know you were there. I am just feeling a little overwhelmed with everything. I think it is my hormones playing havoc." She tried to laugh, but her eyes didn't sparkle, and her mouth quivered with sadness. Alice didn't smile but she looked at Sarah with warmth and compassion in her eyes.

"It is not easy for any of us Sarah, least of all when you are 19 and pregnant and we are leaving dry land to sail across an ocean we don't know, to a place we don't know and the conditions on this ship are beyond belief. The men are so excited about the prospect of an adventure, and in truth, I was until I realized what it was going to be like. It will not be like this forever though - hopefully the hell will end at the Gates of Paradise as Edward has promised me" she said mockingly and smiled as she walked over to Sarah and sat down next to her putting her arm around her.

Sarah was instantly put at ease by Alice's warm welcoming smile and her quiet unassuming ways. She was older than Sarah by about five years, which added to Sarah's trust in her. She had long black hair and bright blue eyes, and turned the eye of many of the men on-board. She seemed oblivious to her beauty. Married to Edward Eaton, the ship's Doctor, she was well liked among the other passengers, and she and Sarah had started to become friends.

Sarah melted into Alice's shoulder. Even now, she missed a mother's touch, and Alice's hug, whilst comforting, had triggered all her pent up feelings. Her whole body rocked with sobs of grief while Alice stroked her hair. Alice continued stroking her hair and rocking her like a baby, until at last Sarah's sobs subsided. Sarah was comforted by Alice's embrace. Despite this, the terror, anger and confusion had not left her. She stopped crying, not because she felt better, but because she had no more tears to cry.

Suddenly, she sat up and pulled herself away from Alice looking straight into her eyes. "Oh Alice, I feel so trapped, I think I have made a terrible mistake... I wish I could go home" she said. Alice sighed.

"You know that is not an option now Sarah. Your baby is going to be born in the New World and the only thing you can do now, is to accept the inevitability of that." She said it kindly but with determination in her voice as she got up from Sarah's bed, and started walking back to her own. Alice lay down and closed her eyes; Sarah's words had triggered memories. Sarah didn't know how lucky she was. She was going to have a baby. Alice's mind floated back to the many miscarriages that she had had. She had given up on the possibility of ever becoming a mother as year after year babies were lost to her. Five in all - three boys and two girls. Edward never knew that she had given each one a name, and they spoke to her in her dreams.

Sarah noticed that her new friend had become quiet and thoughtful, and she realised how self-centred she must appear. The words had just popped out - it was thoughtless. "I am sorry Alice. I know it is difficult for you too." She put her hand in her pocket and furtively, hiding it from Alice, brought out her one precious possession - her rosary. She looked at it and thought back to her wedding day which had been very happy, but tainted by deceit. If she was honest with herself, she still felt she was Catholic, but had married as a Protestant. She did what she had to do to be with her John, but perhaps in God's eyes this meant that she was not married at all. Maybe she was being punished.

At that moment, the ship lurched and the rosary fell out of her hand onto the murky floor in full view.

She jumped up, startled out of her thoughts. She had to retrieve the beads before they were seen. She crouched down picking them up, looking around her. She clasped them to her chest, and looked over at Alice. Alice was lying with her eyes closed, deep in thought. Thank heavens for that, thought Sarah, breathing a sigh of relief. She must be more vigilant.

It was too late though. A furtive pair of eyes took in the scene with malicious surprise, storing it for future use should it be needed. The unseen person slipped from the gun deck, smirking.

Leaving

Plymouth 2nd June 1609

Sir George Somers had arranged for his embarkation on the "Sea Venture" to be spectacular. He wanted everyone to know he was in charge, and to see how elegant and formidable he still was as he walked down the gangway. He knew he had a reputation as fierce and demanding when on a ship, and now he was roaring like a lion ready for anything.

He was dressed immaculately in the full uniform of an Admiral with his colourful, shiny campaign medals twinkling in the sun. His tanned face, full head of grey hair and wiry stature indicated many years spent at sea which had kept him fit and in good shape for a man of coming up to 60 years. His vivid blue eyes were watchful, missing nothing as he strode aboard this wonderful ship. He could feel hundreds of eyes boring in to him as the crew and passengers of the "Sea Venture" and its Pinnace, lined up to greet him, and the trumpeters continued to welcome the new Commander.

He noted with pleasure the large shiny horses being loaded on to the Pinnace attached securely to the "Sea Venture", and gave a nod to the young groom, who, keen to impress his Admiral, was standing to attention, a wide grin on his face at being noticed by such an important man. Sir George broke off from his route and walked over to where the young groom was standing.

"You have some beautiful horses there young man. I hope you are going to look after them well for me." Sir George smiled at the lad, and shook his hand.

"Yes, sir, of course sir. I will guard them with my life." The lad gave a bow.

"What is your name lad?" Sir George loved being a hero, and he could see from the boy's breathless reply that he was making this lad's day by singling him out for attention.

"My name is Davey Jones sir. Davey Jones at your service." He stood ramrod straight to attention.

"I am glad you are with us Master Jones. Give the horses some extra meal for me and tell the galley that you are to have extra rations tonight yourself as you are one of Sir George Somers's most trusted men." Sir George turned to a sailor standing behind him. "See the cooks understand."

Davey was grinning from ear to ear. He had never been spoken to by such a grand person. An orphan from the workhouse never usually gets any acknowledgment, and he had always been treated like the scum of the earth. He had curly black hair, a swarthy skin, piercing vivid blue eyes and freckles, a mixture handed down to him by his black father and Irish mother. The combination had never stood him in good stead, despite his spirit and intelligence. He had been an outcast since his mother left him wrapped in a blanket and placed him gently in a dustbin. Life had always been a struggle, until this moment.

"Yes sir! I am your servant sir!" Davey would walk to the ends of the earth for this man. Indeed, he would give his life for him if needed.

Sir George saluted Davey one more time and turned to continue walking through the crowd. He looked around him, making eye contact with the occasional crew member, passenger or tradesman, and nodding in acknowledgment. Some he recognized, but most were strangers. All had seen the exchange between the Admiral and the lowly stable boy, and all were impressed by the humility the Admiral had displayed. Whilst his encounter with the boy was designed to impress, it was also a genuine act, as he was truly interested in all those who sailed with him, even the lowliest had his respect.

One thing that Sir George noticed with annoyance was that Thomas Gates was conspicuous by his absence. Somers had wondered how he would be greeted by his Co-Commander, and now he knew that definite lines had been drawn between them by his refusal to attend his grand entrance - not that Somers really cared.

He saw Vice-Admiral Christopher Newport standing at attention saluting. As a Navy man, *he* knew his place. Gates would be the problem. Smythe had told him that Gates had demanded to be on the "Sea Venture" even although there were already two Commanders - himself and Newport. Gates's skills were needed as Governor, so in the end the Virginia Company had reluctantly agreed that the three of them should sail together and sort out their differences along the way. Sir George just hoped that it could be amicable.

He raised his hand to stop the trumpeters, before taking a stand on the podium in front of his charges, waving his hand to silence the band.

"I am Admiral Sir George Somers, and I am your Admiral of the Fleet for this voyage. I expect this to be a swift and safe journey, and God willing we will all land in Jamestown in about six weeks time. During the voyage, I expect us all to behave in a civil manner. We have to learn to share space, food and scarce amenities. Anyone that goes against the good of the community will be punished accordingly.

Reverend Buck will conduct religious services every day to remind us of our duty to God. This is a mission dictated by God himself, and we must remember this". He looked at the bald clergyman clothed in clerical robes standing on the deck, and bowed his head in acknowledgement. Reverend Buck was wide in girth and short in stature, with an unshaven unkempt appearance. He returned Sir George's nod and beamed at the crowd.

"As your Admiral, I will do my very best to ensure your safe passage to Jamestown." Sir George stood to attention and saluted the whole community, signalling the band to continue playing as he started to make his way to the poop deck where his cabin was situated.

On his way, Somers' mind fleetingly drifted back to what had happened over the past few months. It had cost him dearly to be here, both personally and financially. Financially, he had contributed two of the smaller ships – the "Virginia" and the "Swallow" as well as mortgaging himself to provide money for the extras needed to make the "Sea Venture" the extraordinary ship that she was. Personally, - he would never see his lovely wife, Joanna again. There was some regret for that.

As he approached his cabin, he became aware of his first possible conflict. He knew this was the only space available for Commanders to bunk down on the ship, as most of the passengers were crammed into stinking cramped accommodation on mats or hammocks in the lower decks. Usually, he would have inhabited this space on his own, one of the perks of seniority, but not on this voyage. He wondered how he, Gates and Newport were going to share this without rancour.

On entering the cabin, he saw that Gates and Newport had settled themselves into the best bunks. Somers had a small flash of regret at joining the ship late. If he had joined the ship in London, he could have laid down boundaries; instead, he did not have a leg to stand on as Gates was making it quite clear that he was not going to be pushed around. He felt that there were probably going to be many battles ahead with Gates, and he decided that this one was a battle not worth fighting. He steeled himself.

"Good day to you Gates" he said trying to appear relaxed and pleased to see him. "I am sorry you were not able to join the celebrations on deck when I arrived." Somers could not help stirring things by being facetious and making a point that he had noticed his absence.

"I decided that my time would be better spent preparing the route." Gates replied starkly. His tone that of superiority.

"Have you spoken to Newport about the route?" asked Somers ignoring the jibe, and at the same time reminding Gates that he did not have the final say in things nautical.

"Newport and I disagree about the route. I think the shorter route is best because we have so many passengers, the quicker we get there, the less likely it will be that we will run out of provisions. I know there might be a slight increase in the risk of storms, but at this time of year, whichever route we take, we risk that happening."

"I agree with you" said Sir George. The other man pursed his lips. He was not prepared to smile, but he nodded in agreement. He had been ready for a fight, but now he could relax, at least over the issue of the route.

Agreement acknowledged, Sir George continued. "The shorter route *is* a little risky, but I think it is a risk worth taking. We must set sail soon though, if not, we will be in the middle of the hurricane season, and that would not be pretty." He paused to see what response he would get. He got none, so merely nodded.

Gates visibly relaxed at the ease with which he and his adversary had come to a decision about the route. "One more thing Sir George… " He picked up a canister sealed with the Virginia Company logo. "I have received a list of the new leaders of Jamestown. I have to keep it sealed until we reach Jamestown. No one, not even you and I are to know who my cabinet leaders will be until we get there. I need to take control before they are appointed, so it puts an end to all the petty rivalries that have so far destroyed progress. I need to place it in the safe, away from prying eyes."

Sir George nodded and pointed to the safe in the corner, he wasn't concerned about the colony, his job was just to get them all there. Let the man have his petty secrets.

At that moment, Christopher Newport entered the room.

"Ah Christopher, we were just talking about you" said Somers, knowing that Newport was not going to like the route that had been decided by his two superiors, but trying to appear amiable and democratic to overcome an argument. "I understand that for some reason you are not in favour of the shorter route going directly West from the Canaries?" His voice was both questioning and condescending.

"We may get caught in the hurricane storms in that part of the ocean at this time of year. In my opinion it would be a grave mistake." Christopher Newport knew argument was futile. He was outranked and he could see by Sir George's stern expression that this was not open for discussion. There was no such thing as democracy on-board ship, it was what leadership was all about, especially with Sir George Somers.

"We are to set sail tomorrow at dawn, heading for the Canary Islands" said Sir George in a voice of strength and command allowing no space for further discussion.

"Aye, aye Sir" Newport saluted Sir George.

At least Gates and Somers had something on which they could agree, Newport thought with dismay. Perhaps they were right, but he said a silent prayer anyway when the anchors were lifted the next day, and they set sail for the open sea, their destiny in the hands of God.

The Open Sea

t last they were sailing on the open sea. England could not be seen.

A small celebration was taking place to mark the start of the voyage. Somers, Gates and Newport had invited a few of the more gentlemanly of the male passengers to the upper deck, to drink a toast to the mission ahead, and to lay the foundations of camaraderie, hoping that friendships might relieve the tedium that ship's life often held.

Somers stood before them, beer in hand and shouted "God speed to us all! Welcome to each and every one of you. We have exciting times ahead. We are a pioneering team destined for riches and a life in paradise.

The wind was blowing reasonably hard as the "Sea Venture" cut a path through the dark sea. It dipped and rose with a regular pleasing rhythm causing a salt spray to permeate the air and mingle with their beer as they all cheered in response to Somers's words which were whipped into the wind as soon as they left his lips.

After Somers had made his speech, Gates took over in a more sombre mood, determined to make his mark. "Thank you Sir George for that stirring send-off. I, too, must add a few words of my own as Deputy Governor. Sir George and I will work together to get us to Jamestown safely. When we get to our destination, I will take over command as Governor of the Colony. The Virginia Company have appointed new Councillors, the details of which are a secret and they are contained in a sealed canister which I am tasked with opening on arrival.

In the meantime, Captain Newport is in charge of the day-to-day running of the "Sea Venture", and Reverend Bucke will be in charge of our spiritual care, both on land and on sea. As you know, there will be a strict Christian routine in place that all must abide." He nodded to the Reverend Bucke, a re-run of what Sir George had done when he boarded. "God Willing, we should reach Virginia in under six weeks from now. We are the lead ship, and we will keep in close contact with the other ships in the convoy every day with a trumpet reverie. Please all raise your glasses and toast to our Good Health, Safety and Happiness."

John stood on the deck, proud to be one of the chosen few. He was excited that now they were really under way, and he smiled to think that all his old troubles had been left behind in England. He had Sarah, and he had "The Sea Venture". What more could he ask for? The wind was starting to get a bit of muscle and he could hear one loud voice above the all the others. John had been told about several of the passengers from Pierce and Yeardley, who had plied him with ale on many an evening after hauling grain and supplies during the long days before they set sail.

He knew from their description that the loud booming voice must belong to the 37 year old William Strachey. Everyone knew he was a bit of a quitter, never finishing law at Cambridge and flitting from venture to venture, thereafter. His literary 'career' had been short and his income insufficient to support his lavish lifestyle of women, wine and tobacco which very quickly turned his sizable inheritance to dust. Now he needed something to keep his ego afloat as the reality of his failure was becoming well known. He had left his disillusioned unhappy wife and sons behind, convinced that he could shine in the New World and that everyone would finally see how wonderful he really was and give him the recognition and income he deserved. John was not looking forward to meeting him.

William spied John, who was talking to Pierce, Yeardley and Alice's husband Edward Eason, and placed himself in front of them, performing a large exaggerated bow, his arm sweeping upwards and then almost touching the deck. "Good day sirs." He smiled broadly. "I am William Strachey, the well-known writer, entrepreneur and Master of the Law, joining you on a mission to find gold and riches. To tell you the truth, I could do with a few nuggets of gold and a Knighthood for placing my life on the line to convert heathens to Christians." He made the sign of the cross in mock deference to the importance of religion.

"Good day to you sir" John bowed slightly in response, taking the lead from his three companions. "These are my good friends, Yeardley, Pierce and Dr. Edward Eason". His three friends bowed in turn.

"Oh, so we have a good Doctor aboard." Strachey stopped to light his clay pipe, pausing as he breathed in the sweet tobacco. "So what is your story Eason? Why is a young Doctor like you venturing into the New World when I am sure you are making packets of money in London?" He gave Edward Eason a mischievous grin, knowing that this probably wasn't the most diplomatic of questions.

Edward took it in his stride. "My wife Alice and I decided that this voyage would be the chance of a lifetime for us. We both wanted a new start, and I knew that my skills would be needed both on the ship and in the colony." He didn't proffer any further information, hoping that Strachey would turn to one of the others. Edward was a quiet and shy man and he did not like talking about himself. He and Alice were leaving behind the memories of five lost babies, but that was not the subject of idle conversation.

"Oh, I see. One of the ones that has brought a wife. Bad decision matey. I left my old girl, and my snivelling children behind. You don't really want women in situations like this. They are too feeble and besides, you need freedom to do what you like on these trips... if you know what I mean." He winked and smiled knowingly tapping his finger against his nose. As he spoke, the wind blew his pipe out, and he swore, trying to crouch out of the wind to light it again. "Damned pipe, this wind might be good for getting us to Jamestown, but it isn't good for lighting a pipe" he said scowling and looking around to see who was watching him struggling. Having stumbled a few times, but eventually lighting his pipe he turned to Edward Eason again. "I had better enjoy this while it lasts, as I don't suppose the tobacco in Jamestown will be up to much."

John tried to rescue Edward from further dialogue with Strachey. "I heard someone in the tavern say that there is plenty of tobacco in Virginia" he said. "The trouble is that the Indians cure it, and it is harsh. Not like the Spanish stuff that we are used to."

"Those bloody Spanish..." shouted Strachey. "Why do they have the monopoly for good tobacco? I say we should steal it from them and produce our own! They are crooks." Strachey's pipe blew out in the wind yet again. "Damned and blast!"

Thomas Gates overhearing their conversation and liking nothing better than to talk about himself, started to bore them as he spouted about his contribution to the introduction of tobacco to England. Small talk was not Gates's strong point, and bored, they all fidgeted to get away as soon as possible, even Will Strachey was lost for conversation and drifted away to find stimulation elsewhere.

John Rolfe turned to look in the other direction. He walked over to talk to a small effeminate man standing on his own looking out to sea. The bright colours and fitted garments that showed off his trim figure suggested a man concerned with his appearance, and possibly no liking for women. His mousy hair was coiffed to excess with a small pony tail at the back secured with a black velvet bow.

"How do you do Sir. I am John Rolfe, and who might you be?" John smiled and held out his hand to shake the other man's hand in camaraderie.

"I am a neighbour of Sir George Somers, Sylvester Jourdain." He said proferring his hand and bowing towards John. "I come from Lyme Regis. You may know of my brother who is a member of Parliament and a successful merchant." He looked at John to see if there was any recognition in his eyes. There was none, so he continued. "Sir George invited me on this expedition as a friend. He thought the opportunity would interest me." Sylvester regaled him with information about his esteemed brother. John was starting to see that Sylvester probably suffered a similar fate to himself - that of a brother seeming to be superior. Maybe his appearance was the only thing that he was remembered for, and John felt a jolt of sympathy for this rather strange man.

"Ah here comes the man himself." Sylvester drew back and smiled as they both saw Sir George Somers coming towards them.

"Hello Gentlemen. Fine day for a bit of adventure eh?" His blue eyes sparkled. "Of course I know *you* Sylvester, but who is this handsome young man you are talking to."

"I am John Rolfe, Sir George." John was a little overwhelmed to be talking to the Admiral himself, and he puffed himself up, hoping to convey himself to be a confident gentleman of standing.

"How do you do, John Rolfe. What do you hope to do for us in Virginia?"

"My specialty is agriculture, Sir. I intend to be involved in ensuring we plant enough food to sustain the colony."

Sir George beamed with relief. At last he had found someone who realised that this journey was not just about finding gold.

"That is a particular interest of mine too John. I have brought along seeds that can be planted, and as soon as we land, I am going to get things started. Perhaps you and I could get together on this…"

John was over the moon. Not only had he been noticed and spoken to, but the famous Sir George Somers was actually asking him to assist him in the planting of crops.

"It would be my greatest pleasure" he said. His face glowed. His eyes sparkled and he felt ten feet taller. He couldn't wait to tell Sarah. At that moment Yeardley and Pierce came sauntering up.

"We see you have met our new esteemed friend, John Rolfe, Sir George" Pierce said, patting John on the back in recognition. Pierce then took on a look of serious contemplation. "Do you really think we will be able to keep close quarters with the other ships in the fleet for the whole voyage, Sir George. It seems a tall order to me."

"That is our plan, and I don't see why we shouldn't manage it." Sir George said, a serious and confident look on his face, as he glanced out to sea towards the other ships. "Every evening, we will have a sounding to make sure that we are all together. The plan is, that if we are split up for any reason, we will meet in Barbuda in the Caribbean, so we can ensure one way or the other that we get to Virginia together with all supplies and passengers intact".

"That is good to know, Sir George." Yeardley had not been married to Temperance for very long, and the separation was causing him a degree of heartache. When he married, he had decided to give up soldiering as it required foreign travel and life threatening situations. Temperance was young and adventurous, and it had not taken much persuasion to get her to agree to a new life in Virginia, bringing up their future children to a new and better world. They had planned to have many children, and had spent long hours discussing what their new life could be like in, what seemed to be, the land of milk and honey.

"It may be a slow journey at this time of year." Sir George remarked. "At the moment, the weather is good, probably too good. We need stronger winds though, so we can make good progress. At least in taking the shorter route, we should be able to get there before our provisions run out."

"I hope so, Sir Thomas." said Pierce, his dark eyes taking on a troubled look. "These things are always a bit of a gamble. Joan and little Jane are very precious to me. I hope I have done the right thing by bringing them on this journey." He looked out over the sea trying to catch sight of the other ships as if communicating his thoughts to his beloved. He kept telling himself that it was only about six weeks that he had to endure, and then Joan and Jane would be safe in his care again. His handsome face portrayed the doubts he had about his decision to place them in this precarious situation. If it paid off, he was sure it would be life-changing for them. England was not a good place to be in these times, and Virginia would offer vast opportunities. His friend Yeardley had made the same decision, so he was not the only one who had placed their loved ones in potential peril.

"It will be a piece of cake to get to Virginia the way we are going. Don't you worry my boy, you will be reunited with your lovely wife before you know it. I am sure of it." Sir George raised his flagon of ale in confirmation as he bowed and turned to walk away.

Sir George walked towards the group of men he was closest to on this journey. His companion Teddy Waters, stood talking to Sir Robert Rich and James Swift. All of them had known each other for years and Sir George was pleased to be amongst friends.

Sir Henry Paine, an arrogant aristocrat sauntered over, clearly aligning himself to those he considered to be of influence. Sir

George's friends all knew him as a bully and a snob. The conversation stalled awkwardly, and in the pause, the sound of angry shouting could be heard coming from below deck.

The reverberations of punching and swearing shattered the peace of the small civilised celebration. This was something more than the usual day-to-day disagreements that were often heard rumbling away in the background.

Walsingham, the young Coxswain, ran on to the upper deck, panting and sweating with panic written all over his face, his eyes searching frantically for someone of authority.

"Sirs, all hell has broken out below deck." He gasped. "They are killing them, and nothing I could do or say would make them stop. They want to beat them to a pulp and throw the bodies overboard." Walsingham was clearly at his wit's end, sweating, panting and hardly able to speak.

"Calm down man" shouted Newport holding Walsingham by the shoulders and shaking him. "Who is killing who and why?"

Walsingham paused, catching his breath. "A whole gang of men are accusing the Indians, Namontack and Matchumps, of stealing their rations, and they will be beaten to death if something is not done. It already might be too late."

The Indian Chief, Powhatan, had trusted Captain Newport to transport two of his men to London and now back to Virginia as a diplomatic gesture. An attack on this precious cargo would not bode well for future relations with Powhatan when they got to Jamestown. Good relations with the Indians was fundamental to the success of the whole project.

There was a crescendo of noise from below. Shouting, crashing and chanting permeated the air. "Kill them! Kill them! Heathens..."

John immediately thought of Sarah. He ran in the direction of the lower decks - he had heard enough to know it was serious.

Rebels

ohn was one of the first to get to the scene. After checking Sarah on the gun deck, he continued to the deck below. What he saw was even worse than that described by Walsingham's hysterical ramblings. The two Indians were lying on the wet deck, the ghastly swill of excess beer, urine, blood and sea water swishing around their bodies. On one side of their heads, their long black hair was tangled, with tufts pulled out where men had obviously yanked at it. The other side of their heads were shaven as was customary in their tribe, and there were huge cuts on their skulls. Their brown painted bodies were swaying backwards and forwards listlessly with the movement of the ship. Deep cuts gaped alarmingly all over their bodies. Their faces were swollen and bruised so much that their features were indistinguishable.

The crazed attackers continued to take turns in kicking and punching them. There were loud cheers, with each punch or kick that landed on the vulnerable bodies - each spurt of blood was a victory. They were past caring who saw them, they were seeing red, and the fury had reached mob proportions - no one really remembered why they were doing this, they were blood-thirsty and mad.

John looked with horror. He was frozen to the spot. The mangled bodies reminded him of Eustace lying at the bottom of the cliff. He shuddered and took a deep breath.

Then he saw who the main perpetrator was. It was Want, the ruffian that had tried to steal his pies in the tavern. They locked gaze. Want was waiting for a reaction, waiting for John to take control.

John shook himself, forgot his memories and marched forwards. He was not a boy any more, he was a strong man in control, and he had to do something to stop this horror happening to the innocent Indians. He was trembling, but controlled his fear, pulling back his fist and ramming it into Want's face. Want stumbled, not expecting the strength of the punch he received. John drew back his leg, kicking Want with full force in the stomach. Want fell heavily and landed on the deck blaspheming.

His men stood back in amazement looking at their floored leader, unsure what to do next.

Christopher Newport arrived not a moment too soon, and took over swiftly and efficiently. "Well done, Rolfe. It is a brave man that takes on this lot alone." He nodded at John in appreciation.

Newport saw Want nursing his bruised and bleeding face, and pulled him up off the floor by the scruff of his neck, pushing him towards waiting soldiers who tied his hands behind his back. He then took another, Christopher Carter, and with great relish punched him to the ground, standing back and daring anyone else to challenge him.

The look in Newport's eyes told them that standing up to him was not a good idea, one arm or not. The ship's dog, Poseidon who was a fierce black bull mastiff kept for occasions such as these, growled and barked menacingly, drooling in anticipation of digging his yellowing teeth into the flesh of unwashed miscreants. He was straining hard against the sailor who was having difficulty holding him with a thick rope, but ready to let him go if order was not imposed. At that point, realising they could do nothing, some of the perpetrators tried to melt away, pretending that they had not been involved. Others, just stood, unsure, their emotions changing from rage to whimpering fear.

"This behaviour is disgusting" said Newport, his eyes blazing with anger. These Indians were his responsibility, and he was going to ensure that the punishments inflicted for this, would deter any future outbreaks of violence. He had commandeered sailors from above deck to arrest a number of the main perpetrators. "You will be put in the hold for a week on scarce rations. I will not have the violence from the streets of London on my ship. If there are any further such incidents, those who take part could be placing their lives on the line, as it will be seen as mutiny. Let this be a warning that I am not going to put up with this either here, or when we reach Virginia".

Want and Christopher Carter looked at each other and rolled their eyes, seeing authority as something to be dismissed. "Who does he think he is?" whispered Want, rubbing his bruised head and turning away so Newport did not hear what he was saying. "It is God that is in charge here - not HIM. We all know that these Indians are heathens, and should be punished... "

The blood spattered men stood with hands tied behind their backs, most joining in the rebellious climate that had been created by Want and Carter. "I for one agree with Want, he is our man" whispered Samuel Sharp, a member of the criminal fraternity who made his living from the misery of others. "I second that" said Robbie Waters. These comments prompted several more grumbling jibes and nods of agreement from most of the rebels, who saw themselves as in the right.

"We will discuss all of this later" whispered Want with a hint of authority, suddenly seeing that his place might be well served as leader and coordinator of rebellion - something that he relished.

Newport did not hear these mutterings, being more concerned with the injured parties. He looked over at the bleeding Indians, who were now being tended carefully by Edward Eason.

"How are they Edward?"

"They are badly beaten" he said. "They have a lot of injuries, and will need constant care for quite a while. They will undoubtedly have scars. If there are internal injuries we will not know for a day or so - if there are, one, or both may die within the next few days. Time will tell."

"The rations that we will take from the guilty will go as extra rations for Namontack and Matchumps and you must take whatever you need from our stores to make sure that they are as strong as possible when we arrive in Virginia. There could be serious consequences if Powhatan is aware that his men have been attacked - if we can show them good care from now on, it may redeem us in his eyes. This is more than just a squabble between sailors - it could affect the future of the colony."

Christopher Newport had transported Namontack and his servant Matchumps to London from their native village of Tsenacommacah in Virginia as a favour to the Chief of the Powhatan Indian tribe. The idea had been for the Indians to become more proficient at the English language, and to learn English customs. It was part of an attempt at integrating the natives with the settlers. An English lad of 13 called Thomas Savage was likewise living with the Indians learning to be an interpreter. The goal was that each could learn the other's language, in the hope that communication and understanding between Indians and British could be improved.

Rumour had it that these two Indians, Namontack and Matchumps had been presented to King James as foreign dignitaries during their visit to London. Namontack was reputed to be the son of the Chief.

To cement good relations with the Powhatan nation, King James had sent mock Coronation robes and trinkets across the water to communicate respect for the Indian Chief's royal standing. Great strides were being made to try and forge good relations. However, it would not take much to throw all of this good-will into disarray.

Newport made a mental note to keep an eye on the dozen or so men that had participated in this abominable fiasco. If they had done this once, they may do it again in his experience at sea. He was not willing to let this happen, and he would keep his word and put to death anyone who carried out violence again.

Want also made a mental note that he would get these bastards that tried to dictate to him.

Who did they think they were anyway? He would have the last laugh with Newport, Gates, Somers and Rolfe. Just you wait and see he chuckled to himself.

* * *

A crisis, all but avoided, everyone went back to their various areas on the boat. John was pleased at his part in saving the Indians and he went to the converted gun deck. Sarah was huddled with the other women, many of whom had been frightened by the noises that had been coming from the lower deck wondering what was happening and bracing themselves to prepare for the aftermath of a mutiny. Such a conclusion, after all the shouting and banging, was not unreasonable at sea, and filled them with horror at what was to become of them. It was not unheard of for rampaging sailors to rape or murder anyone that got in their way.

John took Sarah in his arms. "It is alright now, my love" he said, pushing her auburn hair away from her tear stained face. "Captain Newport has everything under control, and we should not hear much from that rabble for a few days at least." He explained exactly what had happened. He looked over to where Alice was sitting "It is a good thing Edward was on hand to take care of the wounded men. I think a lot of his time will be spent over the next few weeks looking after them. Those ruffians would have killed them if they hadn't been stopped."

"I had seen the Indians at a distance" said Alice, "but I wasn't sure who they were and why they are here. I have been told that Indians are very peaceful people, what must they think of us? We will have to take good care of them from now on."

"They will be bunking down with us until we get to Virginia" said John. Newport had decided he could not put them below deck again and risk a similar occurrence. "I think that is an excellent idea. I can't see the lower deck ruffians accepting them back into their ranks anyway."

Mistress Horton pricked up her ears. *"I* won't be sharing space with heathens" she said, her pinched face devoid of compassion, or any understanding of the situation.

Mistress Horton was one of the grander ladies - a spinster. Speculation was rife as to why she had chosen to be here. Her small erect frame with tiny waist supported the finest of clothes. Trunk after trunk of jewellery and velvet followed her onto the "Sea Venture". She was about 50 years old and stubborn and set in her ways. Her steely grey hair, pulled back into a severe round bun at the nape of her neck, and her pinched face, set with deep lines, indicated years of displeasure and condescension. Her manner did not endear her to anyone. She did not pass the time of day with anyone without a title, and one could tell by the way her eyes inspected each person in turn, that no one was of a calibre that she wished to associate with. She was obviously used to being waited on hand and foot as she did not lift a finger to help either herself or anyone else as she shuffled around her quarters, lifting her fine dresses out of the grime, her nose in the air.

Her shrill voice could be heard demanding Elizabeth Parsons, her 17 year old fresh-faced maid, to act on her slightest whim. She needed to be comfortable, and this, of course, was not possible in these conditions. Poor Lizzy bore the brunt of her bullying, venomous anger both physically and verbally, all of which was witnessed daily by her fellow passengers, who breathed a sigh of relief every time Mistress Horton went up on deck for air.

"Unfortunately, Mistress Horton, we have no choice in the matter." said Sarah, with an abrupt retort, her face stern and set. She was still not feeling well. The swell of the boat, and anxiety about the fight on top of her pregnancy had made her tolerance of this arrogant cold woman finally disappear. She knew they all had to make the best effort not to fall out with one another, as they had many weeks of boredom and discomfort ahead - but this woman was just too much to bear.

"We will make sure that they aren't right next to you" said poor Lizzie tentatively, trying to smooth things over. Everyone else either rolled their eyes or sighed with impatience.

"I will complain to Admiral Somers - he is a man of breeding and will understand". They all ignored her, as they knew that she would be wasting her time complaining but had no energy to argue further.

The conversation was overheard by Sir Henry Paine, who like Mistress Horton, came from an upper class background. He had taken great lengths to bring a full gentleman's wardrobe on-board. No one could forget the loading of his trunks of useless finery, which took up valuable space that would have been better used for provisions and tools. John remembered him with displeasure from the gathering of gentlemen just before the fight had broken out. He had sidled up to anyone with a title, ignoring everyone else with contempt on his face.

Being of a similar arrogant and condescending constitution, Henry Paine understood the plight of Mistress Horton, and empathised with her distress. How could gentlefolk like himself and Mistress Horton be subjected to sharing sleeping quarters with heathens? It was bad enough having to sleep with servants and children. He had been prepared to put up with a few of the hardships on the "Sea Venture", in the hopes of becoming a wealthy gold merchant when he reached Jamestown. Surely this was not part of the agreement? Not something he had signed up to… and certainly not something a Lady like Mistress Horton should put up with. He stood up, ready to fight his corner.

"I feel that the situation is untenable" he shouted, his bulbous nose taking on a bluish tinge as his blood pressure increased with his outrage. "None of you understand how myself and Mistress Horton should be treated." His round, plump face became contorted and began to match the hue of his nose, with the effort of communicating superiority in the face of insubordination. "You are all peasants, and I will not have you disrespecting the gentlefolk on this ship" he said, green eyes flashing, as his rotund figure gesticulated frantically, to the point where his beautiful waistcoat stretched to the limit with the strain of his shouting, and looked like it might pop the buttons that were holding his vast stomach in place. The ship hit a large wave and he had to grab hold of a supporting beam to keep himself upright. All dignity was stripped from him as he stumbled heavily, eventually landing involuntarily on his bed with a look like thunder on his face.

John and Sarah hid their faces. If he saw them laughing, it would be sure to inflame the situation further. As they looked around, most of the other passengers were doing the same.

At that moment the two stretchers arrived containing Namontack and Matchumps, accompanied by Edward Eason, removing any sense of frivolity.

The Indians looked very vulnerable, their almost naked bodies revealing extensive injuries and with their eyes closed they looked on the verge of death. Alice rushed forward to embrace her husband, and to have a closer look at the injured men.

"Are they going to be alright, Edward" she asked.

"I am not sure at this stage, so we must pray for them." he answered, looking sadly at the two figures.

Steven Hopkins, Reverend Burke's pious assistant who also resided with his family on the converted gun deck of the "Sea Venture", looked furtively towards the two still bodies as if they were vermin.

"They are Heathens, and this trip is surely for God-fearing people, as was our contract. Maybe we should not have interfered with the Will of God, and let them die. I agree with Mistress Horton and Sir Henry Paine - heathens should not be placed in the midst of Christian God-fearing people such as us." His vindictive controlling nature was given reinforcement by seeing it as God's Will. He was a member of the London Woolen Guild, and hoped to make his fortune in Jamestown making cloth and hats - but underneath, his true calling was that of Brownism, an extreme puritan religion that saw God as the only true authority.

His children, Elizabeth aged 5, Constance aged 3, and two year old Giles were looking at him with wide eyes, not sure what to do. Their father was a scary person - apparently good and holy - but at the same time giving his children no warmth or closeness. To them he was like a stranger whom they had to obey because he always knew what was right. He never swore but there was always anger in his eyes, and his wife Mary and the children did exactly as they were told so as to keep this unpredictable 'monster' in its cage.

It was not hard for people to see the parallel Steven Hopkins bubbling like a volcano under the surface of the saintly one. He carried a bible with him wherever he went, and had become a self-styled preacher. He had arranged with Reverend Burke that he would help with the religious pastoral care of all the ship's passengers, and he carried out these duties with unsmiling determination, and condescension, feeling a sense of control over the "sinners" who needed his superior guidance. Reverend Bucke was suspicious of his motives, but so far he had no proof of anything untoward, so relied upon him to help with day to day religious matters.

Paying little attention to the ravings of Steven Hopkins and Henry Paine, Dr. Edward Eason directed the stretchers to be placed strategically next to his own and Alice's straw beds.

John could see that something needed to be done to calm this situation. He got up and took control before further disagreements had time to emerge.

"The Hopkins family, Sir Henry Paine and Mistress Horton, can you please remove yourselves from this area, and place your beds at the far end of the gun deck so you do not have to be disturbed by the patients" John said. His voice was authoritative as he directed them to move.

At that, there was a shuffling as the deck was re-arranged. Gentrified protests about the inconvenience were ignored as people rushed to help. It suited everyone to have the complainers at the far end. No one was of any illusion that constant bickering for the whole six weeks would be better at a distance. The only ones that suffered were poor Lizzy, Mary Hopkins (Steven's wife) and their three children whose traveling arrangements suddenly became worse by virtue of close proximity to sanctimonious rantings from dawn til dusk.

For the moment, disaster had been averted but everyone knew it was probably too long a journey to permanently contain the tempers that were already rising to the surface.

This mix of people is like a powder keg, John thought as he looked around at his travelling companions. All we need is someone with a lighted taper - and there are sure to be many of those in the coming weeks, he thought wistfully.

The Rise of Want

Want experienced a good deal of satisfaction knowing that he had been appointed the leader of this rebellious rabble without a word being said. They, instinctively, looked to him for leadership and direction and he knew that he could manipulate the situation to suit his own ends. He wasn't quite sure what those ends were as yet - but he knew that he had the upper hand, and could play his cards whenever it suited him.

Want was used to being in charge, although this had not always been the case. Being an orphan, born in the workhouse, he grew up in a sparse and cruel orphanage where, because of his small size, he had been bullied and beaten by boys older than him. Thoughts often came to him, even now, of himself as a tiny lad. He had longed for the touch of a mother to calm his fears and protect him from the world. He was harmless, a sweet little boy buffeted along by the evils of the world.

For years he saw no way out of his plight. One of his friends was called Robbie Waters. Want and Robbie became like brothers, protecting one another and gaining more confidence as a team. When Want was 9 and Robbie 8, they decided they had had enough of the cruelty meted out the orphanage and they ran away.

Bullies respect bullies, and they soon found that the way to survival was to bully, fight, exploit and lie - they had both been downtrodden and used for too long. Want grew into a large intimidating lad. Over time and with the protection of each other they started to make their way in the world. They had realised the hard way that kindness was a commodity that bought you little respect on the street and any softness and compassion had to be buried deep. The only positive thing that remained was their loyalty to each other.

They robbed and fought as a way to survive, not because they desired wealth - they had no idea what wealth really was. There were three things to remember about Want when you met him - he did not respect authority, he was always loyal to his friends and he had to be in control.

Recent events on board had given him opportunities for increased status. He was a leader with Robbie as his right-hand man, and he had a very powerful force of men before him – they would help him fulfil his destiny. Each and every man aboard was strong, and most were cruel. Many came from the criminal fraternity and would not hesitate to cut a man's throat if it meant personal gain. Want had to ensure that his power was maintained and that he was able to use and control this force for his own advantage. For the moment he could see that he had to strategically calm the frayed tempers of these men until the time was right.

They were all huddled below deck listening intently to what he had to say after his release from the brig.

"At least we have the heathens out of our quarters now. For that we can be thankful." He smirked, rubbing his hands together as if ridding himself of dirt. "Well done everyone for sticking together, and hats off to those who took the hit and ended up being punished - you join me in being real men - men who are prepared to stand up for your beliefs, and for that you are saluted." He nodded to those that had stood by him. Robbie had not been one of them, he remembered. His friend had always had a bit of a cowardly streak in him, he would let it pass for now.

The assembled group all clapped and cheered, Robbie egging them on with wolf whistles and shouts of glee. "Our hero" he shouted, keen to be in Want's good books.

When they had calmed down, Want continued "From now on, we must not lose sight of the reason we are all here. We want to be rich, and there is gold in Jamestown. Each and every one of us can show these toffs who is boss, but we must bide our time. There will be no bosses and servants in Jamestown, and we will not have to put up with such ill treatment once we are there." There was silence as the ship pitched up and down rhythmically.

Want paused as the men started to mutter their agreement absorbing what he was saying. Most were happy to do what they were told, as long as the person doing the telling had their respect. Want had their respect. Letting *him* take control saved them from thinking for themselves, which was too much like hard work. They all knew that their strength lay in numbers, and numbers had to be organised and no one had the intellect or gumption to do this but Want. Gold was the main reason for coming on this God-awful trip - and he was right, they had to box clever to make sure they received what they deserved.

"I want those that are happy for me to be leader to raise your hands." Want would not have asked for this, unless he was sure that they *would* vote for him. Robbie immediately raised his hand, and Want saw with satisfaction, that he had not read the situation wrongly as they all followed Robbie and raised their hands, unanimously voting for him as their leader, all cheering and clapping, their grimy faces showing toothless grins of approval.

"You have all spoken. I am your one and only leader. I will decide when the time is right, and I will direct you. I do not want to see anyone acting without my approval. We cannot let any one of you spoil it for the others, and every action must be planned very carefully and agreed or things could turn into chaos. We can do this, we just have to be smart. Does everyone understand?" He knew that it would take just one ambitious cretin to ruin the whole thing.

A general rumble of assent ripped through the hold, as the men turned their thumbs up and nodded their heads in agreement about what was being said, like a flock of sheep.

"Our time will come. We must remember that our strength is in our numbers, and so we have the upper hand. However, we must be clever and stifle any impulse to act against the good of the group before it is to our advantage. Now I want you to return to your duties, and I will call on you as and when action is required."

He turned to go, clapping Robbie on the back, pleased with the outcome of what had happened. He now had to form a plan, a plan to *really* assert his control. Every army had a leader, and he knew he was the man for the job. Sir George Somers, Sir Thomas Gates... John Rolfe - look out, your 'Just desserts are coming.' He thrust his fist in the air with joy and exhilaration.

* * *

Eddy Samuel, Beth's father, had listened intently to what Want had said. It made sense, but he didn't want to get too involved as he didn't want anyone digging too deeply into his background to discover the secret that he and Beth were harbouring.

After Beth had returned having been caught pick-pocketing, and spending a night in jail, he knew that he had to get her away from London. She didn't tell him exactly what had happened, but he could guess, as her whole personae changed. She became withdrawn and anxious, unable to venture outside and she cried day and night as her appetite diminished. She became a shadow of her former self. It was too dangerous for a vulnerable, pretty girl like her to be on the streets. He couldn't protect her, so he had to get her away.

He had managed to secure passage to the new world, him as a sailor and builder, and Beth disguised as a young lad. She was now a Yonker with short blond hair and boys clothing, helping the sailors with all the menial tasks that needed doing on-board the "Sea Venture".

They were sitting in a corner in the darkness of the lower deck. He rarely had a chance to talk to her, but he could see how she was struggling to keep up with the physical strain of doing the work of a young lad.

"Are you ok Timmy?" He asked, not using her real name in case they were overheard.

"To tell you the truth, I am finding it really hard Da" she said, her sweet face looking at him behind tired eyes.

"I can see that my love, but there isn't much I can do about it." Eddy longed to put his arms around her and comfort her, but he knew he couldn't.

They both sat in the damp and dark, sad that there did not seem a way out for her.

"Hopefully, the wind will pick up soon, and when we get to Jamestown it will be so much better. You will have some of those fancy clothes that you used to wear, and we will have roast meat and lots of cake to eat." Eddy smiled thinking of it.

Beth just looked at him. He didn't really understand. She was almost at breaking point. Having to climb up to the crow's nest and be look-out made her dizzy and sick - but she couldn't refuse to do it, because questions would be asked. It was difficult taking her ablutions as well. The young lads usually kept together, and had no modesty between them. They were starting to think it a bit strange that she did not strip down naked to wash with them.

If that were not all, she had constant leering looks from some of the sailors, which brought back nightmares of her time in jail. She didn't know how much longer she could keep up the pretence - if only she hadn't been caught pick-pocketing, she thought wistfully. That toff had no idea what the consequences had been for her.

Deep in thought and temporarily comforted by the close proximity of her father she sighed. As her mind drifted, she felt the eyes of one of the men boring into her. She turned and saw a scruffy looking man with thin greasy hair and yellowing teeth smiling at her. She quickly looked away and started talking to her father, panic etched onto her face.

"Pa, that man is looking at me in a funny way."

"I know Beth. He's had his eye on you since the beginning. Don't worry, I think he likes young boys, and as you are quite pretty, he probably wants to have a little 'cuddle' with you." This was one of the hazards Eddy had been concerned about. A lack of available women on a ship often resulted in the younger men having to satisfy the carnal needs of the crew. Beth would be easy pickings as she was young and seen to be alone.

"Who is he" she asked, her blue eyes looking intently at her father. She was aware of what a man could do to a woman; flashbacks to her prison experience were very near the surface for her. The thought of it happening again was terrifying. She knew that she did not have the strength to protect herself, and any man could do what he liked with her if he so desired.

"His name is Robbie. Try to keep your distance from him. It is unlikely that he will actually do anything. From what I have seen of

Robbie, he is all mouth and no action."

She was not placated with her father's words. As she caught Robbie's eye again, he smiled a horrible smile. The few teeth he had left were yellowing and crusty giving him the look of an evil Halloween lantern.

He sighed loudly. Beth recoiled with revulsion.

High Seas

⁂

T he days seemed endless, the wind that had been fresh and invigorating when they set off, had now died. Everyone was bored. The passengers wallowed in their bunks, taking the odd stroll on deck to free themselves from the stench and heat of the decks below. The sailors were mostly unemployed, as the winds were so slight and nothing had to be done. It was like walking across the ocean at snail's pace.

On and on they went. John Rolfe had been worried about Sarah at the beginning of the journey, he had noticed that she was quiet and had lost her spark, but she never complained and insisted there was nothing wrong when he enquired. Now he watched her on the top deck with the wind in her hair, smiling. He waved at her and she jumped up and down waving back. Putting her hands to her lips she kissed her fingers and sent the kiss through the air to him. He feigned catching it and laughed, his heart full of love for her.

She had struck up female friendships for support and her sickness had abated as the seas began to calm. The group of young women, who had become her friends, Alice Eason, Mary Hopkins (Steven Hopkins' wife), Elizabeth Joons (a young servant girl), and Lizzy

Parsons (when she could escape from the dreaded Mistress Horton), would often gather around and tell each other stories - cuddling and amusing Mary and Steven's three children who were often sick, tired and crying on the stifling gun deck. Now the women were frolicking in the sunshine, playing with the children like they were children themselves. John sighed with relief.

Lizzy Parsons, one of Sarah's friends, loved going up on deck, and today she had escaped the rantings of her mistress, to feel the wind in her hair, and frolic with the other women and the children. The weather was calm, and as Lizzie held hands with Mary Hopkins and little five year old Elizabeth, circling round and round until they got dizzy and dropped onto the deck laughing, she thought that life might not be so bad after all.

"Look, look" she cried when she got up and saw the other ships in the fleet bobbing up and down on the sparkling blue sea, almost stationary, not far from them. "Give them all a wave everyone!" She shouted.

Mary, held little two year old Giles high in the air to show him the other ships, and he squealed with delight. They could see in the distance passengers on "Falcon" and "Blessing" jumping up and down waving, as eager to make contact as they were.

The big black mastiff dog barked as it chased its tail like a puppy, feeling the frivolity that the women brought to the deck. Giles struggled to be released. "Doggie, doggie" he was trying to learn how to speak, but could only say a few words. He toddled over to touch the dog, but Alice panicked and ran to him quickly scooping him up. Posey was a ratter and a guard dog - he might take little Giles as a morsel of fresh meat. "No Giles" she said sternly.

He looked at her and burst out crying at being told off. "Oh baby," Alice crooned. "Don't cry. It is alright." She held him to her chest, stroking his hair to comfort him, feeling his soft warm form sinking in to her body.

"Look Giles," said Sarah keen to distract little Giles away from his distress. "Pigs and chickens too!" Sarah took Giles's sister Constance's hand and pulled her towards the pen, as the little girl laughed with delight pointing at the livestock. "Look Giles" she screamed.

"Me too, me too" shouted Giles when he saw his big sister being taken towards the pigs. His tears stopped suddenly with the excitement of something new. His big blue eyes were wide with excitement as he tried to bounce out of Alice's arms again, his tiny arms and legs flailing frantically to be released. Alice held on to the little one with difficulty and ran over to the pen to look at the pigs. "Pig, pig, pig... oink, oink" the little boy laughed with pleasure and clapped his pudgy little pink hands.

Her children occupied, being watched by Alice and Sarah, Mary looked skyward to the mast, sails hanging limply with no wind to fill them. "Gosh the mast looks so high from here, doesn't it Elizabeth. I can't imagine what it must be like to climb all that way up." She drew her five year old nearer to her. "Bet you wouldn't like to be up there" she said to her daughter.

Elizabeth smiled. She was a quiet and thoughtful little girl, who had been overwhelmed not only by the journey, but by the constant bullying of her harsh father. She was pleased to see her mother happy for a change. Life on the gun deck with their father was unbearable. She tried to cheer her mother up, but it rarely made a difference. Up here, away from her father, her mother was carefree and happy, and this made Elizabeth happy too. She felt her mother's arms around her shoulders and reveled in the rare chance of closeness.

"No Ma", she laughed. "You won't be getting me up there! Look, there is a lad up there looking down at us." She waved up at one of the Yonkers who was clutching at the mast and looking out to sea. "What is your name" she shouted. The stillness of the wind allowed her words to be carried upwards.

"Ahoy there. My name is Timmy White. At your service Madam" he said smiling down at her.

"Be careful, Timmy White." Mary shouted up at him.

"Look …" Timmy shouted pointing to the stern of the ship. "Davey is exercising the horses on the pinnace. The little ones might like to see them"

"Thanks Timmy" Mary shouted, as they all rushed to the stern to try and catch sight of the horses.

Davey was on the pinnace that was trailing behind the "Sea Venture". He had two magnificent horses. He was riding one bare back, and leading another. Their shiny black coats glistening in the sun, one of them snorted. He waved at the children, looking the picture of happiness, in his element with the horses. He suddenly turned around on the horse's back and rode it backwards, showing off to the children. Elizabeth, Constance and little Giles jumped up and down with excitement. "Can we ride them, can we ride them?" Elizabeth asked.

"Maybe when we get to Jamestown sweetie" Mary replied.

Suddenly there was the sound of splashing. Lizzy, who had not gone to see the horses, had been daydreaming, and she looked around frantically, fearing that one of the children had fallen overboard - but she soon saw that all three were safe and sound waving at Davey and the horses.

She ran over to the side of the ship from where the sound of splashing had come, and saw five men swimming in the deep dark ocean. It was so hot and uncomfortable; they had obviously thought to cool off. It looked so inviting. The water sparkled with the sunlight, and was mill pond calm. She imagined how cool it would feel on her hot and sticky body.

One of the men waved at her. "Ahoy there pretty lady" he shouted.

She blushed with embarrassment, but returned his wave all the same. Encouraged by her response, he swam closer to where she was standing and looked up at her. "What is your name pretty lady" he said with a wide grin. "Why don't you come in and join us, it is very cool and refreshing." He waved his arm indicating for her to join him.

"Go away with you, you cheeky one" She said pretending to be offended. She knew who he was, she had seen him many times in the galley; it was Tom Powell, the cook. He actually was rather nice. He had a dark complexion and a mop of dark hair that fell seductively over his forehead. She had spoken to him from time to time, when she was making culinary demands on behalf of Mistress Horton, and had been entranced by the dark brown eyes, that had always looked at her with sympathy as she apologised for the unreasonable demands of her mistress.

"Well, if you are not coming down, then I will come up" he shouted, laughing.

She was suddenly full of dread. Had the men stripped off completely?

She ran to the other side of the ship, placing her hands over her eyes, but peeping through the spaces in her fingers, naughtily curious.

Tom climbed up the rope ladder that had been placed on the side of the ship, and stood dripping in his breeches, that clung to his body. He wore no shirt, and she noticed his muscly arms and taught brown torso. He looked over at her and laughed. It is ok, he said, I am not going to reveal anything that would offend the eyes of the ladies. He laughed as he stood dripping. His hair glistened with droplets of water, and he shook his head like a dog and stamped his feet to get rid of the excess water.

They stood and looked at one another, spellbound for several moments.

Suddenly, a shrill voice could be heard from below deck. It got louder and louder as Mistress Horton appeared on the upper deck. "Where are you, you lazy girl. I need you to clean my commode pot, and I want it done now" Her voice was shaking with anger.

She caught sight of the group of young women, and spied her victim. "Come here now" she shouted at Lizzy through gritted teeth. The children all jumped with fear and clutched the nearest adult they could find for protection. Giles hid his head in his mother's shoulder.

The rosy colour that had risen in Lizzy's cheeks as she had gazed at Tom drained from her face and her heart was beating with fear now rather than excitement. She slowly approached the rampaging old woman. She was used to abuse from her employer, and knew that she had been taking a risk when she came up to the deck with her friends - but it was worth it to her, to get a tiny break from this harridan of a woman.

"I am sorry Mistress Horton" she whispered, trying not to anger her further. "I thought you were asleep, and wouldn't mind if I came up on deck for a bit of fresh air".

At that, Mistress Horton lashed out and slapped her full in the face. She continued to hit and beat Lizzy, her small frame seeming to take on almighty strength. All the anger for the conditions she had been subjected to over the past few weeks was released in a volcano of emotion. Lizzy dropped to the floor and rolled up like a ball, trying to escape from the blows that were raining down on her. "I am so sorry." Lizzy whimpered through her tears. Everyone stood as if glued to the deck, shocked and unsure what to do about the spectacle before them.

Tom Powell, still standing and dripping on the deck had a clear view of what was happening. He could not believe what he was seeing. He had watched Lizzie Parsons since the start of the voyage, and seen the predicament that she was in with her employer. He fumed whenever he saw Mistress Horton and the way she treated her innocent little maid servant, but he had felt that it was none of his business. He was drawn to Lizzy for a reason he could not explain. Although he was loath to admit it, he had waited patiently to catch every glimpse he could when Lizzy came up to the deck, and any excuse to go on the gun deck was quickly taken just in case he could see her. There was something magical about Lizzy - her laugh, her plump cheeks and her sparkling eyes. When Tom saw what was happening, he could restrain himself no more.

He strode over to where Lizzy was crouched, and placed himself in front of her, grabbing Mistress Horton's hands so she could not move. He was smart enough to know that he had to handle this situation as delicately as he could, because there would be consequences for his actions - and Lizzy would probably bear the brunt of them.

"Mistress Horton" he said gently, but with authority. "I am sure there is no need for you to trouble yourself further. I know things have been very difficult on this long journey, but you should not have to worry yourself with the mundane misdemeanours of servants."

"Indeed I should not" Mistress Horton was not quite sure what to do. This man had interfered with her disciplining of Lizzy. His words seemed to be respectful, but his eyes and his hold on her arms gave a different meaning, and she knew without any doubt that she was at his mercy. How was she going to respond without losing face? She decided to play the game and offer mutual mock respect in return. "Thank you so much for coming to my rescue." She said her voice shaking as he released the grip on her wrists. She was scared of him, but could not let this be seen.

"So - there is an end to this matter then" said Tom, looking at her directly and sternly. "I am sure there will not be cause to punish Lizzy any further on this trip." The meaning was clear as Mistress Horton tried to smile but could only manage a sickly grimace. She had been dictated terms by a mere cook but she knew it was in her interests to agree to them. She saw from Tom's demeanour that there was no going back or there would be further loss of face for her.

She looked over at Lizzy, who was starting to unroll herself from her crouched position. Regaining her sense of authority Mistress Horton barked with a strained voice "I need your assistance below deck Lizzy. Please accompany me now." She had to assert some superiority over the girl - she could not be seen to succumb completely to this loathsome cook.

Lizzy limped back towards the ladder to the lower deck following Mistress Horton. As she did, she glanced back at Tom Powell holding his gaze a little longer than was seemly and mouthed the words "Thank you" as she disappeared down to the stifling gun deck.

* * *

Somers, standing on deck waiting to bark orders should the wind return had seen all the antics of the passengers. "Well, Tom saw to that old witch" he said to Newport who was standing next to him. "Who is that odious little woman anyway?"

"I think her name is Elizabeth Horton. A gentlewoman, I believe - but surely not one with style" he said chuckling.

"I hope *I* never bump into her on a dark night" said Sir George laughing. "Anyway, lovely as this weather is for swimming and playing, it is not doing much for our progress." He was concerned with the calm and hot air - knowing with a mariner's wisdom, that often, as the air rose from the sea in such conditions, it could very quickly turn to a storm.

"Yes, it is a concern." said Newport. This was exactly the scenario he had envisaged when being forced to come the shorter route. "There is nothing we can do now but sit tight and hope that the wind picks up soon without turning into a storm."

"Yes, you're right. I think a storm would be preferable to this though. Bring on a storm, I say" said Sir George, realising that Newport was making his point about coming the shorter route. "We can manage a poxy storm."

Newport looked to the horizon seeing the other ships in the fleet in the distance, and prayed that they could manage whatever was headed their way. In his vast experience he knew that whatever it was, it could be more than Sir George was anticipating.

* * *

The brief interlude on deck had been abruptly interrupted by the incident with Mistress Horton, and the women and children returned to the gun deck deflated by the abrupt ending of a beautiful afternoon. The children were sound asleep from the fresh air, sunshine and frivolities, and Mary sat at the end of the gun deck stroking little Giles' brow as he slept, comforting little snoring noises and grunts emanating from his tiny body.

Mistress Horton was silent for once, and Lizzy Parsons lay on her mat, staring up at the ceiling and reliving every moment of her contact with Tom Powell, her face flushed.

John and Sarah had remained on the deck, hand in hand taking in the sea air and the sunshine, a brief but intimate moment together.

"Ahhh… so good to be in the air" John sighed. "Look over there – can you see the fleet in the distance? Looks like everyone is still with us." She nodded, trying to count the ships.

Are you coping with the conditions Sarah?" John asked.

"Well, it is difficult… I feel so ill all the time" she said. "I just can't wait to get to Jamestown, build our own little house and make a lovely wooden cot for this little one." She said patting her stomach.

John pulled her to him, and gave her a long kiss. "I miss being able to kiss you and hold you Sarah. We will make up for it when we land though." He smiled and touched her breast.

"I hope we will." She said. "I suppose we better not get too carried away up here. You know what happened last time we let instinct take over." She laughed pulling his hand away and playfully pushing him towards the gun deck.

They descended and Sarah went back to her job of helping Alice tend to the wounds of the Indians. The gashes and broken bones were starting to heal. The women were doing everything for the men with supervision from Alice's husband Edward. Alice and Sarah had started to encourage them to sit up and only yesterday the men had put their feet on the floor, standing up for the first time.

"I wonder where these men come from" said Alice as she bathed the brow of the older of the two men. He must have been about thirty years old, and he opened his eyes and smiled at her, nodding his head, and putting his hands together in a bow of thanks. She smiled back at him.

"This one seems very nice. He is always smiling at me, and bowing. Although he hasn't said anything to me as yet" said Alice.

At that, the Indian started to sit up and to speak. "I from Werowoco-moco" he said, his deep brown eyes smiling at her. "My tribe is Powhatan, and my chief is Wahunsonacock, known as Powhatan. Our home near English camp in Virginia. I speak little English, my mother tongue Alonquian. Me been in England with Captain Newport many times."

"Oh." Alice was taken aback. She had not realised that he could speak such good English and she had never heard of Alonquian or the Powhatan tribe. She wanted to know more. "What is your name?" She asked, curiosity etched on her pretty face.

"Me Matchumps" he pointed to his chest that was covered in red tattoos.

"Oh Matchumps, nice to meet you. Me Alice" she said replying. "I am really sorry about what has happened to you." Her face was serious and her eyes downcast. "Some of our men are bad - but we are not all bad. We will look after you and make sure that you get better".

"Thank you. You already been very kind" said Matchumps smiling, putting his hands together and bowing towards her again.

"What about your friend?" asked Alice. "Is he also from your tribe? He seems but a boy."

"Yes, he Namontack. I train him. He son of chief, but..." Matchumps looked over to see if the boy was awake. "He not a good boy." He shook his head. "I take him back to his father, I no like him."

At that the younger man opened his eyes, trying to sit up.

"I Namontack son of Chief Powhatan, brother of Pocahontas. You respect me." His eyes flashed at Matchumps as he shouted loudly in his direction. Matchumps smiled condescendingly and shrugged his shoulders.

Sarah reached over to sooth Namontack in case he did further damage to his wounds, and he shoved her hand away roughly.

"Woman, no touch the great Namontack son of Powhatan" he barked at her, his eyes staring, his face grimacing. "My body sacred. No woman should touch the body of Namontack." He threw his head back.

"But I have to touch you, if I am to help you" pleaded Sarah, palms stretched out in front of her.

"No argue with the Great Namontack" he shouted, looking straight ahead and avoiding eye contact.

Sarah looked at him sternly. She was frustrated. She and Alice had had to clean the most intimate parts of these men, taking off their buckskin breeches and replacing them with rags that they had to change at regular intervals like they were babies. They had had to hand feed them, giving them sips of water and bathing their faces, trying to make sure that the slop of human waste swilling around their feet did not get near the open wounds to cause infection. It had not been a task to relish, and at times, Sarah had to stop herself from retching. She was tired and anxious at her situation. Now this young man, far from expressing gratitude, was rude and dismissive.

"As you will" she whispered as she got up hands on hips and walked to her mat. Despite what she had told John, she had had enough of this bloody journey, and she wasn't going to put herself through the trials of nursing someone that clearly did not want her to. In truth he probably would be alright now. Most of the wounds had healed, although the bruising remained.

Namontack smirked at her. "What in pocket?" he whispered, in a mockingly pleasant voice.

"What do you mean? I have nothing in my pocket, and if I did, it would be none of your business" she said, her face stern.

Namontack smirked again, and gave her a menacing smile. "Need Gold..." he said.

At first she did not understand the meaning of what he was trying to say, and then the reference to her pocket made it start to dawn on her. Her pocket was where her rosary nestled. Namontack must have seen it. She remembered her rosary falling out of her pocket, but she

118

was sure she had retrieved it before anyone saw it... but then again...

The colour drained from her face, and her heart started to beat faster, as reality hit her. They had no gold to make him go away. Her stomach turned over at the thought that this vindictive boy had her and John's fate in his hands. He must realise the importance of a rosary from his instruction in English customs in London. He would also know that Catholicism was forbidden on this ship. She did not know what to do. What would John do? Maybe she could just throw the rosary away. No one would believe his word against hers. Then again, she knew that if she was questioned, she could not lie. It would be like denying God. How could she throw away her rosary? It was her past, her family, her very identity.

"Just leave me alone." She said all power gone from body as images of herself and John being thrown into the brig came into her mind. Her stomach turned again and she felt like she was going to die. She put her arm over her eyes to try and block everything out, to make feelings and thoughts disappear - but it didn't work and a tear slipped down her cheek.

Restless Men

T he men on board were as restless as the women. To pass the time, they would often set up a game of cards or darts wherever there was space. On the gun deck, they had managed to pull together some old crates for a table and would crouch around whenever they could. Sometimes, they took their games up onto the deck for air.

John Rolfe had started to relax now that Sarah seemed more stable, and had made friends of her own. After the attack on the Indians, things had settled down, and he had had no more reasons to seek solace with Eustace's stone. He drew in the fragrant tobacco smoke from his pipe, a rare moment of peace on the top deck before everyone was called to Rev. Burke's prayers, followed by dinner. Things weren't so bad. It was warm and calm with blue skies and the ship almost stationary. They just needed a few puffs of wind and in no time he and Sarah would be acquainted with their new home. He felt a pang of excitement at the prospect. What would their first house together be like? Would he meet Indians and have a black and white pony? Would it be like he and Eustace had imagined? At last his life was going the way he wanted it to.

"John - do you fancy a game of darts?" It was Pierce striding towards him, looking expectant. Poor Pierce was not one to keep still. These calm waters must be driving him mad, John thought with amusement.

"Yes, don't mind if I do" said John. He liked Pierce, and was pleased to see his new friend."I will see if I can round up some of the other lazy bastards so we can get teams going." John smiled, and got up to see who might join the game, walking towards the gun deck.

Want, taking air on the deck overheard the conversation. "How about we have two teams, toffs against plebs" he said laughing. It could be amusing, he could gain some knowledge - and knowledge is power he thought slyly. He smiled and winked at John. "Could give you the chance to get me back for trying to take those pies" he smirked. "I'll round up a few of my men, and you round up some of yours then. OK?" He winked again.

John was full of foreboding. He looked at Pierce and shrugged his shoulders. He couldn't refuse the offer of a harmless game, but was it harmless? He knew Want would have a dark motive. "Alright" he said, trying to disguise the hesitation in his voice, unsuccessfully.

"What's the matter Johnnie boy? One Johnnie against another - what could be better?" He laughed seeing John squirm. "After all, we are all in the same boat – The "Sea Venture!" He roared with laughter bending over to try and contain his mirth at his own bad joke.

They all assembled on the deck. It was a warm evening. The two groups stood in opposite corners looking at one another. On one side John Rolfe stood with Edward Eason the Doctor, Pierce, Yeardley, the bumptious and obese Henry Paine, Sylvester Jourdain, the effeminate adventurer and William Strachey always one to be in the limelight.

On the other side, the grinning Want stood with Christopher Carter, a labourer with high aspirations and ambitions. Christopher had a bald head and strong physique and one would not want to meet him on a Saturday night in an alley. Next to him stood Humphrey Reed, a violent but weak man from the streets of London who saw Want as his route to self-improvement; Sam Sharp, a Northerner with a strong Newcastle accent who had aspirations of wealth in the New World; Robbie Waters, Want's long time childhood friend; Eddy Samuels, and Jeff Briars, a red headed, likeable but cheeky lad searching for fame and fortune.

John looked over at the competing team and sighed. This was going to be interesting, he thought with dismay. There was not one of the opposing team that he would trust, with the exception of Jeff Briars. Jeff was just an innocent lad. He was always laughing and joking, and there was little harm to him. He hoped that Want wouldn't corrupt his young mind.

At that moment, everyone's attention was drawn to a clanking sound coming from the stairs to the gun deck. Heads turned to see what the commotion was, as the head of first Matchumps, and then Namontack appeared. They struggled to stand on makeshift crutches that Yeardley had made in his spare time as they moved cautiously, brown eyes downcast as if they wanted to melt into the scenery. They had not known that Want and his cronies were on the deck when Alice had suggested that they try and come up for some fresh air.

Their tattooed bodies were still bruised, with newly healed wounds from head to toe plain to see. Matchumps had a broken leg that Edward had bound tightly with bandages holding it in place to heal, but with every movement he grimaced. Namontack had suffered head injuries, and his whole head was bandaged to try and stop infection setting in. They looked pathetic and vulnerable. Both of their faces were etched with fear, unsure as to how safe it was to be on the deck confronted by their attackers.

"Oh, my my... " said Want, in a singsong voice. "The Heathens are joining us. Which team would you like to go on 'Your Lordships' he said with a mocked reverence and a bow. "I guess you'd better go on the side of the 'toffs' as they seem to be in league with heathen factions on this ship."

"Leave them alone" barked the usually placid Edward Eason. He was not about to have his patients victimised.

Matchumps and Namontack looked at the deck, not making eye contact with anyone, and limped to the other end of the ship, well away from Want's taunting looks.

"Right" said Want, taking the lead. "Now that we have got rid of that particular scum, let's toss a coin to see who starts. What's it to be Johnnie boy... heads or tails?" He shouted across at John, holding his hand in the air ready to throw a coin.

"We'll have heads" replied John. He deliberately chose to ignore Johnnie's comments about the Indians as he felt it would only inflame the situation, and there was enough animosity already.

Want tossed the coin in the air, it landed on the deck and did a circle round and round until it stopped. "Tails it is!" He said, triumph written all over his ugly his face. "We shall begin then." Want walked over and picked up the darts.

Christopher Carter sauntered up to Want and grabbed the darts from him, .pushing him roughly out of the way. Want fell back, just about managing to stop himself from falling on his rear end, his face clouding over with controlled anger.

"Wow, wow wow... watch it Chris" he barked, composing himself, "I was going to say that you can go first from our team anyway... " Everyone could see that Want was miffed, but not about to make a big deal of it while others were watching. Christopher Carter seemed to be playing some kind of power game with Want and everyone was aware of it.

Want didn't see darts as others did, and had to keep cool to gain his advantage. He saw the games as a chance to observe and get to know his enemies, to forge stronger relationships with his friends and to see which was which. He was starting to gauge each of the opposing team, gaining an understanding of their strengths and weaknesses - he knew this would be invaluable to him when he finally took control. He was also starting get a sense of his own team, and Christopher Carter was one to watch. He sensed a rival for control and had to watch his back. He would ensure a select few of his most trusted men had his interests at heart in case of a power struggle.

Want narrowed his eyes as Chris took his shot. He analysed each person in detail.

First he looked at John Rolfe. An unknown quantity. Seemingly harmless, but was clearly starting to gain confidence. Since the incident in the tavern, he had seen John grow some balls. What a surprise when he threw a punch after the attack on the Indians - he would have to keep an eye on that bastard, he could be trouble.

As for the detestable Henry Paine, with his trunks of finery and his nose in the air - he had never had to roam the streets of London grovelling for food - it would be pure justice to see Henry floundering in the muck. Did he really think he was above everybody else? He needed to be shown his lowlier side. A bit of humility never did anyone any harm, and Want was waiting patiently to do the honours of teaching Paine humility and see him grovel.

Yeardley and Pierce were soldiers, and he would have had a certain amount of respect for them, but for the fact that they both pined and moped for their women. Imagine stooping so low as to allow feelings of that kind to be seen. Soft, not something one would expect of soldiers, but nevertheless these two could be dangerous, and had to be contained if necessary.

Having watched William Strachey, Want thought him to be a puff of hot air. He was loud and brash, full of self-importance but insecure at the same time. He was always writing things down - perhaps trying to make up for a failed writing career. Want had discovered that

William Strachey had no money and had never really worked. He had never managed to write more than a few useless poems. Lazy, and deluded about his literary talents, he was just a bore. Another one that was not a problem.

Strachey's friend, Sylvester Jourdain - well, what could one say about him, other than he looked like a girl, and it was plain to see that his sexual preference was for young boys. Word had it that he was a friend and neighbour of Sir George Somers - so what? Want had often observed him watching with undisguised longing, at Timmy White, the young and pretty lad who did odd jobs on the upper decks. Jourdain would cause no problems in a revolt. He was weak, both physically and mentally. He would just roll over and do as he was told, scared of anything happening to his velvet ribbons and carefully coiffed hair.

As for the big bosses, Want glanced over at the bridge - Somers, Gates and Newport. They squabbled amongst themselves. It was always good to have enemies that were divided. You could set them off against one another, which saved a lot of time and energy. Newport only had one arm - so physically he would be easy to tackle. The other two were so concerned with competing against one another, that their eyes would not be on the ball.

Yes, Want thought, I think I am getting a measure of what I will be faced with when the time comes. I will need to assert my authority before we reach Jamestown, but not too soon, as I need the ship to run smoothly before that. Somers and Newport know the route and how to sail the ship so let them do that. He smiled, his mind wandering to a time when people would respect him, when people would look upon him as a smart and ruthless leader - not just a dirty criminal with no mind of his own.

Just then, he was called to the dart board for his turn. He picked up the dart, looked straight at the board, and threw a perfect bull's eye.

Yes - he thought, that says it all.

As Johnnie's team roared with delight at his shot, the sky seemed to take on an unfamiliar hue. The bright sun that they had seen for so many weeks, seemed to disappear momentarily, before reappearing, but only for a minute. The sun was gradually overcome by a bank of skidding dark clouds.

The game coming to an end with no mishaps, John raised a cheer for the opposing winning team, in a show of good will. "Hip hip hooray" they all shouted, fists in the air smiling.

Want bowed theatrically. "Thank you boys. The best team won." He said. He could not resist a jibe. "Let's all retire for prayers and food" he said, as a rumble of thunder started faintly in the distance. They all stood stock still, listening to the sound. "Sounds like God is pleased with our win too!" he shouted and put his hands together looking up to the sky in mock prayer. His team all laughed, and the other team rolled their eyes.

A gentle breeze started and they all felt a slight drizzle of rain on their faces. It left round dark marks on the deck as each drop seeped into the parched wood. The sky lit up with a lightning flash, showing the outlines of the other ships in the near distance. The air temperature fell as dark clouds blocked out any sign of the sun.

Somers, Gates and Newport drew together.

"Looks like we might be in for a storm" said Somers, his face showing little concern. "Things have been going so slowly up until now, it may be a good thing that we get some speed going"

"Do you know where we are?" asked Gates, looking out to sea. He knew that it was difficult to gauge with any sense of accuracy, exactly where they were in relation to Jamestown.

Henry Ravens, was the ship's navigator. One of the most trusted sailors on the ship. Somers shouted down to him. "How are we doing Ravens?"

"Aye aye sir, I checked with the cross staff at noon, and our latitude was not far off what we had envisaged. " Ravens shouted back.

Somers was delighted. "That being so, using the helmsman's most recent calculations of longitude, with a rough estimate, we should get to Jamestown in a week. If this small storm gives us a helping hand, we might even be there sooner." He was pleased that so far, although the going had been slow and tedious, they now might be able to get some speed up.

Newport's heart was in his boots and a shiver went down his spine. Changes happened on the sea, but when it came this quickly, there could only be one reason.

* * *

The evening started to draw in, and passengers and sailors alike retired below deck for their religious services and dinner, except for those employed in rigging the sails in the increasing winds.

As they all filed below, ready to prepare themselves for prayer yet again, John Rolfe being one of the last to go, felt a tap on his shoulder. He looked around and saw Namontack, the smaller of the two Indians beckoning him away from the others. His crutches clunked clumsily, and John felt a pang of pity for the poor young man. He looked so pathetic and vulnerable. It was starting to rain more heavily now, and he wanted to get below deck as soon as possible.

"Namontack, would you like me to help you? Here, take my hand. He put his hand out towards the Indian. "It is getting a bit wet up here" he smiled at the younger man.

Namontack seemed not to hear John, ignoring his outstretched hand "Sir" said Namontack, struggling to find words in English, his brown face serious, no hint of a reciprocal smile.

"Your woman... "

"Yes" said John, "she helped nurse your injuries." John was starting to get impatient; this wasn't really the time for small talk, the rain was starting to beat down more fiercely.

"She Cat...olic" said Namontack eyes shifty, breath quickening.

John's jaw dropped. He could hardly believe the words that he was hearing. How did this savage know about Sarah's religion? He surely couldn't understand the implications of it, even if he did. John looked around to see if anyone had been listening, and it seemed that everyone had disappeared.

His body tensed preparing for the worst. He looked away from Namontock, his thoughts racing. He paused, looking out to the gradual increase of swell in the ocean, taking in the smell of the sea spray as it coated his face and filled his lungs, he hoped that this was all a bad dream. When he looked back, the strange looking brown figure was still there. It was no dream.

"Don't be ridiculous" John tried to laugh it off, but the laugh was false and hesitant.

"No rid...culus... I *see* she have beads and cross in pocket - I know she Cat..olic, and you give me much gold or I tell." His eyes were wide and his body rigid.

John guessed at this point that the boy must have seen Sarah with her rosary. It was unlikely that the heathen had made this up, as he would struggle to even know what a rosary was. This was very serious and the consequences of this information being revealed were catastrophic. Somehow this Indian whose life had been saved by Sarah and Alice, was using it for his own ends. The implications hit him. Sarah would be imprisoned on the ship if this information was leaked. His stomach turned, and his head filled with violence. He started to tremble and he could feel himself detaching from the scene before him.

At that moment, Matchump's head appeared above the hatch to the gun deck. He gestured his hands frantically at Namontack. "Come boy quick, quick. No rations if don't come quick quick. Leave Mr. John alone." His hands beckoned Namontack frantically.

Namontack limped away from John, his crutches clanking on the deck. Before he retreated down to the gun deck, he looked over at John. He balanced one of his crutches releasing one of his arms. He made a motion around his neck, which John took to indicate death. With that he picked up his crutch again, smirked and retreated.

John grabbed the ships railings, forcing his face into the spray, the wind and the now increasing rain, stunning him into numbness. He slumped onto the deck in a pool of salt water oblivious to the seeping coldness. The lightning was lighting up the sky with increasing frequency and the thunder was roaring, but John saw and heard very little.

No, no, no, he thought to himself. I *have* to keep my head, I have to deal with this rationally, I cannot afford to be weak now - I have a wife and baby to look after. Eustace's face flashed before him. Surely no one would believe Namontack if he and Sarah denied his allegations? He must get her to throw the Rosary overboard. Would she do that though? Her rosary was as dear to her as Eustace's stone was to him. It had been her one condition of marrying him and going to Jamestown. Surely she would see that everything had changed now, and she must get rid of it? A loud clap of thunder brought him back to reality. He had to go down to the gun deck, compose himself and think what to do.

He skidded across the slippery wooden deck, and almost fell into the dry deck below, trying to stop himself trembling. He concentrated on breathing slowly to compose himself as he faced the rest of the passengers for prayers and dinner. He looked at Sarah. She seemed deep in thought, unaware of his presence. He had to talk to her somewhere they could not be overheard.

"Sarah, Sarah" he said whispering urgently. "Come with me up to the deck. The weather is changing, and you must come and see it… " he lied.

She was ruminating about Namontack and started at John's voice. She had to sort her thoughts out before talking to him. "I don't really feel like it right now John she said with irritation in her voice, another wave of nausea flooding through her as her fear and pregnancy combined.

"Sarah, please come with me." He took her hand and pulled her towards the steps up to the deck.

She rose reluctantly, sighing.

When they got up to the main deck, he pulled her to him, cradling her in his arms for a moment kissing her gently, before he released her and held her straight in front of him, looking into her eyes.

"Namontack knows you have the rosary Sarah."

The rain was starting to fall heavier but neither of them felt the cold. She looked at him, her brows drawn together, and shook her head slowly in confirmation.

"He approached me earlier wanting gold. I have been frantic trying to think of what to do. We have no gold. You know I can't get rid of my rosary; it is all I have to remember my family and religion. It would feel like I was throwing away my past and God himself." She looked at John with staring eyes. Suddenly she had a thought and blurted out " I will have to hide it somewhere no one can possibly find it." John had feared this reaction, but knew he had to convince her otherwise. She was so young. He had to take care of her and make her see the reality.

It was getting colder and colder, and Sarah's hair was dripping as the thunder and lightning jolted John back to their surroundings. He pulled her under some shelter.

"Sarah, you have to throw it away. The anti-Catholic feeling could mean that even a hint that you are holding a symbol of Catholic idolatry would have very serious consequences."

She started to shiver. "Maybe he won't do anything." She pleaded.

"He is serious Sarah. We can't assume that he is not going to do anything with this… but he would have no proof without the rosary. You get rid of the rosary, and if he accuses you, just deny it, and there is nothing anyone could do."

"I understand what you are saying John, but I know myself - The proof is in my heart, and anyone challenging me would know that just by looking at me, whether I had the rosary or not. I could not deny my allegiance to the Catholic faith, even on threat of death." Her desperation was showing through. "Could you throw Eustace's stone away John? Could you?" She started to sob.

He was stunned and scared, feeling powerless.

"Please Sarah, I am begging you now. You must throw it away. It is too risky. Think of our baby. It might just give you a chance. I know it will be hard to deny your God, but think of our baby." This was their first real disagreement, and her stubbornness was frustrating him. He was starting to get angry. Could she not see how she might endanger him and the baby as well as herself by holding on to the rosary?

Sarah paused. Suddenly she looked calm, determination on her beautiful face as a thought crossed her mind. "I am being punished for being with you, for giving in to my carnal desires. I know that now. God is testing me. He needs me to be strong and hold on to the symbol of my love for him, no matter the consequences. Only then will our baby be safe. I am sorry John, I will not do what you ask." Her eyes flashed at him defensively.

John could not believe what he was hearing. Was this really his Sarah? She was not thinking rationally and it was as if he had become the enemy. What could he do to convince her? He loved her so much, and he had to make sure she and his baby were safe.

He remembered her hesitation when she had agreed to marry him; something that had been overcome only with the condition of her keeping the rosary. With his overpowering love for her and excitement at the prospect of marriage, he had not considered the true significance of the Catholic symbol. He thought back to when he had chased her along the pier, her hair flying, her eyes sparkling with mischief. His little squaw – his and his alone. Tonight their dilemma had revealed another part of Sarah that he did not know. He shook himself. Surely their love would overcome this dilemma? It was not that long ago when he had felt the centre of her world, when she would have done anything for him. Maybe that had been an illusion. Youthful passion had camouflaged reality. His heart ached, he was angry and powerless. He felt for Eustace's stone.

* * *

Silently they returned to the gun deck, avoiding eye contact as they went through the rituals of prayers and dinner, eventually getting ready to tuck down for sleep as the ship tossed up and down and the wind whistled through the gaps left by the vacant guns.

John kissed her cheek and smiled with sadness in his eyes.

"Goodnight" he said softly, as she turned away from him, an unseen tear falling onto the straw.

As the night wore on and the storm seemed to increase in intensity, John rose, looking at the sleeping form of Sarah with grief in his heart. He went up on the deck, and was greeted with an ocean that had transformed itself from a kind calm and benign friend, to a raging and angry enemy. He stayed on deck watching with fascination for an hour or so, before his mind took over once again. He had to go back down to see Sarah.

He descended once again as everyone who had been able to sleep over the noise of the encroaching storm was starting to wake up. Sarah was lying on her bed of straw, looking lost, rubbing her eyes sleepily. Even through his dismay, John thought she looked beautiful. The pregnancy made her glow. She looked up at him scanning his face for emotions. He walked over and sat down next to her taking her hand, bending over her and kissing her. He felt powerless. What was going to happen? Maybe Namontack wouldn't carry through his threat. Maybe he and Sarah could carry on as they were before. Sarah was carrying his child, he had to get through this.

Tempest

On deck, the skies were darkening further, so no morning sunshine could break through; it was like midnight instead of 7 am. The sea looked like it was starting to boil, large breakers tossed and broke, foaming and writhing, angry and possessed. The wind whistled through every crevice of the ship, a loud wailing screech. The sails strained to contain the captive air that held the strength of a hundred men. The weary sailors ran to and fro trying to harness the energy to best advantage, reacting to orders that could hardly be heard above the competing gale. The bow of the "Sea Venture" dipped and rose, turning the stomachs of everyone on board.

"At last a bit of action." Somers, face was full of excitement. This is what he had been waiting for. This is why he had left Lyme Regis. "We should get some miles behind us now. Maybe even see Jamestown in *under* the week? What do you say Newport". He wanted to prove Newport wrong about the route and as far as he could see, these winds were helping not hindering progress.

"Aye aye, Sir. The men are struggling a bit, but it will do them good to get them working after all these days sitting playing cards. I just hope that things don't get much worse, or we might lose sight of the other ships."

"If we do, we do Newport." said Gates "We are going to meet up with them in Barbuda in the unlikely event that that happens. It will not be the end of the world, will it?"

"No sir, but stronger winds than this, may blow us off course." replied Newport.

"For Goodness sake man. You seem determined to be all doom and gloom. So far, so good. You just keep a track of your helmsman and navigator, and direct the men, and we will be fine" said Gates, enjoying the thrill and excitement of the storm as much as Somers.

"Maybe we ought to light more lanterns at least, so the other ships are more likely to see us. The visibility has gone down significantly." He strained his eyes to catch sight of the other ships in the fleet.

"Oh, alright then Newport, if it makes you happy" said Somers, unconvinced of the necessity. After all, he thought, this storm will not last forever. It will probably pass in a few hours, and then we will be praying for wind again.

Far from abating as Somers had envisioned, he watched as the day wore on. It was like The Almighty was gradually turning the wind up notch by notch as the minutes passed. The rain began to fall like steely sheets, making the hogs and chickens on deck squeak and cry as it landed on their backs like cold sharp knives.

The waves increased in size, so that to look at them, was like looking at a mountain getting bigger and bigger. As the ship climbed the watery peak, everything was driven backward toward the stern by an unseen force. Suddenly on reaching the top, there was a moment of stillness before the wave cascaded over the hull, pulling the ship down in a free-fall that felt endless. This went on and on, mountains and mountains, rising and sinking. Each wave a moment of terror, as everyone below counted the seconds before the ship raised itself again, praying that the next was not going to lead to the bottom of the ocean. The creaking of the ship, and the loud whistling of the wind overwhelmed the senses, and struck fear into the hearts of all aboard. The ship bore the resemblance of a child's plaything in a huge bath at the mercy of angry Gods. It had all happened so suddenly. Somers was starting doubt his estimation of this storm, but he was going to be damned if he admitted it.

The seamen who had laughed and played a few days before, were thrown into high alert. The sails had to be trimmed, and orders were being shouted left and right, carried away by the wind, few reaching the ears of the sailors - no one really knew what to do. The lads perilously climbed the mast, watching the deep and angry sea as it thrashed below them clinging on for dear life.

Beth Samuels was terrified. She had never done anything like this before, and it was one thing to climb a mast in a still calm sea, but another in this raging torrent. Her father watched in fear as his beautiful little daughter climbed with the lads. As he watched, Robbie came staggering towards him, greasy hair blowing in the wind as he looked up at Beth or Timmy as he knew her to be, smiling as if a thought had crossed his mind, and rubbing his hands together.

"I could give a stiff one up the backside to that little lad" he said to Eddy Samuels giving him a knowing wink. "If you know what I mean... " Eddy Samuels stood stock still, trying to take in what he had just heard. "What did you just say to me?" He thought he had heard, but surely not...

"I said... I... could... give... a stiff... one... "his words slow and mocking, as if talking to a child.

Eddy's instincts took over. Before he even had time to really think about it, he drew back his fist to punch Robbie in the stomach.

At that moment, a huge wave crashed over the bow of the ship. The ship gave an almighty shudder as it fought to hold its structure together. Robbie stumbled and fell, leaving Eddy without a target.

Eddy's gaze switched from the ugly sprawling figure on the deck, back to where his daughter had been on the mast. He could not see her. Then he saw a group of sailors surrounding something on the deck. They were shouting and gesticulating "Quick someone, get a stretcher. Is he still alive? Is he still breathing? Someone feel for his heart."

Oh my God, Eddy had an intake of breath. Beth must have fallen.

He ran to the group, and saw his beautiful little girl lying motionless in a pool of salt water that was rapidly turning the colour of her blood. He tried frantically to get to her, but was prevented by the crowds all looking to see what had happened. He saw her limp little body being carefully lifted onto a blanket, the four corners of which were carried by two hefty sailors down to the gun deck, out of the elements. There was nothing Eddy could do, but pray.

* * *

Below deck was chaos with the increasing storm.

"Mummy, mummy, are we going to die?" five year old Elizabeth sobbed. Constance was curled up on the straw bed in the foetal position scared stiff, and her little brother hid his face in his mother's shoulder and cried constantly as Mary tried to soothe him.

"For the Lord's Sake!" Shouted Steven Hopkins. "Will everyone stop the noise. Prayer will help us, but there is so much noise the Lord will not be able to hear us." He grabbed Elizabeth by the collar and shook her. "Be quiet you snivelling little milksop." He shouted, staring at her. "Repeat after me.. The Lord is my shepherd... "

The poor little girl tried to follow what he was saying, but couldn't stop herself from crying, and the words just didn't come. "You are as useless as the others" he shouted as he lashed out at her. He walked over to his wife and stooped to hit her, but she dived out of the way protecting little Giles.

Reverend Bucke, chose to ignore what was happening with the Hopkins family and continued with his duties, holding an impromptu service, praising God, and trusting in him to deliver them all safely to dry ground when he so chose.

Sarah clung to one of the structural vertical poles. John seemed to have abandoned her completely. She could see him on the other side of the deck facing away from her and her stomach turned. He looked so handsome and strong. She longed for him, but knew her choice to keep the rosary had placed a wedge between them. Her distress and fear was gradually turning to anger at his petulant stance as things became more and more difficult for her.

He should be at her side protecting her through this storm. He should understand that it was impossible for her to throw away her rosary. Maybe they did not really know one another at all.

Sarah, partly to take her mind off John, took the screaming baby Giles from his mother. There was a real danger of the children being thrown from one side of the ship to the other if they were not held firmly. Alice had five year old Elizabeth, and Mary took charge of Constance. The women knew that the rocking of the ship could cause serious injury to such little bodies and they had to do something to try as much as possible to shelter them. It was not easy though. The children struggled and writhed, scared and angry, trying to escape the clutches of the well-meaning adults.

Sarah, felt so ill. It did not help that the floor had become like an open sewer again. Toileting was even worse than before, and even Mistress Horton had to surrender the idea of her Chamber pot. No movement was possible as to move would likely end in being toppled over like ninepins. People had to deal with their bodily functions where they were standing, clinging on for dear life to whatever structure they could find.

The stench was beyond imagination. No air circulated as the gun hatches were battened down to prevent water seeping through, both from rain and sea water. No one could see what was happening outside, but the movements and sounds communicated the seriousness of what was happening to them. The screams of passengers and sailors alike added to Rev. Buck's steady and monotonous voice, becoming an overwhelming cacophony of sound.

The sailors had picked up the small body of Beth and moved slowly down the steps to the Gun deck, trying not to jolt the little unmoving figure supported by the sea sodden blanket.

"Careful with him" Edward said, when he saw them approaching with a lifeless bundle. He rushed over to look at the injured form being placed down gently before him.

"Quick everyone, we need help in clearing a space for the patient." He shouted.

Only Alice was able to make her way over, and quickly cleared a space for the small body, trying to hold on as the ship bucked and dived over the increasingly large waves.

"I don't know if he is alive." The sailor's face was serious. "He is very small. I would not be surprised if he broke most of the bones in his body with a fall from that height." The little figure looked pale, but still seemed to be breathing.

Edward sighed. How was he going to be able to do anything in these conditions? The child before him was in a bad way - possibly with concussion, and broken bones, having fallen from such a height.

The lad was quite young though, so may stand a chance.

He knelt down pulling the eyelids to look into his pupils. He started to do a physical examination feeling the lad's slight body. He ran his hand down both of the arms, and across his chest trying to ascertain what was broken and where the wounds were that had to be dressed. As he ran his hands over the chest, he felt slight mounds. His eyebrows raised in surprise.

"What is it Edward?" Alice saw that he was perplexed. "Is he too far gone? Has he stopped breathing?" She whispered.

"No. He is still breathing". Edward looked at his wife with a look of amazement on his face. "I think we have a little girl before us, Alice, not a lad."

"Oh my goodness. How can that be? She must have wanted to get to the New World and impersonated a boy. How did she cope in those close quarters with all those ruffians?" asked Alice.

"Not very well, I would say. Apart from all the broken bones and cuts, she looks undernourished. My guess is she had quite a difficult time of it, even before she fell."

Edward continued his examination of her. He very delicately examined her abdomen and lower body. "Oh poor little thing" he turned and looked at Alice. "There are scars and bruises here that would suggest that she may have been sexually assaulted."

"What - on board the ship, do you think?"

"No the scars suggest possibly a few weeks ago. It must have been before she boarded the "Sea Venture". Let's see if we can bathe her wounds and start binding the bones that are broken. There may be mental scars as well as physical that she has to contend with.

The little body had been muttering confused words as she started to regain semi consciousness.

"Papa, papa" she cried, with tears in her still closed eyes. "No, no, I can't do it. Get that man away from me." Edward looked at Alice and nodded his head.

"I think there is a lot that little girl has to be frightened of" he sighed.

At the other end of the gun deck, Mistress Horton lay listless and depressed, alone with her thoughts, looking up at the ceiling, all fight and dignity gone. Sleep was a commodity that passengers had long since forgotten. Everyone became helpless, forced to accept an unknown fate.

Reverend Bucke still read the bible, trying to give the message that God was with them, even though, he himself, was starting to have serious doubts. Maybe it was God's will that the sea be their watery grave. Maybe the greed of the passengers in hoping to find gold had angered the Lord. Still he read on, his droning voice competing with the wailing and crashing of the sounds of the increasingly rising storm.

Sarah and John remained separated, each wretched with longing for the other, but consumed with confusion over their differing views. How awful it would be if they went to their watery deaths, on such difficult terms, John thought.

John had hoped that this would be a new life for him and Sarah. Was that to be? He sat looking around him at the filth, and people scrabbling for their lives in the tossing ship miles from anywhere. He thought of Eustace as he felt for his stone. What would Eustace make of it? How would Eustace have coped? If they made it to Virginia, and Sarah's secret was kept, Eustace's dream would have been fulfilled. Taking those first steps down the gangplank as he landed in Jamestown would make all of this worthwhile. He felt for the stone to remind himself of his true goal and prayed all would be well.

* * *

No one expected the events of 24th July to be overshadowed by those of 25th - but the new day emerged, worse than its predecessor. Night merged into day without the usual change in light, as evil menacing clouds grew ever higher and thicker, blocking out any possible light from the sun. Lightning forked through the darkness, as the ship continued to be battered and buffeted from mountainous wave to mountainous wave with no relief. Rain continued to pelt down and the decks were under an increasingly rising level of frothing water.

Somers looking out from his position on the poop deck was alarmed to see nothing on the horizon. The companion ships had disappeared from view and there was an eerie sense of being alone with a God that was waging a terrible personal war. He spared a special thought for Pierce and Yeardley whose wives were on the other ships, knowing that their worst fears had come to pass - their families were in the unknown. Who knew if they would ever be seen again?

He looked out again, and breathed in the salt air. He did not get the usual thrill of the challenge, he felt more as if he was in a dark room with an armed and dangerous bully with no weapons or armour. Towering waves continued to sweep over the bow of the ship, and water was starting to leak down to the decks below, despite all hatches being battened down.

His beloved "Sea Venture", was doing her very best - but it was against all odds that Jamestown would soon be in their sights. If the storm abated in the next few hours, they may be able to regroup with the fleet, and estimate positions in order to move forward, but the course that they were running now was a complete unknown.

No stars, no moon, no sun to guide them, and winds that whipped around from all directions meant they were completely powerless to know, let alone direct their route. He ordered all sails to be taken in and reefed, as the energy contained in the winds was just too strong.

The helmsman struggled with the whip staff, trying to maintain control and turn into the wind to prevent the ship aligning parallel to the waves, which would ensure a certain watery death for all of them.

Somers looked at the scene around him, and felt the bile rising. He started coughing. He had been in perilous situations before, but never had he felt so out of control as he did now. He wanted to shut his eyes to it, to make it all go away, to turn the clock back, to be sitting with his wife in Lyme Regis... But he wasn't.

He was responsible for all of the people on this ship, plus the livestock and men on the pinnace that was attached to the "Sea Venture" at the back. He had a fleeting image of the young Davey Jones saluting him, standing next to the two beautiful black horses. He, and the rest of the passengers and crew were innocents in Somers's hands.

"Things are bad, aren't they Christopher" he said, his voice low and serious. Admitting the reality out loud at last, brought the truth even clearer in his mind.

Gates walked over, his face dark with emotion. "What can we do?"

"Sirs," said Newport. "I haven't experienced anything quite like this in my whole career. I think we need to take some drastic measures", he paused to give himself courage before revealing the next devastating course of action.

"We have lost the rest of the fleet, and this ship is struggling, especially as we have the pinnace tied to the stern. We cannot possibly survive with that weight attached to us. We need to set the pinnace free. I know it will be certain death to the men on board the pinnace if we cut them loose, but I think we have to sacrifice the few to protect the many."

"Oh no, surely not Newport." Somers could hardly speak for

emotion. "It will be like murdering them."

"I know that Sir, but if we don't do it, it will be like murdering all the passengers on the pinnace as well as the "Sea Venture". 50 souls, or 200? That is our only choice.

Gates could see that Somers was in a bad way. "Somers, Newport is right. Hard though it is, we would be doing the right thing by cutting the pinnace free. Much as I hate to, I have to agree... and so do you. We will all end up at the bottom of the sea very soon, if you do not act now." Gates looked skywards. "No one, least of all God will judge us for this. This is what leaders have to do. They have to make difficult decisions for the good of the majority."

Somers' face reflected the tragedy of what they were about to do. He thought back again to Davey Jones and his gleaming black horses prancing around the deck. The young lad symbolized the hope and expectations of the whole expedition, and now he had to sentence him to death. He shook his head. "Call Reverend Burke. We cannot just cut them lose to go to their watery graves without a blessing from God."

Reverend Burke came and stood at the stern of the "Sea Venture" looking towards the pinnace that was heaving up and down, straining against the ropes holding it to the larger ship. He made a sign of the cross as he started to pray.

Somers, Gates and Newport stood watching from the Poop deck, their faces. long and drawn, joining in the prayers. There was no time for ceremony, no time to gather the sailors to pay their respects to those that were going to give their lives to save the "Sea Venture", they had to get on with it. They had no choice.

They could see that the people on the pinnace were watching what was happening, at first with bewilderment and then as realisation dawned on them; they started shouting with panic, eyes pleading and mouths screaming. They knew full well, that they were being sentenced to death.

Somers felt like a Roman Emperor, giving the thumbs down in the amphitheatre, although the feelings he had were not entertaining. He signalled for the sailor to start cutting the rope, which was like an umbilical cord between the two vessels. With this command however, death not birth was to be the ultimate result.

Gradually the rope wore thin, and the pinnace jumped back from the "Sea Venture" like it had been thrown away by a large force, as it started to disappear into the rain and waves. The silhouette of the pinnace was exaggerated in a flash of lightning. Somers caught sight of Davey, who was at the point of hysteria, his arms waving, his eyes pleading. Somers had to look away in agony. He knew it was cowardly, but he could not watch the moment when she capsized with all those wonderful men and beautiful animals, all of whom had put their trust and their lives in his hands. He knew he had failed them.

He was sure that it would not take long, as the ship was much smaller and less able to manage the onslaught of such a storm.

Was this the beginning of the end for all of them? He could not let anyone see that he was starting to wonder if they would make it. He had to be positive; there was no point in harbouring negative thoughts. He turned to look at Gates and Newport and all of them made the sign of the cross in silent respect for those that were going to die, wondering if they were soon to have a similar fate.

News of the demise of the pinnace filtered down to the lower decks. People were stunned with the loss. Many remembered Davey and the horses with fondness, and shuddered to think of him at the bottom of the ocean. Fear had permeated the ship as conditions had worsened, but now the loss of the pinnace intensified even more the reality of the situation that they were facing. How much longer did they have? Would they soon be joining Davey and his horses in a watery grave.

Days and nights merged into more days and nights with no one knowing which was which. Nothing seemed to change except the increasing intensity of the storm. It was surreal, like a bad dream that they could not wake up from.

Suddenly, on Wednesday morning, John heard the cry that sent a shard of ice through the hearts of everyone on board the "Sea Venture".

"The hold is leaking. We are taking on Water!" It was Christopher Carter, waking up in his hammock in the lower deck.

"Look… look, it is leaking like a sieve." Humphrey Reed, awakened by Chris's cry saw that the leak was in more than one place. "There and there, and look over there too… it is everywhere!"

Gradually as everyone started to look around, the cries became shrieks of despair, as this was physical evidence that The"Sea Venture" was not coping.

John was frantic. Taking on water could only mean one thing - they were one step further towards sinking to the bottom of the ocean never to reach Jamestown, never to fulfil Eustace's dream.

He thought of rushing to see Sarah and then heard Newport yell "all able bodied men, descend to the lower deck. We have to stem the flow of this water, or we are all doomed."

John did as he was told, and headed down. What he saw, was worse than he could possibly have imagined. The "Sea Venture", had taken so much strain from the relentless bashing from sea, wind and rain, that the infill oakum (unravelled rope seeped in tar for waterproofing) was being pushed out from between the planks that held the ship together. Water was seeping through everywhere uncontrollably. The rate at which the hull was filling indicated that there was probably a larger hole in the hull as well.

The men panicked and grabbed spare candles for light as they scanned the sides of the ship looking for holes, and there were many.

"Look" said Yeardley. "It looks like there are bits of biscuit floating in the water. There must be a large leak in the bread room. Come with me John, let's you I see if we can find that hole and block it, it must be a large one."

Yeardley and John proceeded to the bread room. "Nothing much to see here" John said. "It must just be that there are so many holes, the biscuit is floating around. The best thing we can do is to go back to the main deck. We will have to fill the leaks with dried meat and rags as we don't have anything else.

"Yes, goodness knows how long that will hold - and goodness knows how far we are from land." replied Yeardley.

"It's not looking good, is it?" John whispered.

Minute by minute the water in the hold seemed to rise and rise. They could see that what they were doing was not going to be sufficient and with time, the ship would just gradually fill up with water and sink.

Gates took control. It's no good lads" he shouted. "We are not making any headway here. As soon as we plug one leak, it starts leaking somewhere else. We are running out of meat and rags, and really making very little difference. We will have to start using the pumps to pump the water out. At least that way, we might have a chance to keep things under control." Gates knew he had to organise things.

"I want three teams. We have two pumps, I want one at the stern and one at the bow. Midship, I want the third team to use buckets and pails, forming a line - full buckets to be sent up to the deck for emptying and empty ones coming back. We must work without stopping - this is a matter of life and death, and I don't think there is anyone here with half a brain that needs to argue the point. Any questions gentlemen?"

There was a loud groan of approval. Everyone was working together with the common goal of saving their lives.

Men worked day and night. Gentlemen and ruffians alike sweated and toiled for their lives. Men such as Henry Paine and Sylvester Jourdain worked alongside the half-naked bodies of Want and Robbie Waters. John put all his energies into bailing - his anger and confusion seemed to give him the strength of ten, and as the sweat poured off him, his mind could only focus on the next pail he had to fill.

Matchumps and Namontack joined the working party. Their brown bodies gleamed, and they struggled doing the best they could, backwards and forwards as gallons and gallons of water were pumped and baled. There was little reprieve from the constant battle.

After hours of tedious unrelenting work, Gates could see some of the men doubled over with exhaustion. They would all collapse if they continued at this rate.

"Attention everyone. We are all exhausted. I want each group to take a fifteen minute break in each hour. I will sound a whistle for a group to start and end. We must ensure that we don't take too much time. We can't have this water defeating us now. I don't suggest you go up on deck when you take your break, the chances are that you will be washed into the sea. It is evil up there at the moment and I can't afford to lose anyone. There is too much to do."

John was working with the team with the Indians. He saw Namontack start to climb the ladder. He thought it strange that the Indian would go on deck, especially in such rough seas, when he was already unstable on his legs, having only recently begun to walk without the use of crutches. John was sure he risked being swept into the sea or thrown against the sides of the ship to his death. Namontack, John thought, was a creature of the open air and nature, and he probably needed to breathe the fresh air to hold on to his sanity.

John, unsure at first, decided that he had very little to lose, and this was a chance that he might not get again for a long time, if ever, even if it was dangerous. He had to confront Namontack. So, he too, climbed up the ladder to go out on deck. The deck was virtually deserted.

At that very moment, the largest wave any of them, including Somers, Gates and Newport, had ever encountered rose into the air at the bow and didn't touch down again until it reached the stern, many seconds later. Those few sailors standing on the deck looked upwards horrified to see the glistening wave above them. The whole ship was submerged. It was completely under water for several moments. The icy frothing blanket, was so powerful that the "Sea Venture", a tiny speck in the mighty ocean, became like a piece of driftwood underneath the powerful bank of water. Everyone on deck ran to find anything they could to secure themselves from being washed overboard

It took six men to hold on to the whip-staff, but even with these numbers, the force of the wave threw them asunder, with the whip-staff breaking free. The main helmsman crashed against the side of the ship. His head smashing open, his body limp. Another seaman took the helm, but not before the ship had lurched and dived, throwing all on board up in the air and down again.

Gates, in his position of directing the bailing and pumping in the hold, was himself thrown against the side of the ship with many of his tired and sweating companions. Gates's small, but powerful frame became like a rag doll flailing as he tried to save himself. His eyes momentarily registered panic as he recognised the force at which he was crashing towards the weeping and porous side of the ship.

Stunned, when he came to a halt, he lay for a moment, scanning his body for injury, aware that everyone had stopped working, shocked as it dawned on them that their leader was a human being, capable of injury. Gradually he moved his aching limbs. William Strachey, one of the more solid members of the working party, edged towards him, and gave him a helping hand to slowly rise to his feet. He hobbled gingerly towards a nearby crate, and lowered himself gently.

"What the devil have you stopped working for" he shouted angrily at the men, who were unsure what to do. "Get back to work or this vessel will sink." He held his head in his hands for a few moments, catching his breath and his thoughts. He could not afford to be injured or to be seen as weak. These men could not think for themselves, and he had to be able to direct them. He ached from head to toe, and he had a large gash down the length of his leg that was bleeding profusely, but as their leader, he had to ignore his own pain and get on with the job in hand.

As he sat, motionless, he was able to see the level of water in the hull rising. It was now waist high - they could not let it get much higher, or the weight of it would sink the ship. With that, he rose from the crate, blood pumping from his leg, which turned the salt water pink, and continued bailing.

* * *

John was only half way out of the hatch when the wave hit, so managed to hold on for all of his might, so that he was not swept away. He saw the almighty wave above him, and Namontack in the distance on the deck. As the wave crashed down, John saw Namontack fall, and start sliding, his brown arms waving backwards and forwards, trying to catch hold of something. It was no use, he was being carried further and further away by the torrent of water that had landed on the deck. With the exaggerated movement of the ship, and the depth of the water in the hull, Namontack's slight frame was in danger of being washed overboard.

In a split second, John could see all his worries laid to rest. The demise of Namontack in an accident would mean that Sarah would be safe, without him having to do anything. The problem would just go away. He and Sarah could go back to normal.

Suddenly, he had a flashback of Eustace's hand reaching for his. The slow steady fall, and the limp little body lying at the foot of the cliff. As much as he hated Namontack, could he really choose to be responsible for another death? He would be responsible, because he knew that dangerous and difficult though it was, there was a chance that he could save Namontack.

John pulled himself out of the hold, and gingerly waded through the water, in the direction of the Indian, holding on to anything he could to stop himself falling as the ship continued to rise and fall, it took what seemed like hours. At last, he stood beside the helpless brown body that was not only half drowned, but was dazed and bleeding from the battering that he had received.

John looked deeply into his brown eyes, holding his gaze. The look told them both that John held Namontack's life in his hands. The Indian was helpless. His body only just recovering from the first beating, was battered and bruised yet again. He lay. His brown eyes pleaded with John to grab his hand and save him.

John hesitated...

Choices

~✿✿✿~

Thursday started. The only change from this day to the previous three, was that the situation was becoming increasingly hopeless. Rain, thunder, lightning, bailing, bailing bailing ... Pitching and rolling, pitching and rolling ... There was no respite. It seemed as if despite their determination to stay alive, God had other plans for them. The boat was sinking lower and lower and getting nearer and nearer to the level of the furious sea.

On deck, suddenly, Somers saw through the darkness, what looked like an illuminated fairy light. He was enthralled. Somers called for all those not working, to come and see the spectacle.

"Look everyone" he shouted "out of the darkness, we have dancing lights, beautiful dancing lights." Some came from below deck, despite the warnings they had had about the intensity of the storm. They hung on for dear life and stood in wonderment, pleased they had taken the risk. The light danced and played around the masts, throwing a blue illumination as it went, ducking and diving as the ship continued to toss in the boiling sea. It was like it was touching everything and giving it a playful and teasing kiss in rhythm with the wind.

"Ah, St. Elmo's Fire." Newport looked up towards the illuminated mast. "I am surprised though, usually you can see St. Elmo's fire when the storm is starting to abate - but this storm is far from abating. Maybe it is a good sign though; maybe we will see the storm diminish soon."

"I hope you are right" replied Somers, who was feeling the effects of being awake for so long. He had a sudden coughing fit, covering his mouth with a handkerchief which, covered with blood, he quickly hid. He was hoping that he was well enough to keep going. He had not anticipated such conditions and he knew his health was suffering. He hoped he could last long enough to get everyone to safety.

No one saw Somers coughing and the blood that stained his handkerchief, but everyone that saw the light felt their heart lift a little, before they stumbled back down to continue with the bailing and pumping.

John looked at the blue light, and his mind floated back to a few hours before. He had stared into the eyes of Namontack in the same way he remembered staring into the eyes of Eustace. He did not have a choice in Heacham, as he had only been a child, and not strong enough to save Eustace - he realised this now. This had been another chance for him to save a life. So he had reached for Namontack, felt his hand in his, and instead of the hand slipping through his, John felt the Indian's body being pulled to safety. Namontack had been so exhausted from fear and exertion that he had lost consciousness, but before he did, he whispered "Namontack sorry, Namontack no say anything about wife" and he gave a grateful smile as he closed his brown eyes.

John had carried him down to the gun deck, placing him gently down amongst the other injured, not having time to speak to Sarah. He had not known that Namontack would keep the secret before he saved him, and this made the decision even sweeter. The way things were going, there would not have been much time before he was to meet his maker, and he wanted to do this with a clear conscience. Now looking at this lovely light dancing around the mast, he felt that it was a personal sign. He had chosen a course of action, and the course had been the right one. He imagined Eustace smiling down at him. Maybe the light was a sign? Maybe now he and Sarah could start over. Maybe she could be his little Indian Squaw again, carrying their little baby in her papoose. He smiled at the imaginary picture. He couldn't wait to tell Sarah what had happened, and gather her in his arms, carefree once again.

As St. Elmo's fire danced above them, highlighting the foaming sea, below deck, was continued chaos and there were many injured - Namontack, Beth, the helmsman, and countless more with broken bones and battered flesh, who had fallen or been thrown as the ship was tossed up and down over the angry and tumultuous sea. Patients were tied down to stop them hurting themselves further and the women did what they could to bathe their wounds or bind broken bones. They had not seen the wonderful light, and were gradually being worn down by the relentlessness of everything. There was no time for eating or drinking, even if there had been anything to eat or drink and everyone was getting weaker and weaker.

The children were in a very bad way. The restlessness that had had to be contained a few days ago, was replaced by a staring listlessness. No food, little liquid and constant terror had made the childrens' spirits vanish. They became like shells of their former lively selves. Alice and Sarah still helped Mary to look after them, but this required no more than holding them and whispering reassuring words into their ears from time to time.

Edward no longer cared for the sick. His services were better put to use with the others bailing and pumping, so Alice and Sarah, with the help of little Lizzy Parsons and Elizabeth Joons a young serving girl, became carers of the sick.

Beth had regained consciousness, but was still not making any sense. She constantly asked for her father, and became hysterical when they weren't able to produce him. She wanted to get up, but she was securely tied like the rest of the patients, for her own good.

Sarah did not see John deliver Namontack to the gun deck as she had been so busy, but became aware of the presence of the Indian, when she turned around having finished binding the arm of one of the injured sailors. She was surprised to see the injured Indian, but her feelings were not warm. She knew that he had information that could do her serious harm. She felt her tummy - she knew her baby was there, but was not showing itself by movement or size, to anyone but herself. She thought she felt a little flutter of movement, but was not too sure, as the rocking of the ship disguised all sensations.

She stared at the unconscious body of Namontack. He was an evil Heathen, who had the power to destroy her. She grimaced. She was expected to nurse him back to health yet again. There did not seem to be any justice in the world, she thought.

She started to think about the consequences of Namontack divulging her secret. No doubt she would be imprisoned - John too might be thrown in jail for bringing her on the journey and pretending that she had converted. What would happen to her baby? She was glad she still had her rosary. She felt in her pocket for the smooth beads. God would be merciful, she had to have faith. Her thoughts stayed with her for several hours as she worked tirelessly to help the injured. She was alone with God. It felt as if John had distanced himself from her and the problem.

Baby Giles started to scream. He had awoken from a nightmare, and stumbled across the deck and fallen, his knees streaming with blood and his little face crumpled in pain. Mary and Alice, both ran to his aid, and Lizzy and Elizabeth Joons turned to see what was happening - all focus was on baby Giles.

Sarah went to check on Namontack and from nowhere a dreadful thought occurred to her. Could she solve the problem? Could she finish him off once and for all? No one would ever know, and no one knew that she had a motive. It would be like turning the clock back to before she dropped her rosary. She could save her baby, herself and John. What a wonderful life they were going to have, and if she didn't do this, it would all vanish. Could she? Would she? She hesitated. Taking the life of another was a drastic thing to do, but she was being pushed to the limit – she had to. God was telling her. The thought had come so strongly and so suddenly that it had to have been sent from God himself. If she was going to do it, she had to act swiftly; there would not be many chances.

She quickly pulled up the hem of her dress, looking furtively around her and made it into a wedge of material thick enough to put over Namontack's face. She held it over his nose and mouth for several minutes as although unconscious, his body instinctively fought for breath. His face turned blue and his body shuddered, the lack of oxygen causing his brain and body to react violently as he convulsed. She closed her eyes, her body tense. The shuddering in his body stopped and at last, he lay still. She paused holding her breath, and held his wrist, seeking a heartbeat. There was none. Relief flooded her body. She looked around her, and everyone was busy tending to the children and other patients. No one had seen her, she breathed a sigh of relief.

Sarah turned away from him, and rushed over to baby Giles and the others, as if nothing had happened. It was like a dream. Had she really just killed someone? It was so quick, and there was no going back.

Then she felt her heart beating as shock set in. Remorse started to flood her system. She had become a murderess in one small movement. How could she? She was a Catholic.

Then she remembered that now she and John were free. Their baby could be born in the new world, just like they had planned, and no one would be any the wiser about what had happened, not even John. God had sent her the answer. It had all happened so quickly as in a dream. She had passed the test and kept the rosary and God had sent her the answer. Namontack was a heathen after all. Everything would be fine now. No one would notice that the Indian was dead for a while, as there was so much to do, and so many people to take care of. She would make sure that she was nowhere near Namontack when he was found. They would all think he had suffered an internal injury - the truth belonged to her and to God.

But no, her stomach lurched with the reality. She could try and justify her actions all she liked, but it did not cancel out the stark truth. She was a murderess. She slumped. A tear ran down her face as she looked over at the body of the Indian. Oh God save me... what have I done?

Is All Lost?

O n the top deck, as John looked at St. Elmo's fire gradually lose its strength, he felt as if a weight had been lifted off his shoulders. As soon as he could, he was going to go down to the gun deck and tell Sarah that Namontack was no longer a threat and had agreed to stay silent. They were free again. Despite the world tumbling down around them, at least Sarah was saved punishment and humiliation. Maybe they could start rebuilding trust in one another, even for the short time they may have left.

It was the fifth day now, and things were getting to the point that another day like all the others could only result in the "Sea Venture" sinking to the bottom of the sea. Passengers and sailors started to see the ship that had set out with such high hopes, as nothing but a large coffin. Exhausted though they were, everyone pumped for their lives trying to thwart the power of nature.

John took the first opportunity he could to make his way to the gun deck. He wanted to tell Sarah about Namontack.

As he approached, he saw Sarah sitting slumped and dazed. He ran over to her and crouched down beside her.

"Sarah, Sarah… Namontack has promised not to say anything about the Rosary" he whispered, his heart racing, looking around furtively to make sure no one was listening. He felt that his words were a small gift to ease her suffering even if their hours were numbered in this life. She could go to her rest taking her rosary with her as a keepsake for the next life, knowing that she had not been exposed and shamed.

He looked expectantly at her as he held her tiny hand waiting for a response. He could see shock in her eyes as she registered what he said. She took a sharp intake of breath, her body slumped further, and her eyes squeezed tightly, before the tears poured down her cheeks silently as she began to shake. "No! Oh my God, No!" She wailed.

She held his hand as though her life depended on it and sat stunned, rocking with the movement of the ship. "Sarah, did you hear what I said? We are free. I saved Namontack's life, and he has promised not to say anything about your rosary."

Nothing came out of her mouth except agonising moans. He did not know what to do. Obviously she was in a state of shock, but he had not expected the reaction that he got. Maybe she did not understand what he had said. It was a cause for joy not the pain that she was displaying. He was mystified by her reaction.

He knew that he had to go back to help with the bailing, he felt guilty for being away from it so long, when there was so much at stake, so he prised her hand from his, crouching down in front of her, he looked up at her face. He could see that she was ravaged with despair and he was not even sure she was aware that he was there. She clutched at a nearby post to stop herself from falling.

"I have to go and help again Sarah. I just had to let you know that we are now free. Let's imagine this never happened. I love you." He gave her a gentle loving kiss on her forehead, standing up hesitantly walking away, looking back and catching sight of her slumped body before he reluctantly pulled his eyes away. He hoped that he had been able to convey that he still loved her. He was worried and pulled in two directions - he had to help with the bailing, but he knew Sarah needed him. Reluctantly, he went back to bailing, realising this was their only small hope of surviving, of getting to Jamestown.

They continued to pump and bail - but the effort was becoming too much. No sleep, no food and still the water rose and rose. No headway at all, and it was plain to see that the rate at which the water was rising was not stopping, and if it did not stop, they would die and very soon.

Somers and Newport decided to order all extra weight to be thrown overboard. Men threw barrels of beer, biscuits, cannons, trunks, whatever they could lay their hands on, over the side and watched them being devoured by the hungry sea as they sank into the blackness, swallowed out of existence. As the barrels sank, each and every person on board imagined the cold sea enveloping their own bodies.

Somers watched in horror as the situation deteriorated. He had another momentous decision to make. "Newport, we are really struggling. The mast is a weight that could pull us down. I know it is a point of no return, to hack down the mast, but we have to give ourselves as much time as possible. St. Emo's Fire didn't save us this time" he said shaking his head.

"Aye Sir, a mast is only of use when we have the use of sails and wind to carry us. At this moment in time, our main priority is to stay upright. The mast is so heavy, every sway of it, pulls the ship further and further towards the depths."

He looked up, "It is a question of buying us a few more minutes or hours. Forget getting to Jamestown, we must just concentrate on staying alive."

Newport ordered two sailors to start hacking at the mast with axes.

Everyone on the deck watched with horror, as the mast fell as if in slow motion…

Below, Reverend Bucke and Steven Hopkins still continued with prayers, but even *their* voices were lacking the conviction of true belief in salvation as they mumbled, eyes downcast, no one really listening to what was being preached to them.

The injured passengers and the women looking after them were numb and speechless as they prepared themselves for death. Nursing duties, all but ceased as - what was the point? Mary, clutched her three lifeless children, and Mistress Horton continued her mute, catatonic vigil, lying on her sodden mattress, silently mouthing The Lord's Prayer.

The men below deck pumping and bailing had also come to the conclusion that all was lost. They had done the best they could against all odds, but it had not been enough. The storm had endured too long, and the sea was too angry. Now it was time to accept their fate. Gradually their movements began to slow - no one wanting to give up, but no one really believing it was doing any good

Want had had enough. "All is lost lads" he said resigned and exhausted, saying what every other person was thinking. "I think we need to have one last party to celebrate rather than spend our last minutes toiling needlessly to prolong what we all know is the inevitable. Let's break out what is left of the ale and rum, and numb ourselves. Let's laugh in the face of the almighty who has decided that we do not deserve to live".

Strachey voiced his agreement, and took it one step further. "Hands off the pumps everyone" he shouted with authority. "I for one, aim to end my days drunk" he laughed, but it was not a laugh of good cheer, more of resignation as his large form jumped up, hands in the air to indicate to everyone that he meant what he said. "Come on everyone... a drink to the mighty ship that has fought so valiantly for us. She was just not strong enough... "

Gates stood, speechless. There was nothing he could say. He sat down, head in hands, silently looking at the floor. Maybe all *was* lost.

Robbie Waters, Henry Pierce, Matchumps - every strata of society had become as one. They all cheered, finally accepting their fate, grabbing the barrels that were left, and smashing them open in a frenzy of excitement mixed with terror at what was happening. All were determined to drink as much as possible before the sea water filled their lungs and they became food for the sea creatures.

John Rolfe decided to spend his last moments with Sarah. He was worried about the despair that he had seen on her face, and his stomach churned when he thought of her suffering. Maybe it was his fault, as he had been so hard on her. His disillusionment with her had dissipated, as he realised that all he wanted in life was to be with her, regardless of what she had done. She didn't realise this though. He climbed the ladder up to the gun deck and walked over to where she sat.

"Sarah, my love" John whispered. "We took our vows to love one another until the day we die. I think that day is coming." He took her hand in his, and tried to look into her eyes, determined that they could move on and be as one again, just for these final few moments. He couldn't make her look at him though. She stared at the dirty swirling floor, her face devoid of any expression. She could not talk to him, she could not even move, knowing that she had killed someone, and it had not even been necessary. She did not deserve John's love, she deserved to die - in fact death would be a welcome relief for her. If it wasn't for the new life inside of her, she knew with certainty that she would have thrown herself into the sea. It was what she deserved, but not what this little life inside her deserved, so she stopped herself. She allowed John to lift her chin so that she had to look at him. She had no choice but to look into his eyes as he gently brushed the hair away from her face. She remembered what they had shared and how life had been, such a short time ago. If only she could turn the clock back.

"I know it is scary. I know we will probably die within the next few hours" John said quietly, concerned by the tragic look that Sarah had on her face. "But we love each other, and we can be grateful for the hours that we have had, knowing that we will die together". The ship gave an almighty shudder and tossed into the air with yet another mountainous wave. Sarah fell into John's arms limp and helpless, feeling his warmth and his heart beating against hers. She was going to her death and it was what she wanted and what she deserved."

Shipwreck

George Somers had not moved from the poop deck, despite coming to the conclusion that the end was very near. He still had a job to do, although he knew his ability to concentrate was diminishing, and his blood soaked handkerchiefs increased in number. He was feeling the toll of his advancing years. His body ached, and his mind was dull from lack of sleep and food. Over the past few hours his mind had floated back to Devon and his poor abandoned wife. He tried to draw it back, time and again, but it was a fight to stay with the job at hand without his mind rebelling.

Was it arrogance that had drawn him to this mission? Such folly, to think that he could do such a thing at his time of life and in the state of health he was in. He had come to realise that he was dying. He did not want to admit it to himself, but his blood stained handkerchiefs told the real story.

Maybe a younger, fitter man could have steered a path that kept them together with the fleet, who may, (God willing), have landed at Jamestown by now. Maybe they should have gone the longer way around as Newport had insisted? His confidence and professionalism were the core of who he was - or so he had previously thought. Who was he now? The Admiral who had lost the "Sea Venture" and all those on board? All he knew now was that there was little more he could do. This had shaken him. He did not feel the man he was before he started this voyage. He had hoped to end his career covered in glory, but at present he felt a broken man. Nature had defeated him.

He pulled himself back to scanning the horizon as he had done for hours, despite the fact that there was very little hope. He did not have a clue what part of the ocean they were actually in, having been buffeted back and forth and side to side by the ever changing winds.

"Newport!" He screamed. "Do you have any bloody idea where the hell we are?"

"Sir, we could be anywhere. The wind has kept changing, and we have had to just concentrate on trying to stay afloat. Even if I did know where we are, we have no sail to direct us now. I am afraid we are in the hands of God... and luck" Newport took no pleasure in realising that this route was as dangerous as he had warned.

Somers squinted again, as he had so many times on this journey, but there was something that caught his eye. Was that a dark shape on the horizon? The winds were still very strong, but had abated slightly. The sea continued to swirl and buck, and the spray coated his eyes, making it difficult to see. Whatever it was, it looked like a black blob, and it started to dawn on him that despite the movement of the "Sea Venture", the blob was stationary, so could not be a ship. Could this be land? He continued to stare, his eyes watering with the hope that it was not an illusion brought on by lack of sleep and food. Wiping the moisture from his eyes, it became clearer. His heart quickened, and he could feel the anticipatory tension in his body. If you want something badly, sometimes it can appear in your imagination. He closed and opened his eyes several times and concluded that he was sure - there was definitely something on the horizon.

"Ravens" he called to the Master's mate, trying to hold his voice steady so as not to attract attention too soon. "Come and take over for a minute". Henry Ravens was one of his most trusted men, he was a well-trained navigator and ship's mate who had many years of experience of the sea - one of the best. Somers was not going to say what he had seen; he wanted Ravens to find it for himself as a final confirmation.

"Aye, aye Sir" Ravens clambered up to where Somers was standing, and took the telescope, without any degree of urgency. He looked for a few seconds and then lowered the telescope from his eyes, looking at Somers with hope and amazement in his wide eyes. Both of them looked out to sea, willing the shape to increase in size and form. It was there, quite a way off, but nevertheless, it was something solid. Ravens laughed hysterically, half in disbelief, half in hope, confirming without the need for words, what Somers had hoped to be true.

Somers steeled himself to tell everyone that land was in sight. Whilst possibilities now lay before them, the ship was still in a dire situation. Everyone had stopped pumping and acceptance of a watery fate had taken priority. If they did not re-start the pumping, despite the fact that land was ahead, they would sink before they reached it. How ironic. The Almighty was not making this easy for them.

"Land ho!" shouted Somers, his voice suddenly gaining velocity and energy. Gates and Newport came charging up to the poop deck, having heard the conviction in Somers' cry. Somers pointed to the land that was getting larger and larger so that now trees were visible.

"My God" shouted Gates his eyes bulging, as he stared unblinking to where Somers was pointing. The noise and excitement drew the attention of others from below deck who broke off from their drunken reverie, falling over one another in their haste to see for themselves.

"We are still in grave danger" shouted Gates, determined that they were going to make the most of the chance that they had been given. "I want all men back to pumping and bailing. The water has not stopped leaking into the ship, and unless we bail it out, we will sink before we can reach safety". He was gesticulating and almost hysterical as he had to get things moving fast if they were going to make the most of this chance they had been given.

Everyone that came on deck could see for themselves the incredibly precarious situation they were in. Every second that they stood there looking at the wonderful sight of land, was a second closer to death. Somers continued to direct the helmsman in his job of steering the ship as much as they could without a mainsail, towards the land, and Gates went below deck to ensure that as much effort as possible was put into bailing and pumping. No one was arguing. They had all seen it, from the rebellious Want to the gentleman, Henry Pierce, they all had the same goal. They had to succeed and get to that land.

"Come on lads" Want shouted directing his band of ruffians, "there will be time enough for a dram when we reach land, if we keep this little lady afloat."

They tumbled and stumbled over one another scrambling like rats on a sinking ship to get back to the bailing and pumping, their survival depended on how quickly they could control the balance between seawater inside the vessel and seawater outside of the vessel.

As the men passed through the gun deck on the way down to the deck below they whooped and screamed, the jovial mood of drinking to excess was now turning to panic mixed with hope. Hearts beating and arms flailing they threw themselves down the steps, the haze of alcohol cushioning them from any bumps and scrapes they incurred in their haste.

"What is going on?" Alice had been woken from a dazed state. She had been brought back to reality with a jolt by the loud noise as the men scrambled down to the deck below with energy that she had not seen since the start of the voyage. All the women and the sick were now looking on in anxious bewilderment, not realising what had happened.

"Land! Land!" was being shouted loudly now, although the ship still tossed and dipped, water continuously pouring in like a leaky sieve, as if the news of impending salvation increased the desire of the sea to win its battle to sink the "Sea Venture" as quickly as possible.

For George Somers, excitement was not something he would allow to take over.

He could see that the ship was getting closer and closer to the island. Newport strode towards him with a worried look upon his face. "Is this good luck or something we will regret? His face looked dark and lined. "By my reckoning this must be the Isle of Devils that we are heading towards. There is no other land that it could possibly be - God help us". They both knew that very few had managed to land safely on this jagged pile of rocks, so feared by sailors that it was nicknamed the Isle of Devils. Rumours of witchcraft and horrible deaths for those going near were well known for this island of Bermuda.

Newport had voiced what Somers, through his haze, had not let himself dwell upon. It had been too hard, just focusing on keeping the ship moving, to consider that the glorious land was not so glorious after all. They didn't really have a choice now though. It would be ludicrous at this stage to conclude that the land before them was not worth going for.

"Yes, I am sure you are right Newport, but that is of no consequence. Beggars can't be choosers in these stakes. I suggest that you keep this information to yourself, to avoid panic. My guess is that the more seasoned sailors will know as well as we do what is before us. It is a precarious lifeline but nevertheless it is a lifeline."

The bosun lowered his rope to gauge the depth of the sea. "Thirteen fathoms!" he shouted as the ship steadily moved towards the island. The winds had died down somewhat, but it was going to be difficult to anchor at this depth. Without sails, they would have to rely on floating into shore and hoping to run aground near enough that passengers could get to the land safely on the skiffs.

"Eight fathoms!" the bosun shouted...

Somers could feel the tension in his body lifting slightly. He found himself drifting off again to semi consciousness through lack of sleep, and the illness that he had so far managed to keep from everyone. The strain of the past few days had taken a huge toll on this weathered sea dog. He heard the bosun giving reports of the depth, but was staggering with exhaustion. Suddenly, he was brought back to reality with Ravens shouting loudly, his voice urgent with panic.

"Rocks ahead, rocks head, prepare for collision!"

Somers had not seen that the "Sea Venture" was headed straight for protruding rocks lying menacingly right in the path that he had instructed the helmsman to follow. He had not been alert. He had not been watching. Seduced by the view of the land, he had allowed himself to step back, and now not only were they sinking through the constant leak in the caulking and numerous holes in the hull, now they would be ripped asunder and condemned finally to their Maker by this large reef that barred the way to the island. Somers knew that this had been the fate of so many who had neared this ungodly island, the rocks were made of coral that was jagged, sharp and menacing.

As the ship's hull made contact with the rocks, everyone on board heard a large screeching and splintering as the wood scraped and broke with the force of contact. The ship shuddered and seemed to sigh as though giving herself up to the greater force - she had had enough. She was no match for this jagged reef that stood stalwart and strong in her path.

On impact, everyone was thrown off balance, women and children screaming as they attempted to cling to whatever was near. Somers was stunned as he grabbed the side of the ship to stop himself from tumbling on to the deck. He knew that this was *it* now. He knew that they were done for. The Island of Devils had taken the "Sea Venture" and broken her, as it had done so many before her.

Then there was silence, everyone on board realising that once again the situation had changed for the worse and again they prepared for the end, knowing that the one chance they had been given had been taken away from them so cruelly.

Sarah instinctively clutched the knobbly form of her rosary still in her pocket, and shut her eyes, seeing the body of the dead Indian reflected behind her closed lids. A feeling of calm swept over her. Her wish was coming true - death was not far away now.

Within our Grasp?

⸜⸜⸜

S omers held his breath waiting for the worst. Nothing seemed to happen. The sounds of wood on rock continued to screech and crack, but the ship stopped juddering, and seemed to be rocking gently back and forth. What was happening? It was torture, like being teased and mocked by Neptune looking down on them.

The winds had abated somewhat but floods of water were like a torrent through the hull of the "Sea Venture". Everyone who had gained a semblance of composure following the impact was now scrambling up to the main deck to see what had happened and to get away from the encroaching sea water. Faces were strained with fear. The focus for everyone was getting out, and they scrambled and clawed at one another to achieve this aim.

Reaching the deck, they stood in amazed confusion looking at the incredible scene before them. Desperation seemed misplaced for now, as the ship was not sinking, despite the massive gaping hole that had appeared in her hull, and despite the fact that the lower decks were virtually submerged, everything appeared solid unmoving, although at an angle.

Somers could see that The "Sea Venture" was wedged, in what

looked like, a "v" shaped vice formed by the jagged reef. She was stuck, groaning with the movement of the waves as wood scraped on rock. She was not going anywhere for now, not until the sea could wash her out of the steely grip of the coral reef. She was not going to sink, but neither could she move any further forwards towards the much desired land. They were imprisoned. The beach beckoned about a mile away, the sounds of the sea birds taunting the stranded passengers with their joyful screeches as they dove into the sea and out again showing a freedom envied by the trapped passengers and crew - a powerless audience viewing ultimate freedom.

Gates could feel the cloak of responsibility descending upon his shoulders. He could see that Somers was not up to the job any more. The strain was too much. He glanced over at him and saw the shadow of a man that had set off on this voyage fired up with enthusiasm, an enthusiasm that now seemed absent on his drawn face. He felt at once both impatient and sympathetic, Somers just needed to pull himself together - but Gates knew this was not going to happen.

"Everyone listen!" Gates shouted, determination in his voice as he took command of the situation. It was his duty to show his leadership, and he was not going to disappoint.

"We must ready the skiffs to take us ashore. We don't know how long we have before the ship is levered out of the hold of the rocks. The sick, women, and children must go first and we will all follow as quickly as we can. It will take several trips and hopefully we can also take as many provisions as we can, because we don't know what we will be facing when we land. We have a few hours of daylight left, and that also will be a help to us. Right! Every man and woman must do their bit to ensure this is as quick and smooth as it can be. God help us all." Gates looked to the sky in silent prayer.

Sarah had stayed below deck following the impact. She felt disinterested in what was going on around her, oblivious to the water rising up from below deck. Feelings of blackness and apathy seeped through her very being. She looked around her at those that had been unable to go to the top deck because they were sick and incapacitated, and her eyes drifted over to the prone body of the dead Indian. No one had even noticed that he was not alive in the chaos that had descended since she had killed him. Looking at him, there was no emotion left inside her. Catatonic numbness was a refuge from the searing pain of regret and shame that had ravaged every cell of her body since she had become a murderess.

John had searched the many faces on deck and could not find Sarah amongst them. She must have stayed below deck to care for those that were not able to move, he thought with panic. Most people had escaped the encroaching waters, and John could see that the deck was starting to fill.

He ran down to the gun deck, frantic to see Sarah and make sure she was safe, seeing as he approached that there was at least eight inches of water already rising up. He saw Sarah sitting on her straw bed that was now sodden, with eyes glazed, hair limp and straggly, looking across at the body of the Indian, Namontack.

He was stunned by her appearance. His sparkling and charming little wife, who had always been full of life and vigour, was reduced to a lifeless shell. He knew that everyone's appearance was bedraggled as hygiene facilities were non-existent on the ship, but it was something more than appearance. It was as if her soul had been taken over and sitting before him was a shadow. She had changed so suddenly. Why was she not happy with the news that Namontack was no longer a threat? Surely without that hanging over them they had a bright joyful future ahead of them?

John took Sarah's hand, and looked into her vacant eyes aware that they did not have much time. "We have a chance Sarah, but everyone has to leave the "Sea Venture"and board the skiffs to go to the island.

Look, the water is starting to seep up from below, and soon we will be submerged. Sarah, do you hear me?" He saw a flicker of recognition in her eyes, and she tried to squeeze his hand, although it was not much more than a flinch.

He knew that something was wrong, but now was not the time address it. Hopefully when they reached land, she might improve. He had heard of a state called melancholia, which caused symptoms similar to those that Sarah was displaying. Maybe the trip had just been too much for her. She was young, pregnant and far from home. The conditions on board had been much worse than he had anticipated, and the storm had been the final straw. He was sure that once they got on dry land and he was able to look after her, she would return to her old self. He just hoped that the Isle of Devils proved to be better than the reputation that went before it.

"He's dead." John was startled out of his thoughts by Sarah's whispering voice.

"Who Sarah." John's only thoughts now were of escaping, and her words seemed foreign.

"Namontack" she said his name faltering, tears welling up in her eyes, as if she was grieving someone close.

John just about comprehended what she was saying, and looked over at the body of the Indian. He wasn't moving. What did she say? Surely she was mistaken. Namontack had been injured, there was no doubt, but nothing suggested that his injuries were life threatening. He went over to Namontack and felt his pulse - there was nothing there. His mind struggled to take this in; he didn't have time to deal with this now, and he had to get Sarah out of here. It was a shame the Indian was dead, but it was nothing to do with Sarah or himself, there were bound to be some casualties in these situations.

"There is no time to worry about him now Sarah. His injuries must have been more than we thought" he whispered… "but we don't have time for this. We must get you all out now."

Sarah continued to stare, her tears falling.

"Sarah, we must leave now." He shouted.

"I killed him John." she whispered.

"Sarah, don't be silly, of course you didn't kill him. He was injured and you couldn't save him, but that is not the same as killing him." John was getting frantic now. He had to get her out.

Suddenly the gun deck was filled with men stooping to pick up the sick and injured to take them up to the top deck. Everyone knew the sooner they could get the vulnerable ashore, the sooner they themselves could have the experience of dry land.

John dismissed Sarah's ramblings and ushered her gingerly up the steps to the main deck where Gates was setting things in motion for the disembarkation. It was no mean feat to organise such a large group of people, most of whom were exhausted, emotional and who had been relentlessly fighting for their lives for days. Gates could be heard shouting orders left right and centre, assuming the role that he was used to, aware that Somers was bowing to him as Governor, now that the sea journey was all but over. It would have been confusing if Somers had continued in command, and Gates felt a pang of softening in his stance towards him.

"John Rolfe, I want you to take the first skiff with me. Make sure that you arm yourself. We do not know what is on this island, and we must protect the first load of women and children, should the need arise. Pierce and Ravens, you take the second skiff. We need to take some guns, ammunition and some provisions to see us through, should things be scarce on the island. We can ferry the rest of the people and provisions in due course. Make sure that your guns are ready, we don't know what might greet us."

Last Leg

J ohn was excited to have been chosen to go on the first skiff, but nervous as he had never fired a gun like this before. The only real experience he had of guns was shooting rabbits on the farm. Now he must pull himself together. He felt emotional, and searched for Eustace's stone in his pocket. It was the excitement of the challenge, not the fear of the situation that gave him a surge of adrenaline. Eustace would be proud. At last he could regard himself as a leader, a million miles away from the snivelling boy skulking in the woods. It was his duty to protect these people. He had been chosen, and he was not going to let them down. "Pierce? Could you give me a run-down of how to use this gun, I am not familiar with this model John asked. He had only used guns on the farm, and he needed guidance on this particular model.

"Of course, old man" Pierce was surprised at the request from John, but he realised that John wasn't a military man. He walked over to him and patted him on the back. He went through the procedure step by step until he saw John relaxed and comfortable with the gun.

The rumble of excited chatter was escalating - it was still hardly believable that dry land was within reach after days of fighting for survival.

"Please everyone, calm down. I know this is exciting but there might be dangers that we are not aware of yet, and we must approach the coming hours and days with clear heads" said Gates.

Gates stood tall, looking confident and in charge, when underneath his apprehension was only just beneath the surface. "Bring the last of the sick and injured up, so they can be on the first run" he shouted, determined to get things moving as quick as possible. No one knew how long they had before the "Sea Venture" finally toppled into the sea.

Gates watched the passengers, bodies tense, bringing up the sick and injured from the gun deck and loading them onto the skiffs. He saw the looks of frustration on their faces - everyone just wanting to get to the island, but being forced to allow the sick and injured priority.

"For Fuck's sake, get these bloody cripples moving!" shouted Want, voicing what everyone else was thinking. "They are probably going to die anyway... so why not let some of us able bodied people go first?"

"Be quiet Want" barked Newport. "You will get your turn."

"I just hope it is before this bloody pile of wood disappears under the ocean!" he shouted.

Sylvester Jourdain was standing waiting patiently next to Will Strachey. "Will... Will... " he whispered. "Have you heard what they call this island?" his voice was shaking.

"Yes, I know Sylvester, but it is either take our chances with being eaten by cannibals or hacked to death by angry locals, or drown. Which one are you going to choose?" Will was not joking. He had heard the sailors talking, and he wished he hadn't. He looked at Sylvester whose eyes widened.

"Maybe it's better not to be the first to go on the skiffs. If the skiffs don't return safely, we know it is a dangerous island." Sylvester looked down at his feet that were in a ten inches of water.

"That would be sensible... live the rest of our lives balancing on a rock in the middle of the ocean rather than disembark... I don't think so"said Will.

Matchumps saw Namontack's body being lifted up from the gun deck, and he cried out with distress. He ran over to where Namontack lay and gently removed the beads that were hanging around his neck. He kissed the beads and then carefully placed them over his own neck, placing one hand over his heart and the other over Namontack's eyes, looking to the sky, lips moving in Powhatan prayer. Those of the sailors that saw the dead Indian, stopped for a brief moment, making the sign of the cross. No one had time to give Namontack the thought and prayers he deserved though, as his body was lifted unceremoniously into the first skiff.

"Hey, that heathen is dead. Why is he allowed to take a space on the skiff." It was Want again.

"Just be quiet Want. We are showing respect to the dead" retorted Newport.

"Fuck respect!" shouted Want.

"You are to be in the last skiff to leave this boat Want." Newport said with gritted teeth. He had had enough. His body was rigid and his eyes bored into Want.

Want pulled a face and made a fist that he shook towards Newport.

"If you persist in insolence, you will be clapped in irons, Want." Newport knew this one was going to be difficult either on land or sea.

Robbie stood looking over the side of the ship, down at the young lad who had fallen from the mast. Want was right. Those invalids should go on last.

Gates, Beth, Alice, Sarah, Mistress Horton and Lizzie were amongst those on the skiff that John Rolfe was taking. John looked over to see that Sarah was alright. She looked like a child, doing as she was told, her face white, her eyes unseeing. It came to him - she was in shock. But why? Was it just the trauma of the voyage? He was torn. He had to obey Gates, but he would keep an eye on her and sort things when they landed.

The other skiff held Mary and the children, Elizabeth Joons - with Ravens and Pierce as their protectors. Jeff Briars with his usual cheeky presence had convinced everyone that he would be a valuable asset to go on the first run to the Island. After all, who would make them laugh when they got there? Somers and Gates had become fond of the young rascal from the East End of London, who brought a touch of light humour to a dark and dangerous situation and had given in to his bantering request with smiles of amusement.

John looked over at the little girl that had fallen from the mast. Her face was blank. She was pale and breathing very fast. As the skiff was lowered into the, now calmer sea, he saw her look above her at the ship, and her face changed, with a slight smile spreading. She seemed to recognise a man looking over at her from the side of the ship. Perhaps one of the seamen she had made friends with during her time working with the lads.

He then saw her flinch at the appearance of Robbie Waters who took a position next to the seaman she had been looking at. John knew that Robbie was one of the troublemakers on board, a friend of Want, and he wondered when he saw the look on the girl's face, what had transpired between them. The girl's face turned pale and her petite form stiffened with fear. As she looked around her, her body began to twitch, and she tried to move, looking at the faces on the skiff with panic in her eyes. Thoughts raced around her mind. Where were these people taking her? Was she being captured to be sold?

Suddenly, she became hysterical.

"No no, don't take me away!" She struggled to stand up. She fell, but struggled up again. As she did so, the skiff rocked dangerously. Gates shouted in alarm.

"Restrain that girl, or we may capsize!" His voice held no compassion, only desperation. "You stupid, stupid girl" he shouted frantically as she continued to move erratically towards the edge of the skiff.

Gate's harsh words frightened her even more, confirming to her erratic mind that she was in danger. "No, no. Don't kill me. I am Beth, only a little girl! I will do as you say, I promise." She plunged herself forward with all the might in her little body.

As she moved, panic blurred any sense of perspective, and she tripped. Thrown off balance, she looked down at her feet, and she saw that what she had tripped over was a stiff and cold body. The dead body of a strange looking creature with brown skin and half of his head shaved.

She screamed and threw her arms around, hysterically rocking the skiff to the point that water was being taken in. Her crazed eyes were darting around, trying to gauge what was going on, and who these people were. She was disoriented, clawing at the air like a mad woman, her features distorted and ugly.

"For God's sake Rolfe, do something with that girl, she is going to kill us all with her antics." Gates was too far away from Beth to do anything himself, but he knew something would have to be done as the small boat was becoming increasingly unstable with Beth's erratic gesticulations that were verging on madness.

John had been looking towards Sarah, his mind awash with thoughts, and he automatically jumped to Gate's command, hand on his gun, which he had prepared in readiness for the landing. As he lurched forward to grab hold of Beth, the echo of a gunshot reverberated through the air, leaving a deadly silence in its wake that was filled only by the call of a lone seabird as it circled above, and the sound of Beth plunging like a rag doll over the side of the small boat into the depths. John's gun was smoking.

* * *

The split second silence after the sound of the gunshot, merged into a horrifying scene. The little girl, who said she was Beth, had fallen headlong into the sea, a ball accidentally discharged from John's activated gun, shot her, and combined with her exaggerated movements, forced her over the side of the skiff. She was being swallowed up by the sea, the foam created by her body was now the only thing that could be seen.

John looked on with disbelief at what he had done. Within seconds, instinct propelled him forward and he dived off the skiff to try and save this poor young girl. He was appalled at what had happened and there was no time to think, he just had to act, or she would drown if she was not already dead from the gunshot wound.

He could see the shape of her body under the water, and as the cold liquid enveloped him, he went deeper, opening his eyes despite the saltiness of the water to see Beth's misty form as it floated downward. He reached wildly, grasping at emptiness hoping that he could make contact with her descending body.

He reached as far as he could and finally felt the solidness of her arm. He galvanised all the energy that he had to push himself forwards, grabbing the clothing around her arm. His legs were like lead weights as he fought with his shoes and waterlogged clothing to get a firm enough grasp to stop Beth from sinking deeper. He struggled like he had struggled with Eustace, and again when he had saved Namontack. Now it was like history repeating itself again and this thought instilled in him an energy that felt surreal.

Having secured a hold on her, he then had to combat gravity, and with superhuman strength that he did not know he had, pulled himself and Beth towards the shining mirror-like surface. It seemed so far away, and he started to think that he was not going to make it. The air in his lungs was starting to run out and his heart was racing. It felt like his lungs were going to burst. Just in time, he saw the mirage-like figures of the other passengers looking down at him through the silver water, as he broke the surface. He took an almighty gasp of breath, and then another, and then another. Spluttering and choking. Relief flooded his body as the oxygen seeped into his system. It was a near death experience, but his time was not up yet.

He pulled on the small body that he was dragging and got her to the surface, from where Gates reached over and pulled Beth to safety. He knew that if *he* had almost run out of breath, she would have run out of air before he had, and her chances of survival were slim.

She was unconscious, turning blue. Everyone watching thought it was too late. John watched as Gates knelt over her and as he had done many times before with injured soldiers, felt her pulse and in panic put pressure on her chest blowing oxygen into her mouth. He repeatedly banged on her chest, paused and then blew into her mouth. Suddenly she shuddered as her lungs vomited up the water that had been restricting her breathing, and she took a long deep breath which jerked her back to life. Everyone cheered and clapped.

Alice and Sarah rushed to see what her injuries were. No one knew where the bullet had lodged itself; all they knew was that Beth had been its innocent victim. Sarah could now see that the bullet had gone through her shoulder, and seemed lodged there. She and Alice packed the wound to stop it bleeding, removing some of her sodden clothes and covered her up with a blanket to keep her warm. Beth was shivering and pale. Luckily, although the water was cold, in this part of the world it was not freezing. However, her body had taken a terrible battering when she had previously fallen from the mast, and now she had a gunshot wound and had nearly drowned. She was bruised all over and psychologically traumatised.

It was a far cry from the streets of London where she had escaped dangers of a different nature. The pulsing of the pain through her body was so overwhelming that she could hardly locate its source. Life was pain in that moment, and her thoughts were a jumble. She still didn't know where she was going, or who all these people were. One of them had shot her, but they seemed now to be caring for her. She was in no position to do anything other than surrender to them.

John felt cold and wretched. He sat down with his head in his hands, ashamed that he was responsible for the injury and near death of this young and innocent girl. He knew that he would never forgive himself for what he had done. He looked down at Beth. She was only a youngster of about 15. He was praying frantically that she would survive, promising God that if she did, he would make it up to her in any way that he could and he would look after her.

The passengers in the skiffs had concern on their faces for the girl, but there was nothing more they could do for her now. Everyone took their seats again, and looked towards the island with expectation and fear in their eyes. This piece of land they had prayed for so relentlessly could either be their salvation or their death.

* * *

The sea was now calmer, and looking towards the Island they saw that the colour of the water was like nothing any of them had seen before. It was a bright turquoise green with darker shades of royal blue mingled like an artist's palette, a far cry from the murky brown water they were used to. As they rowed in closer, they could see a beach with the prettiest pink and white sand. They heard the comforting sounds of the sea birds welcoming them to the first land they had seen for weeks. They strained to see if there were people on the island, to make sure that they were prepared to defend themselves against any hostility should they be attacked by cannibals or fierce natives. All they could see so far, was a long empty expanse of sand bordered by prickly grass and a few trees.

They rowed closer and closer. The water became shallower the closer they got to the beach. Looking over the side of the skiff and into the clear water, they could see a myriad of different fish swimming above beautiful coloured and majestic rocks. All colours and shapes of bright and shining fish swam around their skiff, seemingly fearless. No one had ever seen such a sight. The air here was clean, and the sun shone warmly - although it was coming to the end of the day, and dusk was approaching, leaving vivid pink streaks in the bright blue sky.

If there were no obstacles, Gates wanted to get everything landed before nightfall. He knew they would have to find shelter of some kind, and also food. As he had no idea what was on the island, he was concerned that the next twenty four hours were going to be critical to their survival. They did have a limited amount of provisions still on the ship - and they had to ensure that they transported as much as possible to the island. The skiffs could deliver provisions for a day or so, but after that they would have to replenish from whatever they could find.

As Gates looked into the clear water and caught sight of the many fish swimming around, his face softened. At least if they set their minds to fishing, food might not be as much of a problem as he had first anticipated.

As they got nearer Gates said "Rolfe, you cover me as I land. If you see anything suspicious, be prepared to shoot on my command. Ravens and Pierce - you stay put until I give the signal that everything seems safe, and then you can unload the passengers." John was heartened that Gates had not lost confidence in him after the incident with Beth, and readied himself for action.

Gates jumped over the side of the skiff, which was now only in about 2 feet of water. He gasped when the cool water made contact with his hot grubby body and he grabbed the rope and pulled the skiff further towards the beach, until the hull was resting on the sand. So far, so good, there was no sign of human life of any kind on or around the beach.

He sprinted up the beach and looked all around him. He had never seen a place so beautiful; it took his breath away. His feet sank into the warm soft pink sand. The scent of the cedar trees was fresh and inviting, and the sound of gently lapping waves rolling up the beach was soothing after the angry sea that he had been hearing for so many days. He stopped for a minute and breathed in the experience. Peace and quiet were elements Gates had not often experienced in his hectic life. He knew that he had to get on with the job in hand, but this one minute was his and his alone. Probably never to be repeated. This looked like paradise. Maybe everything was not as it seemed, but if it was, he would gladly stay here for ever.

He had to put such thoughts out of his mind. He had a job to do, and people to look after. This still quiet peace was a luxury he could not afford.

He shook himself back to reality, scanning the scene, looking for movements. He jumped when suddenly he saw movement out of the corner of his eye. He stared with anticipation, jumping down onto the sand crouching low. He was aware that whatever it was would be able to see the skiffs in full view which made them vulnerable to a full on attack.

If he could kill the attacker as soon as he revealed himself, he might be able to stop a massacre happening. There was rustling in the undergrowth, but nothing seemed interested in his presence. Gates gingerly started to move towards the bushes. He couldn't make out people talking, but there was definitely something frenzied going on, just outside of his area of vision. Suddenly, he was attacked from behind, being thrown up in the air landing uncomfortably in the harsh prickly grass and left there, untouched. "For God's sake who are you?" He shouted out with shock, paralyzed, like a beetle on his back, unable to see who his attacker was.

Bermuda

hey all stood and looked around in amazement that they had finally made land. Thomas Gates being run down by a stray black hog had lifted the mood. The waiting skiffs full of people had rocked with mirth when they saw what was happening, the tensions of the past weeks evaporated in the soft summer sunshine. It was as misplaced to see Gates laughing as it was to see him sprawling on the sand being stared at by a big black grunting pig. The three children jumped up and down with glee. "Pig, pig," screamed little Giles. "Why is Sir Thomas on the sand" asked Constance. Everyone fell about, unable to answer the question, with tears of mirth rolling down their faces. Laughter had been absent for so long.

The big back hog squealed with fear, and the noise would have aroused anything or anyone within earshot. No natives came to defend their invaded territory so it was assumed that, at least in this part of the island, there were no threats within earshot.

"Right, if you have quite finished laughing… " Gates was hiding a smile as he walked towards the skiffs, beckoning them forward. When the laughter had died down he started his commands.

"Pull the skiffs onto the sand and start disembarking. Put the injured further up the beach on the grass for now until we can sort our some proper bedding and shelter. Don't just stand there!" Gates screamed. He rapidly shook off his newly acquired clown personae and replaced it with that of the humourless and efficient leader that they had come to respect.

Everyone was shaky on their legs, holding on to the side of the skiff as they stood up to disembark.

Sarah stumbled and fell as her feet were swallowed up by the warm sand. She felt the warmth of the glistening granules as her fingers reached out to save herself from full impact. No one noticed her tumble, as everyone had their own long awaited moment to savour and John was focusing on Gates' command to run up the beach and check for enemies. Sarah watched him and knew he had been shaken up by the incident with Beth, but Gates had made it perfectly clear that there was no time for reflection, and that his duties were with setting up the camp and nothing else.

Sarah's previous darkness of spirit was momentarily lifted as she threw her body back and stretched into the gently swirling surf with pure abandon. Looking up at the bright blue and pink sky above her, she sighed. There was no rocking and creaking, no shouts of panic, no lurching of her stomach and feelings of nausea … just the sound of the wind in the trees and the children laughing as they kicked the cool water in the air, watching the sparkling silver droplets fall.

She let her body sway listlessly in the shallow waves. She gradually pulled herself away from her moment of escape, and forced herself to sit up. Her clothes were wet, but in the warmth of the fading sunshine this felt more refreshing than uncomfortable as they clung to her body which was gradually becoming rounder despite the meagre diet she had been subjected to. She looked around at the people who had been her companions on this terrible journey, people who had become a replacement for the family that she had left behind, and with a pang of shame, remembered the dark corner of herself that had destroyed her innocence, and instantly said a silent prayer quietly to herself for Namontack.

Sarah sat with her memories, unable to move, her private darkness starting to descend once again. How was she going to cope with her dirty secret? John hadn't believed her when she had confessed to her crime. Only she knew the depths that she had gone to in order to protect herself and it had all been for nothing anyway. John's goodness had saved her without her knowing. She focused again on the scene unfolding before her. None of them knew what a monster she was nor how good John had been. The accident on the skiff was not really John's fault. He was not used to guns. John had not done anything to deliberately harm Beth and he had been a hero jumping into the sea to save her. John was a good man. She sighed with regret. Their life together was never going to be the same again, she was not worthy of him.

Everyone was carrying on in a world that seemed parallel to her own. Alice was looking after Beth, who was stunned and silent since her ordeal on the skiff, prompting Sarah to feel an increasing sense of guilt for her own self-pity when this young girl had been through so much. They needed to find out who Beth (Timmy) really was and nurture her back to health. She had shouted about her father in her delirium, perhaps her father was on board. Sarah knew John desperately wanted to look after Beth as her accident had been his fault, but he had been ordered to organise the collecting of wood and the setting up of the new shelters, so Alice stepped in to make sure Beth did not feel alone. Alice did not seem to be making much headway though, as Beth stared silently into the distance. She had lost all power of speech.

Mary was looking after her children who, following the initial excitement, were fractious and clingy with tiredness and hunger. No doubt Mary was wishing Steven would be on the next skiff. She was haggard and tired and her face had taken on the pallor and lines of someone twice her age. She needed someone to help her with her little family, but Sarah knew even when Steven arrived, he would be far too taken up with self-righteous prayers and judgments to be of much use. Sarah should step in and help her, but she just didn't have the energy.

Mistress Horton sat on a rock looking out to sea, lost in thoughts of who knows what. Sarah watched as the faded and haggard gentleman, Henry Pierce walked up to Mistress Horton and sat next to her. They had struck up an unlikely friendship based on their self-promoted superiority during the voyage. Together they tried in vain to keep up the appearance of upper class divisions, when under the circumstances, this was ridiculous. No one served them tea and biscuits on a silver tray on this journey. On the contrary - all had to eat together, sleep together and shit together. The journey had been a societal leveller if nothing else.

Henry Pierce's trunks of silk and finery were one of the first sacrifices thrown unceremoniously into the sea as the ship started to sink. Of course he had protested loudly, as he watched his trunks disappear into the swirling abyss. His protests went unheeded; his hatred of Gates and Somers was firmly planted for future flowering. He steadfastly held on to his delusions of grandeur and the only one who understood was the equally deluded Mistress Horton. At least, thought Sarah, Lizzie had been rescued from the clutches of Mistress Horton, who seemed to have mellowed considerably since the altercation with Tom Powell that day on the deck.

Sarah glanced down the beach and saw the most recent skiff as it landed. Lizzie was helping Tom unload provisions and implements for the kitchen. One of the first things that would need to be done was for Tom to somehow organise a meal for everyone. No one had eaten for days and strength was needed to start building shelters and finding additional food - they already knew that fish were in good supply and hogs were certainly to be found, although hunting and fishing would probably have to wait until tomorrow as the light was starting to fade. There were some provisions rescued from the "Sea Venture", so those would have to suffice for tonight.

The men were frantically working to ferry the skiffs back and forwards as more and more passengers were landing. John was working hard, and his face had taken on the look of solid determination. She and John were not the same people that had ascended the gangplank on that cloudy day in London, laughing like two passionate children. She could see John growing with confidence with each new experience he conquered. She realised that his need for her was diminishing. Of that she was glad.

The beach was now a throbbing hum of activity. A fire had been started above the tide mark. This was to mark the centre of the community, provide warmth and also to alert any passing ships. Jeff Briars in his excited explorations had discovered drinking water in a hole that had been dug, and people were rushing to quench their thirst after the scarcity of water they had been subjected to for so long.

Having moved up the beach, Sarah's gaze narrowed and focused as the final skiff rowed its way towards her. Tradition always dictated that the Captain and Admiral were the last to leave a sinking ship and there was a crowd forming on the beach cheering the two commanders on their final approach.

She watched as John ran towards her. His hair had been bleached in the sun and watching him still gave her bubbles in her veins anticipating his arms encircling her. He pulled her off the ground, swinging her around. It felt so nice to be held by him. She treasured the moment, knowing in her heart that there would not be many more chances to be so close to this wonderful, beautiful man.

"Come on Sarah, Somers and Newport are arriving, let's give them a good welcome!" She fought back her tears, trying to summon the pretence of normality. Would the blackness always spoil her fondest moments? Feeling for her rosary in her pocket to give her strength, she grasped only emptiness, the beads had gone. They had been washed away in the turmoil and replaced by pink and white granules of sand; they had deserted her. Perhaps a symbol that God had finally deserted her too. God had not sent her a message, she had killed Namontack all by herself. She bit her lip and felt the pain.

She allowed John to pull her by the hand and start running over to where the crowd was gathering.

They stopped at the edge of the surf, John with his arm around her. Suddenly she felt butterflies in her stomach. She wasn't sure at first, but as it came and went she knew with certainty that the life inside her was starting to move. Perhaps it was reminding her that her only redemption lay in surviving, and surviving well for the sake of the new life that God had placed inside her belly. It was the only purpose for the rest of her tainted life. She must do this; she must protect this child to the end of her days. Pleasure no longer mattered, only duty.

"We made it, Sarah…. We made it!" The crowd were jumping up and down clapping and singing. Jeff Briars was doing loud wolf-whistles in accompaniment. She took John's hand and placed it on her belly. He did not understand at first, but when he stood still he could feel a very slight tremble under his fingers, evidence of the miracle that he and Sarah had created, and he knew that things were now going to be perfect. Sarah was here, the baby was moving, they had landed in paradise, and his ambition to fulfil Eustace's dream had not ended. What more could he want?

Building the Quarter

~~~
⚬◦⚬
~~~

I t had been quite a day for Gates and now, watching his sleeping charges, all covered with large palmetto leaves for protection from the night air, his mind was in a whirl trying to plan the days ahead. He knew that this was what he was good at, but nevertheless it was a daunting task. He had to feed, provide shelter, and keep order among 150 of the passengers that were now the inhabitants of Bermuda, known as the Isle of Devils.

So far this frightening name had seemed to be a misnomer, but their knowledge of their new home was restricted to the small area surrounding the landing place. Who knew what lay beyond the hill above the beach? He gazed behind him at the small mounds of sand. What lay behind these mounds of sand? They didn't even know how big the island was. How were they going to get to Jamestown and reunite with the other ships of the fleet? Gates had a duty to get them there.

It seemed strange that he was thinking of going back to sea just at the moment when the illusive land had offered them refuge, but he was a man that carried out orders and his orders had been to set up and maintain the colony in Jamestown. There was so much to do before that could be achieved though. He expected there to be trouble from rebel factions, he had already seen some evidence of it, and he was ready for it. Structure would have to be imposed as soon as possible.

He knew he would have little support from his own peers. Somers had equipped himself with strength and courage in order to get them here. But as the journey was ending, Gates had watched the Admiral's spirit diminish and he seemed to revert to a shell of a man, almost in another world. It was as if the responsibility had broken him and helplessness had set in. Newport was not much better. He had visibly struggled with the physical demands placed on him during the past few days. His missing arm was finally taking its toll.

Reverend Burke was an important influence and the religious structure he imposed on board had kept things civilised. Gates decided he would have to impose strict worshiping routines on the community to ensure the maintenance of order and to keep track of any possible mutineers.

It would soon be dawn. He looked across the bay to see John Rolfe's pipe glowing in the dim light. Gates was sharing the watch with John and remembered the incident on the skiff with the young girl. It was an unfortunate accident nothing more. The girl had been hysterical and the fault lay with her, and not John. He had redeemed himself by taking responsibility and solving, what could have been a horrible situation. John had acted with decisiveness on good instinct. He seemed to have strong leadership potential, alongside a caring demeanour, which was an admirable combination.

Gates was certainly going to need to build a group of trustworthy men to carry out his orders, and John Rolfe was definitely going to be one of them. He had Pierce and Yardley who he could also rely on, but his key to success was going to be building his "army". He knew he could not maintain law and order alone. His professionalism had taught him that a military-like structure built on trust was the only way to control a situation such as this. He hoped Somers would pull himself together and work with him, but as their relationship had been strained from the beginning of this project, it was unlikely to change. Gates sighed to himself, yes, there was a lot of planning to be done.

He looked around at the sun starting to come up on their first day in Bermuda. The temperature as warm as the hottest summer in England with a harmony of nature seldom experienced. It seemed so incongruous that this was the place that had scared countless seamen. In truth, it was magical.

John walked towards Gates, earnestness on his young and hand-some face. "Sir" he said.

"Yes Rolfe" Gates replied smiling. "I wanted to congratulate you on your quick thinking yesterday with that stupid girl". John looked up suddenly, filled with wide-eyed surprise. He thought Gates would never trust him again, and here he was congratulating him. No one had ever done that to John before. He stuttered "Sir, I betrayed your trust in me, and nearly killed her. I will do everything in my power to make it up to you and to that young girl".

"Nearly killed? Don't be so melodramatic Rolfe. In life things happen, but if you are prepared to act wisely when things go wrong, there is nothing more you can do. I would like to know that I can rely on you to help with the running of things around here. You are one of the few with breeding and bottle. I consider you to be one of my leading men."

"Sir, you can trust me to do whatever is required". He felt like he was going to burst with pride.

Gates smiled.

"Your wife is expecting isn't she Rolfe?" he asked.

"My wife is expecting our first child in a few months" his chest puffing out with pride, his eyes wide at the interest Gates was showing him.

"Congratulations Rolfe." Gates clapped him on the back "your first child will change everything for you, believe me. Let me know if Sarah needs anything during her pregnancy. The first Bermudian... now that is a thought." his eyes sparkled with friendliness. Gates was a firm believer that interest in the personal lives of your soldiers always reaped professional gains. Good relationships fostered loyalty.

"Now on that very positive note, if you will excuse me... I must summon everyone to a meeting to start the ball rolling and to assign duties - they won't be able to do it without being told, unfortunately".

With these condescending words directed at the settlers, Gates created a "them and us" scenario, with John firmly in the "us" camp, which further boosted John's growing confidence. Gates strode to a high point on the beach and blew the bugle. His attention span was sharp but short, and he had moved on from John's pastoral care to bigger and better problems, a talent that had won him respect from many of his soldiers.

Gates waited, his eyes roaming around the motley bunch of passengers he had before him. He would have to keep an eye on Want and his crew, and there were several others like Christopher Carter and Robbie Waters who had been chosen originally for their strength and robustness, but who he would never have chosen as members of a civilised community. Ruffians like that did not take kindly to authority - most having served a life in and out of jail. The incident with the beatings of the Indians had proved this point well.

Newport had reported the volatile mood that was under the surface when the perpetrators had been punished. This was something that would not disappear overnight, and could grow in intensity should the conditions be right for a mutiny. Politics were never far away, no matter how small the community, human beings are selfish, even the most noble, Gates thought.

He drew up his short stature to its full height, and addressed the crowd as he would an army before a battle.

"Congratulations to you all for everything you did to ensure our safe landing on this Island. We now have to survive in a very different environment and we are not yet sure what we are facing. We must pull together. Tasks will be allocated to each of you so that we can address the issues of sustenance and shelter efficiently. Reverend Burke will continue to conduct religious services each morning and evening." Gates nodded in the direction of the portly, dishevelled figure of Reverend Burke in his black clerical robes, who was earnestly nodding his head in agreement with everything Gates was saying. Steven Hopkins stood close to the Reverend, his pinched little face portrayed the self-satisfied, self-righteous look they had all come to expect from this unlikeable, religious fanatic. Gates was surprised that Steven did not display any signs of agreement, just staring into space as if he were above everyone else. Maybe another one he had to watch?

"Compulsory attendances at religious services will be required, with no exceptions, unless prior permission has been granted by myself, and I will give permission only for extraordinary situations. A roll-call will be taken and anyone absent will be severely punished." Gates wanted to ensure that every person on the island was accounted for every day. He did not want factions breaking off and forming secret, unhealthy alliances. This way, he could keep abreast of who was sitting with who and what the general mood seemed to be - not that this was going to stop anything, but at least he could be as informed as much as possible about dissenters.

Even now, as he glanced at the gathered crowd he could see the differing reactions to his resumption of authority. Strachey, as usual was scribbling away, Gates assumed he was writing an account of what was happening - he couldn't blame him, history in the making was a temptation for a failed writer eager to make a name for himself. Jourdain was standing with Somers and talking throughout his whole speech... Want and Christopher Carter, well- known troublemakers, were also carrying on a conversation of their own. Henry Paine, a man not used to taking orders, was looking like thunder; angry that his status seemed to have been thrown into the drink, like his silk waistcoats. Gates took this all in. Managing people was his job. He had to somehow, instil a sense of a common goal in this disparate group, and the first goal for everyone was sheer survival. The strong survive in these situations, so he had to be strong and surround himself with able men as supporters, in order to reach the ultimate goal of getting to Jamestown.

Gates started to organise people in groups, setting each group a leader with a particular task. Some were to start using the nets they had brought for hunting deer in Jamestown to catch fish, others to look for water, and some to start building shelters out of wood, using the massive palm leaves as thatching for the roofs.

"Tom Powell, take as many men and women as you need to start setting up the kitchen. You will have to build some fires, and have a few people scout around to see what vegetation there is that can be eaten. All the fish caught must go to Tom" he said to the crowd. "That way he can either preserve it or cook it for immediate consumption."

"Henry Shelly, Rob Walsingham - I want you to start building some pens for the livestock. When you have the pens, you can also start looking for local hogs to join the ones that we have from the "Sea Venture".

As everyone started to assemble their groups and plan how they were going to achieve their personal targets, Gates noticed Somers slinking off behind some trees with a band of his own allies who had not been commandeered into groups. James Swift, Robert Rich, and

Ted Waters, all men of a higher standing, were dutifully following Somers, who seemed to have his own agenda. Gates chose not to make an issue of this obvious slight. He knew he was going to have to choose his battles, strategically, and this was a battle for another day.

* * *

The days became hectic for the little community, turning the beautiful, but vacant landscape into a home. Gates had instigated a daily routine for everyone, ensuring that each person, man and women had a task and everyone worked towards his goal of stabilising the colony, making everyone safe, well fed and happy, before thinking about the next step, leaving for Jamestown.

The day began with prayers, followed by breakfast. Tom Powell, the cook and his helpers had made long tables and cut big trunks of trees into large pieces as makeshift stools. He served breakfast of gulls' eggs gathered from the ground around the settlement. This was usually followed by fish caught the previous day roasted over a fire that had been lit in a large pit on the beach.

As they ate, Gates stood at the head of the table, issuing orders for the day.

Everyone assembled likewise for lunch and dinner, with Reverend Burke or Steven Hopkins taking another service after dinner, before everyone retired to bed.

Their first impression of the Island had not been wrong. Fish were plentiful, as were plump birds, eggs and hogs. Nothing was scarce and even water had been found in good supply since the initial finding by Jeff Briars, whose job it was to continue to supply Tom Powell with water for the kitchen.

John, like all the men in the community, had gathered cedar wood which was plentiful on the island, sawing it to an even height to bind together for the walls of a dwelling for Sarah, him, and their little baby. Large palmetto leaves, that the passengers had instinctively used when they first landed as shelter, became the obvious choice for makeshift, but waterproof roofs. Palmetto leaves with their large fan-like structures funnelled rain onto the ground, keeping the huts warm and dry in the infrequent summer storms. The climate was pleasant, and since they landed was getting gradually warmer as summer progressed.

John stood back when he had finished his handiwork, hands on his hips sighing. There was something about creating a dwelling for your family that gave a primitive satisfaction. He had made a home for his wife and baby, and he looked at it with pride, smiling.

Now that they were on dry land, he had time to focus on his family, and his nesting instincts were taking over. He was starting to imagine what the baby would be like. It was hard to imagine Sarah's bump as a baby, but he tried. Would it be a girl or boy? He knew the moment he welcomed the baby into the world would be the highlight of his life. His and Sarah's creation. If only Eustace could be here. If only Sarah were happier. It must be her pregnancy that had taken her spirit. She would get it back, he was sure of it.

"Sarah" he shouted "look what we have done. At least the outside is finished. I will make some tables and chairs, and a bed. What do you think? I would love to make a little cedar cradle next." His handsome form, stripped to the waist, brown with the sun, gleamed with the sweat of his labours.

Sarah smiled weakly at him; he was in a world of his own in his innocence about her. He hadn't taken in what she said to him on the ship. She savoured the moment of oblivion. If only it could be like this forever. If only she didn't have to make him realise what she had done. They could have had such a wonderful life together. He was going to be a truly wonderful father, and they both still loved one another. Would that continue? She knew it wouldn't, and her heart lurched. John was a good man, he had saved Namontack. She was evil, she had killed Namontack. John would never resign himself to that fact – she had known him for so many years, she knew his morality. He may put up with her for the sake of the baby, but how could he love a cold blooded killer? She would feel a liar as well as a murderess if she didn't tell him.

"Come on Sarah. Let's go inside and Christen it."

She knew he was trying to instil enthusiasm in her. She got up from where she was sitting on the sand and walked towards him. He took her hand as they opened the door made of cedar and stood in the middle of the one roomed dwelling.

He pulled her towards him, hugging her close. She could feel his hard muscly body, and smell his masculinity. She yearned for him.

"I love you Sarah." he whispered. She forced herself to draw away. The sunlight filtered through the gaps in the wood and the palmetto roof, and the scent of cedar wood permeated the air. John took a deep breath, his brows furrowed. This was not his Sarah. He was hurt and rejected.

"What is the matter Sarah? Do you not love me any more? Is it the baby? Please tell me what is going on; I am going mad not knowing. Maybe you feel sad leaving your family? What is it?" John struggled to offer suggestions for her low mood and the increasing distance that she was creating between them." He thought of their wedding day and how close they had been. It was not that long ago.

"John… " She was bracing herself to tell him the truth. He deserved to know who she really was. It was so hard. Once it was out, there was no going back. No maybe's or what if's.

201

"... remember on the ship, before we boarded the skiffs, when you came down to get me?"

"Yes of course I remember Sarah... " he was impatient, he wanted her just to tell him, not to go into a long discourse.

She took his hand "remember I told you that I had killed Namontack?"

"Yes, but it was only that you couldn't cure him... not that you actually killed him. These things happen Sarah. You can't blame yourself."

"No John." She looked at the floor of the hut, pausing for courage. "I killed him. I held my dress over his face, until he turned blue, and his body twitched." She said the words slowly, with emphasis. "I continued holding until the last ounce of air left his body and he died." She continued to look at the ground; she did not want to see his reaction. She wanted to remember him gleaming, handsome and in love with her. She did not want to see him filled with hatred. She waited.

He pulled his hand away. He got up and moved towards the door of the hut, opening it to feel the soft breeze on his face.

"You murdered Namontack?" he whispered. Sarah nodded slowly. He held on to the door frame staring out, trying to absorb the truth of what she had said.

Sarah knew he was trying to hold his feelings in. She wanted so much to know what he was thinking, but he was not giving anything away. She walked up to him and put her arms around him. He looked at her, and held her for a moment savouring the feel of her familiar body. Gradually he released himself from her embrace and looked at the floor.

"I am sorry. I need to be alone for a while Sarah. Just know that I love you." He walked slowly down the beach, kicking the driftwood that was in his path.

She looked after him with longing and regret. She knew her fears were coming true. She sat down and sobbed. She had spoilt everything.

* * *

John could feel nothing other than the coolness of the water on his body. He tried to make his mind go blank, refusing to think about what he had just heard. He looked down at the white sand below him as he swam around the cove into deeper water. He could see beautiful shells, some shiny and brown with chequerboard markings, others like large horns. He dived down opening his eyes under the water seeing through the mist of his eyes, brightly coloured fish swimming past him unconcerned, and a strange bobbing creature that looked a bit like a horse. It was quiet, like he had never experienced before.

As he rose to the surface, and let the air out of his lungs, it rose like silver bubbles to the surface. He dived once more, trying to hold on to the peace and quiet of the ocean bed. He held his breath for as long as he could, marvelling in the sanctity of the ocean floor, wishing that he could stay there forever, propelling himself towards the sandy bottom to retrieve a shell that was lying there, before rising to the silver surface once more. He swam and swam until exhaustion took over, and he came ashore further away than any of the settlers had ever been.

He sat, feeling the warmth of the sun on his back, and the coolness of the drying water. He tasted the saltiness of the sea water that mingled with the saltiness of his tears. He put his head in his hands, the rocks digging into him as he sat on them. He did not want to be comfortable.

What was he going to do now? Sarah was the love of his life. Could he still hold on to that love knowing this dark secret?

He realised with horror that he did not really know his wife. Her reluctance to throw away the rosary had been his first clue, but he had dismissed it. Religion was the excuse. No doubt in her mind God had told her to kill Namontack. Her God gave her permission to do anything. Religion was supposed to stop people doing evil, not encourage it, wasn't it? He thought of the systematic murders of the Catholic priests in England, all done in the name of religion, and began to wonder about God. What was religion really about? Maybe God had been created in the mind of man to allow him to rescind all responsibility for evil doings? All of these thoughts haunted him… He was full of anger… but he still loved her. She was beautiful, she was kind, and she was carrying his child. It had only been a moment of madness… surely this was not who she was, it was only an indication of the distress that she had been in. She had been cornered, with no way out for herself and her child. Would any mother have done the same? He could not answer that question.

John shook himself and looked at the scene before him. God was good if he had created this utopia. He sighed looking out to sea, remembering how sweet this land had seemed on that first day.

He knew he had to move beyond this terrible thing - they had made a baby together. He would have to swim back to the colony and resume some kind of relationship with her for the sake of his child. He couldn't just turn off his love for Sarah, but it was definitely tainted. He was still the father of her child, and he would move heaven and earth to make sure his child was safe and loved. He would concentrate on the future, making the hut a better place for the baby, working for Gates and Somers, and spending more time with Beth, ensuring that he paid her back for the damage he had inadvertently done to her.

Eustace was still with him, he was determined to get to Jamestown.

He looked at the shell that he had collected from the bottom of the ocean. It was slightly open and when he prised it fully open, he saw a small perfect luminous pearl nestling safely inside the flesh. He pulled it from the shell and looked at it, eyes wide. So beautiful... like his new baby would be... He rose from the ragged rocks clutching the pearl, and dived below the calm waters once again.

Beth Recovers

S he had been transported to another time and place, and had no recollection of what had happened or why she was here. Her whole body ached, and this lovely lady with long dark hair called Alice seemed keen to be her friend and was tending gently to her injuries. The man who had pushed her into the sea had come several times to see her, but she had shrunk away, her reflex for survival taking over. No matter how hard she tried, her voice would not come, it had disappeared along with most of her memory. She was terrified, flashes of seeing herself pushed into the sea kept suddenly appearing, and a slow sensation of falling from a great height played over and over in her mind.

"Here he comes again", she thought to herself as John came slowly towards her. Alice had helped her down to the water's edge for a change of scene. She was still very shaky on her legs, one of her arms was broken and she had extensive bruising. Physical pain was bearable; it was the psychological pain that distressed her most of all.

"Hello Beth, it is Beth, isn't it?" John's eyes were wide, eyebrows raised in concern. He sat down on the sand next to her and stared out at the beautiful scene before them. The turquoise blue sea, contrasted with the fine pink sand. The warm sun beat down, tempered with a cool sea breeze heavy with the aroma of the surf.

He breathed it in and sighed. "This has got to be one of the most enchanting places on earth, hasn't it?" He did not expect her to answer him, or for her to enter into any kind of dialogue. He knew she had not spoken since her ordeal, and he thought he would just be there for her. He had made a pact with God to make it up to this girl, and he was going to do the best he could to honour that commitment to her.

The surroundings triggered thoughts of his childhood in Heacham and playing with Eustace on the beach at Hunstanton. Of course it had never been this warm, but the sand and sea were a magnet for children whatever the weather. Those times with Eustace were magical, he thought, sighing again.

He started playing with the sand, at first running it through his fingers, feeling it's fine texture, then patting the wetter sand into a shape. The three Hopkins children saw John playing in the sand, and suddenly he and Beth were surrounded. John continued making the sandcastle.

"Mmmm… this is looking good children. Maybe I could turn this into a castle? I think I need to make some holes for windows. He put a finger into the side of the firm sand of the sandcastle. "Where do you think I need to put the windows Elizabeth? Maybe you could put some in for me?"

John could see Beth watching him play with the children. Very slowly at first and then with gradual confidence, she positioned herself next to little Giles. She smiled at the toddler, and took his finger, showing him how to make a window in the castle.

"Whats your name lady" Giles asked Beth.

"Her name is Beth, Giles" John replied. He saw Beth looking at him. John turned back to the castle. "I know" he exclaimed, his eyes wide with genuine excitement. "We need a moat. All castles have moats." He started to dig around the outside of the castle. "Can you dig out your side Constance? Maybe we can use the sand from the moat to make the castle a bit taller." He started patting the sand on the outside of the existing rather primitive looking castle. He looked at Beth again. She was now frantically digging and patting with Giles.

"I think I need to put some water in that moat, children." He got up off the sand, "Hold on a minute, I'll be right back. Beth, you keep an eye on them."

He sauntered over to where Lizzie was helping Tom and his team to prepare the next meal. "Can I borrow a couple of those tin cups for a moment" he asked Lizzie.

Lizzie looked at him quizzically, then looking beyond him saw the children and the sandcastle and realised what he was doing.

"You are a surprise; a big strong man being so good with children. I think you are secretly a child at heart yourself John Rolfe" she smiled. "Be sure you bring them back young man, they are very precious and not really meant to be toys."

"Young man indeed. I am a lot older than you… and soon to be a father myself" he laughed.

John walked down to the lapping surf and stooped to fill the cup with water, the warm surf circling around his toes. He thought how he would play with his own baby…

He came back to the sand castle and poured the water into the pretend, moat. Beth watched him intently. It was starting to dawn on her that he had no ulterior motive. He was just having fun, a concept that was unfamiliar but nice. He wasn't coming near her or doing anything to her. He was such a strong man, obviously someone in charge, and yet he was playing sandcastles with these lovely children. She was intrigued, watching as his sun drenched hair fell over his eyes as he stooped to play, laughing. When he looked at her, she could see no threat only softness in his sparkling hazel eyes.

The water seeped down through the sand and disappeared. "Oh no" John cried, mocking anxiety. "what are we going to do, the water is running away. I know, we will have to line it with palmetto leaves". He ran over to one of the large palmetto trees on the beach and proceeded to strip one of the large green leaves, placing small overlapping sections in the castle's moat. It seemed to work and there was a hint of a smile on Beth's face as she watched the delight on the children's faces at his antics.

"I am going back to get some more water" he shouted… "We want to make sure that this castle is safe don't we?" With that, he turned away and headed back down to the water.

"Come on everybody" shouted John. "We have to get this castle finished before lunch". First five year old Elizabeth, then three year old Constance and lastly, baby Giles all started piling more sand on the castle and making shapes and turrets to make it look like a real castle.

The Ship's dog, Posey, interested in what was going on, ran up and started doing some digging of his own. The children burst into fits of laughter, as the pink sand thrown into the air by the big dog, went all over them. Beth continued to observe with a small smile.

Little Giles, not quite two years old, had seen John going down to the edge of the water, and suddenly took it into his head to do the same. He had not been walking that long, and his chubby little legs were unsteady in the sand. As he ran, he suddenly fell down on the soft undulating surface.

In a flash, before anyone else had seen what had happened, Beth got up and ran to him, picking him up clumsily with her one arm, and cuddling him. John noticed what had happened when he heard little Giles whimpering, but he pretended it was not important and let Beth continue her mothering of the little boy. She eventually led him back to the group, and started to help him play with the sand.

There was still no sound coming from her, but she was communicating with the baby with her eyes and very gentle gestures. Giles responded, sensing her warmth, and the two of them became a little team with the common goal of building a rather haphazard annexe to the castle, oblivious to anyone else around them.

John felt that progress had been made, but he knew it was going to take time for her to settle completely. She is a lovely girl, he thought, suddenly realising that not only was she beautiful, the way she handled the baby was compassionate and warm.

John did not see Sarah watching him from afar with silent tears rolling down her face.

Murder

At the other end of the beach, the gentle giant of a figure, Eddy Samuels was watching his flaxen haired daughter playing with the little baby Giles. His heart ached for her, and all he wanted to do was to run up and take her in his arms and give her a hug. He knew this wasn't going to be possible. No one knew he was Beth's father, and he wasn't sure what the repercussions would be should he divulge this now. Beth had obviously not said anything as no one had approached him about her, and he assumed she must want this to be kept a secret. He was determined to keep this confidence for Beth's sake, no matter how heart-breaking it was for him to bear.

It looked as though she was mixing with the little children well, and although he could tell from the way that she was holding her body that she was still in pain, it was clear that she was in good hands. He thought how he had brought her on this mission. He knew why he had done it… but knowing what had happened to Beth, her fall from the mast, and near, drowning - with hindsight he wished they had never set eyes on the "Sea Venture".

Suddenly there was a deep voice from behind him.

"So… he's not a boy after all… I knew there was something different about him… or, I mean *her*." Robbie, the ruffian who escaped a punch for his disgusting insinuations as Beth fell from the mast, had noticed Eddy watching the young girl, and was ready to finish the 'discussion' they had started before. "So why are you so interested in her? Maybe you want her for yourself. She is quite tasty. Very young, but that's alright… " he laughed, winking. "I think I might give her a try." he hesitated. "Unless you want first go…"

Eddy turned around to face the repulsive debauched cesspit of a man, fury showing on his face, every bone in his body tensing for a fight. He was not a small man, but he was carrying a bit of weight, and not fit. He tried to avoid confrontations as he knew he was not as young as he used to be. He was ashamed that he had not been able to protect Beth from the dangers of the world, but he was not going to allow this man to soil her in any way - even through foul thought.

"You animal" he shouted with his fists in the air, his face crunched up, his body shaking. "You ought to be put down like a mad dog for having such thoughts about someone so young and pure."

He was getting closer and closer to Robbie, who moved back, eyes wide with surprise. Most of his mates would have had a laugh about the young girl and joined in with his imaginative banter, but this man seemed very agitated. Maybe just a religious prude, like lots of them on this ship, he thought dismissively.

As Edward got closer he growled "she is my daughter you pizzle!" through gritted teeth, every ounce of energy turned to hate.

Robbie then realised why this man was insane with rage. Insane he was though, and Robbie was going to have to do something drastic to protect himself. This could be a fight to the death. He quickly scanned the area and saw a shovel close by that they had used to dig for water. He ran over and picked the heavy shovel up and raised it above his head as Eddy ran towards him. He brought it down with maximum force, hearing a crunching sound as it hit Eddy's head.

The raving father fell like a stone to the ground, groaning and gasping, blood dripping down his face from the huge open wound on the top of his head. Robbie paused for a few seconds, unsure what to do next, maybe he had managed to finish the bastard. Then, just when he felt it was safe, he could see that despite serious injury, Eddy's bulking blood soaked body had started to stir, and he could see that the crazed madman would be back up in a matter of seconds if he did not take more action.

A man used to street fights, Robbie knew just how to stop this enemy in his tracks. He raised the rusty blood stained shovel in the air once again and brought the sharp edge down hoping to make contact with Eddy's exposed throat as he struggled to get up.

* * *

Beth had looked up from where she was playing with Giles and saw a crowd had gathered. They were all starting to chant, the men raising their fists in the air. She looked beyond the crowd and saw two men facing one another primed for a fight. One of the men, she knew in her gut was her friend. She was frustrated that her mind was so fuzzy. Why didn't she know who these people were? Why was it only feelings she had, and no thoughts? The one thing she did know was that something bad was happening.

She made sure Giles was being watched by Elizabeth Joons, and she ran over to the circle that had gathered around the two men. To her horror, she saw her friend dashed to the ground with a cry like a dying animal. The previously cheering and rowdy crowd stood mute as they saw the scene unravelling before them. The wounded man started to get up, blood spurting from the gash on his head. The crowd gasped, waiting to see what was going to happen.

Beth ran through the crowd pushing and shoving people out of the way, to get to the only person that in her heart she knew loved her - it came to her at last in a flash of recognition- he was her father. The man starting to get up, was her father.

She saw John running towards her and felt his tight grasp on her arm, followed by Alice and Lizzie who went to John's aid.

Beth knew she had to get away and struggled and struggled as if her life depended on it. Her father's gaze briefly met hers in painful recognition as she saw the shovel come down on his throat. Her father's throat was almost severed in two. She watched with horror as the blood bubbled and spurted everywhere in pulses as his dying heartbeats continued to transport the blood systematically through his body. He fell heavily and lay jerking, until the final remains of his life seeped out. She felt spatters of his warm blood on her arm. His glazed eyes stared up at the sky, fixed in the terror of the last moments of his life as he finally lay still. She sank to the ground weeping with despair, pulling herself free to lie across her father's body.

Gates noticed the disturbance from across the bay, and marched with purpose towards the growing circle of onlookers to find out what was happening. When he was a few yards away, he saw who the perpetrators were and tried to gauge what the mood of the crowd was. He was relieved that the event seemed to concern only two men and the noise had died down, with the crowd silent and subdued rather than a mutinous assembly.

"In the name of god what is happening here" he shouted, looking around, taking note of who was there and who might cause further trouble. He could see that it was only Robbie that hung his head in shame, his greasy hair hanging down to cover his eyes.

"Yeardley! Pierce! Arrest this man and bring him to my quarters.

There will be an investigation into what has happened. Law and order must be maintained, and actions such as this will not be tolerated." His voice was strong and loud.

"The rest of you, lay the dead man to rest under that tree. Cover him with something, for his dignity's sake. We will have to dig a grave and Reverend Burke will conduct a burial service as soon as is possible... and for goodness sake do something with that girl" he sighed and rolled his eyes realising that she was the same one that had caused problems on the skiff as they were landing. He had little patience and understanding with women. He felt them to be unpredictable and weak, and they made him uncomfortable as he was not sure how to manage them. He silently wished that he had some support from his fellow officers.

Gates realized that Somers had virtually gone his own way since landing. Somers had spent most of his time surveying the immediate landscape to find what resources were available. Admittedly, he had also caught fish with the help of some of his men and had been able to supply everyone with food for the first few days. What Somers had done was of value, so Gates had not criticised or complained that he was not pulling his weight or working collaboratively. Now, however, Gates felt it was time for Somers to step up to the mark and show the community that they were a united force in leadership. Where was he?

"God damn that pompous oaf" thought Gates as he reminisced about Somers' fanfare when he boarded the "Sea Venture" in his dress uniform, everyone standing to attention, trumpets blazing, to herald the 'great leader'. "What a load of old bollocks, that was." He thought with contempt. "Where is 'the great leader' now, when he is needed?" he was irritated beyond description. "Probably in his useless kitchen garden... chance would be a fine thing for me to be able to do a bit of gardening, fishing and exploring... but someone has to do the real work!" He stomped back to his makeshift shelter ready to deal with the prisoner on his own.

As Gates approached he saw Yeardley and Pierce were waiting outside his hut with the prisoner shackled, and struggling. The prisoner was cursing and shouting "It was not my fault, he attacked me... it was self-defence... I am innocent... Fucking let me go, you have no right... ." Gates, calmly, walked up to him, drew his fist back and threw a punch, winding him. He fell to the ground groaning.

"I don't have time for this" snarled Gates. "You clearly killed a man in cold blood, and under any circumstances that carries a penalty of death."

Gates stared at Robbie as he coughed and spluttered, rising up from the ground staggering after being winded by the unexpected punch in the belly. "I was protecting the honour of my daughter, Beth", he said.

Gates hesitated. To his recollection, the girl had been weeping at the death of the victim. Who knew what went on in the minds of young maids? Maybe the victim had been her lover. Whatever the story was, this man had committed murder and as Governor he had a duty to sentence him to death. The way he handled this, was going to set the blueprint for long-term discipline on the island. They had to know that he was not going to be lenient with wrong-doers. The girl was out of it anyway, and was almost as much trouble as her father having almost caused the skiff to capsize as they landed. So much had happened to her, but it was not really his problem - discipline in the colony came first.

"You committed murder and no excuses can save you from the gallows" said Gates squaring himself up to the quivering man.

"But sir" said Robbie, tears streaming down his face. "He threatened to rape my little girl and then he attacked me... "he dropped to his knees sobbing and grabbing Gate's shins looking up at him with as pathetic a face as he could muster, getting into the role of victim rather than perpetrator. "How will my little Beth manage without her poor old dad if you hang me? She has been through so much already; this will kill *her* as well as me. Do you want that on your conscience?"

Gates looked down at him sighing. He had to convey a message to the others that toleration of violence of any kind would not be countenanced. It was a shame for the girl, but that could not be helped. He had to be firm, he had no choice.

"No. It is *your* conscience that is at stake here, not mine Robbie. You will be tied to a cedar tree outside, and the body of your victim will lie within your view, so you spend the night thinking about the man that you killed. At midday tomorrow you will be hanged. Take him away." He lifted his hand as if shooing away a fly.

What Gates could not see, was that outside, Want had crouched down behind Gate's shelter, listening with rapt attention to what was happening to his friend. He was outraged that Gates had pronounced that Robbie be sentenced to death. His friend would only have done something like this out of self-defence. The real point was that Gates had no more authority in Bermuda than anyone else. He had only been granted authority by the Virginia Company as Governor in *Virginia*, and this was not Virginia. Want was angry as he watched them tying his friend to a tree. He would have to do something about this….

Escape

❧

"**F**or goodness sake Gates, how has this happened? I thought I could rely on you as acting governor to manage law and order. How in hell are you going to manage Jamestown, if you can't even manage 150 passengers? Now we are a laughing stock". Somers was standing with Gates looking at the tree to which Robbie had been shackled. The ropes hung frayed and useless and the prisoner was nowhere to be seen.

Want was observing, interested in the reactions to what had happened, gauging the mood, looking for people of like mind.

A large crowd had formed a circle. He was satisfied to see that many looked triumphant to see that one of their number had escaped the authority of the self-appointed judge. He could hear the sniggers as they watched the confusion of their leaders who were obviously arguing. Officers divided, were officers weakened. Somers and Gates had so far contained their mutual animosity, but it was a doomed relationship from the start and it was overtly starting to crumble with the latest development. Somers was a sailor from head to toe, and sailors didn't see the world in the same way as soldiers such as Gates.

Want was standing with Sam Sharpe.

"Here we go lad." He smiled at Sam Sharpe, whose dirty blond hair and crooked jaw and general appearance of a vagabond marked him out as one of Want's men. "It is good to see the bosses quarrelling isn't it? Divide and conquer is my motto!" He rubbed his hands with glee, chuckling to himself.

Sam returned the smile. "Yea" he nodded eager to please, his vacant eyes looking shiftily around, unsure what his boss really meant. "Do you think they know it was us broke Robbie free?" Sam wasn't bright, but he was easily led, and that was what Want needed.

"For Christ's sake shut up Sam" Want whispered. "If they don't know now, they soon will if you go shouting your mouth off! Listen, watch and learn." He put his fingers to his lips as if quietening a child. "Listen to what the old bugger has to say, we might learn something."

Somers stood and looked at the circle of people, scrutinizing their faces.

"For anyone divulging information regarding the whereabouts of the prisoner, there will be special privileges and for those caught aiding and abetting there will be dire punishment. I hope I make myself clear". His features were taught. "Now let's find this bastard. It shouldn't be difficult."

Somers looked around for men he could trust. "Yeardley, Strachey, Jourdain, Rich, Rolfe, each go in a different direction and look for the prisoner. Take guns with you and bring him back to me. He is due to hang at midday, despite the amateur way this has been handled. The rest of you, for God's sake get back to your duties, we cannot afford to slack, we need to get this community up and running." He glared at Gates, his feelings of disrespect etched into his face.

Somers had chosen the men carefully, thought Want. The best of a bad bunch, but no mind - whether they found Robbie or not, cracks in the leadership were starting to show. His band of rebels could see for themselves how easy it was to get the upper hand; things were going to plan nicely.

Tobacco

ohn was pleased to be, yet again, placed in a position of trust. He and the other four chosen men negotiated the directions in which they would search, and agreed to fire one shot should the prisoner be found. They did not want to waste precious bullets, but there seemed no other way to communicate.

John set off along the coast, tentative but alert. If he found Robbie, he was well prepared. He rambled over the rough ground, Cedar trees framing the coast line. He looked around for places that Robbie might hide. A cave or rock formation would be ideal. The route that John had taken seemed to hold little but open space, sea, rocks and trees. He stopped on a mound of sand to scan the surrounding area, looking out at the deep blue sea that once had been a mortal enemy, but now showed its beauty with colour and movement.

What an amazing place, he thought. He could see the fish swimming lazily in the surf, and saw the reason the nets saved from the ship had captured hundreds of fish at a time with no effort. It appeared that the only predators were "Sea Venture" passengers. The birds didn't move as he approached. The wildlife, having been safe from predation for so long, naively trusted other creatures and their trust had been savagely betrayed with the arrival of the "Sea Venture".

As he sat, a large white bird with a long tail fluttered down and sat on the sand next to him, looking quizzical as it nestled onto eggs nestled in the sand. He felt a pang of guilt looking into the eyes of this bird and thinking of the wildlife that had already been destroyed in such a short time. Gates had directed a system of using the salt from the sea to cure some of the excess meat and fish, should they experience difficult times in the future for any reason. If they escaped the island they would need supplies for the journey, and John knew that Gates already had a plan to leave. To his credit, Gates had been very efficient in the collection of food, and no one had been hungry since they landed. But even so, the numbers killed were far in excess of those needed, and killing the wildlife had become a macabre sport for many of the men.

John paused to breathe in the salt air, thinking about man and his tendency to destroy what is beautiful, just for the sake of it. All thoughts of Robbie vanished momentarily.

His mind turned with sadness to Sarah. He had returned to her after her revelation, determined to try and forgive her, but since that day she had withdrawn herself. She avoided any physical contact with him, and spoke only when necessary. Every now and then, he caught her looking at him with longing, and he tried to reach out to her, but she always turned away. He didn't know how to reach her.

He lay down sighing, and looked up at the blue sky, feeling the warm sunshine on his bearded and tanned face, and said a silent prayer asking God what he had done wrong to deserve such a cruel fate. With eyes closed, he reached up to touch the leaves which surrounded his prone head, and felt their cool smoothness. His hand dropped lower and came upon the crispy dead leaves at the foot of the plant that had been dried in the sun. He pulled one off just to feel the disintegration of it as he crumbled it in the palm of his hand. He had done this with plants on the estate many times as a boy in Norfolk. Feeling the textures and temperatures of the plant connected him to the earth, like Eustace's stone.

Gradually he became aware of the sweet fragrance of the dried leaves as they fell from his hand to the ground. It was reminiscent of the tobacco he used to smoke, supplies of which had long since been depleted. It had a milder and sweeter smell, which was warm and pleasant. Could this be a form of tobacco, he wondered. He sat up and opened his eyes, suddenly alert to the possibility. He did not know what a tobacco plant looked like, but this plant certainly had the aroma of tobacco.

John thought through the logic. Good sweet tobacco was Spanish. The Spanish guarded their seeds carefully to prevent others growing it and undercutting their market. The Spanish had previously been shipwrecked on Bermuda - maybe these plants were a remnant from previous Spanish survivors? Maybe he could cultivate these plants. His thoughts started to spiral and go off at tangents to plans, ifs and buts... He missed the calming effect that tobacco had on him, and the smell of these dried leaves was making his body tingle at the memory of breathing in the lovely fragrant smoke. It would be amazing if these plants were what he thought they might be. Maybe he could make something of this.

He wondered how he could turn these leaves into tobacco that he could burn in a pipe. He could just shred the leaves and experiment, he conjectured. Then he had another idea. The Indian Matchumps, might know what to do with the leaves. He had heard that Indians had smoked tobacco for generations, albeit rather harsh stuff that Europeans refused to smoke. Matchumps might know how to get the best from these leaves. Or maybe Somers would have some ideas about it. He was trying to make things grow in Bermuda - so far with little success, but he was interested in cultivation...

He remembered his lessons in the school room with old 'Chalky'. One of the lessons was about Sir Walter Raleigh and how he had brought the first tobacco to England from Virginia. Maybe John could do the same, but this time a milder Spanish version.

"Bang" John was pulled from his thoughts as he heard the shot that told him Robbie had been found. Hundreds of birds took to the air squawking and fluttering at the unfamiliar sound. He stood up and started to walk back to base, turning around to look back at the plants. This had been an eventful excursion there was a lot of thinking to do. Maybe Robbie escaping had done him a favour. He might have found another kind of gold.

Reprieve

"I know, I know, I know... we *have* to have a united front on this Somers. We need to send out a strong message that we will not tolerate acts of violence... but... " Gates opened out his arms with despair.

"... yes but, if we are inflexible, the mutinous faction... and we know they are the friends of Waters, could start a rebellion. They have more men on their side than we have on ours" said Somers. "It is not that I agree with a lenient stance, but I think we should consider all the options."

Gates paused thinking, pacing up and down. "He is going to bring on the vulnerable father act you know. That might win the sympathies of the other's in the community, which would put us in an even bigger dilemma." He said, his eyebrows drawn together in a frown.

"If only you had handled this better Gates... we could have hanged the bastard before anyone had time to consider that there were options."

"For Christ's sake Somers, if I had more support from you this might not have happened. You are always swanning about, fiddling with your seeds or fishing with Robert Rich and James Swift. I have to do all the hard graft myself. Oh what I would give, just to go fishing!" Gates exploded. "Fighting amongst ourselves is only going to make matters ten times worse."

Somers nodded. "Alright, Alright, Point taken. Let's see what the mood of the crowd is when they bring him in, and then we can make a final decision.

Robbie was brought back to camp with his hands tied behind his back. Yeardly had drawn the jackpot, and it was his dubious prize that stood before Gates and Somers. Robbie was weeping as he threw himself on the sand before them, just as they had anticipated.

"Kind masters, I swear it was self-defence, I am throwing myself at your mercy, I beg you not to hang me. I will do anything you ask. Please think of my poor darling daughter. She is only 15 and alone in the world. She needs me to look after her and protect her from this cruel world". His voice was high pitched and whiny, as he tried to put on the performance of his life. He blinked repeatedly, trying to formulate tears in his eyes.

Somers watched unmoved, and he could see that Gates was stony faced too.

"You have killed, AND you have tried to escape punishment" Somers looked him squarely in the face ignoring his pathetic pleas.

"Free him" the lone voice of Want rang out loud and clear.

"Free him now" several other voices joined that of Want.

"Free him, free him... now" the chorus of voices was getting louder as more and more men found the confidence to be seen as part of the growing number of dissenters. They started to raise their arms in the air clapping their hands as the chant went on and on, stamping their feet in unison.

Somers could take no more. Suddenly he took out his gun and shot it into the air to stop the frenzy from getting any more out of control. The men froze at the sound, shocked. They stood silent, like wild horses being restrained, waiting for Gates or Somers to make the next move. They were out for blood if Robbie was not released.

Somers could see the way things were going in the body language of the crowd.

"Order!" he screamed. He stood erect, his posture communicating his authority. Gates stood shoulder to shoulder with him. Everyone could see that they were now united in their stance.

"Sir Thomas decreed that Robbie Waters should be hanged due to the severity of his crime, which is perfectly reasonable in normal circumstances. However, as these are not normal circumstances and as Sir Thomas is a practical and reasonable man, in the spirit of goodwill for this community, he has decided to re-consider this decision. I back Sir Thomas completely on this issue. When reaching a decision, we have also taken into consideration the issue of Robbie's daughter, Beth, who has been through difficult times since joining the "Sea Venture.

We feel this case is a unique situation. A father, protecting the honour of his daughter, is instinctual and we are compassionate men. For these reasons, both Sir Thomas Gates and I have decided, on this occasion to pardon the accused."

They started to cheer and clap. Somers put up his hand to stop them. "I have not finished." He shouted.

"Let me make it clear that leniency is not the policy in this community, and further incidences of this nature will be dealt with swiftly and harshly with the death penalty." He indicated to Gates to continue.

Gates turned to address the prisoner.

"Do not think that you will get away with any further crimes, just because of your daughter. This is a one off pardon, and should you misbehave in any way in the future, your sentence will automatically be reinstated, even if the additional crime is a minor one. If I hear of any aggression, theft or rowdy behaviour from you, you will hang. Do you understand?"

Robbie sighed. He did not want to appear grateful, but he did not want to queer his pitch with them either. "I understand" he mumbled under his breath.

"I did not hear you Mr. Waters" Gates was losing patience.

"Ok, ok, I understand" underneath Robbie was seething with thinly veiled anger.

"Untie the prisoner, Yeardly" Somers barked, his frown growing deeper by the minute.

Somers could see that they had caught the rebels unaware with their lenient response. Maybe this was a good thing. They had been prepared for a fight, and were actually hoping for the excuse to take these officers down a peg by showing their strength. Somers could see them looking to Want for direction.

Want started clapping and cheering. "Victory!" he shouted. The rest followed suit. They all shouted and stamped their feet clapping. "Victory... victory... victory." Mob rule.

Somers watched with distaste as Yeardly tugged the ropes free from Robbie's bound hands. Robbie did not look at him, or thank him, the appearance of compliance had disappeared once he got what he wanted. Somers expected no less.

Robbie's face was stern, and had turned from that of the pleading victim to that of victorious self-righteous superiority. Why should he thank them for sparing his life? It had been self defence and any way, they did not even have the powers to arrest him as they had only been granted those powers in Jamestown, and this was not Jamestown, this was Bermuda.

Somers grunted. He was disgusted. He marched off.

Robbie shrugged off the ropes and walked towards his friends. They surrounded him patting him on the back as if he were a hero. Robbie smiled and revelled at being in the limelight. He now had another problem though. He was going to have to try and think about how he was going to manage the little white lie that he was Beth's father. If that got out, things might turn sour for him again, as it seemed to have played a large part in getting him released. There were only two other people who knew Beth was not his daughter - Want (and he would never betray his best friend), and Beth (and she was mute and had lost her wits). Maybe he was home and dry. Shame if anything further happened to little Beth.

Temptations

~ C∞ ~

"Sir…" John saw Somers walking down the beach towards his hut. "Sir, can I have a word with you?"

"Of course my boy. How are you getting on with those seedlings of mine?" he replied his eyes smiling. John thought he looked tense after the Robbie Waters incident. He noticed Somers was losing weight and coughing a lot.

"It is quite difficult to get the seed growing, I am afraid Sir. But I have found an unusual native crop up on the hill. It smells like tobacco to me, and I wonder if you would come and have a look at it to see what you think?"

"Is it far Rolfe? I am a little tired at the moment, and I just want to sit down for a bit."

"No, it is only just beyond that little mound there. It will only take us five minutes to walk up there and I really think it will be worth your while. I have shown it to Matchumps and he thinks that it is tobacco."

"Oh, in that case…" Somers struggled up the hill behind John, breathing heavily.

When he got to the top, he bent down and placed his hands on his thighs, catching his breath.

"Are you alright Sir?" John asked, surprised that such a short walk had had such an effect on his companion.

"Yes, yes, Rolfe, just getting a bit older. Being a leader is not always easy." He had a fit of coughing, and quickly covered his mouth with a handkerchief.

John paused until Somers had stopped coughing, and went over to a pile of leaves that he had picked and dried in the sun. He picked a couple of them up, broke them into pieces in his hand, and walked over to Somers holding out his hand. "Smell that Sir." His eyes were wide, and he was grinning from ear to ear.

Somers picked some of the pieces from John's hand and raised them to his nose, taking a deep breath and inhaling the scent. His eyes gradually rose from looking at the leaves, to meet John's. "This smells like good stuff John. How the devil did you find it boy?"

"I just found it by accident. Matchumps thinks that it might be Spanish though, as it is so mild. He says it is definitely not the harsh tobacco that his tribe cures."

"Well, I think you have to make it a priority to cultivate this crop Rolfe. Get Matchumps to help you. It might be something else that we can take with us to Jamestown.

Have you tried to smoke any of this stuff yet?"

"Yes, I tried to cure some of it to smoke, but it is quite primitive. I think I have to play around with it a bit before I get the recipe right."

"Have you got any that I can try boy?" Somers smiled.

"Here Sir." John passed Somers a clay pipe filled with his tobacco, and rubbed flints together to light it for him.

Somers drew the smoke from the pipe slowly. "Ahhhhh... not bad boy." He smiled. "I definitely think you are on to something here. Keep me posted on your progress, and I am happy to try samples." He chuckled, but suddenly convulsed into a spasm of coughing.

"Are you sure you are alright Sir George." John repeated, he could see that Somers was steeling himself to give the impression of normality. Despite this, John sensed his vulnerability.

"Don't mind me. Just got a bit of a tickle from the smoke." Somers smiled, but his eyes were sad. "We better get back to the others now, they will be wondering where we have got to. It will be easier going down." He smiled again.

"I want you to make this one of your priorities John. I am serious when I say that we could have something here that is quite valuable when we get to Jamestown."

"Yes Sir." John was thrilled. His thoughts about it were confirmed. There were definite possibilities here.

As they approached the settlement, Somers and John went their separate ways, Somers back to his hut and John to join the others.

John saw several different groups of people sitting around fires according to their standing in the community and their friendships. Everything looked peaceful. It was getting dark now, and the light of the fires cast dancing shadows on the people sitting in circles. It was balmy, and everyone seemed engrossed in various pursuits, the only sounds were the low hum of conversation combined with the occasional laugh from the children. John looked around each one in turn, thinking how different they all seemed from the days of the storm on board the ship.

Alice and Beth were playing with the Hopkins children and their mother Mary was sitting sewing a pair of torn trousers, trying to see in the fading light. Steven Hopkins had a candle from the ship and was engrossed with reading a religious manuscript, completely disinterested in his wife or children, other than to stop every now and then and shout "Be quiet" in a harsh voice as the children ducked and weaved between Alice and Beth's legs. John noted that Sarah was sitting on her own observing everyone with a look of great concentration and worry on her lovely face, her small round belly starting to protrude under her dress. His stomach turned. He wanted so much to go over to her as he would have done before.

On the other side, William Strachey was writing in his notebook, looking up every now and again as his train of thought halted his writing. Sylvester Jourdain, hair without ribbons now, was deep in conversation with Henry Ravens who looked thoughtful and concerned.

Mistress Horton and Henry Paine seemed to have forged an unusual friendship through their self-perceived superiority, and sat on the rocks behind the circle, as Henry pointed to something in the bushes. Lizzie, Mistress Horton's maid seemed to have escaped for the evening - maybe she was meeting with Tom Powell. Those two were the talk of the community, having started a romance following the incident on the ship where Tom had rescued Lizzie from the bullying Mistress Horton.

Elizabeth Joons and Jeff Briars also seemed to be in love as they sat holding hands and quietly talking to one another. John thought back to the times when he and Sarah had been young lovers. It was so intense, so wonderful. It seemed so long ago now, but actually it was only a very short time ago. He had a picture of Sarah moving her hands down his body, and he had to shake his mind away as the feeling of the loss was too great. There was so much he would never understand of life.

Want and his cronies had separated themselves from the main group and were playing cards around a fire they had built further along the beach, and shouts, spitting and foul language could be heard in the distance, getting louder as the newly found alcoholic drink made from palmetto berries coursed through their veins.

John thought how interesting it was to observe the different groups and what they were doing. It indicated so much about the relationships good and bad that had developed over the past few weeks. There had been no differences when they had all been fighting for their lives, they had all had a common goal, working shoulder to shoulder. John knew with regret that despite the possibilities for a peaceful existence that had been handed to them, greed and conflict would never go away now basic survival was assured. Individual agendas were already starting to show.

Where was it all going? Where would they be, this time next year? Would his tobacco be his future in the new world? John wondered. He would be a father by then. What would happen to him and Sarah? He had a vision of his son or daughter riding beside him with a friendly Indian on a painted pony, galloping through fields of tobacco in Virginia. He felt in his pocket for the jagged stone, that was now smooth. He was on his way to fulfilling Eustace's dream.

As John walked towards the fire, Sarah caught sight of him and got up abruptly and left. She looked away, refusing eye contact as she quietly retreated, all alone, unobserved by everyone but John.

She had been the love of his life. There had been so many possibilities for happiness, and now there seemed only regret and rejection. He looked after her as she disappeared into the night alone.

He walked over to the happy group and sat down next to Beth. She was such a lovely innocent young girl. Her blue eyes had speckles of yellow from the flickering fire, and her flaxen hair shone as she clapped her hands to the sound of the nursery rhyme the children had started singing. She still did not speak, but her eyes were smiling as she looked at him.

There was definite progress in her condition, and he gave himself credit for most of this, because of the time he had spent with her. He moved closer to her, and took her small hand in his as a brotherly gesture. She looked so vulnerable, looking up at him as though she really wanted him to be there with her, protecting her. It was so nice.

John felt strong and needed, feelings that he had not felt since Sarah's rejection of him. As their eyes met, his stomach did an unexpected turn and his heart beat faster.

Taken aback by his unexpected emotions, he suddenly let go of Beth's hand and moved further away so that there was no bodily contact between them. Beth looked surprised and hurt.

He was in a whirl of confusion.

He looked at her questioning face glowing with innocence in the firelight.

He moved close to her again and taking her hand he smiled.

"It's alright. There was a bump in the grass that was digging into me" he whispered, giving her small hand a squeeze.

She nodded at him and shuffled even closer to him smiling.

It had been a while since anyone had needed him or looked at him this way.

It occurred to him that maybe Beth would be better helped by her father, Robbie.

John thought back to when Robbie had tried to visit Beth. She had been terrified. Very strange. That was a while ago though, and Alice had insisted Robbie stay away. Now that some time had elapsed, maybe she needed to get to know her father again and rebuild a relationship with him. Despite the fact that Robbie was clearly a despicable man, he was her father, and fathers always have special relationships with daughters, John thought. Maybe he could help Beth re-ignite her relationship with her only blood relative.

Ravens' Mission

╰♥∽♥∽♥╯

The settlement was starting to take shape now. Gates surveyed all the work that they had done since arriving in Bermuda.

The groups that he had organised at the outset had worked wonders to create a thriving and efficient community. They had the fishing down to a fine art - there were so many fish to be had, that many had been salted and preserved. There was a hog pen, now overflowing with hogs, not only from the "Sea Venture", but those that had been captured when they landed. There were many piglets as well, as breeding had been successful.

There was a row of little huts several yards from the perfectly curved pink sandy beach. All the huts were made of wood, with large palmetto leaves for rooves. So far this had been enough to keep out the soft and gentle Bermuda rain and wind. Creepy crawlies seemed to be at a minimum on the island, and no one had yet seen a snake. All the creatures seemed either beautiful or friendly. Each hut had beds and little tables and chairs, made homely by the inhabitants. Some had even started to plant little gardens, with brightly coloured Bermudian flowers making the community cheerful and welcoming.

The climate was wonderful, if not a little humid for some. It was mid summer, and often when people felt the heat of the mid-day sun, they would just walk down to the crystal clear blue sea and plunge into water that was as warm as treacle.

Gates was pleased, but not satisfied. He had a contract to fulfil, and as delightful as this place was, he could not sit on his laurels and allow things just to tick over. They were still on their way to Jamestown, and he still had the canister with the names of the leaders of Jamestown, and he would not open it until he reached the shores of Virginia. He was going to get there, and he was going to take up the command that had been given him. Looking around him at the people laughing in the sunshine, he could see that he was probably the only person anxious to leave.

He walked over to Henry Frobisher, the shipbuilder, who was standing under a tree talking to Henry Ravens, the Master's mate. Frobisher was one of the older members of the crew, having worked his way up from apprentice. His greying hair was sparse, and he had a shiny bald patch on the top of his head, which was turning pink with the Bermudian sun. His sunken, but clear staring blue eyes, focused unflinchingly on whatever he was doing. He rarely smiled. For him, life was too short for frivolities. He was intelligent though. Gates often felt that had Frobisher come from a different class, he would have made a lot of money for himself with his clever determination and canny ways.

Frobisher, apart from being a serious man, was a perfectionist, to the point of obsessiveness. He could get extremely angry when things did not go his way, and those working under him who were less able than himself, which was nearly everyone, had to learn to ignore his brusque dismissive criticisms. Nothing was ever right and nothing was ever good enough.

"Gentlemen." Gates said as he approached the two men, his

eyebrows drawing together in concentration. "I would like a word with you." His brows were drawn.

Ravens stood to attention. Frobisher, just looked at Gates and nodded.

"I am pleased with the way the quarter has developed and the way everyone is settling in. However, we cannot be content with things as they are, pleasant though it is. We have to start thinking about leaving Bermuda to get to Jamestown as our contractual obligation warrants."

"Oh. It never occurred to me that we could get off Bermuda" said Ravens. I thought we would have to stay here until a passing ship noticed us."

"Well, that could happen. We need to get some bonfires going so that if there are any passing ships they might see us. Mind you, with the reputation that Bermuda has, very few ships actually pass this way. Nevertheless, we should do that Ravens. Good thinking!" He smiled and nodded at the younger man.

"But that is not enough. We need to think of a way to build a boat. Maybe only a small boat to take a few of us to land to get reinforcements and to alert people that we are here. That is why I need *your* expertise Frobisher. You Ravens, would have to navigate the boat." He paused, his face expectant.

"Can't be done sir." Frobisher said blankly, leaving no room for further discussion. His face was stubborn. He looked the other way, almost, but not *quite* insolent.

"Frobisher!" Gates face was thunderous. "Do not turn away from me, and do not dismiss me. I am your commander. What I order you to do… you do."

Frobisher was not phased by Gate's anger. Years of experience told him, that bosses shouted and raged, but they still needed him. "You can order me, and I will do it… doesn't mean to say it will work. I thought you were asking for my expertise, not ordering me to do the impossible." His face showed little emotion, because he didn't have much.

Gates was getting red in the face. "You will do it Frobisher and when you have done that, you can start designing a ship that will take us *all* to Jamestown. We are *not* staying here, and I want you to start building the skiff tomorrow. Do I make myself clear?"

"Aye aye Sir. Perfectly clear." Frobisher turned and walked away. "Idiot", he thought.

* * *

It was the morning of Monday 28th August 1609. They had hoped for a better day to set sail, but it wasn't bad enough to call it off.

Henry Ravens was a good choice to navigate the small boat to Jamestown to bring back bigger ships to rescue them all. He had been Somers' right hand man on the voyage, and he was a seasoned sailor and navigator. He had had an unremarkable career, never shining, although competent and trustworthy. Physically he did not stand out from the crowd. He had the scars of many battles on his weather-beaten face. His sharp features were framed by dull and oily, mousy brown hair. However, he was a man that was liked as he was clever and funny, always the clown in a group of people, and a good friend of the young Jeff Briars.

He was acutely aware of the danger he was placing himself in. He knew he would be a hero if he succeeded, and if he did not, he would be remembered as the sailor that died serving others. He would have a glowing epitaph no matter what, and for a man with no family, he felt he could not ask for anything better than this chance to make his mark.

Ravens chose five other men to accompany him on this small boat, and Gates had ensured that enough water and provisions had been stowed away for more than a month, just in case it took them longer than anticipated. Ravens, being an optimist was convinced that he would be back in Bermuda in under a month, bringing a ship large enough to rescue everyone.

The whole community was assembled on Gates' beach not far from where the "Sea Venture" had landed. Reverend Burke and Steven Hopkins were doing their Godly duty. The passengers stood around in a semi-circle hands together and heads bowed.

Baby Giles toddled down to the beach, and Constance grabbed hold of the dog's tail as it barked and chased the waves. Elizabeth screeched with delight when she saw the dog running and biting at the moving surf. She stooped down and ran her fingers through the water bringing them up suddenly to splash the frolicking dog, who shook himself sending droplets of water over the laughing children.

"Keep those children quiet." Shouted Steven Hopkins. "We are trying to conduct a service here!" No one paid much attention, except the long suffering Mary.

"Come on children, listen to your father." Mary wandered down to the shore and swept the little boy up into her arms, burying her nose in his neck and blowing. Her face showed momentary joy at seeing her children having such a good time. Her long hair was starting to show streaks of grey as each day passed and her husband got stricter and stricter, and less and less helpful to her.

"No, no…" cried little Giles. "Want play…" Mary put him down on the sand, and patted his small white behind. There was no point in him wearing anything in this climate, and his sturdy little body waddled back down to the water.

Most people in the congregation peeped through their closed eyes and smiled.

There was a light rain, almost a mist, which was not unpleasant in the humid heat of the early morning.

"The Lord is sending us a message, he is blessing this voyage." Reverend Burke pointed at a rainbow that had formed from the light rain.

"Praise be the Lord" Steven Hopkins looked upwards and made the sign of the cross. He started chanting "The Lord is my Shepherd" as he continued to look skyward, as if he, and he alone, had a connection to the almighty. The assembled congregation unenthusiastically started to join in with the Psalm, as Reverend Burke signalled wildly behind Steven's back, encouraging greater participation as the boat that was to hold Ravens and his men was lowered into the sea.

The six men boarded the small vessel, smiling. They were going to be the saviours of the community. They gradually started rowing themselves out to sea.

Alice stood with Beth and Sarah, and watched as Ravens' boat disappeared into the distance.

"I do so hope he is going to be alright" she said. "I can't imagine what it must be like to venture out on such a vast ocean in such a small boat after all that we have been through.

"I like it here, but I want to get to somewhere more civilized to have my baby" said Sarah, with downcast eyes.

"When is it due Sarah?" Alice asked.

"Oh not until February. We have plenty of time for Ravens to get us to Jamestown, I hope" she replied.

"I am expecting in March." Alice dropped the bombshell without breaking her stride, wondering if either Beth or Sarah would notice what she had said.

"What did you say? Did you say you were expecting in March?" Oh my goodness Alice, that is wonderful news. It is so lovely to know that we can share our pregnancies together." Sarah had a rare smile on her face.

Beth's face lit up, pleased for her friend. She still did not say anything, but she walked up to Alice and gave her a big hug.

John, at a distance watched the women, his heart aching and his mind confused.

Deliverance

G ates never imagined having to rely on Frobisher as much as they were having to do now - but he thanked the Lord that despite initial misgivings, Frobisher had been allocated to the "Sea Venture". If not, small precarious attempts to leave like the one Ravens was attempting, would have been their only chance - and they could be marooned for years.

Frobisher was duly summoned to Gates' quarters. As Frobisher entered, Gates got up and walked towards him to shake his hand. "Well done with that longboat" he said smiling. Frobisher grunted, he hadn't been pleased with the shoddy workmanship and he had never wanted to do it in the first place.

"Is that all Sir?" Frobisher said, uncomfortable to be the focus of Gates' attention, and eager to get back to the model ship he was making in his spare time.

"No Frobisher. I want you to build a ship that will take us all to Jamestown." Gates thought bluntness was the best way to communicate with Frobisher.

Frobisher's face fell. This was the dream of someone that did not know how difficult it was to build a ship. Gates was obviously an idiot.

"With the greatest of respect Sir, that cannot be done. We do not have the materials or the experienced manpower to embark on such a task. It is a nice idea, but not practically possible. We would need tall straight trees for the stocks and a tree at least forty feet long for the keel. We would have to find something for caulking – you know the trouble we had with the "Sea Venture?" Frobisher stood solidly, looking at Gates, determined to stand his ground on this. He knew his trade, Gates did not.

He had had to give in to build the skiff for Ravens and his crew, but that was a reasonably small job, this was something entirely different. He was not going to put at jeopardy the 150 souls who had survived one shipwreck, to place them in danger of drowning again because his boat was substandard. He had faith in his workmanship - but not in the materials that he had to work with. It was an ambitious pipe dream.

Gates stood his ground. "No. I will not accept that. I didn't accept your refusal to build the skiff and I am not accepting your refusal to build something bigger. For God's sake Frobisher, this bloody island is covered in cedar." Gates was used to getting his own way. He knew how to get things done even when people stood in his way. He had thought long and hard about this and concluded that he had to give this a try. "We also have the materials from the "Sea Venture", and we have able-bodied young men that can be taught how to build the ship. I don't care if we work from morning til night to get the wood for this ship. It will be done. No more excuses Frobisher. We have no choice."

"What if we do build it, and it sinks? Do you want to be responsible for the death of 150 people, when we have already been saved once?" retorted Frobisher his tone becoming mocking and insolent.

Gates ignored his tone. "We have nothing to lose by trying. It will be well tested before it sets out for the open sea, and we will know it's seaworthiness as soon as it is launched. If we build it and you advise me that it is not seaworthy, then we can think again, but until then, I want this ship built." His voice was starting to rise, and he was getting impatient.

The "Sea Venture" was seaworthy when it was launched" Frobisher was determined.

"For goodness sake Frobisher, we had hurricane conditions! No ship could have survived the force of those winds. The chances of a storm as vicious as that occurring again are small. We have to risk it."

"We don't have the materials to build a ship as large as the "Sea Venture" so not all of us would be able to go."

"Well, build a smaller one. We will come back for those that remain."

"It cannot be done Sir Thomas. It is a fool's errand. No one but a fool would attempt it."

"I must be a fool then" said Gates standing his ground, his eyes staring, his complexion turning puce. "Just build the bloody ship man. It is an order. Tomorrow I will pick those I think capable of working on this task to be your workforce. Good day."

The following day, the bell tolled once again. All the assembled passengers stood waiting in anticipation of what Gates was going to say now. The plan for building a new ship was revealed to the shocked crowd. No one had thought such a thing was possible, but no one was prepared to challenge Gates.

"She will be called "Deliverance" Gates said proudly "and she will be built in the bay over the headland in the cove that I have chosen to be called Frobisher's Building Bay". He looked over at Frobisher who was looking slightly happier having a bay named after him.

"Work will commence as soon as possible to transport the materials that we rescued from the "Sea Venture" over to Building bay. This is an ambitious task, but we have a strong young workforce and plentiful resources. Robert Frobisher will be in charge, and anyone shirking from his duty to obey Master Frobisher will be arrested for treason. The list of men required for this duty will be pinned to that cedar tree over there. All boat builders are requested to report to Building Bay after lunch today to receive their first orders."

Gates had to choose the workers carefully. Most were his men, those whose allegiance he could trust. Many of Somers' men were not on the boat building rota. It had been mostly Somers' men that had mutinied over Water's arrest, and Gates was not going to push his luck trying to control them.

Somers' men continued hunting and fishing and attending to the day to day running of the colony. Somers chose to ignore the ship-building, and continued to map the island, the relevance of which Gates could not understand. Yes, mapping and exploring were interesting, and might be of use in the future, but Gates felt that getting off Bermuda was the priority. The relationship between Gates and Somers continued to be cordial, but frosty, splitting the community into two natural factions, those of sailors and landsmen.

After lunch the assembled workers sat on the sand of Frobisher's Building Bay waiting for orders. The spot had been chosen well. It was a small crescent shaped cove with calm still water, waves lapping and caressing the pink and white sand; ideal to start a project that most felt well beyond their capabilities. Some of the men were paddling in the warm sea, cooling themselves down from the heat which became like an enveloping warm wet blanket in the middle of the day. Shoes had been discarded and trousers rolled up. Most of the men wore no shirt and their bodies had begun to turn golden brown after initially suffering red raw sunburn during the first few weeks of exposure to a sun they were not used to.

John sat on the beach with Pierce, Yeardley, Strachey and Jourdain. It was blisteringly hot and they knew the work was going to be hard in the oppressive heat, but the five of them trusted Gates and understood his reasons for embarking on this massive project. John was glad he had been chosen to work with Gates, he needed to keep busy to stop himself from thinking about his personal problems.

John saw Gates and Frobisher arrive over the hill deep in conversation. Frobisher was not looking happy, but Gates was oblivious. "We will start work every morning at 6am when the heat has not begun in earnest. You can then go for breakfast and church service at 9.00am and come back to work at 10.00. We will work solidly every day from morning until 6 at night apart from breakfast and church, until the boat is built. I will be working alongside of you. Do as I do. Slackers will not be tolerated. Frobisher has told me that a ship such as the one we are going to build usually takes years to complete. We do not have that time, and I want to get to Jamestown by March - so we have roughly 6 months until completion. The first task is to gather the materials that we saved from the "Sea Venture" and bring them over to this bay. After that, Frobisher will direct us to build a seaworthy ship, enough to hold most of the passengers."

Ears pricked up at the hint of the ship not being large enough to hold all the colonists.

"So what is going to happen to those that we cannot transport?" asked William Strachey.

"We will ensure that once we get to Jamestown we come back to rescue the others. Unfortunately to build a ship as large as the "Sea Venture" would take a year or more, and we would have to fell and saw more cedar trees to have enough wood to complete it. It makes more sense to do what we can with what we have, and come back again for the others."

There was the sound of murmuring voices, but most of them nodded in agreement, knowing that if they were part of the team building the ship, it was likely that they and their families would be amongst those to sail on her. Some smiled, pleased that they might have to stay on Bermuda.

"Now let's get started, or we will never get off this bloody island!" shouted Gates throwing his fist in the air, acutely aware that Somers was not part of his plan, and would not get any credit when he sailed into Jamestown with the newly built "Deliverance". Gates of Gates Bay would be the one and only hero.

* * *

Captain Newport felt useless. He was a sailor, and his value on land was limited due to the loss of his arm. He was someone that commanded, and these skills were now sadly redundant. Somers had tried to involve him in the fishing and hunting activities, but Newport struggled with the physical aspects of these pursuits. The sea was his world, the place he stood proud and knew his worth. Now, he avoided gatherings and conversed sparingly with his fellow officers, who had each embraced differing roles in the new order of things. The sooner they could leave this Godforsaken place, the sooner he could command another ship. Until then, he would keep to himself but live in hope that they would be rescued. Desperate for something to do which did not highlight his deficiencies, he volunteered to keep the beacons lit in prominent places along the coast to alert passing ships to their existence, and to guide Ravens on his return.

This morning, having lit one of the beacons, he looked out to sea as he had done many times. His eyes scrunched up as he tried to concentrate on a speck bobbing about on the azure blue sea. Maybe it was a large bird taking a rest. As it came into focus, he opened his eyes wide and puzzlement spread across his face. "I'll be damned." He said to himself. It could only be a small boat but it definitely was a boat. How did a small boat manage to get out here in the middle of nowhere? Was it an enemy lost?

He dashed from the beacon to "The Quarter" to alert everyone to the approaching visitor, clanging the ship's bell to summon everyone. Gates and Somers appeared from their huts looking around frantically, their first thought was that something dreadful was happening.

Others also jumped to this conclusion with the women gathering up the children and taking cover and men looking for weaponry with which to defend the colony.

"Over there… " It looks like a vessel of some kind… " Newport could hardly speak as he was breathless from running. "Come quick." He shouted.

In response, the men ran down to the beach to await the first sightings of the newcomer as it navigated towards Gates Bay. They wanted to check whether it was friend or foe, and were ready for both. As a boat came into view, realisation set in, and everyone groaned with disappointment as they saw their old friend Ravens waving frantically at them.

Ravens arrived back on the shore looking forlorn and dejected. "Well, that was a short trip" he said with a false laugh as he jumped off the boat, splashing into the shallow water and starting to pull the vessel on to the beach. "Going North and West, which we took to be the shortest route, didn't allow us to get out of the ring of reefs." He was trying to make light of what happened, but his face showed the despair he felt. He knew that the hopes of the whole colony were placed on him, and he had failed. He sighed, looking at Gates hoping for a friendly response and seeing none.

Gates was exasperated. Hands on his hips, staring eyes, he marched down to where Ravens stood with the rest of his crew. "Did you not try to navigate out of the reefs? I thought you would have had more gumption than just to come back with your tail between your legs. I assumed you were more professional than this, that is why I chose you for the job." Gates disappointment took the form of anger, and Ravens took the brunt of it.

Gates knew that Ravens' journey was precarious, and the chances of him getting to Jamestown were very slim. Ravens had gambled his life for the sake of the colony. He knew he had been harsh with him, but there was no room for sentiment. A soldier had to obey orders and take the action needed to carry the order through.

Ravens' good natured smile faded. What had happened was bad enough. He was now being ridiculed with questions asking the obvious, and he knew as well as anyone that he had let everyone down. "Yes, of course we tried Sir. The swell was getting too high, and we took the decision not to risk the longboat being bashed against the reefs and punctured before we had even left Bermuda. I felt a more sensible option was to return and approach it from a different embarkation point."

Ravens was trying to defend himself meekly as he knew Gates was right. He was angry with himself for failing, and angry with Gates for not giving him a break - after all he and his crew were the ones putting their lives in danger. Surely that bought some respect. He turned away from Gates in a show of dismissal, and helped his men to pull the longboat up the beach out of the surf muttering to himself as he did so…

Those who were eager to leave Bermuda stood stony faced, hopes dashed. Those who were content in Bermuda, looked at one another triumphantly - perhaps God was working in mysterious ways to their advantage, perhaps they were meant to stay. Want and Robbie stood smiling. "I guess Gates and Somers are not going to get their own way" said Want. "Why would anyone want to leave this place... ? we have everything we want here. The only thing we are lacking is good leadership. No one consulted *us* about whether we wanted to go - did they?"

"No Johnnie, they didn't" replied Robbie. "Who do they think they are, dictating to us what we have to do. Our contract ended when they didn't get us to Jamestown."

Gates was oblivious of the feelings of many of the men, and was determined to get Ravens off again as soon as possible.

Having re-stocked the long boat, Ravens and his men set off again two days later.

This time the route, whilst a little more complicated, setting off towards the east, (through what they had come to call Somers Creek) took in the gaps in the reef that they had already navigated on landing. This failure to navigate through the treacherous reefs reinforced the fact that they had previously been extremely lucky when pure chance pushed them through the gap. God had been in their favour, and many (but not all) prayed Ravens was in God's favour as he set off again on the long trip to Jamestown. The beacon was piled high again and kept lit for many moons, in the hope that Ravens would return, rescuing them and taking them at last to Jamestown.

Some just watched him go with hate in their hearts.

Forging Relationships

T he hard work of building the new ship "Deliverance" was
well under way. They were using wood, and fastenings
salvaged from the "Sea Venture". John was with the other
men transporting building materials to Frobisher's Building bay.

Sarah continued to ignore him and he had thought a lot about Beth.
He had a vivid picture in his mind of her sitting beside him in the
firelight, as he pulled away from her. He thought it better that he
stayed away from her, concentrating his efforts on building the ship.
Alice had pleaded with him to visit Beth, and he couldn't explain to
her why he had stopped. He had decided that there was not much he
could do for Beth and that she needed her father, not him.

Robbie was working on the new ship alongside John, but for John
to approach him was counter-intuitive. He would have to think about
what he wanted to say, and to plan his approach carefully. He knew
Robbie could be a dangerous and unpredictable man, although the
threat of the resurrection of his death sentence was not far from the
surface and could be used if necessary.

John caught sight of Robbie picking up some wood and starting to
walk towards him. This was a chance that he could not afford to pass

by.

"So you are Beth's father?" John was trying to be neutral in his tone of voice, he did not want to rile Robbie or put him on the defensive.

"Yea, that's right" said Robbie. "What is it to you?" he answered, his body tensing and his eyes staring. Gentry did not usually talk to the likes of him, and he was suspicious.

"I just wanted to say how sorry I was for what happened on the skiff. I had no intention of harming Beth in any way, it was an accident."

Robbie looked at him, trying to determine what John's motives were. "I don't want to talk about it" he said through gritted teeth. "Beth is fine now, I can look after her. You don't have to come around pestering her any more. I am her father and I will do whatever is necessary for her." He turned to go.

John couldn't leave it like that, although he knew to take it too much further could be pushing his luck.

"Beth seems very anxious when you visit her. She seems to have forgotten most of what happened to her before the accident. I have been trying to help her remember and have managed to get her to trust me just a little bit. Perhaps if we met with her together, we could get her to start remembering and then she might get her voice back."

Robbie's face became flushed and beads of sweat started to appear on his forehead. He stooped down to pick up a log of wood he had dropped, losing eye contact with John.

"I don't need some hoity toity toff helping me with my daughter." He barked, standing tall and scowling, holding the piece of wood threateningly. "Keep out of our business, or you might find yourself with a few broken bones. I have friends who are on my side, and we won't put up with the likes of you." Robbie started walking away again. "She is a stupid little slut anyway, needs a good hiding, and more besides… " He smirked.

John was shocked.

"How can you talk about your own daughter like that?" John's eyes were staring with disbelief.

"As I say, what's it to you anyway?" Robbie snarled. "She's my liddle girl I can give her what she needs, I don't need *your* approval. We had a good relationship before you shot her, now she hates me". He walked towards John with the piece of wood held high. "I said leave me alone." His face grimaced, and the sweat ran down his temples as he strained with the weight of the wood.

John stood his ground. He was not going to be bullied.

"You are walking a tight rope Robbie. Remember what Gates said. I want you to put that wood down now. You will hang if you do anything silly." John spoke with quiet authority. Robbie paused.

"What kind of father are you?" John looked him straight in the eyes.

Waters threw the log with all his might into the bushes, his body slouching with defeat. "Oh fuck off you pizzle, you have no idea what you are talking about, and that little bitch is not worth the effort." Robbie turned on his heels and stomped away grumbling to himself.

John sighed with relief. He was worried though. Robbie was all mouth, but he could be a serious threat to Beth. Had he abused Beth in the past? Would he harm her now? He wondered what the real story was. Whatever it was, it was not good and knowing this, the last thing he should do was to encourage a relationship between Robbie and Beth now.

Eliza

Eliza Horton was a changed woman. She had boarded the "Sea Venture" a privileged and spoilt aristocrat disliked by the majority. Near death experience had awakened a part of her that had lain dormant since long before her cruel marriage and subsequent escape. Her warmth and compassion had been encased with hate for many years but now her gratefulness for being alive surpassed everything and brought her down to Earth. She had had to fight for her life, and these people had fought with her and for her.

In this beautiful place she had found acceptance and friendships, built on a shared need for support that her position had never before allowed her. She looked back with shame at her treatment of Lizzie, and her condescension of all but those of the highest rank, during the long and frightening voyage to Bermuda, and realised that God had reduced them all to a common denominator of fear that had no respect for rank as they tossed and heaved over the waves, sliding in excrement, nearing starvation and suffering hypothermia. The supporting hand of a servant became as welcome as a supporting hand from gentlefolk when despair and the wrath of nature raged its vengeance.

She breathed in the warm Bermuda air, listening to the call of the birds as they swooped and dived in the blue sky. So lucky to be alive, so lucky that sweet nature had turned it's other cheek and was now her friend.

Not only nature, but her fellow travellers had proved their worth. Sir George Somers was such a brave man she thought wistfully. She was not prone to hero-worship, but if she had been, Sir George would have been her hero. She had never had much respect for anyone - least of all men, since her brutal and controlling father had forced her to marry her a man very much like himself.

Her inability to have children after a savage beating, had contributed to the pent up anger that had raged in her soul for years. It had become so embedded in her psyche that she knew nothing else. When she made her escape, she had had to maintain her personae for protection, and had treated Lizzy and everyone else the way she herself had been treated for her whole life, to stop any kind of closeness. She was not respected nor liked, and she was not going to respect or like anyone else. But now she was changing. The constriction of hate was leaving her, with lightness of heart replacing it.

It was after church service and dinner, when everyone had spare time, that she chose to take a walk a little further afield than usual away from the boorish Henry Paine who, whilst initially an ally, was now becoming boring and repetitive with his constant criticisms of Somers' and Gates' audacity at appointing themselves in charge. He repudiated their right to authority, as the Virginia Company had not delivered them to Jamestown thus, so he said, breaking their contract.

As she strolled away from "The Quarter", her senses alive with the sheer beauty of her surroundings, she heard voices in a clearing next to her. She stopped to listen, at first not sure who the loud gruff voices belonged to. She turned her ear in the direction of the sound and held her breath.

"Yes, I bloody well agree, how dare they assume that we should act as their lackeys, building a ship to take us somewhere we don't want to go anyway, and that idiot Burke making us attend religious services every day is a right liberty." The voice was rough and agitated.

"We have been biding our time to take control since we put those heathens in their place. Maybe we should think about it more seriously now Want. We have everything that we need here. Food is better than London, climate is better than London - why the hell would we want to leave."

"You have to be very careful Robbie, they are keeping a special eye on you. If we do attempt something, I think you should take a low profile, and only come in when we have succeeded. If not, they will hang you."

"You have a point Want. You know that I am behind you though." Robbie was not one to put himself in danger unless he had to.

Eliza Horton recognised the voices. Robbie and Want were conspiring with several others, one of whom she knew was Christopher Carter, another of the sailors responsible for the injuries of the Indians. She decided to stay still and continue listening. This could be valuable information.

"What about you bunch of layabouts over there? - are you prepared to put your life on the line for what you believe." Robbie was reluctant to be a part of it himself, but keen to drag others into the scheme.

One by one, Eliza recognised the voices of Frances Pearepoint, Richard Knowles, Billy Martin, Jeff Briars and William Brian all acknowledging that they backed a revolt. Eliza had not had much contact with these men, except for young Jeff Briars. She liked Jeff and she was surprised to hear him conspiring with the likes of Robbie and Want, whose presence in the community had been loud and overbearing. Always being punished for not attending services, being insubordinate and rude, this group did not fade into the background easily.

"We have to play things close to our chest, and plan things very carefully. There is no reason that we should leave Bermuda if we don't want to. If *they* want to, that is fine, but their authority should not prevent *us* from staying." Want's voice was low and serious. He was the obvious leader, being less emotional and more intelligent than the group surrounding him. Intelligent and calm, a dangerous combination for an enemy, Eliza thought with dismay.

"... Maybe when they all go, we might find after a while that we would like to leave as well, but we will do that as our own choice, in our own time, and will *not* be told what to do." Christopher Carter had a sudden doubt thinking about being marooned, but tempered it with indignation.

"That being said" said Want, "we will need to enlist the help of a carpenter and blacksmith should we want to build a boat, even if it is just to get supplies if they run short, although if things keep going the way they have been going, we have food for years."

"Nick Bennit would be a good carpenter to get on our side. I am sure he is one of us. I have heard him cursing Gates many times." Jeff Briars, piped in, striving to contribute and be accepted into the group.

"There are many others amongst us that mutter about staying and curse Gates and Somers for acting in their own interests. I have even heard that religious nut Steven Hopkins grumbling about God being the only authority. That toff, Henry Paine is another one who complains and curses Gates and Somers, and I'm sure there are many more. We have to be absolutely sure where loyalties lie though and whether they can be trusted to act rather than just complain. If we approach people, we may find that they betray us and we don't want to be found out too early, before we have a concrete plan in place."

Want had been keeping a watchful eye on the whole community as he always did, looking for weaknesses and opportunities to exploit. "There are so many people who don't want to leave Bermuda for the lean pickings in Jamestown, that when we make the first move, many more will join us, I'm sure of it…. For now, I suggest that those of us working on the "Deliverance" down tools and stop working tomorrow. We can see what reaction we get, and take it from there. Hopefully many more will join us, and Gates and Somers will be overturned."

They all cheered, and as they rose from their seated positions, Eliza could see their shapes through the trees as she hunched further down into the undergrowth.

She stayed still as stone. She did not want them to discover that she had been listening to their mutinous plans. Goodness knows what they would do to her - they were all thieves and murderers, and if she disappeared, there were always feasible reasons that could be found to explain her death. The wind blew a branch of the cedar tree above her, which being old and rotten suddenly snapped, making a loud cracking sound before it landed with a crash on the ground a few feet from where she was crouched, throwing up dust as it fell. The seven conspirators all looked in her direction as she held her breath in anticipation.

* * *

Eliza breathed a sigh of relief as the seven men dismissed the sound as simply a tree branch, and continued on their way back.

She waited a good fifteen minutes before setting off back to "The

Quarter". As she approached, she saw the familiar camp fires along the beach built more for light than warmth, each with like-minded groups of people surrounding them, some laughing, some talking, some lost in thought.

Want and Robbie and their fellow conspirators were building their fire, ready for the evening of alcohol and card games. Swearing and cursing could be heard as they piled the wood high, eager to get it lit despite the warm damp humid air. They did not notice her returning from the same direction in which they had just come, innocent of what was about to happen.

Eliza knew she had dynamite information to give to Sir George and she was excited that she would be able to give him something, after all he had done in getting them all safely ashore. She unobtrusively made her way up the hill towards his hut. He had built a hut for himself not far from the main quarter, as had Sir Thomas and Captain Newport.

She knocked on the door.

"Enter if you must." Sir George's voice belted out.

Eliza tentatively opened the door, and saw Sir George sitting on a makeshift stool with the glow of a lantern casting yellow light around the room. He was looking at some documents, and he glanced up with irritation, suddenly coughing and raising his handkerchief to his mouth. He saw Eliza and groaned loudly. He did not really know her and he couldn't be bothered with her right now. He had a vague recollection of the disturbance on deck with this witch berating a young girl, and he was even more irritated when the image came to mind.

"Yes" he barked. "What the bloody hell do *you* want? I haven't got time for petty complaints."

"Sir George…." At first she faltered, having second thoughts about being bold enough to approach him. She had not expected such a gruff reception. Then she started to bristle, and the "old" crotchety

Mistress Horton could not help but respond.

"Well, I have some very important information for you, but I really don't expect to be spoken to in that tone." Some of her old confidence was returning and her voice was strong and as harsh as a school mistress. She had forgotten that this was the man that had saved them all, the man that moments earlier she had regarded as a hero. In that moment, she felt him looking down on her, and she was not having any of it, she would not be bullied. "I think I will come back when you can find a more civil tongue in your head. Then again, I think I will just forget it." At that, she turned to leave.

Sir George was not used to being spoken to like this and he was pulled up sharply. He realised he had overstepped the mark with her and had been blatantly rude.

"No, stop. Come back. I apologise." He got up from his stool and went towards her to grab her hand which she pulled away violently. "I really didn't mean any disrespect to you, it is just that I have a lot on my mind, and I am in the middle of something. Perhaps we can start again?" He smiled, trying to win her over, and his blue eyes twinkled. This was a feisty woman with a lot of insecurities, he thought to himself. He would have to handle her carefully, she was definitely better as a friend than an enemy.

Eliza looked at him smiling at her, and she could not help it as her face relaxed she returned a brief smile. Perhaps she had overreacted. She was fired up with excitement that she had something to give him, and his grumpy mood had momentarily crushed her.

"Right then." She said. She paused before continuing. "I have just been for a walk and I overheard a group of men who were talking about a mutiny". There, she had said it… that should get his attention, which is really all she wanted.

Sir George put his papers down, looking squarely at her, a deep frown furrowing his brow. He was now taking her seriously. "I see,

come and sit next to me and tell me exactly what you overheard."
He and Gates were constantly on the lookout for rebellious factions,
as they both knew that mutiny could end the mission completely,
and it sounded as though this woman had stumbled on something
important.

Sir George pulled up another stool and she sat down. She explained
everything that she had heard, and who the culprits were. She was
enjoying being the focus of Sir George's attention, and she elaborated
over and over as she didn't want to miss anything and she didn't want
the conversation to end. Her eyes were wide with excitement at being
the provider of something important. He was not looking at her as a
lowly women now.

Sir George let out a long sigh. "I was expecting something like this
to happen. We have kept a watchful eye on a few of the men, especially
Robbie, Carter and Want after the debacle with the Indians. Thank
you Mistress Horton. I am sorry I was so dismissive. I should have
known that a woman such as yourself would not be coming to me
with trivialities."

Eliza could feel her whole body inflating with pride. She looked at
him with a relaxed open smile that for the first time, in a long time,
didn't seem false. She felt free and accepted. She felt like the little girl
who had won first prize. It was an unfamiliar feeling, and one that
she liked.

Sir George felt the tension in the hut disperse as they recognised a
surprising connection between them developing. When he looked at
her and really *saw* her, there was something about this woman that
touched him. He was curious about her. He had been introduced
to her at the beginning of the voyage, and had just pegged her as a
pinched, tight-lipped, dried up spinster for whom he had no interest.
Then he had seen her as a harridan, but it seemed that she was not
really that person.

She was not young, maybe a few years younger than himself. Her hair was loosely tied with a rag, and escaping wisps of fine grey hair framed her thin, but rosy face that shone in the flickering light of the lamp. Her figure was slight with a tiny waist that could not be hidden by the rags that she was dressed in since she had had to abandon her finery. He instinctively knew that whatever she wore, her presence would be one of elegance. As her blue eyes looked at him, expecting him to say something, he could feel the blush rising in his face at his evaluation of her.

"Why don't you stay awhile and tell me about yourself" he said with a whisper.

Eliza looked at the floor. She did not want to tell him about herself, she just wanted to have this moment of friendship. She looked up and smiled, her heart was beating with the thought of staying longer.

"No. I must go Sir George. I will soon be missed, and I don't want people to know that I have been here. If the rebels found out that I have betrayed them, there could be consequences."

As she rose from the stool, she did something that she had never done in her life to anyone before, she reached over and touched his cheek tenderly, feeling his rough beard under her small delicate hand and looked searchingly into his blue eyes. It was a moment of calm intimacy, the meaning of which they both understood.

As she made her way down the hill towards the quarter, her head was in the clouds. She did not see Henry Pierce's look of disgust as he watched her come out of Sir George's hut.

Jeff and Elizabeth

⚜

Elizabeth Joons was in love with Jeff Briars. He was funny and clever. He was not handsome, but he caught one's eye with his bright red shiny and floppy locks that glistened in the Bermuda sunshine. She loved the way his green eyes flashed at her when he was teasing her, something he did with religious monotony. She didn't mind, she knew it was done out of affection. She was a plain girl who was not used to attention. Jeff kept everyone in the quarter smiling, and was often seen frolicking with the dog and the children in his spare time - a child at heart. Elizabeth thought he was wonderful.

Since landing on Bermuda, they had spent more time with one another, and she had learnt about his harsh upbringing in the workhouse in the East End of London, which bore some resemblance to her own. Bermuda, to both of them, was like a paradise neither had even dreamt existed. Both were dreading the onward journey to Jamestown, where their new found freedoms would surely evaporate back to that of servitude and poverty. They had talked for hours of what it would be like to stay here, maybe even getting married and having children.

They had not explored the physical side of their relationship. A baby at this stage, when they were both 15, would not be a welcome prospect. So they enjoyed the odd kiss and cuddle, holding themselves back from the throbbing urges that could easily have taken them to another level of closeness.

Elizabeth had been very concerned when Jeff had started to become interested in Want's plans to stay in Bermuda, rebelling against Sir Thomas and Sir George. Much as she wanted to stay, she knew the dangers of keeping such company.

"It is such an opportunity for us Elizabeth. Just think, we could stay here and never serve another rich bugger for the rest of our lives. We could build ourselves a real stone house by the beach and we could enjoy making lots of babies. I could fish and hunt, and you could look after the babies."

"It is very risky joining that bunch of ruffians. Robbie is still being watched carefully and the others will probably be hung as traitors if the scheme is found out. It seems that Gates hears about these things sooner or later. Please don't do it Jeff. I am begging you." Her eyes were pleading.

"I have promised that I will be part of it now" he said, grabbing her hand and pulling her towards him as he gave her a deep soft kiss, caressing her ample bosom and making her melt into a heart stopping silence. "Don't worry. I am a big boy, I can take care of myself."

* * *

The next day, 1st September 1609, Elizabeth woke up in the morning to the toll of the ship's bell. The bell always tolled in the morning summoning everyone to roll-call for the morning service. This was far too early for that though. She put on her clothes and walked down to the beach curious to see what was happening.

To her horror, there stood a line of men shackled together, heads down, obviously having been arrested; amongst them, stood Jeff. He looked terrified, and the smile that was always on his face had turned to quivering fear. Sir Thomas Gates and Sir George Somers stood with Captain Newport waiting for the rest of the community to arrive, so that the proceedings could commence.

Once everyone was assembled, Sir Thomas started to speak.

"It is with the greatest of displeasure that I have to announce that the men standing before you have planned to betray the community. They have decided that their authority outranks that of myself and the Virginia Company, that they are no longer going to contribute to the building of the "'Deliverance'", and they will not sail with us to Jamestown. They have decided that Bermuda is to be their home from now on, and the rest of us be damned! For crimes of mutiny, I have the authority to sentence these men to death."

Elizabeth sucked her breath in with horror at his words. She felt as if she was going to pass out. Her beautiful Jeff sentenced to death, just because he wanted to stay in Bermuda - surely this could not be right.

Sir Thomas continued … "However… Sir George and I have decided that if these men are so keen to inhabit the island on their own, that is exactly what they shall do. We are preparing a skiff to take them to one of the far off islands without provisions, so that they can set up their own community in accordance with their own wishes. They do not have to be troubled with the likes of us."

The crowd was so silent, one could have heard a pin drop. Each individual had thoughts about Bermuda, and many were in agreement with Want. The under-classes had never experienced the plentiful food or the ambient temperatures. Some felt that it was God's wish that they should stay, as He had led them here for a purpose.

Gates had had to act swiftly when Somers had told him of the impending revolt. He did not want to give the rebels time to garner support, as he knew that there were many people that secretly didn't want to leave Bermuda. He wanted to put fear into the hearts of those that harboured unspoken desires to align themselves with this group. If confidence for these ideas grew, it could mean real trouble. Hopefully this banishment might stall any future ideas that they might have, and he would gain support for not being too harsh. His first thought had been to hang them, but Somers and Newport had come up with this idea, that they felt was more appropriate, and less likely to cause uproar, whilst at the same time communicating a strong message.

As Gates finished his speech, Captain Yeardley brought up one of the skiffs that had been taken from the "Sea Venture". Gates ordered that the group be loaded into the skiff with nothing but what they stood up in. Jeff glanced over at Elizabeth, and could not smile. Her heart broke as she saw his red rimmed watery eyes.

She fell on the sand wailing. "Please, Sir Thomas, please don't send Jeff away. You know in your heart that he is not a bad lad, he has just been led by Want and Carter. He would never have done this on his own."

Gates knew that what she said was right, but he could not make an exception for the lad. He was very fond of Jeff, but he knew that the assembled crowd needed to see a strong leader who was no longer capable of being swayed. He had already gone back on his word by pardoning Robbie, and he was not going to do it again. He appeared to ignore Elizabeth, although he had heard what she said, and he walked back up the beach with Somers and Newport to their respective quarters.

Captains Yeardley and Pierce rowed the skiff out to sea, until it could be seen no more.

* * *

Arriving on the Godforsaken island that was miles from where the "Sea Venture" had landed, the motley crew of rebels were faced with having to make shelter and find food as a first priority. The weather was starting to transform from the soft warm sun and summer breezes to something a little fresher as they moved into Autumn. Rain and wind were more common now than in the Summer months. It was still not cold, but it was getting distinctly cooler, and because they were unfamiliar with this part of the world, they could not be sure how cold and stormy it was going to get in the coming months.

"For Fuck's sake" shouted Want. "We can't even do any fishing, we have nothing to fish with!" His tanned face was incredulous at having been exiled in this way. "You think they could have at least given us *some* tools so that we could catch food… "We will have to scout around and see what berries there are, to at least keep us going until we can think of something better."

"Trouble is, it is such a small island. There is not much here. There aren't even many palmettos to make shelters from." Said William Brian, one of the more practical amongst them.

"Shut up Willy, we can all see that" replied Christopher Carter. "We don't need obvious comments, we just need solutions, for Christ's sake."

"The one thing we can do, is collect some firewood and start a fire. It is going to start getting a bit cooler, and we need it for light as well." Willy replied, trying to be helpful.

"Alright, alright, lets start with the fire. It is not going to be easy to even do that because of the rain, but we have to give it a go." said Want.

They struggled and struggled, until at last they managed to get a very weak fire going. They huddled together around the fire, damp, and miserable, just looking at one another in despair.

"Does anyone know where the hell we are?" asked Frances Pearepoint.

"None of us are navigators, so we haven't a clue. I know we are in rowing distance of where we landed on the "Sea Venture", but as we don't know which direction to row in, and we don't have a skiff, that is not much help to us" replied Want sighing. "They have really done a number on us. It didn't seem too bad when he announced it. In fact, I thought it might be a good thing. But we are helpless, no better off than in a prison - and he knew that, the bastard!" Want clenched his teeth with hatred. "I will not be defeated though. I am not sure what to do yet, but I will decide tomorrow."

"Well, I think they damned well have defeated you" retorted Christopher Carter. Having a jibe at Want, who had appointed himself leader yet again. "We need a plan tonight. I think it *is* possible to escape to another island that is a little bit more hospitable than this piss hole. It can't be that far, and if we start one way and don't hit land, then we just try another way. For God's sake Want, use some imagination! If we got to the big island we might then be able to go overland and get near enough to the "Quarter" to steal some tools and food and then really start the colony that we are dreaming of despite those bastards." Carter could feel the mantel of power being transferred to him.

Want was not pleased. He was not going to surrender control. He did not like Carter, who was obviously a cut above the others, to interfere - he was the only one who should be telling people what to do. He turned to Jeff Briars.

"Jeff, tomorrow morning, I want you to scout around the island for bits of wood suitable for building a raft. I also want you to look for large thick vines or roots that would be long enough to tie the wood together. Do you understand?" Want thought that giving orders was the best way to indicate authority.

"Yes Sir!" Jeff did a mock salute. Carter smirked, he knew that Want was clinging to his position, and that was alright for now, he would play along until the time was right for a change.

"The rest of us will continue trying to make this bloody arse of the universe habitable, and see if we can produce food other than these disgusting berries. My stomach is already complaining."

* * *

Jeff whistled as he left the others in the morning. He had a day to himself, looking for materials to build the raft. He was pleased that he had been included, and had a useful job to do. He was missing Elizabeth, but felt that one day he would be back with her - he was sure this was just a temporary situation.

Want would make sure that they succeeded, and the option of staying in Bermuda was becoming more of a possibility. They had to go through the motions of this punishment, but they were not really far away, and whilst it might take them time and effort, Jeff was sure that these difficulties would eventually be overcome and they would find a place in Bermuda that was as plentiful as the original landing place that they could start to call home. He could get Elizabeth to come to the new settlement, and who knows, more people might join them.

As he sauntered over the hill from the new quarter that they were building, he came across a little bay. The sand was pink, and the waves gently lapping on the shore, made him feel that he would like a little dip in the ocean before he started the hard work of transporting wood. A slight drizzle was starting, but this did not deter him, in fact it made the dip in the ocean even more appealing.

He looked up in the sky and saw the bright and colourful ark of the most vivid rainbow he had ever seen. A new start at the beginning of a rainbow. Who knew what he would find at the end of this journey. He smiled, thinking that the rainbow was a positive omen - what a wonderful day. He stripped off his shirt and trousers and walked down to the small beach his taught young body glowing white in the sunshine. Jeff, like the others, couldn't swim, so he just lay down in the surf. He could feel the tepid waves gently washing over his body, as the light rain pattered on his face mixed with the warmth of the competing sun. He breathed in the experience as his mind floated back to Elizabeth and her plump body with its wondrous curves, yet to be explored. He was almost drifting off to sleep, when in his peaceful state he suddenly felt something wrapping around his leg.

He tried to sit up, but whatever it was had also wrapped around both of his arms and his neck. He shouted out in despair. The pain was like barbed wire digging into his flesh, so deeply that the blood was starting to ooze. He tried to grab what he thought were tentacles, frantically pulling them off his body shouting and crying with pain and fear as the tentacles clung fast.

He saw several small blue and pink balloon-like creatures with very long tentacles floating in the water, surrounding him, the largest of which, seemed to be his captor - he had no idea what they were, but he knew that he was in grave danger unless he could get himself up to standing and start removing the tentacles from his skin. He could feel the poison being pumped into him with every second that passed.

Gradually, he rose. He looked down at his body that had red lines where the tentacles had stung him leaving wheals from head to toe. Everything throbbed with pain as the poison found its mark. He was exhausted, and lay down on the beach to try and catch his breath. He felt that he was going to die unless he could get himself back to camp for help. Then he remembered in his confusion that there was no proper camp, and there was no doctor. They would have nothing but salt water to treat his numerous wounds. He started to cry, but shrugged off his self-pity and summoned the energy to get on his knees, and from there struggle to his feet; standing on wobbly legs, trying to focus.

His mind was hazy, and he could feel nothing but pain, as he stumbled on up the hill shouting "HELP! HELP!" He wasn't sure if he was going in the right direction because his thoughts were a jumble and consciousness was coming and going, only just allowing him to stumble forwards in a controlled falling motion.

Billy Martin, Will Brian and Frances Pearepoint were sitting on a log, talking about how they could fashion some kind of fishing implement, when they heard Jeff's weak voice floating through the air. They rushed in the direction of the sound recognising it as a panic call. As they neared the top of the hill, they saw Jeff fall to the ground and sprinted to reach him.

"What the Fuck?" screamed Frances, looking down at Jeff's thin white body covered in red lines of weeping wheals. "He looks like he has been attacked by a monster or something."

Billy bent down and took his pulse. "He is alive" he said, "but we have to do something. I have no idea what though." He lifted Jeff's head slightly and looked at his face.

Jeff opened his eyes whispering "It was a sea monster like a blue balloon, with long tentacles hanging down into the sea. It hurts so much, I can hardly bare it."

"That sounds like a Portuguese Man O' War" said Will. "They can be deadly, and there is not much one can do. Let's get him back to the the base at least, and then we can think of something to make him more comfortable."

They carried him back to camp and lay him on a bed made of grass. Billy and Will patiently bathed the red lines on his body with sea water. There was nothing else that they could do. Jeff floated in and out of consciousness, groaning and muttering.

Over the next few days, his condition deteriorated. The wounds left by the tentacles started to become infected, with smelly yellowing puss seeping through the bandages that they had made by tearing his clothes into rags. His face took on a grey pallor as beads of sweat broke out over his whole body. They were all fond of this cheeky young lad, and they were doing the best they could to keep him alive. They all knew that he should not have been banished with them, he did not deserve this. He was not a troublemaker - he was just a harmless boy trying to show that he was a man, and everyone knew that Gates was fully aware of that when he ignored the pleas of Elizabeth to pardon him. Now, with conditions on the island this young man's life was in the balance.

* * *

Elizabeth had been upset when Gates had ignored her pleas. Sorrow had turned into anger, the force of which she had never experienced. Determined to use the energy of her anger, she decided that she was going to take matters in her own hands. She sought the help of Captain Yeardly who had transported the rebels to the far off island, and knew where to find them.

"Please help me Captain Yeardly. Jeff did not deserve to be banished. I know you know that, everyone knows it, but no one does anything." There was desperation in her eyes, as she put her hands together pleading with him.

"I sympathise Elizabeth. I promise I really really do. The trouble is, I don't have the authority to take you to him. If I countermand Sir Thomas's orders, I will be court marshalled and who knows what will happen to me." His eyes were soft with sympathy for her.

"Please, you must be able to do something. Can't you go and ask Sir George? He might be more sympathetic. If you just asked him if you could take me to visit Jeff, nothing more... surely that would not be going against Sir Thomas?"

"Well..." George was faltering. Perhaps she had a point. If she just wanted to visit, there wouldn't be much harm in that... surely... if he had gone to prison, he would have had visitors, so there couldn't be much harm. "Ok, I will ask Sir George" he said at last.

"Oh thank you, thank you Captain Yeardley. I will never forget this." Elizabeth was smiling with hope.

That afternoon George Yeardly carried out his promise and approached Somers with Elizabeth's request. Somers recalled with shame how Gates had waived his hand dismissively at Elizabeth., and he had done nothing.

"Women," he said. "Help her if you wish, my boy. The punishment was always too harsh for that boy in my opinion anyway."

Yeardley had not expected Somers' backing for such a plan, but having received it, he agreed to take the skiff with Elizabeth to find Jeff.

It was a stormy day when George Yeardly and Elizabeth Joons set off to find the rebels. They had to navigate around the coast of Bermuda to find the Island. When it came into view, Elizabeth stood up shouting and waving, hoping to see a freckled faced red headed lad, running down the beach towards her. Instead, everyone was there but Jeff. Maybe he is on the other side of the island fishing, she thought to herself as she waved back at them.

As they approached the beach, Want and Christopher Carter ran down to pull the skiff onto the sand. "Are we glad to see you" said Want. "Your lad is in a bad way."

Elizabeth's face changed from joyous anticipation to incredulous fear. "What do you mean" she stammered. "Is he alright? Where is he?" As they led her up the beach to the little hastily made hut, her heart was in her throat. She had never thought that anything would happen to Jeff. He was so young, healthy and vibrant, he could withstand anything.

She opened the door of the hut, and cried out with horror at what she saw. His beautiful body was ravaged by red wheals oozing yellow puss and he was skin and bone as he had not eaten for days. His eyes were sunken, dull and staring. He looked up at her, and a flicker of recognition for a moment brought a smile to his lips. She took his cold damp hand in hers, and leant down to kiss it.

"My darling. We must get you back to the Quarter and let Dr. Eason have a look at you. I think I came just in time." He closed his eyes and sank into a restless sleep.

* * *

His death had been a painful one, but his last moments were spent in the arms of Elizabeth. She cradled his head as they rowed back towards the quarter, praying with all her might that he would survive. He had briefly opened his eyes one more time, and looked at her, knowing that his end was near. He tried to squeeze her hand, but all she felt was a slight pressure before his hand went limp and his eyes closed for the final time.

Elizabeth was stunned. She looked down at the only person in the world she had ever loved, and gave out a wail that could be heard by everyone at the quarter, even though they were still quite a way off. She bent down and cradled him in her arms, tears pouring down her face, stricken with grief.

The rebels, hard men as they were, could not help but feel her loss. They had been fond of this cheeky little rascal and every one of them felt as though they had been punched in the stomach when they saw him give in finally to the infections that had been ravaging his body for days. They were silent with respect as they watched Elizabeth rocking backwards and forwards holding Jeff like a baby. The scene was too heart-breaking to bear.

Landing was a sombre affair. Gates, who was the first to see them coming back, was enraged when he saw them arriving. He had not known that Yeardly had taken Elizabeth to the island, and was affronted that his decision of permanent banishment had been overruled by a mere soldier and a servant. "What the bloody hell has been going on" he shouted. When he saw the men quiet and respectful, and Elizabeth weeping, he instinctively knew he had to find out the whole story before acting.

Those on the beach ran down to the shore to see what was happening. What they saw stunned and humbled them. They had had two deaths on the island so far, that of Namontack and Edward Samuels - but Jeff had been someone that everyone had taken to their hearts.

Jeff was gently carried up the beach and placed in the nearest hut. They covered him with a blanket and left Elizabeth alone with him to say her final goodbyes. She crouched down beside him, tears rolling down her cheeks. She wanted to look at him for as long as she could to remember every freckle on his face, and every eyelash as it lay on his cheek. She looked at his mouth and imagined his cheeky grin. She looked at his hands and wrists, and imagined how warm and soft they had felt as they roamed her body. After today, she would never see him again, and she did not want to forget.

The funeral took place the following day. Rev. Burke assisted by Steven Hopkins, directed the proceedings. This death had brought everyone back to the reality of being thousands of miles from anywhere. For a time, all barriers appeared to disappear, and they were united in their grief, silent as his slender body was lowered into a grave in the red earth of Bermuda. Elizabeth wept, as the congregation sang. No one was unmoved by the proceedings, all were thoughtful with heads bowed, even the hardest amongst them had been touched by the charm of this young lad. Gates too, bowed his head in prayer, feeling for a moment, a sense of shame at his part in the boy's death. Maybe he should not have been so harsh? Maybe he should have listened to his little girlfriend? There was no doubt that the lad would still be alive if he had not been banished. He would still be cracking jokes and playing with the children.

He had to put these feelings aside, leaders always have difficult decisions to make, and there can be little time for regret. As soon as it was seemly, Gates called Captain Yeardly to his quarters.

"So tell me on whose authority you took the skiff and rescued those men, when I had given strict instructions that they were to stay there in perpetuity." Gates had found his anger again, and was prepared to punish Yeardly if necessary. His face was stern, eyes flashing.

Yeardly was ready for him. "Sir George Somers gave me his blessing. Elizabeth was concerned about Jeff, and I told her that it was not possible to see him. I told Sir George of the conversation, and he suggested I take her just to visit. Obviously when we found the state he was in, we could not leave him there, and we brought them back". Yeardly knew this was going to cause a further rift between Somers and Gates, but he was not prepared to take the flak for their petty rivalries."

The wind was taken out of Gates's sails. He did not have a leg to stand on, and he felt as if all his powers had been taken away by Sir George. He tried to hide his feelings from Yeardley, and abruptly ended the conversation.

"Dismissed". There was no point in getting into the whys and wherefores with this underling, he would have to confront Somers himself.

Patience and Confrontations

Gates marched over to Somers's hut and banged on the door with both fists, the door shook.

"Enter" Somers barked.

"You have undermined me yet again Somers. We agreed the punishment, and you went behind my back. This can't keep happening. I am trying to instill respect from a bunch of rowdies, and you are thwarting me at every turn. No doubt we will have to let those rebels stay now - which further undermines my authority."

Somers eyed Gates up and down.

"Respect is something that you have to earn Gates" he said. "It was only a visit by a young girl to her swain. Anyway, if we are talking about respect, I have a bigger bone to pick with you. Something infinitely more important. How do you expect anyone to respect you or take you seriously when you plan and plot behind people's backs to build a ship smaller than that required to take us all to Jamestown. You may not think people realise that you have commandeered all the best building materials to build a ship that is only big enough to carry yourself and your cronies, but it has not gone unnoticed. You are a self serving bastard, Gates. We are well aware that "Deliverance" will not be big enough to take everyone – we are not that stupid." Somers had started, and he continued to let his venom out. "You only have yourself to blame if this incites conspiracies and rebellion… I had expected more from you…"

Gates's face went red, and his eyes were staring. He felt like a volcano about to blow. How dare Somers talk to him like this. Indeed, he recognised that Somers had excelled in managing the "Sea Venture" in a treacherous situation on the sea, but he had hardly excelled since they had landed. He had swanned around with his friends fishing and hunting when the colony was about to implode through vicious infighting.

Gates's instinct was to respond with aggression, putting Somers in his place, but he told himself he was a better man than that. He paused to compose himself ensuring his response was measured and coherent.

"The reason we are building a smaller boat is that it would be almost impossible to build a boat the size needed to carry everyone with the meagre materials that we have. If we can build one that can carry a goodly proportion of the people safely, then we can sail back and pick up the rest. "

"People are confused Gates. On the one hand you are decreeing that we all go to Jamestown and on the other, you are not building a ship big enough. I don't get it. You are sending mixed messages."

"Well that is why "'Deliverance'" is smaller. We only have a certain amount of fastenings, wood and caulking - it is folly to try and do anything more ambitious, you can ask Frobisher" said Gates.

Somers thought he had him on the run. "That's as may be, but it is not beyond the realms of possibility to build another ship. If you really are committed to fulfilling the Virginia Company contract, another boat will have to be built and if you are not going to do it, I will. I will not allow you to take over Gates. I know you want glory, but you will get it over my dead body!

I demand two out of your four carpenters, and twenty men - I will have mariners, you keep your 'tinned' soldiers. I also want some of the building materials taken from the "Sea Venture". We need to instruct everyone that there will be a place on the boats for all of them and everyone is contracted to go to Jamestown. There will be no exceptions." Somers knew Gates did not have a valid counter argument.

Gates sighed and shrugged his shoulders. "If you must build a ship Somers, so be it. I warn you that most of the good materials have already been utilised on the "Deliverance", though, and I am not about to deconstruct anything. You will have to cut more wood and make fastenings. I will let you have the men and whatever is left of the materials. That is the best I can do."

Gates knew he had to give him something, but he was not prepared for him to have the best materials, even if some of them were still unused. This had been *his* grand plan, *his* project, the success of which would have people remembering *his* name for years. Somers' boat was just an afterthought, a copycat idea. He had been too busy swanning around fishing and drinking with his chums to seriously consider how they were going to get off this island and now after the fact he comes swanning in thinking that he can take over. Somers never wanted to leave anyway, he was only saving his image with the Virginia Company.

Gates knew he was handing Somers only leftovers to build another boat, and it would not go down well with many of the rebel factions, but it couldn't be helped, the 'Deliverance' *had* to be the superior ship at all costs, in the same way Gates was superior to Somers.

The building of another ship to be called the "Patience" began the following day.

Autumn Unrest

“So how are you feeling today Sarah?” Alice had been increasingly concerned about the withdrawn state of her friend. She had noticed that John was not often around, and when he was not helping with building the boats, he was tending the tobacco plants or playing with the children.

“Much as usual” was the non-committal answer from Sarah. The women were assembled in a large hut that had been built as a community gathering place when the weather was inclement, passing the afternoon before service and dinner. It was not as cold as England, but it was damp with driving rain and high winds were a regularity.

“I think you are looking well Sarah” said Mary, “looks like your bump is coming along nicely.” She was trying to engage Sarah whilst teaching little Giles to clap his hands.

Sarah looked at the floor with an expressionless face. If only they would leave me alone, she thought. I am six months pregnant, I don't sleep at night because of this bloody lump in my belly, I am not talking to my husband, I am a murderess and I wish I was dead, what do they want from me? It is not their fault, I know they are only trying to be friendly to me. She gathered up her strength to try and give a civilized reply.

"Yes, it probably is fine, but it feels like I have a boulder under my ribs." she said quietly. "I think I would just like to be by myself, if you don't mind. I don't feel particularly well and I don't feel like talking to anyone right now. I am sorry." With that, she got up placing her hands on her lower back and went out.

They all looked at one another and rolled their eyes. "What have we done?" said Elizabeth Joons. "We were only trying to be supportive."

"I think she might be suffering from melancholia" said Eliza Horton. "I have suffered from it in the past, and it is the most awful illness. You have no motivation to do anything, and it feels as if you just want to die."

"Oh gosh… do you think so…? What can we do for her" asked Alice.

"There is nothing that can be done for her, poor love, she will just have to get over it herself. Her husband could be more attentive, I must say, but men just don't understand. Maybe when the baby comes, she might start seeing things differently. I hope so. In the meantime, we just have to give her some space."

Eliza had started opening up to her new friends. Her transformation had continued. Her friendship with Sir George had also blossomed. She often visited him at the regular gatherings he had in the evenings with James Swift, Ed Waters and Robert Rich - sometimes John Strachey and Silvester Jourdain also joined them. She had never visited him alone again.

"What about you then Missy… " Eliza directed her attention to Lizzy Parsons, who had just become engaged to Tom Powell. "At least we have some happy news around here for a change. When is the wedding to be? Surely you don't want to leave it too long - after all, the nights are getting a little cooler now." She said with a grin.

Eliza and Lizzie now had a good relationship. Lizzie was no longer her servant, and they had put the past behind them. Lizzy looked

down at the ring made of bark that was on her engagement finger, and smiled wistfully. If only he would suggest a date…

"You are a bloody lucky cow" a sullen voice piped up from the shadows. "At least your man is alive." Elizabeth had been bad tempered since Jeff had passed away. She was angry at Gates and she took it out on anyone that was near. "I don't know what that bitch Sarah Rolfe has to be depressed about either. She has a lovely husband and a baby on the way. I would give everything to have what she has. No one understands what it is like for me. Maybe *I* have melancholia too because *I* often feel like dying."

They were all silent. Each one of them had a separate secret pain. Mary was struggling with her marriage to the violent and bad tempered Steven, and trying to manage three very small children under extremely difficult circumstances. Alice was struggling with the tiredness of pregnancy. Eliza struggled to contain her feelings for Sir George, and Beth had still not recovered from her trauma and was not speaking, confused about her feelings for John. No one knew what to say to Elizabeth.

"We must try and stick together," said Eliza, as the eldest of the women, feeling the tension in the group. "There are only a few of us amongst the men, and we can be strong and survive or we can start falling out because of the difficulties that we have been through, and end up very alone. We must be a team. We have two babies due over the coming months, and we must gear ourselves up to make sure that those babies are safe and looked after well. If anyone has a problem, we must feel free to discuss it here, knowing that it will go no further than these walls. We must learn to trust each other and become like a family. It is fine for the men - they drink, play cards and have a natural camaraderie, we must make an effort to have the same bonds in order to survive."

"You are right Eliza" said Alice. "Elizabeth, we have been very neglectful of you since Jeff's death. I think we were all so stunned and upset that no one wanted to bring it up. That was selfish of us. He was a lovely lad, and he is sorely missed by all of us. You mustn't think that your grief has gone unnoticed... Maybe you can tell us a little bit about him. I know he was a cheeky rascal" said Alice, smiling, trying to clear the air and get Elizabeth to talk.

At that moment, the bell for evening service tolled. Elizabeth shrugged her shoulders. She knew that they were only trying to help. It was not *their* fault in the first place. Gates was the one to blame; he was the one that had murdered her lovely Jeff. She would not let him get away with it.

* * *

Beth was starting to feel better. Her physical wounds had almost healed completely. She still didn't talk, but now this was more of a choice as she had found that her voice had come back slowly over the weeks. No one knew though. It was quite useful, people believing that she could not speak. It allowed her time to figure out how she was going to manage the unfolding situation.

John Rolfe had been very attentive to her. He was so handsome, and kind and sweet as well. So tall and strong. His sun bleached hair, and rippling muscles made her feel tingly inside. The night on the beach when he had held her hand so tenderly and looked into her eyes with such emotion, told her that he was very fond of her too, and she turned on the vulnerable and appealing personae when he was around, because he responded to it with warmth.

She knew that he was married, but this did not stop her having fantasies about how she and John might spend the rest of their lives together. Sarah was not really up to giving John what he needed. It was just a matter of time, until John realised that Sarah was not the woman for him. Elizabeth had been right - she was a bitch.

Robbie had killed her father and made everyone think that *he* was her father. During the weeks since arriving in Bermuda, she had had time for the fuzzy images to take clearer shape in her head, until she knew just what the situation was. She hated Robbie with a vengeance and missed her dear sweet father. Her grief for him was unrelenting. She wanted to take care of things, protect herself, and avenge her father. Now that she could talk, she could just tell everyone that he wasn't her father, and he would be dealt with - but that would be too easy. She needed time to calculate and scheme.

Beth's repressed feelings were like an unexploded bomb - a mixture of love, grief and hate. Love for John Rolfe, grief for her father and hate for Robbie Waters.

She had been planning what she was going to do with Robbie. She knew that he worked on the ship-building with the others, and they left in the morning to go down to Builders Bay at about 6 in the morning and worked all day. Gates kept an eagle eye on them and worked with them, not only guiding but grafting himself. There was not much time in the day when Robbie was alone. Sometimes, she had noticed that when he came back at 6pm, before evening Service, he wandered off up the hill - probably just for a bit of peace and quiet.

Perhaps this was the time when she could catch him unawares. It would have to be on the spur of the moment though, as his routine was not always the same.

Beth left the hut after Mistress Horton had given her speech with the other women. She agreed with all she said, but she had more important things on her mind. She caught sight of the men starting to come back from Building Bay, and crouched down behind a tree in a dip in the sand, waiting to see what Robbie was going to do. Sure enough, he peeled off from talking to his friends and started to walk up the hill. Beth let him go for a few minutes to be sure that he did not hear her coming behind him.

She then took her chance. She ran softly and quickly after him, waiting until he disappeared over the brow of the hill. She did not want anyone seeing what she was about to do. Suddenly she quickened her pace, and catching up with him she launched herself at his grubby sweat drenched back. She had a long knife that she had stolen from Tom's kitchen, and she tried to dig it into his back with repeated strong thrusts of her arm. But nothing seemed to happen. Even though he was scrawny, he was too big for her, his skin too tough, her arm too small.

He turned and grabbed both of her hands in his as she struggled frantically, mute with fear. He threw her down on the ground. This was his chance. Stupid little bitch, she was going to get what was coming to her. He hadn't really been serious about having her, but she had handed herself to him on a plate and who was he to refuse a good meal when it was offered? He held both of her hands in one of his big hands and fumbled with her undergarments as she kicked and struggled. "Come to daddy little darling" he smirked.

She could feel his large looming body on top of hers, and was powerless to do anything. This is what he wanted, this is how he liked his women, weak and begging for it. How he loved the struggle when he knew she was so small and could do nothing. He felt like a real man - in control and taking what he wanted. She screamed, finding her voice at last and struggling even more as she felt him heavy, his body fully on top of her, his stale breath hot on her face.

The knife was long since thrown into the spikey grass, leaving her powerless as her mind flashed back to the moment in jail when the two men had raped her. She finally went limp and gave up the fight waiting for the inevitable, it had happened before, and it was now happening again.

Suddenly, Beth felt his body lifting away from her. She saw a brown arm grasping Robbie around the neck, pulling him away. "You bastard. Get away from her! How could a father do such a thing to his daughter." John shouted.

Beth could contain the truth no longer. "He is not my father" she cried pitifully. "He killed my father. He almost raped me." She started crying, frustrated that Robbie had survived her attack and she had not been strong enough to finish him off. She wanted so much for him to die like her father had, she wanted to be the one who did it. It would not be the same if he hanged.

John had retrieved the knife from the scrub, and was holding it against Robbie's throat.

"Stupid little bitch attacked me." said Robbie. He was hoarse and could hardly speak, panting and gasping for breath after the target of his rampant desire had been taken away so suddenly at the point of climax. He stopped to catch his breath. "I was minding my own business, when she came up behind me with a knife." He was feigning surprise, hoping that John would relax his guard long enough to be overpowered. He knew he was stronger than John and that stupid little bitch was not going to be of any help to him.

"Do you really think anyone is going to believe that story, especially when I caught you with your pants down." John found it hard to believe that Beth had been the attacker, but looking at her unrepentant face, a flicker of doubt crossed his mind. He wouldn't blame her, especially if what she said about her father was true, and he had no reason to doubt that. It all started to become clearer.

"Kill him... kill him" Beth screamed, her face red and tears running down her face. "I hate him, he is a murderer, I did attack him, and I am just sorry that I didn't finish him off."

John pierced Robbie's neck with the knife, to let him know he meant business. Robbie had had enough, he knew he could pull back and throw John on the ground with very little difficulty. Street fighting taught a person many techniques. As this thought was forming in Robbie's mind, John pulled away and grabbed the gun that he had carried since landing.

Robbie was not expecting the gun, and instinctively lunged towards John to take it away from him.

The shot rang out in the early evening Bermuda stillness. Bird distress calls, as they rose startled from the trees, were all that could be heard in the aftermath. The small community gathering for evening service, always alert for intruders and enemies stood stock still, waiting for clues as to where the gunshot had come from and who had fired it.

Speculation was rife, as fear descended.

* * *

Gates, Somers and Newport were the first to move towards the sound. They ran in the direction of the gunshot, with their own guns at the ready. They had no idea who it was, but if there was a gun involved, it had to be hostile men.

Gates was the first to see three figures approaching them, and recognised them at once, breathing a sigh of relief. Rolfe had Robbie Waters held captive, with his hands behind his back, tied with vines. He was holding a gun to his head. Robbie was limping, with a large wound in his thigh that was dripping blood. What really surprised everyone was that the young and recuperating Beth was following behind Rolfe and Robbie, holding a long knife that pressed into

Robbie's back as he walked.

"What the bloody hell is going on? We thought we had hostile intruders." shouted Gates, relieved that there was no danger.

"It is a long story" said John, who was breathless and shaking. "This scumbag was trying to rape Beth. He is not Beth's father as he claimed - he killed her father, and he was going to kill her before she found her voice and could give the game away. He wanted to take a little pleasure before he killed her though."

"It is not true" shouted Robbie. "She attacked me." He pulled away, pointing his finger at Beth. "She is a vixen and a liar. All sweet and innocent, and not able to talk... it is all an act. She is a lying little bitch, and she knows it".

Beth looked at the ground, eyes staring and innocent. "I don't know how you can say those things Mr. Waters." She started to cry. "I found that I could speak only after you attacked me. I was so scared, my voice just came. And no, you are not my father". She paused, regaining her composure. "You killed my father, and you tried to rape me. If it were not for Mr. Rolfe, I would be raped and dead and probably floating in the sea by now." Beth started to cry again, dropping the knife and moving towards John and throwing her arms around him. "You saved me again."

"Oh pretty boy gets the prize. I am sure she has given you more than a hug in the past." Robbie smirked. "Your father was a wimp you little fraud. He couldn't take it that his little girl had grown into a whore. I am sure half the crew had a go at you - even although you were supposed to be a boy."

"That's enough Robbie." Gates got the picture of why Edward Samuels had died. He was not going to have this bastard besmirching this young girl and her father's name any more. "I am disgusted to the core." He spat.

"Take him back to the quarter. We will have to decide what to do with him there. He is skating on very thin ice, and it will take lot of persuasion for me not to hang him."

* * *

Gates and Somers had another dilemma. Surely, they had to hang Robbie this time as a message of strength to a group whose only rule was the survival of the fittest. However, he also had to remember that his primary goal was to get all the passengers to Jamestown. Any decisions had to reflect that aim.

Gates ordered that the prisoner should stand on the makeshift platform that they had erected for formal speeches. Robbie stood, defiant and looking like thunder, his hands tied behind him, blood congealed around the gunshot wound in his thigh. The community of settlers stood silently, waiting to hear what had happened.

Gates began. "Robert Waters has been found trying to rape and murder this little girl. He has also lied to us about being Beth's father. She is not Beth Waters, she is Beth Samuels. The man that he killed was Beth's father."

There was a loud intake of breath from the crowd as Robbie's lie was laid bare.

Gates continued. "This man is never to be trusted again and he should face a swift hanging for the despicable things that he has done." He paused. The crowd were silent, waiting.

"I have to consider what is best for this community. We need all the men we can muster to get the two boats built as quickly as possible for our escape to Jamestown. I have decided, therefore, to spare his life for now, so that we can use him as a workhorse. When the project is finished, I will re-evaluate the situation and he may hang then. For the moment, he just has a stay of execution, not a pardon."

Beth gasped with disbelief. What did it take for Gates to condemn a man to death. Perhaps he was just not capable of it. Robbie hanging would have been a secondary pleasure to her stabbing him to death herself, but at least he would be dead.

Gates continued. "Robbie Waters will be manacled. The blacksmith will make leg irons from the materials we have salvaged from the "Sea Venture". He will wear these at all times, and be supervised during the working day. At night, he will not only have leg irons, he will be handcuffed and tied so that there is no chance of escape. I will not have him escaping like the last time."

Gates glanced down at Waters with a meaningful stare. "This is his very last chance. If anyone tries to free him, or he tries to free himself, it will be an immediate hanging for both himself and his rescuer."

"But I am innocent" cried Robbie, now anticipating the discomfort of the irons, and the captivity that was as good as jail. His body was starting to slump with the thought of final defeat, and he spat in the dirt in frustration.

"You are past the stage where anyone will listen to your pleas Robbie. Look at Beth. Think of what you have done to her and her father. Any man that condones those actions has no morals or conscience. The punishment that I have given you is meagre for such sins, and you and everyone here knows it." Gates got down from the platform. "Take him away, and start making those leg irons as soon as possible."

"This is your fault John Rolfe. I will get you one day." Robbie cried in his last attempt at grasping some power back. No one paid him any attention.

Beth ran to Alice and the two of them hugged.

"So your voice has returned now Beth." Alice smiled at the younger girl.

"Yes, at last I can thank you and John for all that you have done for me. John was so wonderful, I just don't know what I would do without him. If I were Sarah, I would be so happy. I wouldn't be a miserable cow like she is if I were married to John."

Alice thought it a strange thing to say. "Sarah isn't a miserable cow, she is ill. And yes, she is very lucky to have him" she responded, starting to wonder where the conversation was going, remembering the distance that seemed to have been created between John and Sarah lately.

"She doesn't know how lucky she is." said Beth. "I could look after him a lot better than she could, I am sure of it."

Alice could see that Beth had a teenage crush on John as he had been her hero and saviour. She put on a serious face, and looked Beth straight in the eye, taking her hand.

"Listen to me Beth. Sarah has been very ill, and she is carrying John's baby. They love each other very dearly. I am sure you would like to look after John after what he has done for you, but that is Sarah's place and John and Sarah are very happy with things the way they are. They will be happier when the baby is born. I am sure Sarah would love you to help her and John with the baby when it arrives." Alice smiled and gave Beth a hug, she understood what it was like to have a crush at that age, it would pass.

Beth scowled; her pretty face looked dark and sulky. She knew Alice was being patronising. Her feelings were real, and she would not be deterred by such condescension. What would an old person like Alice know anyway?

"I like toddlers, not crying babies". She threw a stone in the water and watched it splash, a frown on her lovely face.

Murder of Innocents

⚜

The days became shorter, and the weather worsened. It was not the paradise that they had first been introduced to. The sea had turned from pale shades of turquoise to dark, stormy and dull, white caps lashing the coral rocks with spray. No longer were they able to sit on the beach around fires, laughing and chatting well into the evening. Nowadays, after the religious service and dinner, all retired to their own separate huts, mostly tucking down to sleep after the day's toil.

One October night, everyone was roused unexpectedly by a very loud and scary sound. It was haunting and ghostly, filling the air so it drowned out even the sound of the crashing sea. Gates, Somers and Newport opened their doors to see a sight never before witnessed.

A flock of large birds swarmed in all directions. The noise was deafening, and the numbers of birds overwhelming. They were very large and black with a white underbelly, web feet and long hooked black beaks. "COW, COW, COW"

Everyone emptied out onto the beach looking at the spectacle, fearful at first. No one knew what these birds were, or whether they might attack humans. If they did attack they could do serious damage as they were so big. Want tiptoed towards one of the birds that was sitting on the ground, and grabbed it. The bird looked at him stupidly, unsure what was happening. "COW, COW". Want suddenly broke it's neck with a crack.

"That was easy" he laughed as he held up the limp bird for all to see. "The birds are slow and stupid. We can have a lot of fun here tonight boys." He shouted. "They are plump and juicy too - a lot of foul for the pot Tom Powell" he cried.

At that, others replicated his actions, many of the men held out their hands, mocking the birds with loud cries. To their astonishment the birds landed on their outstretched arms. Men danced around, squawking and flapping arms as more and more birds landed. As each one landed, it's neck was broken and a pile was started, collecting the birds for the cooking pot.

More and more birds arrived, and more and more were killed. The pile became so big that more killings weren't necessary, but by this time, the men were having a great time laughing and killing like gruesome children in a sweet shop. There was blood and death everywhere.

Gates could see that things were starting to get out of hand. He blew the bugle, and everyone stopped and looked. "I think we have enough birds for one tonight. Tomorrow is another day, and it looks like the supply of these rather strange creatures is not going to stop any time soon."

Reluctantly, everyone stopped what they were doing, surveying the pile of dead birds that had literally dropped from the sky, innocent of their fate. This was truly a fertile place. It reaffirmed the views of many that the trip to Jamestown should never be made. Five year old Elizabeth Hopkins broke away from her mother's grip and ran towards the pile of warm dead birds.

She picked one up that was not quite dead and cradled it in to her chest. It's large black eyes looked up at her with bewilderment before it finally died. The little girl stroked it's lovely head, a tear falling silently down her cheek as she stared at her father.

Her outrage overcame her fear of her father as she yelled at him."Why have you killed them? They are God's creatures." Her little face was contorted with pain. With the innocence of a child, she understood the pointless enormity of what the men had done. It was a massacre.

"For God's sake child, we need to eat. You would be the first one complaining if you were hungry. Put the damned thing back on the pile and go to your mother. It is none of your concern. God has provided us with food, and who are you to question it!" Steven Hopkins was embarrassed that his child had been so stupid questioning what was obviously God's will.

"You didn't have to kill so many!" the little girl shouted as she ran avoiding a cuff from her father. She stooped down to stroke a bird that had landed on the ground beside her.

"I am sorry they have killed your friends" she said in her childish manner. Everyone could see that her little heart was broken, but everyone thought the killings were necessary. They had to eat after all - who cared if a few more than necessary had died, they were only birds and killing them was fun.

The following days, the birds continued to come at night. It became a nightly routine that the men went out, shouted and waved their arms around, and birds flocked to them. They were easy pickings. There was too much food. They kept on killing, hoping that they could preserve some of the meat in the salt that they had been collecting from drying out the sea water, but if not, who cared. It was good sport - a sport they knew they could win every time.

Little Elizabeth hid herself in the hut, unable to bear the constant massacre of these lovely creatures with large black bewildered eyes.

Despite a thorough thrashing from her father who demanded that she have nothing to do with the creatures, she had rescued the bird that she had stroked, and secretly looked after it in the corner of the hut. She fed it and talked to it, hoping that it would understand that she had nothing to do with the killing of its friends. Her hatred for her father deepened as her love for the bird grew and she began to understand the cruelty of man. Surely if they continued to kill so many, there would be no more left?

Tom and Lizzie

om Powell and Lizzie Persons were getting married. It had
been decided weeks ago, but the arrangements were yet
to be made. There was always some crisis or another that
prevented a ceremony. It was the first celebration in Bermuda, and
seeing the plentiful amount of food that was appearing in his kitchen
in the form of Cahows, Tom was excited.

"We can get married as soon as possible Lizzie" he had blurted out,
grinning from ear to ear. "We could have a feast, like never before,
like the gentry." he gushed. "What do you say?"

She laughed. "Of course" she said. "What took you so long? I have
been waiting for weeks, but I needed *you* to suggest a date - a girl is
never really sure until that is done. I am glad the birds have forced
you into action - although I hope 'forced' is not the word you would
use." She smiled, dimples showing in her plump and rosy cheeks.
She looked at him, so handsome with his large masculine frame and
gentle ways. "I love you so much Tom. I knew it that first time on
deck when you rescued me from Liza. What a changed person she is
nowadays. Perhaps I will ask her to be Matron of honour. Oh, I will
have to think about bridesmaids, and the children must be involved

too..." she drifted off into thoughts of her wedding and what she would wear and what it would be like.

The first Bermuda wedding, Tom thought, they were going to make history.

Lizzy could not stop talking. "You must tell Sir Thomas, Sir George, and of course Reverend Burke that we will be getting married soon - what about the day after tomorrow? We don't want those birds going bad before we have had a chance to feast on them, do we?"

She ran over to him and threw herself into his arms. He enveloped her, feeling her warmth and her ample curves, his body responded as he anticipated what was to come after the wedding. He felt her pull away. "Tom, behave yourself!" she smiled.

Without further ado, preparations for the wedding had started almost immediately and the wedding day finally arrived. Liza was the Matron of Honour, and Alice, Mary and Sarah were bridesmaids. Five year old Elizabeth Hopkins and her little sister Constance were both Flower girls, and little Giles, carried the ring (with the help of Mary) in a basket made from intertwined palmetto leaves.

Lizzy walked towards the waiting congregation with her brides-maids and flower girls, looking down at her wedding dress, smiling." I never would have believed that an old day dress that had been through the horrors of the "Sea Venture" could be turned into something as beautiful as this." Her eyes were wide with surprise.

Mary had made holes in shells that she sewed all around the neckline and hem of the dress. The mother of pearl of the shells sparkled with a rainbow of colour. The veil was made from an old net petticoat that the children had adorned with small daisies, and a crown had been made of wild flowers.

Lizzie walked barefoot on the warm pink sand, her tiny ankles and wrists were adorned with daisy chains, all picked and assembled by little Elizabeth and Constance.

The day was mild with the sun shining weakly in the autumn sky. The smell of the birds cooking in a large pit on the other side of the beach, sent the delicious fragrance of sizzling wildfowl over the crowd. The waves lapped lazily on the shore, and birds of many different species sang as the congregation waited for the bride to walk to the front. Lizzy's face was aglow. She had always imagined what her wedding would be like, and it was nothing like this - this had to be the finest wedding there ever was. She felt like a princess.

As they all gathered together, with Reverend Burke standing before them, everyone was silent as the bride approached with her bridesmaids and two little flower girls hand in hand.

"I would like to welcome you all here today for the joining in Holy Matrimony of Elizabeth and Thomas. Elizabeth has requested that we say a special prayer of thanks to God that we are here in this place of beauty". Everyone bowed their heads in prayer, all thinking how things could have ended so very differently. God had chosen to save them, and they were truly thankful.

At the end of the prayer Rev. Burke raised his hands and made the sign of the cross, blessing the whole congregation. "I bless you all, and I bless those who are no longer with us. Namontack, the heathen friend who shared so much with us, Edward Samuel who God chose to take to his bosom, young Jeff who is missed by all and of course all in the pinnace that had to be released to save us. Rest in peace." He made another sign of the cross and paused.

"Before I start the ceremony, the law dictates that I ask the congregation if anyone has just cause as to why these two people should not be joined together in holy matrimony?"

There was a pause as he waited the required time for a response. This was purely a formality. No one ever objected, but the law decreed he had to offer the opportunity.

"I bloody well object". A voice from the back of the congregation shouted as whoever it ran from the beach.

* * *

She had had enough. 'Missed by all' - what was he talking about! Jeff needn't have died if someone had lifted a finger to protect him. Gates was to blame for his death, but they *all* had to take responsibility. She was the only one that had stood up to Gates's decision and said what everyone else was thinking. No one backed her up, and they allowed Gates to continue with his stupid plan of banishing Jeff when he was not even part of that awful gang.

Now there was a marriage ceremony and everyone was being 'nicey, nicey' as if the world was a wonderful place... well it wasn't. It should have been her and Jeff getting married. They *would* have done it one day, but now they would never have the chance. She doubted if she would ever marry. No one would match Jeff and no love could ever be as strong.

Her anger had propelled her away from the stunned crowd as she ran up the hill to Gates' quarters. She had a knife in her hand that she had grabbed as she ran past Tom's kitchen. Storming into Gates' hut, she began frantically to destroy everything in her sight. Exhausted, she slumped to the floor. Holding the knife firm, she ran it over her wrist, watching her blood start to ooze in pinpricks and then gush as the cut went deeper. Blood had to spill for her Jeff. She would have liked to kill Gates, but this was even better as soon they would be united in death, if not in marriage. As she looked down and saw her life's blood pumping, peace settled on her. She laughed to herself. Now Gates would be responsible for her death as well. Let him rot in hell! She had made sure that her blood spattered all Gates's possessions, so he would never forget what he had done.

She lay down and closed her eyes feeling her heart pumping her body free of life.

The wedding was halted. Lizzy and Tom held hands and looked behind them at what was happening. Alice and Eliza Horton ran from the ceremony, recognising the voice as Elizabeth's.

They ran up the hill following in the direction of where she had gone. As they entered Gates' hut they saw the limp and bleeding body lying on the floor.

"Quick, get some rags to stem that bleeding" Eliza was taking charge.

"No, please leave me, I want to die" whispered Elizabeth.

"There is no need for you to die Elizabeth. We are here. We are your friends, and we can help you get through this." Alice was wrapping rags very firmly around Elizabeth's cut wrist and putting pressure on the wound to help it stop bleeding. "Hold your arm above your heart Elizabeth" she said curtly, anxious to stop the bleeding.

Elizabeth knew they were trying their best as her friends, but she just wanted them to leave her alone with her searing pain. She knew she was in a bad way, but that didn't really matter. The sooner she died the better. She might be reunited with Jeff or it might just be like dark dreamless sleep - either would be better than life without her beloved.

She could feel them putting pressure on her wound as she started to feel woozy from loss of blood.

"My poor darling" said Eliza. "You should have told us you were feeling so bad."

"I did tell you, but you can't do anything... What is the point. My beautiful Jeff is gone, and I want to join him. You have stopped me doing that, and I hate you." Her voice was weak, but still passionate with the conviction of her beliefs.

"Alice, let me take over here and you run down and get Edward and tell everyone to continue with the ceremony. Although Elizabeth has objected, there are no legal grounds for her objection, so Reverend Burke can marry those two young people as soon as possible."

Alice ran down the hill. Everyone was sitting on the sand, waiting to find out what had happened and whether it was appropriate to continue the ceremony. Lizzy was slumped sobbing in Tom's arms.

"You can continue Rev. Burke" Alice shouted. "There are no legal impediments as to why Lizzy and Tom should not be married. Elizabeth Joons is not feeling well, and she was a bit confused when she objected. She should be fine, so please continue."

She rushed over to Edward whispering "Edward... Edward, Elizabeth needs medical attention. Eliza is with her, but she will require stitching to her wrist if you have the materials to do it."

Everyone stood up, looking around. Tom offered Lizzie his hand as she stood up, brushing the sand from her dress. She smiled at him and he kissed her on the cheek before leading her back to Rev. Burke. Signalling the congregation to follow.

"We will continue with a prayer" said Reverend Burke.

The service proceeded with no further interruptions, and as Tom Powell lifted Lizzie's veil and kissed her, Rev. Burke pronounced them 'man and wife'. The crowd clapped and whistled. Rev. Burke patted Tom on the shoulder.

Tom then lifted Lizzie up and carried her, smiling, to the waiting feast. A shelter had been hastily made of large palmetto leaves, as the weather in November was still quite unreliable. Everyone huddled together, sitting on the ground as the golden roasted fowl dripping with fat and sizzling from the fire pit was carved and passed around. The alcohol flowed and the fragrant smell of tobacco floated through the air. The murmur of conversation hummed as contentment descended.

"That was a close call" said Henry Paine, juice from his dinner dripping from his fat face. "I thought the whole ceremony was going to collapse." He said with a laugh, amused at the misfortunes of others.

"It's not funny Henry" Strachey said. "I think the poor girl is quite ill, after what happened to young Jeff."

"Well, she just has to get over it. He is dead and that is that. There is nothing more to be said. Although I do think that bastard Gates has a lot to answer for. I have certain sympathy for those rebels - they only want to stay in Bermuda. Surely that isn't a crime. Look around you; it is not exactly Newgate here is it? Who do they think they are, dictating terms to us?" He picked up another leg of cowcow, dripping fat all over his, now grubby, stained emerald silk waistcoat.

"Gates has to maintain order, or the community will break down into chaos Henry" replied Strachey as he took a puff of tobacco to calm his rising anger.

"Well, I don't see it myself. Gates and Somers both, haven't a clue about the real world. They don't know anything. They aren't acting for the good of the majority, they only want to get to Jamestown so they are not sued for breach of contract by the Virginia Company. Fat chance of that even happening though. The Virginia Company broke *its* contract the moment they landed us here and not in Jamestown. I know a thing or two about the law." He puffed himself up to look important.

"That's as may be. But we have to stick together. The truth is, there is nothing to stop people coming back here, after we get to Jamestown." Strachey was picking at his food between puffs of tobacco and sips of berry wine. He wished he had not sat down next to this odious little toad.

"Nothing except money. Anyway, I don't think Somers really wants to go. Anyone can see he loves it here. He has even managed to get himself a lovely and willing mistress in Eliza Horton. I think such a thing is disgusting, but who can blame him if she is willing… She is a bit of an old slut really, no one seems to know her background, and I am sure her past must be seedy." Strachey's eyes opened wide. "Oh dear, maybe I shouldn't have said anything" he said in a mocking voice. "You look a little surprised that Somers and Horton are together, Strachey. Old people still have urges. Keep up with the gossip man, sometimes it is useful to know these little titbits. You never know when they might come in handy. You heard it here first." Paine smirked.

Strachey was shocked. He didn't believe that what Paine was telling him was true in the slightest. He had been with Somers and Eliza many times, and there had never been a hint of that kind of relationship. He decided to ignore it. Paine was only baiting him and if he made an issue of it, Paine would have succeeded. He got up, and 'accidentally' spilt his wine on Paine's waistcoat as he passed in a gesture of disgust, adding to the grime that was already encrusted on the protruding belly.

Steven

~~~~~~

Tedium, tedium, tedium. A routine had been set -
breakfast, morning service, ship-building, lunch, ship-
building, evening service, supper and bed. The daylight
was shorter, and Christmas came and went with only a few slight
alterations to the daily routine. Reverend Burke held a special
Christmas service, and the children had been involved in creating a
small Christmas play.

Prayers were said for Ravens on his voyage to Jamestown, who
no one spoke about, but everyone thought of. They knew that he
had probably been lost at sea, but to talk about it would make it
a certainty. The usual dinner was served, a few psalms were said
and hymns sung to commemorate their first Christmas in Bermuda.
Everyone was wondering if they would see a second Christmas in
Bermuda or whether the ships that were being built would actually
be sea-worthy enough to take them all to Jamestown.

Sarah and Alice's babies continued to grow, their bellies swelling
with every month that went past. The birth of the two babies was
something for everyone to look forward to, the first two Bermudians
would be born. Sarah's mood was muted, but she disguised her

feelings well from everybody but John who continued to try to be superficially supportive, but turned more and more to perfecting his tobacco and slaving away at building the 'Deliverance'.

Poor Elizabeth Joons had taken weeks to recover, both physically and psychologically. Gates had been uncharacteristically touched by her show of emotion. He had always felt deeply sorry for the loss of Jeff, but never shown it. Elizabeth's demonstration had brought this to the fore. He realized that Elizabeth was young, and just needed to know Jeff's life had not been swept under the carpet and forgotten, and he tried the best he could to communicate this to her. Her anger subsided, but her sadness remained.

Somers and Gates managed a cold tolerance of one another as each was in charge of a different building project. Gates was building "Deliverance" in Buildings Bay with his landsmen, and Somers was building "Patience" on the other side of the island three miles away with mariners at Shelly Bay. The separation of the two allowed for a semblance of calm underneath the turbulent waters of restrained feelings. Communication between the two leaders was done by messenger between the camps, so even talking was kept to a bare minimum.

Steven Hopkins, Mary and the children loved Bermuda. The freedom given to the children, even in the gusty winter, bore no resemblance to the enclosed and restrictive life they had left in England. Steven felt he had a certain kudos and power in Bermuda, and would be reluctant to give it up to return to his role as a merchant in Jamestown. Steven was getting more and more agitated as the progress of the "Deliverance" and "Patience" became a reality.

Prior to building the new ships, escape to Jamestown had just been theoretical, but now there was a real danger of it coming to fruition. He knew as well as anyone else that Ravens must have been lost at sea, as despite manning the lookout points tirelessly, there had been no sign of him. This increased Gates's determination and Steven's unease.

"This is absolutely ridiculous." Steven said to his wife as they sat one evening, staring at the fire as the children slept.

"Many of us do not want to leave this island, and Gates has just taken it into his own hands and overridden the views of the majority. We have a right to stay if we want to. God landed us here, and he is telling many of us that we should stay. There is no authority above that of God." He was getting angry, throwing a twig on the fire. "I will not be ordered around by that idiot." His voice started to get louder, and Mary shrank back, it was not unheard of for him to lash out at her when he was incensed about something.

"I agree with you Steven, but there doesn't seem to be anything that we can do." Her voice was faltering.

"Yes there is. I am sure we can do something." He shouted, "I am not the only one that feels this way. People have tried to rebel before. It just needs more careful planning next time. The last time, it was just a bunch of ruffians without a brain cell between them. If I could somehow get them all together, organise them and present Gates with a fait accompli, things would be different. I don't care if some people want to go to Jamestown, that is their choice. I don't want it for my family. How do we know that those ships are even going to be seaworthy? I have had enough of shipwrecks for one lifetime."

Mary tensed, looking at the floor. "It is a bit dangerous to go against Gates, he might not be so soft the next time someone tries to rebel."

"Oh you stupid, stupid, woman, you have no backbone at all. Do you really want to leave here? For once in your life perhaps you could back me on this one. It is the best idea for the children." He grabbed her arm and looked into her eyes. "Listen to me you whore, this is not business for women, so I don't want you blabbing to your little witch friends. Do you hear me?" Mary shrank back.

He was sick and tired of his wife – and his children at that. He should never have married her. His greatness was in his ability to rule and spread the word of God. His family held him back.

Mary at a safe distance ventured, "…But most of the men that would be willing to rebel are not really your sort of person, are they Steven? They are all lowlier types. Do you think they would respond well to a man of your standing?"

"You are such a negative bitch Mary. I have God on my side, and he is telling me that I must do this. I am going to start approaching people like Want, Carter and Reed - and all the others that were banished to the island. I am sure they will not have changed their minds about wanting to stay. They are just keeping a low profile for an easy life. When push comes to shove and those two ships are ready to sail, I bet they would revolt. This just brings things forward a few weeks, and gives me a chance to make my name."

He could see it in his mind's eye – he could rise to the top, he could be the leader. Governor Hopkins had a ring to it.

"Well, maybe it is worth trying to sound them out and see what happens. At least we know they are sympathisers, so it is unlikely that they would betray you to Gates."

"You are not so dumb after all Mary." He laughed a cruel laugh. She was starting to understand, he thought. Not that it really mattered.

Over the coming weeks, he did just as he said he was going to do. He approached men, individually, men that he would never usually stoop to talk to, trying to ascertain their views. It was looking good. Most of the men at first turned away from him, but as he probed a bit further and started talking about how nice it would be to stay in Bermuda. They gave him the respect he was due, and he knew he had them hooked. If he had enough support, this was going to be easy, and he felt excited at the prospect of being the instigator of the demise of the Gates regime.

"So what does everyone think" Want said, looking at the assembled group. Everyone knew that he was still in favour of staying in Bermuda, but this approach from Steven had come out of the blue.

"Well, nothing has changed about the way we all feel about this issue" said Christopher Carter shrugging.

Want felt that Christopher Carter's view was important. He was the one that was most likely to question his opinions and stand up to him. Unfortunately Christopher Carter wasn't scared of Want the way the others were, he was scared of very little and this is what made Want wary, detecting a strongly dismissive undertone when Want tried to assert himself. Would Christopher back a partnership with Hopkins? Want knew he needed his support to get the backing of everyone.

Christopher cast his eyes around the group, ensuring he had their attention. "... But we have to make sure that the time and place are right. I have my doubts about that religious little pizzle Hopkins - I don't think he is trust-worthy, and we could get ourselves hanged for conspiring with him. Partnering with him gives him a lot of control."

"That may be true," said Want, he knew this was going to happen. Bastard Carter was challenging him... "but it is our one chance to have the support of someone that has the ear of Rev. Burke, and through him the respect of many of the gentry. I am not sure we can really afford to turn this opportunity down."

He had to save face with the group. He had to win this argument. "On our own, overturning Gates is going to be difficult, as we have already found to our cost. But with Hopkins' support, I am sure we have more of a chance of it working. I am thinking it is now or never."

There were murmurs amongst the assembled men. Want knew that none of them wanted to go to Jamestown, but neither did they want to hang for mutiny - which is what everyone feared, should the details of a conspiracy with Steven Hopkins be leaked back to Gates or Somers. Who did they trust - him or Carter? Want watched their faces trying to guess what they were thinking.

He had always been their leader and they had backed him all the way since the first situation with the heathens on the boat. They had pledged allegiance to him, and were usually reluctant to start making changes, but what Carter was saying made very good sense. It *was* really risky. Who were they going to back Carter or him?

"Mmm… you may have a point there Want" said Carter. "We probably won't have this opportunity again." Want saw him looking at the group analysing the mood. He paused. "I say we do it!" Chris Carter said.

Want looked at him askance. He wasn't going to question him, but there was something very fishy going on. Why had he contradicted him and then suddenly changed his mind? Still, at the end of the day, they had all agreed, so he could start setting the wheels in motion to plan the next steps.

He looked over at Carter who was smiling to himself.

* * *

The bell tolled on the morning of Sunday 24th January 1610. What was going on thought Want?

Gates stood on the platform before the crowd of assembled citizens of Bermuda, his face like thunder. It was Sunday, and they had all been getting ready for the Sunday service and a hearty breakfast.

"It grieves me to stand before you once again with news of treachery and mutiny. This time, I was shocked to hear of betrayal by one who has been close to the formation of the colony and the establishment of religious standards. Bring the prisoner on to the platform please."

Everyone gasped, as Steven Hopkins, manacled and sobbing, was pushed on to the platform, where he stumbled and fell to his knees.

Mary was standing with an ashen face, clutching her children to her breast trying to stop them looking at their father in chains. Giles was wriggling and crying. Elizabeth held onto her bewildered tame cowcow, who fluttered with panic.

"Oh my God." Mary gasped. "What has happened. Not my Steven. He is a good man. He cannot have done anything to warrant those chains" she whispered to herself. Although doubt crossed her mind as she remembered their previous conversations about rebellion.

Want stood aghast. What the bloody hell had happened. It was only last night that they had decided to conspire with this idiot, and now he had gone and got himself arrested. Thank heavens his meeting with Steven had been scheduled for later on that day. No one could accuse him or his mates of being a part of *this* particular scheme.

"Reed, Sharpe come to the platform please." Gates beckoned two of Want's so called, mates that had only last night pledged their allegiance to him and agreed to co-operating with Hopkins. What were *they* doing there? Surely they had not been arrested as well? Want could see all the men who had been at the treasonous meeting blanching with fear. If Henry Reed and Sam Sharpe were involved, it could mean that they too could be branded as mutineers.

"You two brave men have been loyal to me and to the Virginia Company in divulging this man's plans. The whole community owes a debt of gratitude to you, which will be remembered when we get to

Jamestown."

The two men smiled weakly. Want guessed what must have happened as he watched the two men avoiding his eyes. These two were not capable of putting together a plan or having the courage to thwart Hopkins. It must have been Carter. He must have convinced them to sabotage the plans. Bastard.

Want looked around and caught sight of Carter. He was giving the thumbs up to Reed and Sharpe with a large grin on his ugly face.

"Now for sentencing." Gates carried on with the proceedings. "I have given the perpetrator of crimes the benefit of the doubt in the past. Sadly, this time, Mr. Steven Hopkins will not be so lucky."

The crowd began to rumble with exclamations.

Steven broke down. He raised his manacled hands in prayer crying out with anguish. "My dear God, please save me from this cruel fate. All I wanted was a civilised community for my lovely wife and our three young babies. Look at the faces of those children - do they deserve to lose their father this way? I am not evil - just wanting the best for my family."

Mary ran up to the front with the three children. "Look at the faces of these children Sir Thomas" she pleaded "they are innocent of crime, and yet you are sentencing them to a life without a father in a foreign land. He has been the backbone of this community, providing religious counsel to all. Surely God would not condone such an action as this. Steven is not a criminal, and has never stolen or murdered, and yet he gets the harshest sentence so far in Bermuda." She dropped to the ground, her long hair trailing in the dirt, her body convulsing with the uncontrollable tears, her children draping themselves around her body in fear.

Want wondered if Gates would give in, yet again.

He saw William Strachey walk forward, obviously touched by the scene of the mother pleading for her husband and children.

"Sir Thomas, I crave your indulgence. You know that I respect you and will obey you until the end. As a staunch servant having witnessed your past compassion, I beg you to reconsider the fate of this man. It is the children that I am thinking of. Both Steven and Mary have been positive influences in this community up until now. This is *one* stupid error of judgement. Please reconsider the death sentence.

Captain Newport stepped forward to join Strachey.

"Sir Thomas, I have to agree with William Strachey. We understand the gravity of this crime, but these children are just starting their lives. I beg you to reconsider, not for the sake of the father, but for the sake of the children. You have shown us in the past that good leaders have compassion and understanding as well as power. Please listen to your compassionate side today."

Elizabeth Joons walked slowly to the front of the crowd. She looked at Gates with piercing blue eyes that were confident and unflinching.

"Sir Thomas, I am begging you as I once begged for mercy before. Do not be hasty in your decision. You have the power to change the lives of these children for ever, as you changed mine. I am asking you in the name of Jeff Briars, to think again."

Gates looked at her and paused.

Everyone could see that he was starting to feel a twinge of conscience. He looked again at the children and the sobbing mother. He looked at the bedraggled and unlikeable Steven Hopkins. He looked at Elizabeth Joons and thought of Jeff Briars and sighed. He looked over the heads of the Hopkins family to the silent crowd beyond.

"My patience is wearing thinner with each show of rebellion that I have to put up with. Let me assure you that if Steven Hopkins' life is to be spared, this is the last time that I am showing mercy. I cannot have people taking the law into their own hands, as this would lead to chaos and anarchy. In this case, for the sake of these poor children,

I am prepared to listen to my honourable friends.

Let me make it clear that this is the very last time." He marched off the platform.

Christopher Carter looked over at Want and gave him a wink.

"Deliverance" Disaster

I t was a very stormy night in January 1610. John lay on his bed and looked up at the ceiling of their little hut. The wind was high, and the palmetto leaves sheltering them from the pouring rain rippled and hummed. He hoped the large leaves were strong enough to stay in place. He could hear Sarah's restless breathing as he watched her swollen belly rising and falling. Every now and then she tossed and turned one way, then the other - and although he knew she was semi-conscious with the discomfort of her pregnancy, she did not acknowledge him sitting there looking at her.

She rarely spoke to him during the day these days, so he did not expect her to turn and look at him and ask him what was bothering him like she used to. He knew she was in turmoil, but he felt he could not comfort her. Any show of affection towards her nowadays was met with rejection to the point of anger. So he had stopped trying.

Eustace's stone was still a comfort to him, and touching it gave him strength to carry on, remembering the pledge he made, determined that he would do something good in his life to right the wrongs of his past.

He was frightened when Sarah told him that she would not be

around much longer. What about the little child she was carrying - did she not care about it? His feelings for her were turning darker by the day. He tried and tried to think of a solution, his mind going round and round in circles. It was difficult to accept that his relationship with Sarah was over. Flashes of Beth's face came to him, and he dismissed them rapidly.

He could stand his thoughts no longer, and got up from his bed to walk in the rain, hoping the coldness would stop the pain.

Outside, it was still dark. The yellow moon flickered in and out of sight as the clouds scooted past her, driven by the howling wind. John felt the rain on his body, and the soaking coldness of it was an uncomfortable but peaceful diversion. He was shivering, but there was a freedom in being cold and alone on the pink beach, hearing the waves crashing and watching the war between sea and land as each struggled to maintain their superiority.

He set off in the direction of Tobacco bay, buffeted by the wind and struggling to maintain his balance as he walked. This was a familiar route for him. The tobacco plants had been doing well, and he was able to supply the colony with as much as they could smoke. It had been a good experiment, and over the months he had learnt a great deal about the cultivation and curing process. He wondered how the plants were surviving the storm.

As he climbed up the hill from the beach, he could see that the plants were swaying and dancing in the wind and rain. Their flexible stems laughing at the wind and soaking up the rain. He stopped at the top of the hill to watch the rolling, boiling sea in all its beauty.

The sea of the summer months, which had been a range of blues so beautiful and calm that it made you want to dive into it, had been transformed into a dark, almost black demonic syrup, topped with white spraying foam. The power of it never ceased to amaze him. He sat down, breathing in the salty smell of the sea which mingled with the deep, earthy smell of the red soil as the rain turned it to mud. All of this was accompanied by a chorus of miniature tree frogs that whistled their loudest, trying to be heard over the sound of the sea and the wind.

After a while, John decided to take a stroll over to the "Deliverance". He walked back to Gate's bay and continued on over the headland to the small bay that they were using to build the new ship. Then he saw it…

The half built "Deliverance" was lying on her side. The sea, in its fury had encroached further up the beach and surrounding the ship, was pulling her backwards and forwards in the surf. With each retreating wave, "Deliverance" was being pulled further and further out towards deeper water. If this continued for much longer, John could see her sinking without trace.

He ran back to 'The quarter' and rang the ship's bell as loud as he could. Sleepy colonists appeared from their huts, and Gates, Somers and Newport staggered to where John was standing.

"What is going on?" shouted Gates.

"The "Deliverance" is being washed away sir. If we do not do something, we will lose her."

"All men to Building Bay NOW!" shouted Gates. He was not going to ask any more questions, he could see by John's expression that this was very serious.

All the male colonists ran to Builders bay to see the pathetic sight of "Deliverance", unable as yet to float, rolling backwards and forwards like a helpless piece of driftwood.

"Surround her, and start pulling her up the beach" shouted Gates.

It was no easy task. "Deliverance" was half-built, and very heavy. The sea was battling to pull her into its foamy depths, and they had to use all the strength they had to combat the rhythmic pull of the waves. It was still raining, and the wind was still howling. The men were cold and stunned, having been woken up so early.

"We will have to use the force of the waves to help us," shouted Gates. "every time there is an incoming wave, I will shout "PUSH", and I want you to use all the strength that you have to get this boat up the beach and away from the sea. One, two, three... Push!"

At first this technique gave them a bit of leverage, but as they got her closer and closer to the beach, and into shallower water, it became more difficult as the hull dragged on the sand. "Keep going. Keep going... Push! One, two, three... Push!"

At last, "Deliverance" was more on the sand than in the sea, and they wedged her with planks of wood and tied her to stakes buried deep in the sand to stop her slipping back into the grips of the thwarted sea.

"Our first task after breakfast is to gather stones for a breakwater, and to start building a cradle further up the beach that will hold her firmly out of the water. We do not want this happening again. Thank the Lord that John Rolfe came up here to check on her, if not we may have lost her entirely."

The men were tired. They should have been cold as the rain was still beating down and the wind blowing, but the effort that it had taken to rescue "Deliverance" made each man feel like a glowing furnace. They all trickled back to the Quarter to rest and clean themselves up for breakfast and church before re-starting the building work.

Gates walked over to John and patted him on the back. "Good work Rolfe. We would certainly have lost her, if not for you. You saved the day. Thank you."

John smiled. He should have felt pleased with himself. Instead, as he watched Gates walk away, he punched his fist into the side of the newly secured ship inflicting pain trying to drown out his continued misery, but it didn't.

* * *

John's adrenaline was still high. He could not go back to his hut and Sarah - her sullen negativity was too much for him to bear this morning. He headed back over Gates' Bay and back up the hill to Tobacco bay and sat down on the familiar headland overlooking the water. The rain had stopped, and the furious wind had died down to a gentle breeze.

He closed his eyes, leaning back. He felt himself drifting off to a pleasant floating sleep that was welcome after all the tensions of the night.

His mind took him to a leafy glade in Norfolk. Sarah was there, her beauty filling his senses. The birds were singing, and the East Anglian sun was weekly warm on his body as he lay prone. He relaxed, as he saw Sarah moving closer to him, bending over him to kiss him. Another time, another place.

Suddenly he awoke to the sound of approaching footsteps. He looked up and rubbed his eyes, which were bleary from sleep. Standing before him, silhouetted against the light from the rising sun, stood Beth. Her blond hair was luminous and her blue eyes were smiling at him.

He sat up as his heart started to beat. He had promised himself that he would never be alone with Beth.

"Hello John." She looked at him, and walked over, sitting on the ground next to him. "I hear that you are hero of the day, you should be back at the quarter, everyone wants to give you a clap on the back. If it were not for you, the "Deliverance" would be lost." She reached out and touched him gently.

He felt the warmth of her small hand like a lightening bolt. His mind was racing, his body tingling. He wanted to pull away, but he could not fight his attraction to her. He did not want to fight it.

"Beth...? " he said.

She moved closer to him. He put his arm around her shoulders protectively and drew her towards his body as if she were a delicate china doll. He felt her warmth against his chest, his heart was beating. Maybe he could just enjoy a moment of closeness with her. What was the harm?

They did not move.

He could feel her breathing getting faster, and he bent down, putting his finger under her chin and lifted her face, looking into her blue eyes. She smiled up at him, willing him to come closer to her.

He lowered his head. She pulled him closer, her small arms rising to encircle his neck.

Carter

The surprised expression on Want's face at the trial of Steven Hopkins confirmed to Christopher Carter that he was now in charge of the rebels. He was determined that he was going to overthrow Gates. Clearly he had overthrown Want by his clever little deception. A little manipulation here and there... The rebels would never trust Want again. Carter knew he had always been the better leader, he was just biding his time. Luckily, most of the like-minded mariner rebels were now working in Shelly Bay with him, building the "Patience", so he had daily contact with them, able to brain wash them as he wished.

"I know that we have talked of this before, but I think the time is right to take matters into our own hands." Carter had called a meeting out of earshot of Somers, to discuss his plans.

"You know what happened last time Christopher. We just escaped being linked to that religious fool Hopkins - imagine what could have happened. We could all have been hanged!" said Want. Carter had expected this from Want. He would have done the same in his shoes. "I think we should learn from our mistakes. If word gets out Gates will never be as lenient again, he has been pushed too far too many times. It could lead to the gallows for us all." Want was struggling to save face.

"Timing and balls are everything, my man," replied Christopher with a knowing smile that put Want firmly in his place. "This time, *I* will be in charge, not some namby-pamby religious freak." Carter did not want to overtly blame Want, but everyone knew this was a put down. "I understand what we want, and I know how to get it. If everyone follows me, we will succeed. There is no doubt in my mind." Carter knew he was strong and charismatic. He had the attention of the whole group who were all mesmerized by his bold and confident approach.

Carter continued, seeing that he had them eating out of his hand. "We must act tomorrow so no one has time to betray us. If there are enough of us, and we lay down our tools and refuse to do as we are told, there is not much they can do to us. We out-number them, and I am sure many more will follow us when they know what we are planning. Gates has NO right to make us leave if we don't want to go. It is outrageous in the extreme. Jamestown is the pit of the earth, why would anyone in his right mind want to leave an island of plenty to go to that shit hole? Even Somers knows it doesn't make sense to leave. He just doesn't have the balls to confront Gates. We could easily build a new colony here and be the first citizens, claiming Bermuda for the Crown. What is Gates' problem? We are not saying HE can't go!"

"Maybe we should talk to Somers and see if he is willing to back us?" ventured Robert Chard. "If he is so keen to stay, he might be persuaded to support us, and we would have even more of a chance of succeeding."

"It is a reasonable suggestion Chard, but I am loath to trust someone like him. He is just as likely to turn on us and send us to the gallows. Sir George and Gates are not the best of friends, but he has never publicly denounced Gates. Our best chance is to go it alone. That way, we retain all the control." Carter really meant that *he* would retain control. He was determined he was going lead the mutiny. He wanted the glory of founding the Colony. He might even become Governor, he thought wryly. If Somers was involved, he would take all the credit. A thought suddenly occurred to him. "Gates is an enemy of the Colony, imposing his will on us and in effect making us prisoners. I think he needs to be taken out of the picture completely."

There was silence. He was suggesting that they kill Gates, to gauge a reaction to how serious they were.

William Brian, keen to be seen as a supporter of Carter, nodded in agreement. "I think you are right Christopher. We don't want anything getting in our way this time, and sometimes strong measures have to be taken."

Frances Pearepoint piped up "The only thing is that we want to avoid *killing* him if possible, as we want this overthrow to be something that becomes recognised by the Authorities. If we commit murder, the Virginia Company is likely to take a dim view and arrest us."

"Mmm... I hear what you are saying" said Carter. He had been way ahead in realising that killing Gates could only be a last resort. It may come to it, or it may not - but he wanted 100% backing to do whatever he felt was needed, no half measures.

"We should have enough supporters to overturn Gates' rule." said William Brian. "We have all of us, and many of them over at Building Bay are undeclared sympathisers. Robbie, for one will be glad to be back with us and have his leg irons removed. Poor bugger, he has had a rough time of it since that situation with the little blond bitch. Billy Martin has also had to work on "'Deliverance'" against his will. I am sure there are many more."

"Alright, we are all decided that we can do this, and there are others who will join us. The first thing to do is steal supplies and equipment to arm and feed ourselves. We are an army now, and we have to get as much advantage as we can by taking what is rightly ours" said Carter.

There had been very little disagreement, other than a little whining from Want who had been efficiently put in his place. Carter stopped and looked out to sea imagining himself being sworn in as the first Governor of the new colony of Bermuda - he might even meet the King! His mother had always told him he was destined for greatness, and he had always known she was right.

Want had faded into the background. Carter had outsmarted him again - or had he?

Want's Revenge

Robbie was thoroughly fed up with his lot. He had been slaving away on this bloody ship "Deliverance" all day every day for several weeks, when he didn't even want to sail to Jamestown. His leg-irons dug into his legs causing pain every time he moved, and his thoughts were consumed by hatred of John Rolfe and lust for Beth. He had almost got what he wanted from her, and even the thought of it made his head spin. That bastard Rolfe.

Most of Robbie's mates were working three miles away in Shelley Bay on the "Patience", so he couldn't even have a laugh with them anymore. There was only Joshua Chard, a rugged outlaw from the slums of Dublin to talk to. Joshua held radical beliefs, and he and Robbie, having much in common, had spent hours talking about the injustices of having to leave Bermuda.

As he sat on a rock breathing in sweet warm tobacco taking a ten minutes respite from his back breaking work, he saw Want appearing over the headland. He raised his hand to wave but Want seemed too preoccupied to see him. He wondered what Want was doing over here - he was firmly in Somers' camp building "Patience", and rarely did the two workforces mix.

Robbie watched as Want walked over to Gates who was, as usual, hard at work, his muscular form rippling with the effort of sawing wood for the "Deliverance" sweat pouring off his red face.

Gates paused with the look of strained effort turning into puzzlement when he saw Want approaching him. He turned and paused while Want said something to him. Robbie could see the two of them engaged in deep animated conversation, Gates nodding and Want gesticulating with his hands. Obviously something was going on, but he couldn't hear anything from where he was sitting. He slowly and quietly moved off the rock and moved towards the two men trying to hear what was being said.

"Are you sure about Carter?" Gates' eyebrows were drawn together. He seemed to be taking Want seriously.

"I swear to you, Sir Thomas. I know we have had our differences, but I have had a change of heart. I think that you are right about leaving Bermuda. Carter is a dangerous man, and he has the support of all of Somers' mariners at Shelley Bay. They are going to attack the store room and steal weapons and food. Your life is in danger too, Sir. If you want to save the Colony you must act as soon as possible."

Robbie did not have to hear any more. He had to get word to Carter. His friend, Want was betraying the cause that they all believed in. He could not understand it, Want had always wanted to take power from Gates, now he was colluding with him. Want must have selfish motives for doing such a thing, as he knew Want of old, but he didn't have time to think too hard about it.

Gates and Rolfe were the main enemy, and no matter how close he had been in the past to Want, his hatred of these two surpassed his loyalty to his friend. He knew that having heard of a mutiny, Gates would act quickly. All the rebels would hang, and there would be no chance of anyone staying in Bermuda, it was up to Robbie to save the day.

As he was still watched constantly, and with his leg irons, the three mile trek to Shelly Bay would take him too long, he could not tell Carter himself. The wiley Irishman Joshua was quick and nimble and loyal to the cause. Just the man to warn Carter, thought Robbie as he limped over to charge him with the task of betraying Want.

"Make sure you run as fast as you can Joshua. Gates will be there very soon, and no doubt they will be hanged if they are caught, so they have to leave *now*. Go, Joshua. Go..."

Robbie watched Joshua disappearing over the headland. Thwarting Gates and that bastard Rolfe had become Robbie's main goal in life.

* * *

As Gates arrived at Shelley Bay, he knew by their absence that someone had warned the mutineers. He spied Sir George Somers standing next to The "Patience" hands on hips looking quizzical.

"What the bloody hell, Sir George!" Gates shouted. "Where are all your men, and why are you not looking for them?"

Sir George looked up as if at a pesky insect. "I have no idea where they are my good man. I just came back and found everyone gone."

"For Christ's sake George, you should have been here supervising them. What game are you playing? If you haven't realised it, our lives are at stake here, and you seem totally unconcerned!" Gates eyes bulged, and his face was red.

"I am *very* concerned Gates, but there was nothing that I could do" murmured Somers. Gates was now speechless. Somers clearly must be on the side of his men. He had not helped them, but neither had he done anything at all to stop them. How was he expected to maintain order when his fellow officer was so obviously working against him?

As soon as Gates returned to the Quarter, the bell tolled again summoning the community.

Everyone stood expectant, yet again.

"I am sorry to say, there has been yet *another* revolt in our community. The men in Shelly Bay building the "Patience" have decided to take matters into their own hands.

Christopher Carter and his men have decided to risk a hanging in order to defy me. I want vigilance amongst those of you that are left. Anyone that wants to join the criminals, feel free to desert with them - but know that if you do, your life will be in the balance. Anyone who is caught aiding and abetting or even talking sympathetically about these rebels will be arrested as mutineers. This will have serious consequences, and as you know, I am at the end of my patience with insubordination. The consequences will be swift and harsh. We must guard the stores, and arm ourselves in case the rebels attack. For the moment, we will let them stew in the woods - they have chosen to reject the comforts that we have worked for, so let them start their Colony alone. They have tried it once and failed, and they will fail again."

"Aren't you being a little dramatic Sir George?" Henry Paine looked fed up with Gates. "Surely they are not criminals, they are only men that want to stay in this beautiful land?"

"Watch what you say, Henry. It is talk like that which will get someone at the end of a rope. I do not want to hear that kind of talk from you or anyone else. I will let it pass this time, but never... I say NEVER again. So much as a breath of sympathy will have serious consequences."

Henry Paine smiled to himself, a look of pure insolence on his face.

Gates was tempted to punish him, but he had more important things on his mind at the moment.

The other passengers stood, looking a little sheepish. Gates knew that some had sympathy for the rebels, but were scared to be open about it now.

The question in most people's minds was "What about Somers"? Everyone knew there was a serious rift between the two leaders, and that Somers loved the island. Perhaps there was still some hope that they could stay. Maybe they would have to wait to see what transpired, before committing either way.

Henry Paine smirked. Who did Gates think he was anyway?

Paine

～⚬ഉⓥℂⓥ⚬～

P aine was not used to taking orders. He was becoming tired
of all this hassle. He had only signed up for this wretched
journey as he thought it would make him rich. So far, he had
lost most of his treasured clothing and no one recognised his status.
No respect. At least if they stayed in Bermuda, he had a chance of
making something of himself. He would be one of the only gentrified
men staying, and that could be advantageous.

He had been disappointed with Eliza Horton. He had thought that
she was of like mind, but since he had seen her slinking out of Somers'
hut, she appeared distant with him, as if he was not good enough
for her. Imagine the effrontery! She was a slut anyway. At one time
he thought they could have made a good team, but he did not want
Somers' soiled hand-me-downs.

He lay back on his makeshift bed, smoking and watching the smoke
rise to the ceiling of his hut. He should have been on guard duty.
Guard duty indeed, he had never done a day's work in his life, did
they not know who he was! Anyway it was a pointless task. He was
not going to take part in guarding the provisions against people he
felt had done no wrong - it was absurd.

He heard someone walking towards his hut. "Sir Henry, you should be on guard duty. Maybe you have forgotten. I can escort you there now." It was the duty commander who had noticed his absence.

"No thank you. I think I will stay here for now." Paine replied with mocking respect, smiling and raising one eyebrow to signal the laying down of the gauntlet.

"Sir, I don't think you understand. Sir Thomas has ordered everyone to take part in patrolling against the rebels. He will not take kindly to you refusing your shift."

"Not take kindly eh? Why don't you come in here and make me then?" Paine was determined not to be spoken to by riffraff in this manner.

The Commander walked into Paine's hut and saw him lying complacently on his bed. "Please Sir, please come with me, I have orders to ensure everyone complies with Sir Thomas's orders."

"Come over here you little pizzle." Paine began to get up off his bed, putting aside his pipe.

"Sir, I don't want any violence, please just come with me... " the commander tried to reason with Paine, but he could see Paine's face distorting with anger as his large body lurched forwards lashing out, his fists flying randomly in the air as he shouted at the soldier "You little shit. Take one of the best from one of the best." Paine's fist, more by chance than skill, connected with the Commander's nose, causing blood to spurt everywhere. Paine tried to lash out again, but the commander was too quick for him, and he caught both of his hands, forcing Paine back down onto the bed and pulling his gun out.

"Oh mummy's boy has to resort to guns now does he?" Paine chuckled. He may have been beaten, but he was not going to give in. "What you gonna do now 'Soldier Boy'" Paine mocked.

The commander held the gun on Paine while he blew the whistle for help. Three more soldiers came and unceremoniously marched

Paine out of his hut and tied him to a tree. "Sir Thomas Gates will see you when he comes back from Building Bay this evening."

Paine was a large man, and his fat form rolled around awkwardly as he tried to get himself free. "Bloody fucking bastards!" Paine resorted to the language of the streets, forgetting he was a gentleman of the realm. "Do you know who I am?" He thrashed around wildly.

"Richards, keep constant guard on this man, and alert us if you need assistance." The commander turned on his heels nursing his bleeding nose, to inform Gates of what had transpired.

The bell tolled. Once again, everyone stood assembled. Most knew of Paine's arrest. Eliza was sorry, as he had been her friend at one time. She knew that he would get the punishment he deserved though, and the way he had been carrying on recently, it was his own fault.

Sir Thomas looked at the crowd. Everyone could see that he was weary.

"I am sorry to announce that one of the gentry amongst us has chosen to defy my orders. I am fed up with insubordination. I cannot go through this charade any more" he said.

Henry stood on the platform, hands tied behind his back looking at the crowd. He was attempting, and failing, to stand tall, reflecting his diminishing place in society. He still didn't think his punishment was going to be too harsh. Maybe a few days tied up with meagre rations. That should do it.

"I sentence the prisoner standing before us to death by hanging." Gates pronounced.

"What? No, it can't be. I haven't done anything. Kiss my arse you pumped up bastard of a whore." Paine shouted. He was starting to panic. He could see now that he was the sacrificial lamb intended to bring everyone else into line. "What about that lily-livered Somers, what has he got to say? or maybe he is screwing his old hag Horton!" He wanted to do some damage, to get some revenge on these power hungry pompous megalomaniacs and this was a accusation that would get attention!

The crowd stood silent, Paine could tell that they were shocked both by the pronouncement of his sentence to hang and his outburst about Eliza. It was starting to dawn on him that he may have gone a bit far.

He saw Eliza Horton run from the assembled group, unable to face the questioning faces that were gazing at her. She has as good as confirmed the truth, Paine thought. He looked around for sympathy, remembering how Steven Hopkins had been pardoned. No one was smiling. He had no supporters amongst them. He started to panic as the reality hit him. Paine looked at Gates and saw only resolve, with no mercy.

He fell to the ground, his hands still bound behind him. "Please Sir Thomas" he begged. "Please spare me."

"No."

Paine could see that Gates' mind was firmly set.

"If this is the end for me, please allow me to be shot as a gentleman and not hanged as a commoner." Proud to the end.

"Very well Paine." Gates was prepared to concede this one detail.

"Take the prisoner into the woods at sunset, and shoot him until he is dead."

The Colonists were in shock and many were scared for their lives. They were not prepared to stand up for Paine, but it made them realise that Gates had finally taken a stand. This changed everything.

Demands

Following the execution of Henry Paine, Robbie and a few others had escaped to the woods to join the rebels. They sat in a circle waiting to be told by Christopher Carter what to do next. Christopher observed the substantial numbers with satisfaction.

"Now we are all together, we must take this plan forward." He knew he had to act swiftly to out-manoeuvre Gates. "I think it is reasonable that we demand that The Virginia Company provide us with two sets of clothing each and enough food for a year. It is what they would have given us if we had gone to Jamestown. Somers has always covertly been on our side, so we can negotiate through him."

"Are you sure they won't follow the messenger and just come and arrest us and hang us?" shouted Robbie.

"We have to take that risk" replied Christopher. He didn't entirely trust Robbie as he had always been a trusted friend of Want.

"We need to let them know of our demands, and we need to let them know that we are confident that we are in the right. There is nothing in our contract about this situation. The Virginia Company have absolutely no hold over us. We are only obligated to them if we are in Virginia... and we aren't, so Gates can go stick the contract up his arse!" Everyone laughed and clapped in agreement.

Carter threw another log on the fire and watched it burn.

The next day Carter sent a note to Somers with the demands of the rebels.

Gates kept them waiting for several days, knowing this would cause anxiety. At last Carter saw the messenger approaching and smiled. He knew Gates would have to give in.

"So what does he say boy?" he smiled at the young sailor, who stood quivering with the message from Gates.

"Sir, Sir Thomas Gates refuses to give in to any of your demands. He has declared all who refuse to work on the new ships as outlaws and mutineers who will eventually be hanged. He is not prepared to spend valuable time searching for you and arresting you, so you will have to fend for yourselves, awaiting the wrath of the Virginia Company when they eventually come to get you.

However, he extends to those that are willing to come back, an amnesty. Anyone that has joined the rebel faction, but is now willing to resume work on "Patience" and "Deliverance" will be granted their freedom with no further questions asked. He says to tell you that this is his final offer and he will accept no further negotiation." The young sailor bowed, turned and ran back to the quarter, his mission complete.

The rebels looked at one another. "A good try" laughed Carter. He was disturbed by the silence in the group. They were all looking at one another, fear in their eyes.

"Come on people. Don't let one little threat worry you. He has made threats before. Don't listen to him. We have rights." His eyes were pleading now. He could tell from their wide eyes that they were starting to have doubts.

"It's all very well for you to say Chris... but if we stay, we will be marked as criminals" said Joshua. "I am not sure it is worth it. Maybe we can come back again after we reach Jamestown."

"Don't be ridiculous Josh! We are here now. Why go to all the bother of building a ship and going somewhere we don't want to go?"

The men continued to look at one another, their eyes shifty with doubt, analysing what the mood of the group was.

Two days later, Carter and Robbie sat looking down the hill towards the quarter. They were alone, having set up camp a few miles away to create maximum distance between themselves and the settlers. They could see anyone coming from the high ground, and were prepared to flee if there was any chance of Gates trying to arrest them. All of the other men had decided that the risk of becoming criminalised was too great to stay. Carter knew that they were just sheep. None of them wanted to go back, but all of them were scared to stand by their principles.

"Well, we are the only ones with any backbone then." Carter shrugged his shoulders. The two of them could not risk going back as, even with the amnesty, they both had, in one way or another, defied Gates one step too far. Bermuda had become their permanent home. This is not exactly the way they had imagined it turning out, but at least they were not going to Jamestown and they had avoided being arrested for now.

Baby Bermuda

Alice could see Eliza Horton running down the beach.

"Where is John Rolfe!" She was shouting, picking up her long skirts as she ran. "John Rolfe… has anyone seen John Rolfe?" She grabbed Will Strachey. "Will, can you go down to Buildings Bay and see if John is still there, Sarah has come into labour, and we need him to be here."

She ran towards Alice "Can you tell your husband, and get him to come to Sarah's hut as soon as possible, and could you go over to Tobacco Bay - I know John often goes over there to tend to his plants. He can't be far away. I will start boiling water and preparing for the baby."

Alice was breathless with excitement, the baby was coming. How wonderful. Maybe Sarah would get back to her old self now. The birth of Sarah's baby also marked the fact the Alice's own baby would be here soon, she could hardly contain the joy she felt. She ran up the hill and over the crest to Tobacco Bay.

Suddenly she stopped in her tracks. There was John, his arms around Beth. Alice was so shocked that she waited for a moment, not believing what she was seeing, unsure what to do.

Alice ran up the hill standing with her hands on her hips. "I cannot believe my eyes John Rolfe" she shouted, tears not far from the surface. "Sarah is down there crying with pain trying to deliver your baby, and you are here with that little fifteen year old slut, taking your pleasure! How can you be so low, no wonder Sarah is melancholic! Get yourself off the ground.

And you, Beth - how could you? This is not a game, this is a family that you are breaking up. No doubt he forced you into it, but you did not have to go along with it." Alice thought back to the conversation that she had had with Beth. She knew Beth had a crush on John, but she had never expected John to take advantage in this way.

"I want this to end now. I will say nothing to Sarah, as it will upset her and she is a dear friend." She stared at them both, hardly able to contain her anger.

John had no words. He was ashamed.

"I want a promise from both of you, that this will never happen again."

John knew how it looked, and he could not argue any further. "Yes, you have my word that I will never touch Beth again." His words were mechanical as he looked at the ground, his face was long and drawn.

Alice looked at Beth. "I know this is not your fault, but I want you to promise me that you will never be alone with this man or encourage his affections."

"I promise Alice" said Beth meekly, but with little sincerity.

"Now we must hurry, Sarah is in labour and the baby will be born soon." Alice was concerned to get John back to Sarah's side, where he belonged. She never thought John could stoop so low. It was disgusting.

They all scrambled down the hill, with Alice and John making their way to Sarah's hut.

As John and Alice entered Sarah's hut, they saw her lying on a bed of leaves, her lovely freckled face red and dotted with beads of sweat, her auburn hair lying in a tangled damp mess around her shoulders. As they entered, she looked up with pleading eyes. "John, I don't want you to see me like this." She was panting. "I must do this on my own, please go, and we will call for you when the child is born."

Alice felt for John, despite his recent indiscretion, as she could see the sadness on his face.

He passively nodded agreement, approaching her slowly and bending down, stroking her cheek and moving her hair aside to kiss her on her damp forehead. "I understand Sarah." He whispered gently. "I will leave it to Eliza, and Alice to let me know if you need me." He turned and walked out of the hut, starting to pace up and down. "No, no, no" he was whispering over and over to himself.

Alice turned to look at Sarah. Her heart was aching for her friend. She couldn't get the picture of John and Beth out of her mind.

"It is alright my love" she whispered to her. "It won't be long now. Eliza and I are here. Alice saw Sarah's face tighten with pain as her body had another contraction.

"I can't bear it Alice" she said.

"Yes you can. I am going to be doing the same thing in a couple of months." She smiled, and wiped the sweat from her brow, as Sarah convulsed once more.

* * *

As John went outside, he felt in his pocket for Eustace's stone. It was gone. He must have dropped it at Tobacco Bay in his haste to get to Sarah. He could not go and look for it now.

He heard screams coming from the hut, and knew that Sarah must be having a rough time. "Oh dear God, be kind to her" he said looking up at the sky. She had done a terrible thing, but he still wanted to protect her from pain. He grabbed his pipe and sucked hard to receive the comforting warm taste that momentarily diverted his attention. Where was that stone? He had had it since that fateful day his "Little Mischief" had died. It was only a stone after all. There are bigger things to worry about now, he thought, pacing, pacing, pacing as more screams rang through the air.

It was a long day. John sat outside the hut leaning against a tree, with his head in his hands. He sobbed quietly as the reality of the day's events filtered through his mind. When he thought of Beth, he smashed his fist into the tree with anger. It was his fault, he led her on... She was too young to understand what she had done and the consequences. He was the adult, he had to take responsibility for what had transpired between them.

Suddenly the cries that had been going on all day ceased, replaced by the sound of an infant wailing.

John stood up, expectant. He needed to know that everything was alright. Alice appeared holding a little form wrapped in a blanket. "You have a beautiful little girl John." She smiled at him and handed him the little bundle.

He felt the baby's little body through the blanket. So small and light. He looked down at her face and saw bright blue eyes staring at him in bewilderment. She was the most beautiful and perfect little creature he had ever seen. She was a miracle.

"Welcome, my little one" he whispered, tears of joy shining in his eyes.

As he held her, she started to wriggle and wail. John looked at Alice in panic thinking he had done something to hurt her.

"It is alright John" she said. "Babies always cry. It is their way of communicating with you."

"How is Sarah" he asked.

"Sarah is doing well, although very tired. She has said that you can come in and see her now if you want to."

As John went into the birthing hut holding his tiny baby, he saw Sarah lying exhausted. Her weary eyes looked at him as he entered, and she gave him a weak smile. "I did it John. She is alive."

"Yes, you certainly did Sarah. She is very beautiful. What shall we call her?"

Sarah smiled. "I think as she is the first baby born in Bermuda, she should be called Bermuda Rolfe. She is yours John, I know that you will look after her well. She deserves better than a mother like me." With that Sarah turned her face to the wall.

* * *

Sarah watched as Eliza shushed John out of the birthing hut to allow her ablutions to take place in private. Alice gave her some Cahow egg, to start getting her strength back, and she coaxed her onto her side. Alice brought the little wailing baby Bermuda to suckle on her breast which was flowing with much needed milk. Sarah lay passively as the baby was placed next to her. Alice took over and put Sarah's nipple in the baby's mouth.

Sarah sank into the makeshift bed, propped up like a zombie, doing what she was told, but not looking at the child or making any attempts to encourage the sucking. Her heart was bleeding. She felt the tickle of the little mouth on her breast and the flowing feeling as the milk poured and nurtured the perfect little baby. She loved the baby with all her heart, and because of this, she did not deserve the honour of being her mother. Others would be far more capable and worthy of looking after this helpless little girl. She did not ask to be born, and she should not have to endure a murderess as a mother.

Sarah could see Alice's alarm when she was reluctant to engage with the baby, but she knew what she was doing. She knew it was for the best.

"Oh Sarah, she is so lovely, isn't she?" She tried to spark a reaction. There was nothing. Sarah looked past the baby to the door, almost as if she wanted to be transported somewhere else. She heard what Alice was saying, but she knew there was no point in trying to explain her feelings.

Eliza looked at Alice. "She is in a bad way, Alice. I am not sure she is going to be able to look after this baby. Very often with melancholia, the birth of a baby increases apathy. I think this is what is happening here." Sarah could hear them talking, but she continued to stare into space.

"We can try to make sure that she feeds the baby, but we are going to have to have a round the clock shift as small babies need regular feeding. I only hope that her milk doesn't dry up. John is not going to be able to help, men and babies don't really mix, and anyway he seems to be overwhelmed by all this. I think it is better he leaves it to us."

"Yes, I agree." said Alice.

Sarah observed in a haze of sadness as Eliza and Alice tried everything to get her to engage with Bermuda. They stayed with her and the baby constantly, attempting to latch the baby on to Sarah's breasts when Bermuda cried with hunger. Over two days, despite all their efforts, Sarah's milk gradually dried up, and little Bermuda's howls could be heard by the whole community. They didn't know what to do. She was going to die if they could not get milk for her. Perhaps they could feed her with hog's milk?

Sarah sank further into herself. God would not let her baby die now that she had survived her birth. But God did not want Sarah to be a mother, she didn't deserve it.

On the evening of the second day, Alice noticed that when the baby cried, she felt a tingling sensation in her own breasts. She looked down and saw a damp patch on her dress. God had answered their prayers. She was producing milk for her baby, but it had arrived early to save little Bermuda. She held Bermuda to her breast and as she did so she felt a surging release as the milk started to flow. Sarah raised herself enough to watch Bermuda guzzle hungrily at Alice's breast, sighing with each tiny gulp. She watched as Alice held her tenderly and the little wizened face relaxed and snuggled into her ample breast, little hands seeking the comfort of human flesh.

Sarah was moved but didn't show it. She could see Alice feeding Bermuda, but no emotion showed on her pale and drawn face. "Thank you, Alice" she whispered in a monotone, and turned to face the wall again. She felt overwhelming grief at the loss of her baby, mixed with relief that someone so gentle and kind had taken her place. She knew God would provide someone better than her. She silently cried tears of pure agony, squeezing her eyes closed to try and shut everything out.

Alice continued to feed the restless and scrawny baby, who struggled to put on weight or achieve contentment. As much as John and Alice tried to comfort and nurture Bermuda, what she craved was her mother's touch, and her mother was too ill to offer her anything.

Sarah heard Bermuda's cries, and saw her little fists tight and thrashing with rage. All Sarah knew was that anything she could give her baby would be tarnished with evil, so she closed her eyes and ears and faced the wall.

John was frantic. He did not know what to do. He could see that Alice and Eliza were doing their very best, but he knew it was not enough. He kept coming to the hut, pleading with his eyes at Sarah, but she just ignored him. He held the little soul in his big hands, holding her to his chest firmly to try and make her feel secure and loved. Despite this, her cries were becoming weaker and weaker. His heart was being torn in two, unable to stop her gradual deterioration. Alice's milk was welcome, but she could not supply enough, so he tried to spoon feed her hogs milk that Lizzie gave him from the kitchen. He looked down at the beautiful face, stroking her brow with one finger as he tilted the spoon against her rosebud mouth. Her eyes met his and focussed for a second. He held his breath, hoping that she would take the milk from him, but she spluttered and spat it out.

A tear welled up in his eyes as he caressed her small head, feeling the soft downy white hair, willing her to understand that he loved her; that he wanted her to survive. He saw her spirit getting weaker and weaker as he struggled harder and harder to make her engage with life.

Day by day, the little soul was tormented in a life that offered her no solace. The milk that Alice offered was rich and flowing, and that given by her father was given with love, but Bermuda was now too weak and did not have the strength to take it. Gradually she lost more and more weight.

Two weeks later, Bermuda finally gave up her fight to live and passed quietly in John's arms. John was distraught that he had not been able to save her. He walked over to Sarah who was sitting in the corner silently, and placed the warm dead baby gently in her arms so that she could say her final goodbyes. "Sarah, our little one is with God now." He had anger in his heart for Sarah's abandonment of his child, but he stifled it, looking at Sarah's pathetic form.

Sarah looked down at the baby, as if for the first time, and gently ran her finger over the perfect little face, feeling every outline of her features. She looked at her little fingers and toes and ran her fingers around her pink shell like ears. Lifting the dead baby to her heart, she rocked backwards and forwards, her eyes closed, singing to her, silent tears rolling down her cheeks, soaking the baby's head with her mother's pain. Alice, Eliza and John watched unable to move.

* * *

The next day, the whole community was assembled, everyone, even the hardest of men were touched by the passing away of such a small and innocent life. Tiny Bermuda lay in a miniature casket made of woven Palmetto. Alice had wrapped her up warmly in a blanket and placed her tenderly on the flower petal mattress that Constance and Elizabeth Hopkins had collected for her.

The little baby looked like she was sleeping peacefully after the strain of her short life. Her pale white skin was luminous and looked like the finest porcelain, her eyelids were touched with the palest of purple, and her perfect little hands and fingers with tiny shell like fingernails, were placed gently across her chest. The children had made a crown of purple Bermudiana daisies mixed with fresh yellow Bearsfoot that adorned her tiny blond downy head. She was beautiful and at peace at last.

Alice brought the tiny casket to the graveside as everyone stood mute with sadness. Every now and then a sob could be heard, and even the children realised the gravity of the situation and stood quietly bewildered.

John stood with Sarah, holding her hand. Stunned with grief. It was a grey and damp morning. Bermuda had been so wonderful in her short time on earth. He would never forget her - she was safe with Eustace now, and he prayed that Eustace would take her to his heart and play with her and love her, two little ones taken to God's breast before their lives had really begun. He felt a lump in his throat, trying to control emotions from today, and from long ago. He did not have Eustace's stone as a comfort, he had to manage on his own.

He felt Sarah's limp hand in his, and glanced down at her. She was a shadow of her former buxom and healthy self. Her face was drawn, the brown freckles that had been so endearing to him, faded and dull. Her eyes were lacklustre, and silent tears were streaming down her face. Despite everything, in an act of humanity, he pulled her closer to him. She resisted, pushing him away. "No!" she shouted.

His anger started to surface. *He* had lost a baby too, but men were expected to be strong. No one understood the searing pain in his heart from the loss of this tiny life. Bermuda, Sarah and all his dreams were gone.

As the service finished, and John and Sarah walked towards the little casket, John stooped to kiss the cheek of his lovely daughter. "Bless you my little one. You will always be in my heart. He placed the little pearl that he had retrieved from the sea into her tiny hand." He turned to Sarah "Sarah, you can say your last goodbyes." He said woodenly.

Sarah looked at him with madness in her eyes, and turned and ran as fast as she could. John was distraught.

He looked up. Beth's young and eager face was looking at him with love and concern.

A tear slipped down Beth's cheek.

Somers

S omers stood facing Gates. Up until now, he had not been involved with the disciplining of the rebels or supporting his colleague. He had been told about Paine and what had been said about Mistress Horton, and he was furious.

"Damn it Eliza and I have done nothing wrong - she comes to my hut sometimes with Strachey and Jourdain just for an evening of chat and pleasantries, but nothing more. We have never met alone." He knew that this was a lie as he thought back to the evening Eliza had come to his hut with the news of the rebellious chatter - but that was a one-off, and nothing had really happened between them.

"Well, I think any contact between you has to stop. Most people thought Paine's ravings were a fruitless attempt at revenge, but she didn't help matters by fleeing. We don't want tongues wagging any further by seeing you anywhere near her. We have to maintain self-respect if we are going to hold on to any sense of authority.

"It does seem a little harsh, but I don't want Eliza's reputation to be tarnished - she is a woman of the highest moral standing." He knew that he would have to stop socialising with Eliza. His heart ached, he cared for her more than he dared admit to himself.

Gates continued. "Whilst we are being open and honest, I have been disappointed that you have not openly supported the plans to leave Bermuda. For all anyone knows, you might want to stay here yourself. You haven't even said much about your men deserting. I managed to save the situation, and I think Paine's sentencing had a big impact. Your men are all back now, apart from Robbie and Carter, but I think your backing for me has been lacking. "

Somers knew that what he said was true. He had been sitting on the fence because he *did* support his men in what they wanted. However, it would have been a bold move to openly go against Gates, and the consequences of a complete break between the two of them would be catastrophic. So he had decided just to do nothing.

"You realise that if we do not stick together, it will allow the rebels to take over again and our command will be in jeopardy. The Virginia Company will put it down to weak leadership and blame us. If I were in their shoes, I would do the same. We will be disgraced, our careers will be over and no one will want anything to do with us ever again."

Somers considered what had been said. "I am not sure it will come to that Thomas, but I suppose it is a possibility."

"For God's sake man - you can always come back to Bermuda after we reach Jamestown. You don't have to leave here for ever, but support me now when our reputations are on the line. You might even be able to come back here on behalf of The Virginia Company as Governor when we tell them the bounties that exist here."

Sir George was thoughtful. " I will try and support you from now on." He looked down at the ground, knowing that Gates was right and that he had not given things enough consideration. He started to cough again a fit that was difficult to suppress. He looked at his blood stained handkerchief. He was getting older, he was clearly sick, he just wanted a bit of peace - and he had it here on the island. To him it was like paradise, and he would gladly die here.

* * *

Eliza was so ashamed. She had been humiliated by Henry Paine, a man she had once called her friend. Just when she was starting to trust people, she felt like she was back at square one - no one would respect her again. What he said wasn't true of course, it was thought, not deed that she was guilty of.

Perhaps in God's eyes they were one in the same. She could control her actions, but how could she control her thoughts and emotions when they were so strong? She was sad that Henry had had to die, but her anger was paramount. He had destroyed her.

She heard someone coming towards her hut. It was late and dark, and she started to get a little worried for her safety.

George Somers appeared before her. Her heart skipped a beat. In his fading years he was still handsome. His eyes were the bluest eyes she had ever seen, and on his face was etched the perils of many battles, making him rugged, masculine and authoritative.

"Eliza, I had to come and see you, just to apologise for what happened, and to make sure that you were coping. I know such a slur on a woman's character can be quite devastating, and I feel somewhat responsible."

"It is not your fault, Sir George." She stood up brushing the creases out of her dress and looking at the floor. "I had a friendship with Henry and although it was not of the romantic kind, I think that maybe he felt rejected by me latterly as I spent so many evenings with you and your friends. He wanted to punish me. It is nothing to do with you." She smiled, unsure what to do or say next, she knew what she wanted to do - but that was out of the question.

"I think his hatred was more directed at me than you…" said Somers. "but that is by the by. As much as I regret having to say this, I have decided that I must never meet with you again socially. Even our evenings with my friends when you join us, innocent as they are, obviously cause wicked minds to fabricate lies. Our friendship will always stay in my heart, but for both of our reputations, it is best that we become estranged from one another publicly."

Eliza's face fell. She knew it was the only thing to do, but she felt as if her heart had been ripped out. "As you wish Sir George" she said quietly, feeling the tears welling up in her eyes.

"Damn it… it is NOT as I wish!" He marched over to her and took her in his arms roughly. He could feel her heart beating as her tiny form was crushed in his embrace.

She was surprised, but not that surprised. She knew that when two people feel as strongly about one another as they did, there was no stopping it. She did not want him to go, she did not want him to stop. She wanted him.

He pulled her to the bed and he sat down beside her. Her hands were cupped in her lap, and she was looking away from him. Her breathing was fast and her chest rose and fell betraying her feelings. He touched her face, and gently turned it towards him, looking deeply into her eyes. They sat for what seemed like ages, just looking at one another. He took her small hand in his large rough one and just held it.

He leant in to kiss her. The kiss of her lifetime, Eliza thought as she surrendered completely, the sheer bliss enveloping her. She was his, and there was nothing that she wanted to do about it. No one had ever kissed her with affection in this way.

Eventually, he gently pulled away from her and lay her down on the bed, lying next to her. He held her hand and she put her head on his chest. As he stroked her gently, they listened to one another's breathing, aware of nothing but their love for one another.

This one stolen moment had to last them until the end of their days.

Alice

I t was 18th March 1610. Alice felt her tummy. She cried out. A sharp pain joining the dull aches that had been with her for most of the night and morning made her double over. It was getting intense. She felt a gushing warm liquid on her feet and realised with excitement, tinged with panic that her waters had broken, and her little one would soon be here.

She had a flashback to the other little one, Bermuda, who had never had a chance in life and her heart did a flutter. Babies can die, she thought as the next pain punched her in the stomach.

Beth, Eliza and Elizabeth Joons were with her. Beth soothed her brow with cold sea water and Elizabeth stroked her hand. The day was blustery, and she could hear the rain falling on the palmetto leaf roof "pat, pat, pat", as she stared up at the overlapping lines of leaf veins above her, the edges of which were pouring streams of silver rain on the red earth outside. Oh how she hoped this little one would live. Too many babies in her life had died, and this one was a gift from God that she never thought she would have, after her five previous miscarriages.

She thought back to poor Sarah, how in the beginning they had talked for hours about their little bumps, planning and giggling together. How sad that it had not turned out the way they had imagined. Alice had given Bermuda as much as she could, but it was not enough, she was not her mother. She still remembered the thrill of feeling the little mouth sucking at her breast, and how she had loved little Bermuda in the short time she had been on the earth.

Another wave of pain throbbed through her body as the muscles contracted around the tiny bump in her stomach forcing it downward. "Ahh! " she tried not to scream. This was not a bad pain, it was a pain that was welcome, as it meant she would soon be holding her baby in her arms.

"God help me… " she cried as the agony of childbirth peaked to indescribable proportions.

"You are almost there Alice." Eliza was monitoring the progress of the baby, and could see that birth was imminent. "One last push my lovely" she coached.

There was a cry. All three of her friends gave out a chorus as one. "It is a lovely little boy!"

Alice strained to catch a glimpse of him, and was handed the perfect little baby who screamed healthily, his eyes startled by unfamiliar surroundings and light. Alice held him tightly as his mouth sought the comfort and food from his mother. He suckled gustily, and Alice smiled. All the unhappiness of the past was erased by that one moment. Everything was going to be fine.

Edward entered the hut smiling as he saw his beautiful wife and little son.

"Are you alright Alice. I was worried when I heard you screaming and the baby crying"

Alice laughed. "For goodness sake Edward. You are a doctor… you should know that that is normal." She took his hand and placed it on the baby's cheek.

"What shall be call him Alice?" He could not take his eyes off his little son who was still gustily sucking his mother's full breast.

"I would like to call him Bermudas in honour of the first little baby that was born on the Island." Alice had a pang of sadness and felt that the little girl could live on in spirit through her little son.

Elizabeth, Eliza and Beth left the little family to get to know one another, and walked down to the beach. Edward sat with Alice and held her hand. Alice thought of John and Sarah, and how different things were for her and Edward. She felt joy mixed with sadness.

* * *

Bermudas was going from strength to strength, and even in the short time that he had been on the earth, his personality was developing. Alice loved him with such intensity that it hurt. Maybe it would help Sarah to see him, she thought suddenly as she walked towards Sarah and John's hut. He is so wonderful, he cannot but instil happiness. She knocked on the door.

"Come in" John shouted.

As Alice entered, she saw John sitting on the bed next to Sarah who was staring at the floor unmoving.

"I just wondered if Sarah would like to see Bermudas? It might cheer her up to see a baby now it has been a while since… " Before John had a chance to object, Alice walked up to Sarah and placed the baby in front of her eyes.

Sarah looked down at the little face, and a smile flooded her face. "Oh my little Bermuda, you look so lovely. They told me you had gone." Sarah grabbed the baby from Alice and held him to her chest, looking hunted and aggressive. "Go away, all of you, I want time with my baby" she shouted. She started singing a lullaby.

"Lullay, mine Liking, my dear Son, mine Sweeting,

Lullay, my dear heart, mine own dear darling.

saw a fair maiden, sitting and sing,"

Alice was alarmed. Sarah held Bermudas too tightly, frightened that he was going to be taken away, and he started to whimper. She was looking furtively at Alice and John as they came near her. "Leave me alone" she growled through clenched teeth.

This was not the reaction Alice had expected.

"John, please do something." Alice was scared.

John jumped up and knelt in front of Sarah, looking up at her face. "Sarah, this is not Bermuda my darling. This is a little boy who belongs to Alice and Edward. You can hold him for a moment, but then you must give him back to Alice." He was whispering gently, hoping his words would get through to her.

"NO! This is Bermuda. This is MY baby. I will not have anyone take her away from me." She shouted as she held the baby in one arm and tried to shove John roughly away. The tiny baby's head lolled backwards as Alice looked on with horror, unable to do anything.

John was terrified for the safety of Bermudas, as Sarah was so unstable, he could not anticipate what she was going to do next. He lurched forwards, catching Sarah unawares and wrenched the baby from her arms, handing him to Alice.

"No, no, no... she is mine." Sarah threw herself on the floor screaming and crying, arms flailing. John stood back. Alice held Bermudas to her chest and looked with horror at her friend, unable to do anything to comfort her.

"You had better go Alice. I will see if I can calm her down once you are gone."

"I am so sorry John. I had no idea how bad things had become."

Alice left the hut with Bermudas. She felt so powerless. Sarah had been a good friend, and it was as if losing her baby had made her go mad. Poor John, maybe that is why he had turned to Beth, not forgivable, but understandable.

The Launch

There was no doubt that it had been an eventful few months. Now, things were settling down and the passengers, all thoughts of staying in Bermuda put well out of their minds, focused all their efforts into preparing to leave Bermuda.

John watched Gates rushing about doing the final preparations for the launch of the two ships. Good progress had been made, with extra attention paid to the caulking - one of the things that had let them down on the "Sea Venture". Food, in the form of Cahow meat, fish, turtle meat and hog was being salted and packed, ready for the journey. No one knew what conditions would be like in Jamestown, or indeed how long it would take them to get there. It should take under a week, but experience had taught them that nature had a way of altering plans.

Gates and Somers, who despite initial stubbornness, at last appeared to be co-operating, and the route between Building Bay and Shelly Bay was becoming worn with the constant communication between the two camps. "Deliverance" was ahead of "Patience" in development, but it had been decided that the two ships would sail together.

As the final touches were made to "Deliverance", everyone from all camps assembled to launch her into the water, where she would wait for the completion of "Patience". She had no sails or rigging as yet, but they would be added once she was in the water

Gates was shouting "Heave... heave... heave!..." Some were pulling, some were pushing, and small boats in the water had ropes tied to them and were pulling the larger ship into the waves. The weather was getting warmer, although it was not hot as it was still only April. The sea was a calm, lapping azure soup. There was excitement in the air with the final launch of the first ship.

The women and children stood on the beach watching the procedure, shouting along with Gates to add encouragement to the straining muscular men as they put all efforts into getting the ship where it belonged. No one really knew whether she would float and many a finger was crossed and prayer said. Henry Frobisher was watching, proud of what he had achieved, but anxious to see if she would be seaworthy.

Finally her hull dragged free of the beach and she was pushed deep enough to leave the sandy bottom. She was completely suspended by water, moving backwards and forwards with the lapping of the gentle waves.

"Deliverance" was half the size of the "Sea Venture", but still impressive. Frobisher stood, his legs up to his knees in the surf and stared at what he had achieved. He had thought it was impossible. He had made it happen though, and he was proud, even though it was not as perfect as he would have wanted it. Maybe there could have been a little more head-room for the passengers - maybe the hull could have been a little longer... he knew he would never be totally happy with his handiwork, but it was floating, and that was all that really mattered.

Everyone cheered and clapped. All united again with one goal.

Henry Frobisher was surrounded with everyone clapping him on the back. Suddenly he was raised into the air and there was cheering from everyone.

John Rolfe looked up at the ship towering above him. He would be so glad to get away from this island. The island had saved their lives, and for that he was eternally grateful - but his life had changed immeasurably during the ten months they had been here. Things had seemed to be looking up for him when Sarah and he had married and set sail, but now everything he had thought he had achieved, and all the hope he had had for the future was gone. He didn't even have Eustace's stone any more.

The enthusiasm he had had for taking tobacco to Jamestown had deserted him, perhaps he wouldn't even bother with that - what was the point. Everything he wanted to do was for his little daughter and Sarah, and one was dead and the other was so ill that any relationship they had had was gone. He thought of the little casket containing his tiny baby, her beautiful little head crowned with flowers, and his heart pounded in his chest with grief. He had to leave her here, the perfect pearl his only legacy to her. He was alone again.

Beth was playing in the surf with Giles, Constance and Elizabeth. She looked up and saw John, and their eyes locked. He turned away.

He sat in the sand, his head in his hands staring at the sand in his own world trying to block everything out.

"I am so sorry John, for the death of your little baby. She was truly beautiful" a voice said.

He looked up with blurry eyes, trying to take in who it was that had spoken to him and what she had said. He paused. "It doesn't matter now Beth. Nothing really matters to me any more."

Her heart was breaking. "Don't say that John. Things will be better in time."

"How the hell do YOU know, you have only been on the earth 15 years - you know nothing of time or heartbreak." He was angry. Not with her, but with life.

Beth drew back, not expecting her lovely John to be so cruel. "Oh, I know of heartbreak enough. First my mother, then my father, and now you. I know we should never have kissed but I love you, and I thought you loved me."

John looked up. She had had a lot to deal with in her 15 years. He managed to pull his thoughts away from his own self-pity. She was only young. "Beth, what happened was my fault. I should not have taken advantage of you. Perhaps there is something special between us, but you are too young, and I am married. I cannot deny that I have feelings for you, but it can never be."

"I know John. It is alright. I understand."

She smiled and held out her hand sheepishly. "I took this from you" she said as she held Eustace's stone in her hand. "I am sorry, but I only wanted something of yours to hold next to my heart. I don't need it any more. You will always be in my heart anyway, with or without the stone, whether you like it or not."

He took the stone from her and turned it around and around with his fingers, remembering where it came from. "Thank you for returning it Beth. It means more to me than you will ever know." John got up from the sand and made his way back to the hut to see Sarah, leaving Beth staring wistfully after him.

Alice had seen the brief encounter between Beth and John and she watched as John slowly returned to his hut. Maybe the two of them had come to their senses.

Leaving Paradise

⁓ ❧ ⁓

The Island had been their saviour, but despite being provided with food, shelter and seemingly no cares in the world, the happiness of many was sabotaged by the vagaries of human nature. The passengers assembled on the beach for one last service of thanks, each deep in thought about what the last ten months had meant for them.

Some, such as Tom Powell and Elizabeth Parsons stood hand in hand treasuring the memories of their blossoming romance and wedding. Others, like Elizabeth Joons, Sarah and John Rolfe had been deeply scarred by their time on this beautiful island. There was regret for many, including Sir George Somers, at leaving a paradise too good to be true.

As Reverend Burke read the bible and blessed the island, thanking God for landing them there safely, he thought how ironic it all had been. God had given them paradise and what had man done with it? He had over-fished, killed far too many birds and turtles for what they needed and fought amongst themselves incessantly. Maybe it was true, the Garden of Eden could not be cherished and loved by man. Man was compelled to destroy. Reverend Burke sighed with despair. If men could not be peaceful and kind here - there was no hope.

If only the island could be left alone now, without further disturbance from man, nature could rebuild the damage that had been done. He knew this was a forlorn hope though. There were too many resources for the greed of man to leave her in peace. Only the children understood - but sadly they would grow up to be like their parents, except for little Bermuda who would stay here forever in her bounteous paradise. Christopher Carter and Robbie Waters were the legacy that they were leaving in Bermuda to further destroy this paradise.

The ships were ready for embarkation. Days had been spent loading food and supplies, and now the passengers started to board. It was like a flashback. The last time they had boarded a ship, they had not realised what lay ahead, any more than they did today.

John led Sarah down the beach to board "Deliverance".

"No, leave me alone John. I cannot leave my baby" she struggled and kicked him. "I will not go!"

"Sarah, please… we have to go my darling. Little Bermuda is dead." He tried to pull her arm, but she struggled and ran back.

John ran after her and grabbed her. She fell on the sand screaming and crying. "No, no leave me alone. I have to stay with Bermuda."

John shook his head looking down at the writhing figure on the sand. "Please come with me Sarah. I can't leave you here in Bermuda with two criminals. We have to go." He bent down and picked her small wriggling form from the sand, and carried her down the beach sobbing into his shoulder. He took her down to the passenger deck and made her as comfortable as he could. She was as far away from Alice and her baby as she could be. "Mary, could you keep an eye on Sarah for me." He looked at her with pleading eyes, he had to get some air.

Eliza stood up. "It's alright John, I will look after her." She smiled, her eyes soft with compassion.

John went up on deck to help Newport who was commanding "'Deliverance". Somers was commanding "Patience" which was following behind.

John stood watching as the anchor was lifted and all the ropes untied.

Two faces stood on the beach out of reach of the now departing ships. Christopher Carter and Robbie Waters watched as the ships made ready to go. "Well good riddance" grumbled Carter.

"Now we have a chance for a bit of peace." Replied Robbie. They looked around at the empty beach. They could have their pick of huts, and there was plenty of food left. Still… could they survive with only each other? They both looked at one another, there was no going back now, they were imprisoned in paradise.

The ships moved away from the place they had called home for ten months, circumnavigating the shore until finding the escape route through the dreaded rocks. At last, Bermuda was fading from the horizon. Everyone could remember the excitement of seeing the landmass from the "Sea Venture". Now it was all hands on deck to re-commence the voyage to their original destination, and John for one, had no regrets about leaving. John was feeling so desperate just to get away from this 'Devil' island, that he had deliberately left the tobacco. He wanted as few memories of this place as possible.

As he stood on deck, he saw Matchumps approaching him. Matchumps had stayed away from the settlers on Bermuda, preferring to be on his own, in his little den, modelled on Powhatan design. He had helped John with the growing of tobacco, but once John had established the crop, he had disappeared once again. John thought with regret that the Indian may be missing his dead friend, the cause of Sarah's breakdown.

"Sir" stuttered Matchumps. "Sir, I think you forgot something." Matchumps smiled at him handing him a container". His brown eyes were twinkling.

John looked down at what he had given him, surprise on his face. "Oh what is this Matchumps?" he asked looking into the brown eyes. John had been the only one that had spoken to Matchumps during their stay in Bermuda, and although they were not friends, they held a mutual respect for one another.

"It is your seeds and some of your tobacco." Matchumps smiled. "I think you forgot to bring it."

Matchumps had seen John two days previously, collecting a container of tobacco seeds which suddenly and without provocation he had thrown angrily to the wind shouting "it is all useless". Matchumps guessed this to be an act of defiance against a God that had taken his little girl from him. Even the white man's God was cruel, but sometimes friends can see things more clearly. He had decided to collect more seeds and give them to John. He knew the tobacco was special, and John had worked hard to learn about its cultivation and curing, and such knowledge should not be wasted. Something good should come of these white men invading this island.

"Thank you Matchumps." John was surprised that the heathen had approached him. He had not even been aware that anyone knew he wanted to cultivate the seeds in Jamestown. He took the seeds and shook Matchumps' hand. "I wish you well, my friend" he said.

Matchumps bowed his head, putting his hands together in front of his heart.

"And you" Matchumps replied.

John smiled at him as Matchumps walked away. It was strange that everyone had referred to Matchumps as a 'heathen'. John thought of the irony of the behaviours of the white men in Bermuda. He wondered who was the more civilized race – Indian or English?

He looked down at the seeds that Matchumps had given him. He had left them, but maybe he could not avoid what was meant to be. Maybe they would be the one thing that he took from this island of heartbreak, which was positive – there was nothing else.

The ships were making good progress. The wind was strong but tame, in stark contrast to the hurricane that had last whipped through their sails ten months previously. Life on board ship resumed with Reverend Burke holding his services and meagre meals being served. They wanted to preserve as much of the food as they could, as they did not know what was going to face them when they finally reached Jamestown. The hope was that all the other ships had reached their destination, and that there would be upwards of 600 people and a thriving and plentiful community waiting for them.

Sir Thomas Gates had kept the Virginia Company orders safe, so that he could resume command as soon as they arrived.

The "Deliverance" was ploughing through the waves, spray flying, hull rising and dipping with the swell, dolphins diving and surfacing, grinning at them as they passed. John stood for a moment, feeling the freshness on his face and smiling at the friendly dolphins as they raced. He was brown and healthy from the outdoor work and the plentiful food, although the strains on his face from the emotional burdens that he had carried were etched deep.

He looked over to where Beth was playing with little Giles, and smiled at her. She had taken on the role of nanny to the three children. Mary had been so impressed with her talents with the children that she had asked if Beth would live with them and help her with the children, when they reached Jamestown.

Beth smiled back at him, holding his gaze.

He pulled himself away, and decided that he should go down below deck and see how Sarah was doing. Perhaps a stroll in the fresh air would do her some good, maybe seeing the good natured dolphins

5

might bring a smile to her face. He wandered down to the passenger quarters.

John looked to where Sarah should be, and the space was empty. Mary Hopkins was reading to Constance and Elizabeth, the large white Cahow flapping around lazily. "Mary, where is Sarah?"

"Oh, I didn't realise that she had gone. She must have gone to relieve herself." Mary said. John had a sudden panic. He had provided her with a bedpan so she did not have the indignity of relieving herself elsewhere. He turned to find Eliza.

"Eliza, Eliza... have you seen Sarah?" John's face showed his panic.

"Oh, she was there a second ago. I just came over here to help Alice with little Bermudas, but Sarah can't have gone far, I am sure." She smiled, trying to hide the guilt and panic that was written all over her face. She should have watched her more carefully.

John went back on deck and scoured every inch of it with his eyes, and eventually caught sight of her. She must have come up on deck and with his preoccupation with Beth, he hadn't seen her before he went below. He started to walk over to where she stood. She was holding on to the side of the ship, the wind blowing in her hair, and a smile on her face, looking calm. As John walked towards her, she turned and looked at him, inching away from him. "Don't come near me John" she shouted over the wind. She laughed hysterically.

John could see from the determination on her face that she was set on her plan. She had told him weeks ago that she was going to leave him, and he had not believed it. He believed it now. "Sarah, please, let's talk about this. We can build a life for ourselves in Jamestown." He could feel the lies. He knew the truth. Their relationship had died long ago.

"You are strong now John. You can manage without me. I have seen you grow, and I am no longer needed. You don't love me, and I don't blame you. I am an evil person, and I cannot live with myself. I want to join our perfect little baby now. I was not able to care for her in life, but I can care for her in death. I wanted to die lying on her grave, but you stopped me. I am sure God will unite our souls though, he can't be cruel enough to keep a mother from her baby forever."

John started to run towards her to stop her. As he did so, she climbed up the wooden side of the ship and jumped into the surf, her dress billowing like a sail in the wind.

"Nooooo!..." John shouted. He reached the place where she had been standing and looked over the side of the ship. He saw Sarah's slight body slip beneath the waves as "Patience" sailed over the spot where she had been. John was wailing, throwing his hands in the air, despair in every crevice of his body.

"Help, help, man overboard " he shouted. Newport heard the cries and came running down to see what was happening. He signalled for everything to slow down and rang the bell to warn "Patience" that was coming up behind.

"John, what has happened?" cried Newport.

"Sarah has gone! Sarah has gone!" He knew it was only her physical self that had gone into the sea, her soul had left many weeks before. There was no point in looking for her. They would not know where to look in this vast ocean.

John was numb. He had suffered with the grief of losing the woman he loved, his little playful squaw, over many weeks - weeks that had culminated in the death of his beautiful little Bermuda and now Sarah herself. All the pain he had suffered in his life could not compare with the depths of his present agony. Losing Sarah was a symbol of all his losses in Bermuda. That night, he went below deck and lay on Sarah's bed, quietly crying. He would never let himself love again.

Little Giles Hopkins toddled over to where he lay.

"Where RaRa. Why you sad?"

"Ra Ra is gone Giles" said John, looking with watery eyes at the little boy. Giles climbed up on John's lap, and put his head on John's chest, snuggling down. "Giles wait for RaRa" he said as he snuggled in to John and fell asleep. Mary looked over at her baby snuggling into John, and a tear ran down her face.

Everyone on the gun deck was silent. No words could express how they were feeling. Eliza was wracked with guilt at not having watched Sarah more carefully. Alice held little Bermudas tightly, her grief mingled with love for her baby as her tears fell silently. Elizabeth Joons, thought back to her hatred of Sarah with regret as she shed a silent tear. Beth looked at John with longing, wanting to comfort him, but knowing it was not possible.

John's mind wandered to scene after scene of Sarah laughing, teasing, loving... Then to the day that Bermuda had been born. The feel of her little body as he held her, the sound of her squeaky plaintive cries, her soft unblemished new skin... her little coffin. Why had God been so cruel?

For most of the journey, John went on deck and looked out to sea, imagining Sarah rising to the surface and waving at him with Bermuda in her arms, then ducking below the waves, only to rise again and duck again. His flashbacks to Eustace's accident were very infrequent nowadays, now he had something else to replace them with.

Land

20th May 1610 Sir Thomas Gates noticed floating debris and the smell of earth. He realised that it would not be long before they saw Virginia. He had done it. Against all odds, he had achieved his aim. Whilst no land was in sight, the passengers could also see evidence of land and were starting to get excited but apprehensive.

"I wonder what we will find when we land" said Will Pierce. He had never stopped hoping that the ship with his wife and daughter aboard might have made it to Jamestown. He wondered how much bigger his little daughter Jane might be.

"I am praying that the other ships have landed" replied George Yeardly. "I hardly dare hope that our wives will be safe and sound and jumping up and down to welcome us."

"There should be more than your wives" said Somers. "At least 600 settlers inhabit Jamestown. Thank God there should be plenty of food and accommodation. We can let them look after us for a bit before we start the real work."

"At last civilization is around the corner" sighed Gates picturing a well-structured settlement, organised and efficient. "As soon as we land, we must have a meeting to open the casket and appoint the rest of the leaders of the colony." He smiled. He knew their arrival here would not have happened without his leadership and persistence. If he had left it to Somers they would still all be lounging about on the beach and squabbling amongst themselves.

"Look, look - Land ho!" Newport shouted. "There seems to be a fort there that is not on our map."

"We must be cautious. If it is not on the map, it could be an enemy outpost" said Gates. "We will drop anchor and see what this place is. Just in case there are hostiles, I will disembark alone, with John Rolfe as my guard."

They lowered the skiff into the water, and Gates and John rowed towards the fort. There was a group standing waiting for them looking suspicious. Their clothes were shabby and their faces drawn, Gates could see that they had guns, but when he raised the white flag, the guns were lowered. "Something strange going on here John, be on your guard even though they have lowered their guns."

Gates and John pulled up at the dock. "Sir Thomas Gates at your service." He said to the waiting party. He was still not sure whether they were friend or foe as he looked around at their stricken and hollowed out faces.

"Welcome Sir Thomas. I am Sir George Percy, Governor of Jamestown." He smiled. "Please come to the fort for some refreshment." George Percy was not a strong looking man and Gates had not heard good things about him, but he went with him nevertheless.

They entered a tumbledown fort that was in much need of repair. Gates was not encouraged by what he was seeing.

"So, Sir Percy, have you any knowledge of the other ships in our convoy?" He looked at the other man with hope in his eyes.

"Why yes, all of the other ships landed at Jamestown." Sir Percy didn't seem to be as pleased with the information as Gates felt he might have been.

"Oh that is good news! We will be re-united with some of our kin, and we can, no doubt, help continue the good work that everyone has been carrying out over these past ten months." Gates was starting to feel hopeful. If the ships had survived, what more needed to be said.

Sir Percy lowered his eyes and shook his head. "Sadly, the colony is a shadow of its former self." He sighed.

"What do you mean man?" Gates shouted, starting to panic with the look on the other man's face.

"We have had a run of bad luck. Many of the settlers have been killed by the attacks from the Indians. There have been several massacres. Others have lost their lives through disease and some through starvation." He could not meet Gates' eyes.

"What do you mean... starvation?" There should have been the cultivation of crops, people should have been farming. There should have been natural resources!"

"I am afraid there has been a few years of drought. This has meant that even the Indians have struggled to grow any crops. When John Smith, the previous Governor was recalled, the new regime was not able to forge a good relationship with the Powhatans, and any prior cooperation between Indians and settlers turned into competition. The Indians all but demolished us. On top of that, many of our settlers were more concerned with finding gold than raising crops. The result has been devastation. There are very few left."

"I don't believe what I am hearing" shouted Gates, his eyes wide. He sank down on a chair, his head in his hands. "There should have been at least 600 people at Jamestown." His voice was screeching with horror.

"I would say we have less than 70 left." Sir Percy hung his head.

"Over 500 people died? Why are you here then? Why are you not with your community fighting for them and instilling some order?"

Sir Percy didn't even bother to reply. They both knew the ugly truth.

John listened silently. Everything had been taken from him, and his last ray of hope – a life in Jamestown, was being added to his list of losses.

* * *

Gates and John re-boarded the "Deliverance" to continue the journey to Jamestown.

"So... what news of the other ships?" Somers asked, breathless with anticipation.

Gates's eyebrows pulled together, and his mouth turned down. "The bastards have all but destroyed the colony." He whispered as he did not want to spread panic.

"What? Did our ships land?" asked Somers.

"Oh yes. They landed alright. For all the good it might have done them. Poor leadership combined with Native aggression has all but wiped them out."

Somers looked to the sky, trying to take in what Gates was saying. "Well, let's keep this to ourselves, we don't want people going hysterical at this point. Looks like it would have been better to stay in Bermuda."

"Don't even mention that Somers. I don't want to hear you say that again." Gates was furious at Somers' below the belt jibe at such an important time, despite the fact that it had a ring of truth to it.

People stood on deck curious to see this New World as they

navigated towards their long awaited destination. Would they see Natives? Would they see wild animals? How many of the other ships in the fleet had followed this same route? Excitement abounded.

"Is there any news of the other ships? Yeardly shouted to Gates.

"Yes" Gates replied. "The other ships made it to Jamestown." He said with no further elaboration.

As they sailed up the river, at last they caught sight of Jamestown in the distance. Everyone was on deck fighting for a vantage point. There were whispers amongst the passengers that there seemed to be no movement coming from the settlement - but this could be because they were too far away to see the people.

As they got closer, they realised that Jamestown pier appeared to be deserted. There were cries of anguish when they saw a skeleton that was propped up against a tree, flies swarming around it's empty eye sockets. Why had the body not had a Christian burial? Where was everyone. Gates closed his eyes and said a silent prayer as the first evidence of Percy's horror story unveiled itself. There was silence apart from the sound of the ships moving through the water, and the mariners preparing to land.

There was no welcoming party as they docked, and no dockers catching ropes to help them secure the ships. It was like a ghost town. The colonists were shocked.

As they disembarked and walked through the gates of the fort, there were gasps of horror. The new arrivals struggled to take in the scene that was unfolding before them. It was clear that this had once been a thriving settlement. Now the parched earth and countless dead bodies told an unimaginable tale. Those that they found alive were emaciated and riddled with disease, lying helpless, hardly able to speak. A young lad lay in the street looking up at them with vacant eyes.

"What has gone on here?" George Yeardly said as he gently raised the boy's head off the ground.

"There is no food." The boy croaked. "Some have even resorted to eating the dead bodies, or killing those on the verge of death, for food. You cannot imagine how it has been for us. Please give me some food and w..a..t…." He pleaded, his voice petered out as he almost lost consciousness.

Yeardly lay the boy down. "Unload food and water - the people that are left will not last much longer". Frantic to find his wife, he ran on looking in every dwelling place, finding more and more, either dead or dying. He was losing hope of finding his lovely little blonde Temperance. "Quick Pierce, we must search everywhere just in case we can find them alive."

Yeardly and Pierce were now resigned to finding the worst. If so many had died, it was unlikely that their families would have been spared as they were young women, and not robust.

"Yes I know George, but my heart is sinking. There must only be about fifty people left here. There should be at least 600!"

"I know, but we have come this far, if they ARE alive, we need to find them quickly."

There were dead bodies everywhere as the remaining people were either too sick or emaciated to give the dead a Christian burial. The smell of rotting bodies permeated the air, and rats openly feasted on the fresh meat of the poor souls lying on the ground unprotected.

As the two soldiers turned a corner they saw a young Indian Squaw. She was stooped over, administering food to a little girl. As Yeardly and Pierce approached her, the squaw ran away, revealing the hardly recognisable figures of Temperance, Joan and little Jane. The two men ran to them, crying out.

"Joan, my darling, darling." Pierce picked up her small figure, no more than skin and bone and laid her head upon his chest, kissing her head tenderly. "What have they done to you?" He looked over at little four year old Jane who seemed almost on the verge of death, and tears poured down his cheeks as he ran to her.

Yeardly was cradling Temperance in his arms. She too was skin and bone, the lovely curves that he remembered, long since disappeared.

"We had almost lost hope that we would find you alive" said George. "How have you managed when so many others have died."

"That little Indian Squaw saved us." said Temperance, so weak she couldn't open her eyes. "She disobeyed her father, Powhatan and came as often as she could, sneaking into the camp to give us food. She loved to play with little Jane before the rains stopped when her people used to do trade with us. When trade stopped, she kept coming. She could not bear to see what was happening to us and wanted to help." Temperance drifted out of consciousness. The effort of speaking had been too much for her. George panicked and felt for her pulse. He felt a faint pulse, but knew that unless she had some water and food, she could easily slip away. He shouted for help, silent tears streaming down his cheeks.

Suddenly a shot rang through the air setting everyone screaming and running for shelter.

Two highly painted Natives ran up to the gate, which was off its hinges, and threw two bloody corpses onto the ground. As the settlers ran forward shooting at the perpetrators, they were just in time to see the two men riding away at full speed on brown and white horses, cheering and whooping as they went, spears high in the air in triumph, feather headdresses fluttering.

So, not only was there famine - there was murder. The settlers tentatively approached the two corpses. What greeted them was like nothing they had seen before. Frances Pearepoint, and Richard Knowles, rebels as ever, must have decided to venture further than the walls of the fort to see what they could find. For their trouble they had lost their lives in the most grisly way possible.

The Indians had taken their time in the art of torture. The two men were unrecognisable at first. Their eyes had been gouged out. Most of the flesh had been scraped from their faces and every limb in their bodies had been broken. Large blue-bottle flies swarmed frenetically around the bloody lumps of humanity that lay oozing on the ground.

Many of the Colonists screamed when they saw what had happened to their comrades. Some ran away, vomiting at the awful spectacle that was before them. The Natives had achieved their aim - they had put the fear of God into the newcomers, just in case they didn't understand the nature of Native/English relations.

Gates had not expected any of this. He, as commander, took responsibility for bringing his passengers to this inhospitable land. He was going to have to save them and the remaining colonists with the decisions he was to take in the following few days. It was no good soul searching for what might have been had they stayed in Bermuda, the reality was that he had taken the decision that he felt to be right at the time. No one could never have envisioned the bountiful land in Newport's description turning so quickly to hell on Earth.

First the food had to be shared, and the fifty starving Virginians taken care of, then he would have to think about his options, one of which was returning to England in disgrace. Hopefully it would not come to that, but looking around him, he could see little to salvage of "Nova Britannia". His heart sank.

They had brought *some* food, but it was not going to last very long, as they had to feed their own passengers as well as these few starving skeletons. The supplies that they had were only intended for a ship's voyage, plus a little extra. They had anticipated arriving to a thriving community of plenty. This was a gamble that had not paid off. There was no way that they were going to be able to start to grow and hunt enough to keep everyone alive in this dust bowl.

Somers stood next to him deep in thought. "We have to leave. There is no way we can salvage this carnage" he said coughing, thinking wistfully of the lovely waters of Bermuda.

"We have to at least try, Somers" Gates replied.

"Try if you must; then leave. If you don't we will be responsible for the deaths of the rest of the settlers as well as our passengers" said Somers.

With no exception, passengers and crew, conformists or rebels thought back with regret, to the bounties that they had left behind in Bermuda. Were Carter and Robbie right? Should they have stayed in Bermuda? It did not take a fool to know the answer.

John Rolfe was exhausted. He had helped unload the food from "Deliverance". It had to be done quickly, as lives were at stake. His muscles ached as he wandered around the settlement, offering water and rations to anyone that needed it. There was so much to do here - and not much to do it with. God had saved them, only to take them to this land of the devil, where men had lowered themselves to eat other men in order to survive. Maybe this was a punishment for him. What had he done to deserve tragedy after tragedy in his life? Maybe he should have gone with Sarah to be reunited with little Bermuda. He was sure that that would have been a better option than this. He had had too much pain.

He looked around him at the people who had been his companions for the last ten months. Beth was busy trying to entertain the children and keep them away from the decaying corpses. Elizabeth Joons also helped with the children. Mistress Horton was standing bewildered, in tears looking around her, and Alice cradled her new baby. Tom and Lizzy were busy seeing to the sick and dying. All must be wondering what was to become of them. All were reflecting on the sparkling blue waters of Bermuda, and the gentle call of the birds floating in a clear sky.

As he moved on through the fort, he saw an Indian squaw kneeling down tending to a child that was nearly dead, feeding him water and stroking his head. She did not hear him as he came up behind her, and he stood and watched the tenderness with which she ministered to the child. A small morsel of compassion in a world that was otherwise wracked with cruelty. He was touched, and could not pull himself away from watching the scene. An enemy helping an enemy. In that moment, it struck him. He saw that there could be kindness in the world, there could be compassion amongst people, something that had been missing for him for a long time.

Suddenly the squaw felt someone watching her, and turned. John saw large dark brown eyes framed with long lashes looking at him with fear. She was beautiful. She had long glossy dark hair, like a waterfall hanging down her back, and smooth coffee coloured unblemished skin.

She crouched, waiting to dash.

"Please, don't go. I will not harm you." His voice was soft. He didn't expect that she would understand the words, but she might understand the meaning by his tone.

"I should go" she replied in English, looking towards the gate.

John was taken aback. He didn't expect her to understand, much less speak English. "Who are you?"

"They call me 'Little Mischief'" she said. "My real name is Pocahontas. I am the daughter of Powhatan."

John gazed at her in disbelief. He felt in his pocket for Eustace's stone. 'Little Mischief' - it couldn't possibly be! He knelt down beside her taking in every feature of her beautiful face. Eustace and this girl both had the same nickname. Surely this was a sign that she had been sent to him. His heart was beating with emotion as he took her hand and kissed the creamy golden skin. She smiled at him, her eyes softening.

"I must go now, I am not supposed to be here" she whispered. He put out his hand to help her up. He felt her tiny hand in his. Her warmth mingled with his and he didn't want to let her go. They paused, looking at one another, hands held. For a moment there was only two people in the world. As he let her hand go, she put both of her hands together and bowed her head to him. Turning, she ran towards the gate, looking over her shoulder at him, unable to relinquish her gaze until she turned the corner.

He watched her go, his whole body shaking, suddenly he felt energized like he had never felt before. Maybe this could be his beginning, not his end, dare he to hope? Would he ever see her again? He would make sure he did. How had he found a moment of joy in a place one could only liken to hell? He felt in his bones that, despite all the evidence, this place would flourish. He would flourish. He just knew. She had told him with her eyes and he believed her.

That night as he lay sleeping he saw Eustace in his dreams. "You are not to blame, John. Soul-mates cannot protect each other from life, they can just love one another without end. Our love will never die." Eustace smiled. "Remember me with joy, not pain." Eustace opened his hand to reveal the stone. "This stone did not help me, and it didn't help you. You did it on your own, I am not the better twin. We were just different." Eustace smiled and threw the stone away. "Live your life."

As Eustace's face faded, the image of the beautiful little Indian squaw Pocahontas appeared and took John's hand in hers. They walked away together smiling. He felt he had come to where he belonged at last.

THE END

Epilogue

John Rolfe

Read the continued story of John Rolfe and Pocahontas in my next book -

'Peacemaker's Dream' - The True First Lady of America

The Virginia Company- Jamestown

The spectacle of the starving humanity in Jamestown that greeted the passengers of the "Sea Venture", "Deliverance" and "Patience", was shocking in the extreme. Gates had sworn that he would do his duty to The Virginia Company, and would not return until his job was complete; to do otherwise would be humiliating. However, he knew there was not enough food for the numbers of people, and there was little chance of getting enough in time. The people wanted to go home, and Gates had to listen to them.

On June 7th, 1610 the ships were loaded and they set sail for Newfoundland. Gates' plan was to transfer some passengers to fishing vessels, and others would travel in the four ships laden with Newfoundland fish to make the onward journey to London.

Many wanted to burn the fort as they left. In their eyes, it was an evil place that had cost the lives of many of their loved ones. The horror of it was too great to be left standing. Gates ordered that it be left intact, feeling that it might be of some use at some point in the future. He had still not lost all hope that a Jamestown colony would survive one day.

They boarded the four ships to the sound of drum beats. Gates commanded "Deliverance", Sir George Somers commanded "Patience", George Percy commanded "Discovery" and James Davis commanded "Virginia". On July 8th they espied a longboat coming up the river towards them. The longboat's crew bore a letter from Thomas West, the third Lord De La Warr, who had brought 3 ships of supplies and arrived at Point Comfort on 6th June 1610. Gates, to the horror of many of the settlers, ordered that they turn around and go back to Jamestown to await the arrival of De La Warr and the supplies. The Colony was saved, yet again. Many saw this as a message from God, some saw it as their worst nightmare.

Over the following years, the Colony limped along under several leaders, existing rather than thriving. Leadership and laws were often harsh and penalties for misdemeanours unforgiving. Indians continued to clash with the settlers and many lives were lost in the wars between the two cultures. The Virginia Company was weary of ploughing more and more resources into a venture that seemed to be going nowhere.

Brutal leadership over the years did not lead to a thriving community, and despite the first profitable shipment of tobacco in 1617, in 1624 the Virginia Company finally collapsed.

Sir Thomas Gates

Sir Thomas Gates returned to England in 1610 and convinced The Virginia Company to re-invest in the colony. He went back to Virginia accompanied by Sir Thomas Dale, a former soldier, who was respected by the well to do in London. On the crossing in 1611, Gates brought his wife and daughters. His wife died on the crossing.

March 1614, Gates finally returned to London, leaving the brutal Thomas Dale in charge of the Colony. In 1620 Gates protested at the appointment of his old colleague George Yeardly to Governor, seeing his leadership as too soft. He began selling his shares in The Virginia Company, finally losing faith. He moved back to the Netherlands and died around September 1622.

Sir George Somers

Sir George Somers had been reluctant to leave Bermuda, but had listened to and complied with Sir Thomas Gates' reasoning. When De La Warr arrived in Jamestown, he needed all the help he could get with the continued feeding of the starving colonists. Sir George Somers volunteered to go back to Bermuda to get more supplies. Many thought that his motives were anything but altruistic, and that he had conspired with the two remaining rebels, encouraging them to stay to preserve the Island for Britain, until such time as he could return. No one knows.

He left on "Patience" for Bermuda accompanied by Captain Samuel Argall in "Discovery" to find further food and resources for the Jamestown settlers. They were blown off track and ended up near the coast of Maine where they fished to retrieve supplies for Jamestown. On the way back, they were separated, and Argall was unable to find Somers. Somers had continued the voyage to Bermuda where he met with the two rebels who had stayed behind in Bermuda. He was accompanied on his voyage by his long time servant Edward Waters, Joshua Chard who had been one of the reformed rebels, and his nephew Matthew Somers who had landed safely in Jamestown. In November 1611 George Somers died. It is reported that he died from eating pork. Despite his request that his nephew return to Jamestown with supplies, Matthew defied him and returned to England after burying Sir George's heart in Bermuda and hiding his body in a barrel (as having a dead body on board was superstitious for the sailors) for the return journey to his home at Whitchurch Canonicorum, near Lyme Regis where he was buried.

Sir George's aide, Edward Waters stayed in Bermuda with Christopher Carter and Joshua Chard. (they became the Three Kings of Bermuda). Robbie Waters returned to England with Matthew Somers, being tired of his time in Bermuda.

Steven Hopkins

Steven's wife Mary died in Jamestown in 1613. He returned to England that year. In February 1618 he married Elizabeth Fisher. He signed himself and his family up as passengers travelling to the New World in the "Mayflower".

Steven did well in Plymouth, New England, having one of the largest houses in the settlement, housing his wife and five children. He died a wealthy man in 1644

Christopher Newport

Christopher Newport had sailed many times to Jamestown, but became disillusioned with the lack of progress that was made by The Virginia Company. In 1610 he sailed, finally, to England.

1612 he joined The East India Company and sailed to Java, India and South Africa before dying in Java in 1617.

REFERENCES

Bernhard, V. "A tale of Two Colonies, What really happened in Virginia and Bermuda"
(2011)

Doherty, Kieran, ""Sea Venture" Shipwreck, Survival, and the Salvation of the First English Colony in the New World"
(2007)

Glover, L. & Smith, D.B, "The Shipwreck that Saved Jamestown"
(2008)

Jourdain, S. "A Discovery of the Bermuda, Otherwise Called the Isle of Devils"
(1510)

Strachey, W. "A True Reportory of the Wreck and Redemption of Sir Thomas
Gates, Knight" (1510)

Thank you for reading

I hope that you enjoyed this, my first novel. If you ordered this book through Amazon, I would be extremely grateful if you would leave an honest Review.

The link to the review page is: https://amzn.to/3tOtgOS.

Any comments or suggestions can be directed to me at: suewrightauthor@gmail.com

If you liked the story of John Rolfe so far, his true life journey continues in "**Peacemaker's Dream**" - The True First Lady of America about the Indian Princess, Pocahontas and her relationship with John Rolfe.

It is a tale of Romance, Spiritualism and Historical Tragedy that reveals aspects of Pocahontas's life, previously only documented by Native Americans, denied by the invading Colonists, and gives pause for thought about what *really* happened during the founding of America. Prepare to be shocked!

A SAMPLE OF PEACEMAKER'S DREAM :

"I think we have met before, Sir" she said, her face softening. He looked at her, drinking in her beauty. He had thought of her many times since that awful day in Jamestown. He had hoped that one day they would meet again in better circumstances.

"I wondered if you would remember me" he said quietly, searching her face, hoping for a positive reaction from her.

She looked at him with sorrow in her eyes. "For many years I fought to bury thoughts of those terrible days" she said, "but the cries of children haunt me still." She looked at the floor.

There was silence between them as both, filled with the emotions of the horrors surrounding their first meeting, were lost for words. Pocahontas was surprised as she felt an invisible bond with this stranger. From where had this come? Perhaps sharing the horrors of that day had set them apart from others. Perhaps the bond arose out of having known him when she was a carefree teenager with her life ahead of her. Perhaps it was just the Gods showing her the way.

John broke the silence. "It is a long time since those days. Things are very different now. My heart is sad that the relationship between my people and yours seems to have taken a turn for the worse, and that you have been wrenched from your family and your people in such a way. But Sir Thomas Dale tells me that you want to learn about the Scriptures, and improve your English to improve the relationship between our people."

Pocahontas sighed. She looked closely at him. She hardly knew anything about him, but could feel his unexpected concern for her. Obviously, he did not know the reason she was learning about the Scriptures. He was looking at her, unable to hide the anticipation written on his face as he waited for her to respond to him.

Find your copy of 'Peacemaker's Dream' at Any good book store or:

www.Amazon.co.uk   www.   Amazon.com   www.amazon.ca
www.amazon.de

Printed in Great Britain
by Amazon

82994411R00233